# LONG LIVE THE DEAD

## TALES FROM BLACK MASK ©

**Hugh B. Cave**

(Photograph © 2000 by John L. Coker III)

# LONG LIVE THE DEAD

## TALES FROM BLACK MASK©

# HUGH B. CAVE

WITH AN INTRODUCTION AND INTERVIEW WITH THE AUTHOR BY
KEITH ALAN DEUTSCH

Crippen & Landru Publishers
Norfolk, Virginia
2000

Special thanks are extended to Bill Pronzini for providing copies of the texts found in this volume.

Cover design, book design and production by Tom Roberts
Crippen and Landru logo by Eric D. Greene

ISBN 1-885941-49-8 (limited edition)
ISBN 1-885941-50-1 (trade edition)

FIRST EDITION
10  9  8  7  6  5  4  3  2  1

Crippen and Landru Publishers, P.O. Box 9315, Norfolk, VA 23505 USA
e-mail: CrippenL@Pilot.Infi.net
Web: http://www.crippenlandru.com

Dedicated to my readers for
the past seventy-one years.


Hugh B. Cave

# CONTENTS

# INTRODUCTION

## Hugh B. Cave on His Ninetieth Birthday

H ugh Barnett Cave's writing career spans all the important changes in
20th century American publishing:

— The invention of the terse narrative sentence pioneered in the 1920's,
according to Gertrude Stein, not by Hemingway, but by Dashiell Hammett in
*Black Mask*.

— The explosion of the pulp magazine, and the invention of all the pulp
genres and sub-genres that have become staples in every medium of popular
entertainment — from radio, television and movies to computer games, and
web sites.

— The demise of the pulps and the reign of the slick magazines for short
fiction starting in the 1940's.

— The invention of the paperback format, and the original paperback novel,
which encouraged a move from short fiction to novels in the 1950's.

— The growth of formalized international publishing and film conventions in the 1960's and 1970's, which encouraged foreign sales and the export
of American popular culture.

— The rise in the late 1970's and 1980's of a new mass market of fandom,
with well-organized conventions, and specialized genre societies, and the creation of new genre writing awards.

— And finally in the late 1990's, the growth of the World Wide Web and
cyber publishing, and web magazines, and sites devoted to single authors.

## Hugh B. Cave's Lifetime Career Achievements

Hugh B. Cave was there from the beginning, and at 90 years old (July 11, 2000) his career is still in full swing. Two new novels by Hugh Cave are about to be released, *The Dawning* and *The Evil Returns: Mindstealer* (Leisure Books, 2000) as are a number of story collections, including *Bottled in Blonde*, the Peter Kane stories from *Dime Detective* (Fedogan and Bremer, 2000) and *The Lady Wore Black and Other Cat Tails* (Ash-Tree Press, 2000). New web sites have sections devoted to him (vintagelibrary.com). Mr. Cave will participate in cyber publishing on the new *Black Mask Magazine* web site. In addition, awards for individual stories, story collections and many other international honors of recognition for Mr. Cave's extraordinary career keep coming along, including Lifetime Achievement Awards from The International Horror Guild, The Horror Writers Association, and The World Fantasy Association.

I want to bring to the attention of the reader the breadth and scope of Mr. Cave's achievement. He has published 37 books, many of them novels, between 1942 and 2000, with three or four currently in the hopper. His collection *Murgunstrumm and Others* (Carcosa, 1977) won the World Fantasy Award as Best Collection. The volume is also listed in Jones and Newman *Horror: 100 Best Books*. *A Summer Romance & Other Stories*, a collection of Mr. Cave's romance stories published in *Good Housekeeping Magazine*, was published by Longman in England and reissued in Japan by Eichosha-Longman in their Simplified English Series where it is used for teaching English in schools — and is in its twelfth printing in Japan.

According to his detailed but sadly incomplete records (fire damage), Mr. Cave published over eight hundred stories in every genre of pulp magazine. And he wrote for tough markets that were hard to crack like *Black Mask* (10 stories), *Dime Detective* (20), *Street and Smith's Western Story Magazine* (20), *Weird Tales* (12), *Argosy* (9), *Terror Tales* (13), *Detective Fiction Weekly* (63), *Spicy Mysteries* (26), *Spicy Adventure* (18), *Spicy Detective* (16), *Short Stories* (41), *Dime Mystery* (19), and too many more to mention. Beginning in the 1950's he also wrote often-reprinted stories for *Ellery Queen's Mystery Magazine* (4) and *Alfred Hitchcock's Mystery Magazine* (7).

Starting in the late 1940's, Mr. Cave wrote at least 350 tales for the slicks like *The Saturday Evening Post* (43), *Good Housekeeping* (40), *Cosmopolitan* (9), *Elks* (16), *Boy's Life* (21), *Esquire*, *Ladies Home Journal*, *Scholastic*, *Redbook*, *Woman's Home Companion*, and *Liberty*.

From the earliest pulp days, Hugh B. Cave's stories were of a quality to be reprinted and reprinted again in magazines in thirty-five countries, in anthologies, and in school books. Several have been adapted for radio and television. One *American Magazine* short story, "Two Were Left," has been reprinted in school books, worldwide, more than one hundred times.

I can think of no other American author who has been so prolific in so many different fields. Many popular and extremely prolific authors worked primarily in one genre: for example, Frederick Faust (Max Brand) in Westerns, and Erle Stanley Gardner in mysteries. Other prolific pulpsters like Frank Gruber, who wrote for a wide variety of markets, and made the transition to novels, do not approach the longevity, the consistency, the scope, the breadth, the variety, and the reprintability of Mr. Cave's story-writing achievement.

## The Black Mask Tradition: Hugh B. Cave's Achievements

The pre-eminently American style of detective story, the hard-boiled private-eye tale, was a creation of one of the greatest of all pulp magazines, *Black Mask*. *Black Mask* published 340 issues under six editors from 1920 to 1951. Two of the editors were women. At least thirty-one published writers were women, too. To put Hugh B. Cave's *Black Mask* achievement in perspective, more than 2,500 stories appeared in the magazine over 31 years. William F. Nolan, hard-boiled historian and editor of *The Black Mask Boys* (Mysterious Press, 1985), estimates that *Black Mask* printed thirty million words during those thirty-one years. Hugh B. Cave is not associated by scholars and critics with the classic "Black Mask Boys" like Dashiell Hammett, Raymond Chandler, Frederick Nebel, Raoul Whitfield, Carroll John Daly, Horace McCoy, Paul Cain, and Erle Stanley Gardner. However, Hugh Cave is among only a dozen or so *Black Mask* authors (out of total 640 contributors) to have stories accepted by all of the magazine's last three editors: Captain Joseph T. Shaw, Fanny Ellsworth, and Kenneth S. White. In the famous group of contributors listed above, only Erle Stanley Gardner and Carroll John Daly can make that same claim of continuous appearances. Mr. Cave is also among a very select group of authors to have more than one story published in a single issue of *Black Mask*. Only Raoul Whitfield appeared regularly with a second story in *Black Mask*, featuring his popular series character Jo Gar. These stories and novels of intrigue in the Philippines were published under Whitfield's famous pseudonym, Ramon DeColta.

Few writers' careers in *Black Mask* span the major transitions that took place in the magazine during the tenure of its last three editors from 1934 to 1941 and later. Of particular impact was the broiling international scene prior and during World War II. Hugh B. Cave integrated this wartime background into his fiction in a more subtle and satisfying manner than most pulp writers of the 1940's did. Many wartime pulp stories now feel dated, jingoistic, or melodramatic. Cave's tales of this period, particularly "Lost and Found," use international intrigue unobtrusively as an integral, secondary element to a satisfying reading experience. These *Black Mask* stories, written by Cave in the late 1930's and early 1940's, remain as fresh today as they were when first published.

Hugh B. Cave's *Black Mask* tales represent the style of the magazine, particularly as it evolved over the years of his appearances. In its own way, this collection of all of Hugh B. Cave's *Black Mask* stories, brought together for the first time, represents a special kind of writing achievement within the *Black Mask* tradition.

Doug Greene (who with his wife Sandi is Crippen & Landru's publisher) and I are honored to have worked closely with Hugh B. Cave on the production of this book. Hugh answered our questions, provided frank, revealing evaluations of each of the tales, wrote his own brief prefaces to each story, and freely shared reminiscences of his pulp writing days. In addition, Hugh B. Cave provided meticulous records, now stored on computer disks, that span the breadth and depth of his extraordinary writing career. The interview that follows, the appended checklists, statistics, and bibliographic materials which augment this collection of *Black Mask* stories derive almost exclusively from Hugh's own detailed files. Despite his considerable achievements within the pages of *Black Mask*, however, Hugh B. Cave is such a widely versatile and endlessly entertaining writer that the full range of his talent, and his astonishing staying power, are more interesting and significant than even his impressive *Black Mask* accomplishments, and the interview touches on many aspects of his career.

This collection is offered as a small tribute to the great career of an extraordinary writer, active as ever, and still at the peak of his form as he celebrates his ninetieth birthday.


Keith Alan Deutsch
July 11, 2000

# THE BLACK MASK INTERVIEW

*Hugh B. Cave*

## "You Learn to Write by Reading."

Hugh Barnett Cave was born in England on July 11, 1910, but he grew up in and around Boston, Massachusetts. The *Boston Globe* published his first story in 1925 when Hugh was a 15-year-old student at Brookline High School. "I wasn't paid for it," Hugh makes sure to set the record straight. The story was called "Retribution" and it won an Honorable Mention in the All High School Short Story Competition. "But I did sell one or two stories while still in High School to a Sunday-school paper published (I think) by the D. C. Cook Co. I do remember a letter I got from the company, saying the story was much too long for them but they would use it as a serial, and please would I double-space the next story I sent them!"

Of course, Hugh had been writing stories long before he became a published author, and he made up tales to amuse himself long before that. But in his opinion, the most important aid to his development as a writer was the avid reading of exciting, classic novels and great short stories he did when a youngster. From the very beginning of our correspondence and telephone conversations, I wanted to know what Hugh's earliest pulp fiction stories were like. I had a comprehensive list of the titles, and suspected that Hugh was immediately drawn to the genres of horror and fantasy. I asked. He answered. No, he was not drawn immediately to horror!

When I began writing, I wrote adventure stories. I was born with adventure in my genes, I guess. My English mother was born in India, where her English engineer father, George Barnett, built the Great Indian Peninsula Railway and was made a C.I.E. (Companion of the Indian Empire) by Queen Victoria for doing so. He was also Mayor of Bombay. As a nurse, mother served in the Boer War in South Africa. The man who became my father, Tom Cave, followed her to Africa and married her there. The first of their three children, my brother Tom, was born there. Then they returned to England. My brother Geoff (the original Geoffrey Vace) and I were born there in Chester.

Geoffrey Vace was a pseudonym Hugh and his brother, Geoff, shared for a few early pulp stories. Then Geoff (the brother) dropped out of the game. But Geoffrey (the pseudonym) made many pulp magazine appearances.

Geoffrey Vace became my second most used pen name after my favorite pseudonym, Justin Case. It was fun to use. Ironic without being obvious. I wrote all my "spicy" stories, more than seventy of them, under that name. I also occasionally used Judy Case. My output was so great, once I hit stride in the early 1930's, that I needed pen names because I often had more than one story in the same issue of a magazine.

And this is why the title story of this Hugh B. Cave *Black Mask* collection, "Long Live the Dead," was written by "Allen Beck" — because "Smoke in Your Eyes" appeared in that same December 1938 issue of *Black Mask* under Hugh's real name.

For Hugh B. Cave, having two stories the same issue of a magazine was a regular occurrence. "It happened a lot," he wrote.

But not in *Black Mask*. Getting two stories into the same issue of *Black Mask* was quite a feat, particularly under the strong editorial hand of Fanny Ellsworth who was editor in 1938. This use of pseudonyms has led to some errors and omissions in standard sources. For example, in E. R. Hagemann's *Comprehensive Index to Black Mask, 1920-1951* (Bowling Green State University Press), the meticulous index of record, Hugh is listed as having written only the nine stories that appeared under his own name. Professor Hagemann missed the Allen Beck pseudonym used for the title story of this collection. When I wrote and pointed out Hageman's Allen Beck error, Hugh replied:

I'm glad you set the record straight. You are right. All of us successful writers for the pulps used pseudonyms, and often they do get hard to untangle. Then there is the problem of house names. Some publishers kept pet pen names in reserve when they wanted a different name on the cover for whatever reason. And the reason wasn't always clear to me. I preferred to use my own pen names. But a couple of times a few of us wrote under a house name, and we still can't figure out who wrote which story!

## A Brief Aside on Pen Names

No matter how popular a pulp author might be, pulp editors *never* wanted to appear to publish two stories by one author in the same issue of a magazine. Although I am certain some alert *aficionado* of pulp history will write in with a few examples that are exceptions to this rule (and I welcome such letters), there was sound marketing psychology behind this standard industry policy. Pulp readers wanted as much entertainment as possible for their change. Harold Steeger built one of the greatest, longest-running pulp publishing empires, Popular Publications, with a just such a bargain strategy. He started a line of different genre magazines featuring "Dime" in each title — *Dime Detective, Dime Adventure, Dome Western,* and so on. In the early 1970's when I met with him on an almost daily basis for a number of months, he told me that the appeal to value was one of his great strategies that led to his extraordinary publishing success. In fact, Steeger's *Dime Detective* became *Black Mask's* only true rival. Over time, the summer of 1941 to be exact, Harold Steeger finally acquired what he told me was he prize acquisition of all, *Black Mask.*

Steeger explained to me why it was accepted pulp wisdom never to include two stories under one author's name in a single issue:

> One Erle Stanley Gardner story featured on the cover of any of my magazines guaranteed an increased sales of 50,000 copies. I learned to increase my print order by about 60,000 copies to cover the assured extra demand of that name on the cover. However, two Erle Stanley Gardner stories in one issue would not increase sales one more issue above that initial 50,000 boost. I'll tell you why. The reader wants a sure thing *and* a bargain. A second Erle Stanley Gardner story would only dilute the impact of the first Gardner story. Almost all readers would rather get a story by a different big name writer, rather than two stories from one big name writer. Now two stories by two different major writers *is* an obvious bargain. However, two stories by one major writer may also be a bargain, but it starts many potential newsstand buyers to thinking. And the last thing we want a potential buyer holding one of our magazines in his hands at the newsstand to do is to start thinking. The buyer may think: well they spent the dough to buy two Gardner stories, so why not an original Ian Fleming James Bond story, instead?

Or maybe the potential buyer starts thinking: maybe one of the two Gardner stories isn't as good as the other. Or maybe they are both second-rate Gardner tales and they threw them both in one issue to kind of equal one great story.

It doesn't matter what that buyer is thinking. Thinking is bad at the newsstand. We want that reader to *buy!* If our potential customer stops on his way to a purchase for any reason, another magazine may attract his eye and the sale will be lost.

So we at Popular, like many of the other pulp houses, invented house names. Famous phantom authors, who didn't exist, but who appeared regularly in our magazines. Any good writer who knew the genre of the magazine could write the story that went with the house name. The stories had to be good stories if a Popular Publications house name was used. However, many of the second or third level pulp houses just used house pseudonyms as a convenience. When any author had two stories in the same issue, one story went out under a favorite house name. Or when an editor needed something written fast to fill an emergency gap in an issue, many writers turned out a story that would serve, but it wasn't a work he'd want associated with his own name. So the editor would roll out one of the house names of the magazine. Or the writer would roll out one of his favorite pseudonyms.

(*Note:* A list of pseudonyms of Hugh B. Cave follows this introductory interview.)

**A**fter pondering the problems of keeping track of pen names, I asked Hugh when he started keeping records. Did he have a system for sending stories out, and if rejected, sending them along to the next appropriate magazine?

I have tried to keep very accurate records, but I have some blank spots, too. It is a hard job for a beginning professional writer. Before Lurton "Count" Blassingame became my agent in the summer of 1931, I used to send stories out to the highest-paying pulps first. If they were rejected, I went on down the line until they sold. Of course, once I sold to a good market I tried to keep that market well supplied. Then I followed the same procedure in the late 1940's for the slicks, where in the beginning I didn't use an agent. So my record keeping grew out of my method of getting my early stories placed.

I asked Hugh to go back to his early experiences as a writer. By July of 1929, the same year Dashiell Hammett's *The Maltese Falcon* was serialized in *Black Mask,* he made his first professional pulp sale, "Island Ordeal," to *Brief Stories*. He followed that up the next month with "The Pool of Death" also in *Brief Stories*.

By 1930 and 1931 he was selling stories all over the place in many diverse markets. He favored *Short Stories*, a general pulp, just a tier below *Argosy* and *All Story*. (I should point out, however, Hugh did sell to *Argosy* as early as 1931 with "Steal a Dog's Bone," and made nine more appearances in the great magazine through 1950.) Even at this early stage in his career, the titles of many of these stories conjure visions of horror and fantasy: "The Pool of Death" (1929) and "Condemned to a Living Tomb" (1930) in *Brief Stories;* "The Corpse on the Grating" and "The Murder Machine" (both 1930) in *Astounding Stories*. And two tales in *Ghost Stories* in 1931, "The Strange Case of No.7" and "The Affair of the Clutching Hand," that were collected 46 years later in Hugh's award-winning horror/fantasy book *Murgunstrumm and Others*.

Within two years of turning professional, Hugh B. Cave had dozens of stories published, and in tough markets. How does he explain such an early and immediate success as a professional writer? Did he study the markets, analyze what editors were buying, or use successful short stories as practice models — as so many of the great early pulp writers report they did?

> I have to tell you and the readers more about myself and my early experiences to explain the influences that I believe made me an early and successful writer. When I was not quite five years old my adventurous parents decided to move to America, where they knew no one. The ship landed in Boston. I grew up around Boston in Cambridge, Winchester, Brighton, Brookline (I went to Brookline High School), Malden, and Back Bay.
>
> As a boy, I sang in Boston's Emmanuel Church choir for several years. For two weeks every summer we choir kids went to a church camp on Cape Cod. The choirmaster, Mr. Albert Snow, who also played the organ for the Boston Symphony, taught me a love for music. At camp, he also read to us every evening around a campfire — creepy stories by Poe, Bierce, Conan Doyle, etc. Is it any wonder I wrote for *Weird Tales, Strange Tales, Terror Tales,* and all the others, when I began writing for the pulps? Or that I wrote stories such "The Silent Horror" for *The Saturday Evening Post,* and similar tales for other slicks? Or that I wrote detective-mystery tales for *Black Mask* and other publications?
>
> When I was in grammar school, living in Brighton, we kids used to walk a couple of miles to go to the movies every Saturday afternoon at a theater, which, if I remember right, was called the Billy Woods. (Also, if I remember right, admission was a dime!). My favorite movies featured Tom Mix and William S. Hart. I read Owen Wister and other fine Western writers also. Is it any wonder I wrote for Western pulp magazines?

In Brookline, where I graduated from high school at age 16 (just a month short of 17) we lived within walking distance of the public library. My brother Geoff and I spent many hours in that library. (My brother Tom was then away at sea, all over the world as a radio operator on ships.) Also, the various homes I grew up in were always filled with books. My mother knew Kipling.

I read Kipling and Conrad, Arthur Conan Doyle, Hugh Walpole (I was named after him), Stevenson, Dickens, Maugham, London, Dumas, Conrad, Wells, Scott, and many other fine writers. You learn to write by reading, not by taking courses in "Creative Writing." If my memory serves me well, a fellow war correspondent, J. C. Furnas, once wrote an article to that effect that was published in *Atlantic Monthly*.

At Brookline High I won a scholarship to Boston University, but had to go to work, instead, because my father was nearly killed by a runaway street car. A vanity-publishing house in Boston gave me a job designing book jackets and editing manuscripts. That lasted about a year. Then I began selling to the pulps and turned to writing full time, attending college evenings.

I later went from the pulps to the slicks to books — war books first, as a correspondent in World War II, then a book on Haiti where I lived for several winters, and one on Jamaica where I bought a run-down coffee plantation in the Blue Mountains and restored it over the years to produce prize-winning coffee. Then I moved on to mainstream novels, paperback novels, and collections of short stories. All this time I maintained a home base in the States, first in Rhode Island, then in Florida to be closer to the islands.

Did Hugh have to do much rewriting for editors to get his early stories placed?

No, I didn't do much rewriting, but I never hesitated to do so if an editor suggested changes in a story and I agreed with him. The idea was to get those stories out and move them from the highest paying markets to the lower until they sold.

## WRITING FOR BLACK MASK

### *"The Reader Has to Feel Something"*

Things changed for Hugh in 1931 when he acquired an agent to do "the story moving" and "accounting" for him. In an August 1931 letter, Hugh wrote to his good friend and fellow writer, Carl Jacobi:

I'm letting one of NY's best agents handle my stuff (some of it) just now, and the son of a gun sold a dud, which had been out 17 times, to *American Boy* (slick paper) for three cents per.

In correspondence with me, Hugh explained how he acquired his new literary agent to help sell his stories and to aid in the massive job of keeping records for so prolific an author as himself.

Rogers Terrill, an important editor at Popular Publications, told me I ought to have an agent, and he recommended Lurton Blassingame. Everyone in the business knew Lurton as "Count."

I was lucky to interview Lurton Blassingame in 1974. At that time, Robert Heinlein was his major client. His brother, Wyatt, was also a writer, mainly for the horror pulps. The "Count" and I talked about the pulp publishing days. I remember that he was impeccably dressed and very cordial. He knew a lot about the history of Harry Steeger's Popular Publications, the publishing house I was most interested in because I was gathering material about *Black Mask* and *Dime Detective* and Popular's shudder pulps at the time.

Hugh described how his relationships with the folks at Popular Publications were strengthened through "Count" Blassingame:

"Count" was a Southerner. Always a gentleman. Born in Alabama, I believe. We hit it off from the start and became close friends. He introduced me to a good buddy of his, Ken White. Ken became one of my closest friends of all time. The "Count" and I came to call him "Dr. Livingstone." I had a house up in Rhode Island by then and I loved to go fly-fishing in northern New England and Canada. So the three of us would go fresh-water fishing all the time. And we invited various friends and acquaintances, mostly in the publishing business, to join us. Once Whit Burnett, the famous editor of *Story* magazine, the fellow who taught and discovered J. D. Salinger, among others, went fishing with us. But the best adventure we had was when we hired two Indian guides and explored and fished the Canadian wilderness in canoes. We went to places the Indians had never seen before. The experience became the background for my first novel called *Fishermen Four*, published by Dodd Mead in 1942. I turned the story into an expedition by four boys in Kekekabic country in Minnesota.

By all accounts, Harry Steeger gave Ken White *Dime Detective* to edit in 1932. By that year, Hugh was already writing for a number of Popular Publications' shudder pulps, including *Terror Tales*, *Horror Stories*, and my favorite, *Dime Mystery Magazine*, which featured a kind of hard-boiled detective terror tale. Hugh reminisced fondly about Ken White:

> Ken was a great editor. And very kind. Much loved and loved by others in return. I am sure I had him in mind when I suggested to my wife that we name our first son Kenneth. Ken White later became editor of *Adventure*, then fiction editor of *Esquire*, and finally an agent. He died much too young.

Back in 1975, Harry Steeger told me his plans for *Dime Detective* when he gave Ken White editorial responsibility for the magazine. Steeger told Ken to compete head on with *Black Mask* with a two fisted strategy. First, he told White to offer a penny a word more to the *Black Mask* authors to pull those star writers over to *Dime Detective*. Secondly, Steeger told White to get the new *Dime Detective* writers to create original series characters that could appear only in *Dime Detective*. The strategy worked. By 1936, the year Cap Shaw left *Black Mask*, Raymond Chandler was writing exclusively for *Dime Detective*, and although he did write a few stories later for other magazines, Chandler never returned to *Black Mask*.

Hugh's response to my *Dime Detective* history was concise:

> Well, I invented my alcoholic, hard-boiled detective, Peter Kane, for Ken's *Dime Detective*. It was in August of 1934 that my first story, a Peter Kane tale, appeared in *Dime Detective*.

I tried to get more *Black Mask* information from Hugh. His first story for *Black Mask*, "Too Many Women," was published by the most famous editor of *Black Mask*, Cap Shaw, in May of the same year Hugh first appeared in *Dime Detective*, 1934. I asked what he thought of Shaw as an editor:

> Well, he bought my first story offered to him (Hugh answered succinctly). But I never had any personal dealings with Shaw. The "Count" was handling things for me by then.

In some ways, that is a shame. Hugh is the last living author to write for Captain Joseph T. Shaw.

A letter from Hugh to his writer pal, Carl Jacobi, postmarked February 27, 1933, reproduced along with four others in Audrey Parente's brief biography of Hugh, *Pulp Man's Odyssey* (Starmont, 1988). The leter includes some interesting observations by Hugh on *Dime Detective*, the toils of a pulp author, and on the *Black Mask* school of writing:

*Dime Detective?* As you know, I wrote a novelette for them. Got it back with the comment "too much woman." Mowre, of *All Detective*, refused it because it was too long. Dorothy Hubbard, of *Det. Story Mag.*, said too much sex. Right now it's at *Rapid-Fire Detective*. You're right in thinking *Dime Detective* uses weird plots. They like the weird element, but — as they say — the story must have a logical conclusion. . . . Their best writer by a million miles is Fred Nebel, who has also written for the *Saturday Evening Post*. Nebel uses the Dashiell Hammett style, but does Hammett one better. Economy of words is the secret, plus brutality of treatment, bluntness, and vivid character portrayal. His Cardigan is a better character than Hammett's "Spade."

Apparently at the time this letter was written the "Count" had not taken over the story sending chores from Hugh. And perhaps Hugh's sexy novelette was rejected before Ken White fully took over the reigns of the publication. In any case, Hugh published 10 stories for Ken White's *Dime Detective* during his three year hiatus from *Black Mask*.

I asked Hugh whether he thought those lost years from contributing to *Black Mask* happened because Harry Steeger's strategy for *Dime Detective* was successful. Hugh got a penny a word more from *Dime Detective*, and a sure slot with the six popular Peter Kane stories that appeared during his absence from *Black Mask*.

Well, it could be. The "Count" was handling the submissions by that time. And Ken and the Count and I had become good buddies, and it *was* a penny per word more. But I also contributed many stories for less money than *Dime Detective* during this same time to *Dime Mystery*, and *Horror Stories*, and *Terror Tales* for Popular Publications, where I was well-known. The reason wasn't that I didn't have time to write the stories for *Black Mask*. I was aware of the prestige of *Black Mask*.

It is a good question and I'm not sure what the answer is. From 1934 to 1937, I didn't return to *Black Mask*. Then I appeared regularly for five more years under two different editors. And even after Ken White took over *Black Mask*, I never appeared again after 1941. And I never created a series character for *Black Mask*.

Many authors spoke of the extra care they put into writing for *Black Mask*. Dashiell Hammett (over 50 appearances) and Raymond Chandler (11 stories) spoke of the special attention they brought to the creation of a good *Black Mask* story. Yet these two most famous creators of the *Black Mask* tradition narrated very different, but, at the same time, very typical *Black Mask* stories.

Hammett wrote fast, terse tales that revealed character through action — and through the dialogue, especially the natural speech each character used. His narration was objective, flat, and realistic — despite the underlying melodrama of his very well-made plots.

For Chandler, as reported in his essay "The Simple Art of Murder": "The scene outranked the plot, in the sense that a good plot was one which made good scenes." Chandler's tales were fast, but confusing. His narration was beyond realistic to the point of graphic poetry. He used similes like sledgehammers to describe a world gone wrong, a world filled with fear. But his dialogue was amusing with clever repartee that Hammett never used until he wrote *The Thin Man*, after his *Black Mask* days.

I asked Hugh if he did anything special to prepare to write his *Black Mask* stories. Unlike Chandler and Hammett, Hugh wrote for just about every fiction magazine genre that ever existed. Did he develop special strategies for each different kind of story? Did he ever emulate Hammett's, or Chandler's, or Fred Nebel's writing strategies?

Hugh gave a very interesting, and I believe, a very revealing answer:

> I really don't know what strategies different kinds of stories require. I've read so many tales of all kinds — good ones, I mean, by great authors — that when I get what seems to be a promising idea, I just start writing. I have a very developed sense of how a good story is supposed to work on a reader.

In Hugh's correspondence with me about his ten *Black Mask* stories collected in this book, he used a rating system. I asked him to tell us how he rates and evaluates his own stories.

> How do I rate my stories? I simply re-read them and rate them on a scale of 1 to 10. A story has to be pretty darned good to win a 10 from me, whether it was published in *Nickel Western* or *The Saturday Evening Post*.

Hugh and I reviewed some of the comments he originally sent to me as he first re-read and rated the stories in this collection. I wanted to pull out some specific standards Hugh might use when he analyzed what made a story work for him. I think an important idea about good story writing is revealed in Hugh's first comments to me for "Smoke in Your Eyes," from *Black Mask*, December 1938. Hugh wrote in part:

> The hero owns a greeting card company. Girlfriend is a lovelorn columnist. Their hobby is detecting. *There is a complicated plot here on several*

*levels, but I didn't get much feeling of suspense or urgency.* The story is cleanly written, however, so I gave it a 5. (My emphasis, KHD)

Despite the fact that this long tale (10,000 words) is cleanly written, and the central characters are unique and engaging with lots of background color, Hugh severely faulted the story, it seemed to me, primarily because it didn't make him feel any strong emotion. I thought this such an important topic that I dropped Hugh's rating review of his other *Black Mask* stories to follow through on this point. I thought I was really on to something. Here is what I wrote to him:

Hugh, tell us about the importance of creating emotions in the reader — what kind of emotions are needed for a successful horror/terror story vs. a detective tale, or a western, or a romance. You have written hundreds of great stories in all these different fields. Does each type of story require a different set of techniques to create the appropriate emotions in the reader?

I was surprised and educated by Hugh's written response:

I'm not sure the word "emotions" is the right word here. Obviously, the reader has to *feel something* if a story is to be successful. And the reader is going to feel different things when reading different kinds of stories. A sense of adventure for a South Seas tale, for instance. Of the great outdoors when reading a western. Of suspense and mystery when dealing with a detective yarn. And so on. It is very important, essential to a satisfying reading experience, essential to a successfully written story.

That is an important answer for me. I think it speaks for itself and touches a chord that runs through all satisfying fiction. My misguided focus on "emotion" contrasts sharply with Hugh's understanding of what a good story must do, at minimum, for the reader.

I next asked about one of Hugh's areas of expertise:

You are associated with horror and terror stories of every kind by a very large audience of readers and fans. Despite your enormous achievements in so many other fields, you do seem to have a great affinity for the frightening, the "scary" fantasy story. And you've won more awards in the horror and fantasy fields than any other. Is there a difference in your mind between "terror" and "horror"? Harry Steeger, publisher of Popular Publications, and inventor of the shudder pulps, told me "horror" was the emotions of disgust, fear, etc. the reader feels watching what happens to a character in the story. He said "terror" is what the reader feels when he identifies with the evil forces or the villain, and feels the fear that terrible things might happen to him. What is your opinion?"

> Harry Steeger had it right, Keith (Hugh responded). "Horror" is what you feel when you see a monster devouring a stranger. "Terror" comes when the monster is about to devour *you*.

What about villains? (I asked.) Alfred Hitchcock said something like the hero is nothing without the villain, and the story, no matter how interesting, will only make as strong an impact on the audience as the villain is interesting, dangerous, and threatening.

> Villains? (Hugh replied.) They have to be convincingly villainous, of course. If the monster in your previous question about "terror" and "horror" is merely papier-mâché, nobody is going to feel either horror or terror. Hitchcock, of course, had it right. There has to be tension between conflicting forces for a story to create suspense, and a sense of urgency. The more real and interesting the evil forces are, the more opportunities the writer has to create exciting moments of action filled with suspense, or fear, or mystery, or horror, or terror, or adventure. Even in stories that don't require villains in the traditional sense, like some romances, there have to be conflicts to create anticipation or surprise or a satisfying resolution. Boy gets girl — or boy doesn't get girl because he doesn't deserve her. Just like Hitchcock's villains, if these conflicts are not interesting, or do not seem real, then the resolutions will be duds and the story won't work.

My last question to Hugh related to traditional villains. My next:

But in horror/fantasy stories, instead of a human villain, there is often an evil force. Something like what Hitchcock tried to do with birds, but often more obviously sinister and fantastic. Evil taken to an inhuman level. If that assumption is true, what can you tell us about story teller techniques that will make that evil come alive for reader?

> Well, Keith (Hugh answered), in the best horror-fantasy, the evil force is a threat all through the story and the reader is kept constantly aware of it. H. P. Lovecraft was good at this sort of thing.

I wrote back:

So are you, Hugh. And for me you create the same sense of fear and dread in a much more accessible, realistic style. But let us quickly finish the *Black Mask* story comments because there are a few new elements you mention when you rate your other *Black Mask* stories. Of the title story, "Long Live the Dead," *Black Mask*, December 1938, you wrote me: "This is a pretty good crime tale, rather well written, with interesting characters." But you only gave it a 7. It had very good characters, a solid plot, and it was well written. Why not a higher rating?

I found Hugh's answer very revealing. It also gives insight into what it means to mature as a writer, even within the confines of a popular pulp genre:

> Just look at the stories that followed in 1940. "Lost — and Found" was a *Black Mask* novelette published in April of that year. It was a fast-moving tale, with a swift action climax. And a great locale. The hero is a well-drawn and interesting character. War profiteering plays an important part in the plot, but there is much more going on. Then there is the top off with the hero spanking the young gal who tries to flatter him into making love to her on the ride back from the successful mission. This is good *Black Mask* stuff. I gave it a 9. I think the mood of the magazine was changing. The depression had faded, war was on the scene, and there was an interest in foreign places. And that story is representative of its time
>
> "The Missing Mr. Lee," *Black Mask*, December,1940, is narrated unlike anything I have ever written. A man named Paine is found stabbed to death, and each of five or six other characters comes forward to tell what he or she thinks happened. This is a one-of-a kind story — I don't believe I ever wrote another like it — and it's a good one, well written, with an unexpected ending. I gave it a 10. Then came "Front-Page Frame-Up," a novelette for *Black Mask* in February 1941. Detective Jeff Cardin, investigating a blackmail racket on a wet, nasty night gives a lift to the Anderson girl and she starts screaming for help the minute they reach a populous crossroad. Jeff is forced to quit his job. He becomes a private dick. This complex story is told in the first person in a lively, sometimes humorous style, and could be one of my best stories for *Black Mask*. Everything works. I gave it a 9 or 10.
>
> Finally there's "Stranger in Town," my last story for *Black Mask*, about 5000 words in the April 1941 issue. A clever story, very different. Corey, a

cop, is back in town from a sanatorium. All the crooks are scared. In trying to cover themselves, they . . . but it is such a good story I won't give any more of it away. A very well written, different, hard-boiled detective tale. 10.

I commented:

I like the way that story unfolds, Hugh. It reminds me of *High Noon* in reverse. It is a story that is difficult to analyze exactly how it achieves its effects.

I agree with you (Hugh replied). In some ways you can't take apart a great story like it was a mechanical device, Keith. When a story really works, it is like a living thing. If you cut it up to analyze it, you just won't find the spark that makes it so good.

# Pseudonyms Used by Hugh B. Cave
## and other names under which his works have appeared

*Supplied with annotations by the author*

PERSONAL PEN-NAMES —

C. H. Barnett

Cary Barnett

Hugh Barnett

Allen Beck

Judy Case

Justin Case

> (The jokey "Justin Case" was by far the most frequently used of my pen-names, with some 70 stories originally appearing under that name in the *Spicy* publications.
>
> Some of my Justin Case stories were also reprinted by the editors of the *Spicy* magazines under the various house names Paul Hanna, R. T. Maynard, William Decatur, J. C. Cole, T. V. Faulkner, Max Neilson, and — gasp! — John Wayne.
>
> I still use the name Justin Case occasionally.)

Carl Hughes

Geoffrey Vace

> (My second most frequently used pen-name. But the first three Geoffrey Vace stories, appearing in *Oriental Stories* and *Magic Carpet Magazine*, both edited by *Weird Tales'* Farnsworth Wright, were actually written by my brother, Geoffrey Cave.)

HOUSE NAMES OR OTHER BYLINES —

Ace Williams

> (I believe this was an editorial house name for the Standard Publications *Thrilling* line of magazines. I had one story appear under this byline in the May, 1932 issue of *Thrilling Adventures*.)

Jack D'Arcy

> (This was the name of an actual pulp writer but two of my stories somehow appeared under his name.)

Maxwell Smith

> (This also was the name of an actual pulp writer whose stories appeared in many Street & Smith titles during the 1920s. For whatever reason it appeared as the byline for a story that my brother Geoffrey wrote for *Amazing Detective Stories* in 1931. Later it appeared as the byline on a few of my overseas reprints of pulp stories as well.)

# TOO MANY WOMEN

THIS STORY ABOUT GUMSHOE BILL EVANS AND THE DEAD LADY APPEARED IN *BLACK MASK* IN MAY 1934 AND WAS THE FIRST TALE OF MINE TO BE PUBLISHED IN THAT MAGAZINE. I WAS 23 YEARS OLD AT THE TIME AND HAD BEEN WRITING FOR THE PULPS SINCE I WAS 19. *BLACK MASK*, EDITED BY THE LEGENDARY JOSEPH T. ("CAP") SHAW, HAD DEVELOPED THE HARDBOILED PRIVATE EYE STORY, AND, DURING THE EARLY 1930s, AMONG ITS REGULAR CONTRIBUTORS WERE DASHIELL HAMMETT, RAYMOND CHANDLER, ERLE STANLEY GARDNER, RAOUL WHITFIELD, PAUL CAIN, HORACE MCCOY, AND FREDERICK NEBEL. BY THE TIME *BLACK MASK* FELT I WAS READY TO MINGLE WITH THESE AUTHORS, I HAD BEEN PUBLISHED IN SUCH PULPS AS *ACE HIGH*, *ALL DETECTIVE*, *ARGOSY*, *ASTOUNDING*, *DIME MYSTERY*, *GHOST STORIES*, *SHORT STORIES* (23 TIMES!), *STRANGE TALES*, *TOP-NOTCH* AND *WEIRD TALES*, TO NAME JUST A FEW.

HBC

*Gumshoe Bill Evans finds that the murdered girl was only one of many*

WITH RAIN slapping his face and more rain drooling from the turned-down brim of his gray hat, Bill Evans swung left off Atlantic Avenue and hiked methodically across the Eastern Star Wharf. Teetering along a wet plank to avoid slopping through a pool of goose-pimpled water, he stood staring at the weather-scarred words, *Ritoli's Fish House*, painted across the front of the endmost wharf shanty. Scowling, he pushed in the door, and said impatiently to the shack's occupant: "You Ritoli?"

The man said he was Ritoli. He stood behind an enormous counter packed with clams, fish, lobsters, ice. He wore a wet black apron and his hair was greasy and his bare arms were hairy. His face was round and fat and smeared with fish blood.

"Where's the stiff?" Bill said.

"Huh?"

"The stiff you phoned in about. I'm a cop."

Ritoli said: "You a gop? Huh? Yez, zir. Yez, zir, mizter." He took off his apron and wiped his hands hard on his thighs. "She iz out back. I zhow you." He put on a dirty brown hat and a blue sweater with leather elbows, and limped to the door. Bill trailed him.

"She wuz float in ze water, mizter," Ritoli explained, limping to the end of the wharf. "I find her wazhed up againzt my clam boat when I go out little while ago for zum clamz. I keep clamz in ze water after I dig zem. Zey keep frezher. Zey —"

"All right, all right." Bill scowled. "Forget the clams."

Ritoli turned and said: "Watch out here, mizter. Ze rain make ze stepz zlippery." He limped carefully down a crude stairway to a long float where a half-dozen flat-bottomed boats were upended. Bill slipped on the bottom step, crunched one foot into a pile of clam shells, and slouched on again, muttering maledictions. Ritoli scuffed to the end of the float and bent over to drag back a sheet of canvas. He said: "Here zhe iz."

The girl lay stark naked beside an upturned dory. Her eyes were wide open and glazed. Her body was rigid. She was not more than twenty years old, Bill guessed.

"W'en I find her," Ritoli shrugged, "I pull her up out of ze water and put her here. Zen I call ze police station."

Bill put his hands in his pockets and stood staring. He forgot it was raining; he felt sick. Leaning forward slightly, he examined a whitish mark in the girl's breast where the flesh had receded from a deep gash. He fingered the water-soaked rope around the girl's ankle and studied the frayed end of it, frowning. Then he stood up and swallowed the thickness that came into his throat.

"All right," he said. "Cover her up."

Ritoli said anxiously: "You will not leave her here like zis, mizter, please? I don' want —"

"Where's your telephone?"

"Tel'phone? Yez, zir," Ritoli said quickly. "Yez, zir, mizter."

Bill used Ritoli's phone back in the shanty behind the fish counter, to call headquarters. He said into it: "O'Brien? Evans talking. Listen, Jay — the stiff's a girl. Young girl, stabbed, rope around her foot. Looks as if she was murdered and thrown in the drink with a weight to keep her under. Rope broke or frayed, and the body got loose. Case for some guy with imagination . . . . Yeah? Well, maybe I have, but not enough to see the joker behind this . . . . Okey. I'll hang around until Macy gets here."

Bill lit a cigarette and slouched to the door. To Ritoli he said: "Listen. If a big Mick with size seventeen feet and a mush-melon face asks where I'm at, send him to the one-arm lunch around the corner. I need coffee and beans — something simple and homelike — after looking at that thing you found."

"Yez, zir," Ritoli nodded. "Yez, zir, mizter."

"And save that," Bill said "for Macy. He'll get a kick out of it. No one ever called him Mister before."

J AY O'BRIEN said across the desk at headquarters, two hours later: "Well, where's the tie-up? What's back of it?"

Bill played an imaginary piano with the tips of his fingers and again read the penciled memo on O'Brien's desk pad. He scowled, massaged his chin slowly, looked up into O'Brien's scowl.

"That's her all right, Jay. Twenty years old, five-foot-seven, dark hair and eyes, attractive, Italian-looking. That's her."

"Listen," O'Brien scowled. "I been a flatfoot twenty years, and this fits too easy. See? It smells. You find an undressed stiff at four in the afternoon without a ghost's chance of identifying it, and at five the phone rings and a guy gives you all the info it would take you two months to dig up. Ain't that lovely now? Better check up."

Bill nodded, tore off the memo sheet, stood up. The phone rang. O'Brien clamped the receiver between ear and shoulder, said "Hello" through his cigar, then listened. He forked the receiver slowly.

"Macy," he said to Bill, "calling from DePisa's office. The girl was stabbed. Been dead not more than twenty-four hours, probably less."

"Yeah?"

"Go out and smell around. Find out who phoned me that identification."

"Yeah."

Bill went out and climbed into a taxi.

T HE NAME on the memo sheet was Rose Veda, the address 154 Vernon Street, South End. Bill climbed the high wooden steps, knuckled the doorbell, stood scowling at a frosted globe with *Board and Rooms* painted on it in black. The door opened and a smallish woman with thin dry lips and a checkered house dress said: "Yes?"

"Does Miss Rose Veda live here?"

"She rooms here, yes," the woman said.

"Home, is she?"

"I don't believe so. I haven't seen her today. Is there any message?"

"Mind showing me her room?" Bill suggested.

"Her room? Who are you?"

Bill put two fingers in his vest pocket and brought out a nickeled badge. The woman said: "Oh. You're a — a policeman."

"Yeah."

The woman said "Oh" again, and then: "Yes, surely. The room is upstairs, Rose hasn't —" as Bill stepped past her into the hall — "done anything wrong, has she?"

Bill shrugged, waited for her to close the door, then followed her down the carpeted hall. The room was on the second floor, midway down the corridor The woman produced a bunch of keys unlocked the door. Bill entered slowly.

The room was small, stuffy, with an old-fashioned chiffonier, wooden bed, one window, two rag rugs. Bill walked to the chiffonier and picked up a photograph in a cheap tin frame. The woman said: "That's her. Those pictures on the wall are her too. She posed for them."

Bill put the photo down and stood with his hands hipped, gazing at the pictures on the wall. They were magazine covers, all four of them, mostly carmine and yellow. The first was a nude girl holding a parrot; the second was a nude girl looking at canaries in a cage; the third was a nude girl stroking a Pekinese; the fourth was a nude girl fondling a large cat. The woman said: "She's posing for a whole series of them for that magazine. It comes out every two weeks and she's on the cover of every issue. The next one has her lying beside a bowl of goldfish. She's working on it now."

Bill squinted at the artist's name and said, scowling: "I'll take these, May need 'em."

"But —"

"She won't mind. Has she got any friends?"

"You mean boy friends?"

"Yeah. Either kind."

"She has a boy friend," the woman said. "Edwin, his name is. I don't know his other name. He comes here often."

"To her room?"

"Well, yes, sometimes. I don't allow my girls to have boy friends in their rooms, but Rose and Edwin are such good friends."

"On good terms?"

"Oh, yes. That is, all except her posing. He doesn't like that, and I don't know as I blame him. After all, it isn't very nice for a girl to pose with no clothes on. They were having an argument about it only night before last. I didn't try to listen, you understand, but he was talking loud. He said he wouldn't stand for it any more and if she didn't stop he'd —"

"He'd what?"

"He — well, he said he'd kill her. But he was just talking like that, of course. They were going it hot and heavy, and he was excited."

"Where does this chap work?" Bill frowned.

"Why, I don't know. She has a picture of him somewhere, though. Maybe I can find it."

The woman looked through two chiffonier drawers and found the picture in the third. Bill took it, glanced at it, thrust it into his pocket. He took the girl's photo, too, and the cheap prints on the wall. "Thanks," he said. "Got a phone here?"

"We've a phone downstairs."

Bill walked downstairs and dropped a nickel in the slot. He called Jay O'Brien. He said with his mouth close to the tube: "Listen, guy. Tell this one to Macy and watch his eyes glitter. The girl was posing in the nude for an artist bird by the name of Jules Valliers. Ever hear of him? Yeah, I thought so. Good-by, sweetheart."

JULES VALLIERS was a thin, ascetic-faced foreigner with raven hair and shifty black eyes. He was, Bill decided after casual scrutiny, the type commonly known as pansy. Women might think him ultra.

Valliers built a church and steeple with his hands and said jerkily: "I quite understand your point, Mr. Evans. She was working for me. But I assure you she left my studio yesterday afternoon precisely as usual. I know nothing of her home life. She was merely an employee."

"In the nude," Bill shrugged.

"But an artist attaches no significance to that, Mr. Evans."

"She posed for you in the nude," Bill said, "and she was found in the nude."

"But surely you don't think —"

"Cops don't think. All I know, Valliers, is that she was murdered and thrown in the drink. Outside of the murderer — assuming you're not him — you're probably the last man saw her alive. What time'd she leave here?"

"Shortly after five o'clock," Valliers said precisely.

"M'm. Know where she was going?"

"No. Yes — wait a moment. She had a gentleman friend. I believe she intended to meet him."

"Who?"

"Krauss was the man's name. Edwin Krauss."

"Ever meet him?"

"Yes. He has been here on several occasions. You see —" Valliers fingered the crease in his trouser leg —"he is employed in the shop which supplies most of the er — live pets for my work. I have been doing a series of covers —"

"Yeah. I know. What shop?"

"Matthew Fern's Pet Shop, just below here," Valliers said. "Krauss is Mr. Fern's assistant."

"Did the girl ever tell you," Bill demanded slowly, "that her boy friend, Krauss, threatened to kill her if she didn't cut posing in the nude."

"Good heavens, no!"

"No. She wouldn't. When'd you last see Krauss?"

Valliers did mental arithmetic. "This is Thursday. He came Tuesday morning to bring" — he smiled sheepishly — "some goldfish in a bowl. I needed them for a new picture."

"Let's see 'em."

"What?"

"Let's see 'em."

"Why, certainly. But surely a bowl of goldfish —" Valliers walked to the door, opened it. "My studio is at the rear of the house." He proceeded down the corridor, taking two short mincing steps to Bill's one.

The studio was a junk shop with three huge windows. Valliers switched on light and said womanishly: "I'm afraid I ought to apologize for the condition of the room." He led the way through an array of easels and canvas squares, switched on another light, and said: "There it is, Mr. Evans."

The model stand was low on the floor, draped with black velvet. The goldfish bowl stood front center. Bill stepped sidewise to the unfinished canvas and saw the same layout reproduced in oils, with Rose Veda added. She was nude, lying on her stomach and elbows with one leg kicked up. She was apparently smiling down at the goldfish.

Bill strode to the stand and stood scowling. He walked around it to the rear, put his hand on the knob of a door, and said to Valliers: "Where's this lead to?"

"To the back stairs," Valliers said. "I keep it locked."

Bill tried it, found it locked, and turned away. He stopped, scowled, stooped slowly to pick something like seeds up off the floor, then straightened and put his hands in his pockets.

"Well, I guess that's all."

"If you care to see anything else, Mr. Evans —"

"Later. How do I get out of here?"

Valliers said: "This way," and walked to the head of the carpeted stairs. "If there is anything at all I can do, please feel free to call on me."

"Thanks. I even might."

Bill descended the stairs alone and stopped in the lower hall to light a cigarette. He heard Valliers walk back along the upper corridor; then a door slammed. Then a woman's voice behind him said: "Please. May I speak to you?" and he swung around sharply.

The woman stood in a doorway, beckoning. She wore dark green and she was exceptionally good looking with a severely slender body and precise features. Perhaps twenty-five years old, not more. She stepped backward into dining-room as Bill walked towards her. Closing the door, she put her hand furtively on Bill's arm and said quickly: "I heard what you and Mr. Valliers said. I listened deliberately. He was lying."

"Was he?"

"He didn't tell you all that happened."

"I didn't expect him to, little one," Bill scowled. "Who're you?"

"I'm Katherine Mitchell, his housekeeper. That is, I'm everything. I'm a secretary of sorts and a maid and — well, everything."

"And what didn't he tell me?" Bill said.

"Yesterday — it was about four o'clock — I was in my room writing some letters, and I heard a girl scream upstairs. I ran out of my room and up the stairs, and the studio door was open. Mr. Valliers was bending over the model stand and I could see Rose Veda lying there. Then Jules — Mr. Valliers — saw me and slammed the door shut."

"And after that?" Bill said quietly.

"I — I went back to my own room, and a little while later I heard Mr. Valliers go out. I was curious, so I went up to the studio to ask Miss Veda what had happened, but she was gone, too."

"Thanks," Bill said. "That'll help. Anything else?"

"No. I don't think so."

"Okey." Bill put his hands in his pockets and paced to the door. Frowning, he turned back again. "You said you heard a scream and ran upstairs and the studio door was open. Does he usually leave it open when he's working?"

"No," the girl faltered. "But —"

"Left it open so you'd be sure to catch him at his dirty work, eh?" Bill said casually. "Thoughtful of him." He strolled down the hall, opened the front door, and closed it softly after him.

OUTSIDE, the rain was a cold drizzle and the clock in the Park Street Church began to boom nine while Bill slopped across Vernon to Charles. He pushed into a corner drug-store and pawed through the yellow pages of a phone book, looking for the address of Matthew Fern's Pet Shop. He found it and scribbled it on the back of an envelope. Five minutes later he hammered on the door of the shop itself, three streets distant. The place was closed up.

Sucking a wet cigarette, Bill took a cab to a hotel in Park Square, saluted the doorman, and used a phone in the lobby. He called Jay O'Brien. He said, grinning:

"Listen, sweetheart. I got enough to give Macy a nightmare. Hot and how. You and him going to the fights tonight? Okey. See you ringside and tell you the whole works. What? Me dine with you? Listen, flatfoot, I'm only three steps from the sweetest little waitress in this man's town. With you along, she wouldn't see me with sunglasses. Nope, I dine alone. As Ritoli the clam man would say: "Yez, zir, mizter. 'By now.""

**M**ACY, large of fist and small of brain, rubbed moist palms together and said importantly: "It's a cinch. It's open and shut. What I don't get is why you passed it up when it was right in front of your face."

Macy paced the floor. Jay O'Brien used a pencil to draw pictures on the butt-scarred headquarters desk. Bill sat on the desk with his legs crossed.

"The girl says she heard a scream," Macy argued. "She ran upstairs and found Valliers leaning over the dead body. Valliers slammed the door in her face. Couple of minutes later he left the house and took the body with him."

"The point is," Bill said, "that he slammed the door."

"Huh?"

"He slammed the door in his secretary's face. Get it? The door was open."

"Well, what of it?"

"You're dumb, Macy."

"Yeah? I'm dumb? Well, I'll have Valliers here in an hour, see? And he'll talk. He's been in a jam with dames before. I'm dumb, am I?"

Bill said: "Yeah, you're dumb," and scooped up his hat. The hands of the wall clock pointed to ten after ten. Halfway to the door Bill turned and said to Jay O'Brien, grinning: "So Schaaf wouldn't last three rounds, hey? Twenty bucks you owe me. Yez, zir, mizter. Don't let it slip your memory."

"Where you goin'?" O'Brien demanded.

"To look at canaries."

"What?"

"Three rounds," Bill grinned. "Tsk, tsk. You and Macy should be in business together, selling gold bricks."

Outside, the sun was shining for the first time in two days. Bill took a cab to the South End, walked up Charles Street, and entered Matthew Fern's Pet Shop. The shop was small, musty, full of noises and queer smells. Matthew Fern himself, shabbily dressed, near bald, eagle-eyed, was arguing with a fat Italian woman who talked with her shoulders and brandished a box of bird seed in one hand. A thin, worried looking young man came from the rear and said to Bill: "Yes, sir. Can I help you?"

Bill said: "I guess you're Krauss."

The young man stared, stepped backward, and said in a low voice: "What do you want?"

"Talk to you."

"I'm only the assistant here," Krauss said quickly. "Mr. Fern will be through in a minute and he'll —"

"Never mind Fern. Want to talk to you. Private."

Krauss licked his lips. "Yes, sir."

"Got a back room here?"

"Yes, sir. Yes."

"That'll do. Let's go."

Krauss glanced furtively at Matthew Fern, turned, and walked quickly to the rear. He opened a door and said: "There's a step here." His thin fingers groped along the wall for a light switch.

Bill trailed him inside and sat in an old rocker. The room was small, low ceilinged, choked with piled-up boxes, floor covered with oily black dirt and cigarette butts. There was a window, but the lower half of it was painted black. Bill sucked a pipe and began to crumble tobacco in his left palm. Krauss, breathing heavily, sat in a straight-backed chair, leaned forward, and said: "Well, what do you want? Who are you?"

"You're in a jam, Krauss."

"Why? Why am I?"

"I guess you know why."

"I didn't do it!" Krauss said. "If you think I did it, you're crazy. I'll admit she was my girl friend, but —"

"Well?"

"I guess I better keep still. I'll only get myself in worse."

"How'd you know she was dead?" Bill said casually.

"I — I had a date with her last night. She didn't show up, so I went over to her house. I was sore. I talked to Mrs. Vail — she's the woman who runs the house and she told me what'd happened."

"And she, I suppose, got it from friend Macy."

"What?"

"Never mind, never mind. Some guys are born dumb." Bill pulled his mouth out of shape with the stem of his pipe. "You didn't like the idea of your girl posing naked; did you?"

"No, I didn't."

"Had some pretty strong arguments about it, didn't you?"

"Well — yes."

"Maybe you even threatened to kill her if she didn't cut it out, hey?"

"I didn't mean it," Krauss faltered. "I only told her that because I was sore; that's all. You'd be sore yourself if the girl you were going to marry was posing —"

"Yeah; I know. Don't think much of Valliers, do you?"

"No, I don't. He's no good. He's got a rotten reputation with women."

"Ever talk to him about Rose?"

"No."

"But you went to his house a few times?"

"I — yes, but I went on business. I had to take some stuff over from the store, and —"

"All right," Bill said. "That's all."

He knocked his pipe out on the arm of the rocker and stood up. Krauss stood up, too. Suddenly Krauss took a step forward.

"You don't think I did it, do you? You don't think I'd kill the girl I love, just because —"

"You're in a jam," Bill shrugged. "What I think won't get you out of it."

He opened the door, scowling. In the store the fat Italian woman was still talking with her shoulders and Matthew Fern was mopping his bald head with a handkerchief. Outside, Bill hailed a cab and said to the driver: "Hello, Ricki. I'm having tea with Jay O'Brien. Three Rounds O'Brien." He stretched his six foot-two bulk-in the seat and laughed softly. "And with Macy. Dear old Macy, the Great Brain. Don't hurry, Ricki. Take your time."

THREE MEN were in the back room at headquarters when Bill strolled in. Macy, the Great Brain, was striding from wall to wall, both hands wedged in his hip pockets, words growling from his mouth. Jay O'Brien sat sidewise on a table, pensively studying the shaft of smoke from a fat cigar. Jules Valliers cringed in a straight-backed chair, feet braced, eyes wide, hands rigid in his lap. Macy was saying:

"You'll talk. Yes, sir, you'll talk. There's ways and ways. Well put the screws to you, mister. Tighter guys'n you have opened their traps. What'd you kill her for?"

Valliers said shrilly: "I didn't. I don't know anything about it."

"You know, mister. You know, all right. You'll tell what you know, too. You'll come clean or you'll sit here and rot."

Bill closed the door behind him and said softly: "My, such language."

Macy jerked around and said: "You're just in time, guy. Have a seat, ringside."

Jay O'Brien said: "Greetings, gorgeous. When did school let out?"

Bill found a chair near the wall and sat down with his feet sprawled in front of him. He said: "Go ahead. Don't mind me." He took a match from his vest pocket, stuck it cornerwise in his mouth, and stared across at Valliers. Valliers' hands were kneading imaginary dough.

"Now get this straight," Macy growled, standing stiff-legged. "You're gonna talk, see? You're gonna talk if it takes all night. You killed the girl, didn't you?"

"No," Bill said. "He didn't."

"What?"

"I didn't!" Valliers whined. "I don't know anything about it!"

"All he did," Bill shrugged, "was get rid of the body."

"Yeah?"

"Yeah. The dead body."

"He says," Jay O'Brien murmured, lifting both hands palms upward, "he don't know anything about it."

"If you know so much, wise guy," Macy rasped, "maybe you know all the rest of it."

"Sure."

"Yeah? Well, what?"

"Let him tell it," Bill shrugged. He spat out a chewed match-end and nodded to Valliers. "Better tell 'em about it. Begin where the phone rang."

Valliers pressed both fists to his forehead and rocked from side to side. He said thickly: "I tell you I don't know anything about it!"

"Don't be a sap."

"I don't *know,* I tell you! I had nothing to do with it! I —"

"All right," Bill shrugged. "All right. It's not my funeral. Listen, you guys. He was painting the girl's picture, see? And the phone rang. The phone's in the den at the other end of the hall. There's no phone in the studio. Yeah, I been snoopin'. The phone rang, and this guy hustled out of the studio to answer it. He left the door open. Who was on the phone, Valliers?"

"I don't know anything about it!"

"Okey. You will later." Bill tipped his chair against the wall and put his hands in his pockets. "While this guy was talking on the phone, he heard a yell from the studio. He charged down the hall again and found the girl sprawled out on the stand, stabbed. You wouldn't call me a liar, Valliers?"

Valliers sobbed: "I don't know what you're talking about! I —" Then he put his face in his cupped hands and stopped rocking back and forth. He said almost inaudibly: "It's true. I — I admit it."

"Who was on the phone?"

"No one. No one answered it. Then I heard a scream and I ran back to the studio and — But she was dead when I got there! I didn't do it!"

"If you didn't do it," Macy growled, "why all the fancy lyin'?"

"I — I was frightened."

"Been in a tough spot with women before, haven't you?" Bill said quietly. Valliers nodded, sobbing.

"Figured it looked bad for you, so you got rid of the body, hey?"

Valliers nodded again.

"All right, mister," Bill shrugged. "Who killed her?"

"I don't know! I tell you I don't know!"

"That straight?"

"It's the truth. It's the God's honest truth. She — she was dead when I found her."

"Okey," Bill said. "Better let him go, Macy."

"The hell I will."

"Don't be a sap. He admits he didn't do it."

"Yeah? Well, I got to be shown."

"Okey," Bill said. He got up and strolled to the door. "While you're doing the Missouri, a guy by the name of Edwin Krauss is giving you the horse laugh. And don't forget that phone call. When a phone rings, flatfoot, it means somebody dropped a nickel in a slot somewhere."

**M**ALONE of the *Times-Herald* was lapping thumb and forefinger over the pages of a city directory when Bill strolled in. He looked up, grunted, and lapped some more. Bill pulled up a chair and said gently: "Listen, scribe. Who's working on Rose Veda?"

"Marshall and young Meade," Malone said. "Yez, zir, mizter."

"I see you've been snooping around," Bill grinned. "How much did O'Brien spill?"

"Enough for this." Malone pushed a pile of typewritten sheets; much penciled, across the desk. "Why? Got any more?"

Bill read the sheets slowly, scowled, squared them together again, tossed them aside. He took a cigarette from an open box of flat fifties. He said casually: "What do you know about Valliers?"

"Plenty," Malone said. "He's news."

"His women?"

"His women do things to our circulation, mister." Malone shrugged. "We keep a standing list. Want a look?"

"It might help."

Malone pawed through the bottom drawer of the desk, found a worn sheet of copy paper, glanced at it and handed it over. Bill studied it, eyes narrowed.

"Want to do me a favor, Malone?"

"What?"

"Get some nice black type and a fancy border and box some hot syllables on page one of tonight's paper. Something like this: 'Police mum on list of suspects. Refuse to name person they believe guilty of Veda killing until positive proof is obtained. Watching every move of those under suspicion.' Got it? And throw in some hooey about a knife. 'Police seeking murder knife. Will comb all possible hiding places in search of weapon which may prove killer's guilt. Believe they have definite clue as to knife's whereabouts.' Okey?"

"You'd make a hell of a newpaperman," Malone grinned.

"Yeah, I know, I know. But I got good ideas, mister. Do that for me, will you?"

"On the level?"

"On the level," Bill said. "Print that and you'll have the rest of it by this time tomorrow."

"Okey," Malone nodded. "Anything to oblige."

Bill walked from the *Times-Herald* building back to headquarters, stopping in *Peroni's* for fish-cakes and beans. He found Jay O'Brien scowling over a letter.

"Get a load of this," O'Brien said.

He shoved the letter across the desk and Bill picked it up. The writing was feminine, in purple ink on gray paper. It said:

Dearest Ed:

You won't have to worry much longer, I'm sure, and I suppose we'll both be happier when I'm through working for Valliers. He got fresh today as usual while I was posing for him. He tried to maul me and of course I told him where to get off. I've told him the same thing before and he just laughed, but today he got real sore and told me if I couldn't be nice he'd find a way to make me. I guess he's always had his own way with girls who worked with him before, because he got awfully nasty. I guess I won't be working much longer, but maybe it's all for the best. I was real scared of him today. Gee, Ed, I'll be glad when we can get married. I'm so sick of working for men like him. Love me, Ed? Loads? I hope so because I'll always love you.

Rose.

"Krauss brought that in half an hour ago," O'Brien scowled. "He was nervous as a rabbit and had the shakes. Said she wrote it three days ago. Said he thought we ought to have it because it might throw some light on the case."

"He's not so dumb," Bill said.

"Looks bad for Valliers."

"Yeah? Where's Macy?"

"Out feeding his face."

"Valliers in the back room still?"

"Nope. I let him go and put Kennedy on his tail."

"When Macy shows up," Bill said, "give him this letter and send him over to the girl's boarding-house. Send some guy with him that knows handwriting. There's a scrapbook in the bureau drawer with writing in it. Her writing. Tell Macy to check up."

"You think Krauss wrote this letter himself?"

"I think Krauss is a wise guy."

"Yeah? Well, why send Macy? You on a vacation?"

"I got a date," Bill said.

IT WAS three-forty-five when Bill climbed out of a cab and walked up the street towards Jules Valliers' house. On the opposite sidewalk a short, thick-set man leaned against a brick wall between a neighborhood grocery and a delicatessen store. Bill strolled over, nodded, and said: " 'Lo, Kennedy."

"Greetings," Kennedy growled. "Gimme a cigarette. If there's a lousy job around, I get it every time."

"Valliers home?"

"Yeah."

"Let's go," Bill said.

He crossed the street again, climbed stone steps, and pushed the button above the brass name plate. Valliers' good-looking housekeeper, Katherine Mitchell, opened the door.

Bill said: "Good day. Valliers in?" The girl nodded and stepped aside. Bill and Kennedy walked in and waited. A moment later Valliers, in lavender dressing-gown and leather slippers, descended the stairs and stood staring. "You want me?" he said slowly.

"Want to look around," Bill shrugged. "Kennedy here has an idea the evidence is still in the house."

"The evidence?"

"The knife."

Valliers said: "Oh," and looked at Kennedy helplessly. "If there is anything I can do, I hope you won't hesitate to — But I'm afraid I'm not much help." He summoned a weak smile. "The whole affair has upset me?"

"I'll get along all right," Kennedy said.

"Then if you won't need me, I believe I'll —"

"Yeah. Okey."

Valliers walked upstairs again, holding the banister. Katherine Mitchell said calmly: "You prefer to be alone, gentlemen?"

"Talk to you later," Bill nodded.

She said: "Certainly," and paced down the hall without looking back.

Bill glanced at his watch. He said to Kennedy: "Listen. I gotta scram. All you're supposed to do is mope around dumb like and keep an eye on Valliers and the girl. Especially the girl. You'll get wise when you see the papers."

"Give me the low-down," Kennedy grumbled. "What am I, anyway?"

"Some other time, mister. Some other time."

"Say, listen —"

"Keep an eye on the girl," Bill said, and closed the door behind him.

**D**OWN the street a newsboy was hiking across front lawns, tossing papers on verandas. Bill went towards him.

"What one does Valliers take, Bud?" he asked the boy.

"The *Globe*," the boy said.

Bill fumbled in his pocket and slapped a half dollar into the boy's hand. "Here. Throw a *Times-Herald* on his porch, too. And give me one."

The boy gaped and said: "Sure. Thanks, mister."

"Been over by Fern's Pet Shop yet?"

"That ain't on my route."

Bill snatched the paper, looked both ways for a cab, swore under his breath, and ran down the sidewalk. Five minutes later, at the corner of Matthew Fern's street, he saw more newsboys climbing down from a truck and catching bundles of papers that a man heaved out to them. He exhaled slowly and stopped to light a cigarette. Then he grinned. Farther down the street a wide shouldered man with a derby was waddling along on big feet. The man was Macy.

Bill strolled towards Fern's Pet Shop, ambled past, and glanced inside. Fern was talking to a customer. Edwin Krauss was on hands and knees among an assortment of wire cages. Bill strolled past again and casually tossed his *Times-Herald* on the sidewalk, in the doorway. A moment later the door opened, the customer came out, and Matthew Fern picked up the paper.

The shop was midway between the ends of a one-story block. Bill ran to one end of the block, plunged down an alley, strode along a cement walk at the rear. The back door of the shop was locked; so was the rear window. Bill hauled out a clasp-knife, finger-nailed the blade open, poked the point into the door-lock, and slapped the heel of the knife sharply with his palm. He opened the door, stepped inside, and closed the door quietly.

The room was dark; the door leading into the shop was closed. Bill tiptoed past a mound of empty boxes, squatted with one eye to the keyhole, and saw Matthew Fern standing near the counter, staring nearsightedly at a spread newspaper. Krauss was wiping birdcages with a white rag.

Fern laid his newspaper down and walked along behind the counter. The front door opened, and he stopped. Macy came in. Macy and Fern stared at each other, and Fern took a step backward. Macy said: "Hello, Fern," put one hand in his coat pocket, strode to Krauss, and said: "You're wanted, Krauss. You're comin' with me."

"What for?" Krauss said, staring.

"Never mind that. Come on."

Krauss said in a shrill voice: "But I haven't done anything! I —"

"Come on."

Krauss continued to stare, then mumbled: "All right. I'll — come." Without looking at Fern he walked slowly behind the counter, took his hat from underneath, and paced stiffly to the door. Macy strode out behind him.

Fern peered at the door. He took the newspaper, unfolded it, and bent over it again, fingering his cheek. He looked at the door again, frowning, then paced quickly to the rear of the shop.

Bill flattened against the wall just in time. The door creaked open. Fern entered, pushed the door shut quickly, stood blinking in the semi-dark. He began to mutter to himself, then groped nervously along the rows of shelves. In the far corner he pushed aside some empty cardboard cartons and tin cans, reached his whole arm behind them, and stepped back, holding a roll of newspaper. He pawed the newspaper apart, took a knife out of it, and stared at the knife intently, still muttering. He jerked a handkerchief from his pocket, wiped the hilt and blade of the knife carefully, and rewrapped the knife in the crumpled newspaper. Reaching up, he moved the empty cartons back into place. Again muttering, he thrust the newspaper into his pocket and started towards the door which led to the back alley.

"Thanks, Fern," Bill said. "You're a big help."

Fern spun around and stood rigid, and Bill paced quietly into the open. Fern took a step backward, stopped, and stood rigid again, eyes wide, mouth twisted. His fingers clawed the newspaper in his pocket.

"I'll take that," Bill said. "Then we'll go for a walk, mister. A long walk. Your own fault. You shouldn't believe all you read in the papers."

Fern said: "What are you talking about? What are you doing here?"

"I'll take the knife, Fern."

"Knife? What knife?"

"This one, wise guy." Bill stepped closer and reached for the newspaper. Methodically he stuffed it into his own pocket. "Let's go, Fern."

Fern put his hand out timidly and said: "Listen. Why do you come here? What have I done? What —" Then he leaped. Breath exploded from his mouth. His head rammed Bill's jaw and his fist made a loud crunching sound against Bill's face. Bill stumbled back, gasping, turned on one toe and tripped into a cairn of piled-up boxes. Fern struck again blindly, and struck a third time, snarling viciously. Bill groped up. Fern pushed him back with both hands and kicked him. The mound of boxes toppled, smothering Bill's oath. Fern whirled and ran.

Dazed, Bill rose on one knee and elbowed himself free. He stood up, swaying. He said: "Well, I'm damned," and limped slowly to the rear door. He stood there, scowling, and said: "Of all the fat-head fools."

He limped back again, entered the store, and looked for a phone. There was one on a shelf behind the counter. He lifted the receiver, dialed a number, and said a moment later: "Listen, Jay. I just had a complete massage, from a guy named Matthew Fern. Yeah, the same Matthew Fern. He got away. Smacked me down and took the first train. Yeah. Send a couple of blood-hounds after him and pass the good word along."

He forked the receiver and opened the phone book, looking for the name Jules Valliers. He dialed again and Katherine Mitchell answered the ring.

"Kennedy there?" Bill said.

"Just a moment, please."

Bill waited, then said scowling: "Listen, Kennedy. Matthew Fern just gave me the works and got loose. He's in the neighborhood. See what you can do."

"If there's a lousy job around," Kennedy growled, "I get it every time."

"The girl make any trick moves?"

"Naw."

"Okey. Find Fern."

HALF AN HOUR later Bill limped out of a cab on LaRonge Street, climbed the stationhouse steps with painful awkwardness, and found Jay O'Brien, Great Brain Macy, and Edwin Krauss in the room behind headquarters. Macy was standing on spread legs, hands hipped, neck outthrust, over the chair which held up Krauss. Jay O'Brien was sucking a fat cigar, slipping the paper cigar-band on and off his little finger and listening without interest to Macy's harsh syllables.

"Now listen," Macy was rasping. "We got it on you, see? You bring a letter in here and hand it to us in a nice, sweet way, and the letter's a fake. The girl didn't write it, see? You did. You wrote it to hang suspicion on Valliers, see? And to clear yourself. But you're in a jam. You're gonna come clean."

"I wrote it because I was afraid," Krauss mumbled.

"You wrote it because Matthew Fern told you to," Bill said.

Macy spun around and growled: "What?"

"Didn't you, kid?" Bill said quietly.

"Y-yes," Krauss said, licking his lips. "He — he said it would clear me and it wouldn't do any harm. I was afraid I'd be accused of the murder. I took some old letters I had from Rose and — and —"

"And faked the writing. Give the kid a break, Macy. He's just dumb."

"You'll be tellin' me next he didn't kill the girl, wise guy," Macy said irritably.

"I even might," Bill shrugged. He leaned against the table, looked at O'Brien, and said softly: "You get Fern yet?"

"I don't get anything," O'Brien said pleasantly. "I'm in a complete fog."

Macy exhaled loudly and swung back to face Krauss. He hipped his hands again and rocked back and forth on stiff legs. He said savagely: "Well, are you gonna talk, young feller, or do I have to show you how?"

"Lay off, flatfoot," Bill said. "He didn't do it. Fern did it."

"What?"

"Save it for Fern."

"What else do you know, wise guy?" Macy scowled.

"Plenty."

"Well?"

"All right," Bill shrugged. "You asked for it." He put a cigarette in his mouth and took a light from O'Brien's cigar. "Valliers and the girl are in the studio, see? The phone rings. Valliers hikes out to answer it. Fern is waiting at the top of the back stairs outside the studio's other door, which is kept locked. Fern has a key. He lets himself in, the girl screams, he does his dirty work, goes out the same way and locks the door after him. He does all this to frame Valliers with the killing. Instead Valliers gets rid of the body. So Fern calls up O'Brien here and reports the girl missing, to put the cops wise."

Macy said: "Now isn't that nice? Isn't that just lovely?"

Someone else said bitterly, from the doorway: "You're clever, Mr. Evans. Damned clever." Kennedy and another man came in, holding Matthew Fern between them. Fern's face was convulsed.

Kennedy said: "He was walkin' down Vernon Street near Valliers' house. When he spotted me he dove for a cab. Your pal Ricki was parked on the corner, and him and me chased this guy halfway across town before we got him. He had this on him." Kennedy took a gun from his pocket and banded it to Bill. "There's two shots been fired out of it.

Matthew Fern said again, standing with feet wide apart and fists clenched: "You're clever, Mr. Evans You think you know everything. I hope it does you some good."

Jay O'Brien pulled the cigar out of his mouth and said, scowling: "What is this, anyway?" Macy walked away from Krauss' chair and stood staring, eyes narrowed and a sneer widening his lips. "Yeah," Macy said. "What is this?"

"You're right, Mr. Evans," Fern said viciously. "I killed the girl. I planned it right. I stole the key to the studio door when I went to Valliers' house for money, a week ago. I knew he'd never miss it. At the same time I learned the layout of the studio and the rear stairs. The whole thing was planned right. Maybe you'd like to know the details."

"It might save time," Bill shrugged.

"Then you don't know everything after all."

"You killed her," Bill said through his cigarette, "to send Valliers to the chair. You hated Valliers for playing around with your wife."

"So you know that, do you?"

"And more."

"Good," Fern said. He was enjoying himself. His face was flushed and his eyes smouldering, and a little mad. "Then I'll tell you the rest. My wife was one of his women. I wasn't supposed to know. They thought I was dumb."

"Why the hell, then," Jay O'Brien grumbled, "didn't you kill Valliers? Why the girl?"

"Killing was too easy. That's why."

"So you picked on an innocent girl."

"I'd kill a dozen innocent people to see him hang."

"Oh, you're a tough guy, hey?" Macy growled. "Well, I'm no sap. I don't go for fairy tales, Fern. What about that phone call?"

"My wife," Fern said precisely, "telephoned her lover at exactly the same time each day. I made my plans accordingly." He swung on Bill. "What I should like to know is how Mr. Evans discovered me."

"Should you?" Bill said quietly.

"Yeah. And so would the rest of us," Macy snapped.

"Your wife," Bill shrugged, looking without emotion at Fern, "is listed on the *Times-Herald* scandal sheet as one of Valliers' latest attractions. Also, when you charged out of Valliers' studio after killing Rose Veda, you stopped to wipe your fingerprints off the doorknob. You took a handkerchief or something out of your pocket. And you spilled some bird seed on the floor, little one."

"Bird seed," Fern repeated slowly, mouthing the words.

"Right. Bird seed. So it was either you or Krauss, sweetheart, and the scandal sheet pointed to you. Then you did your own pointing. You read what the *Times-Herald* said about the knife, and you fell for it. Psychology, feller, psychology."

"What about Valliers' secretary?" Kennedy said.

"Couldn't be sure of her," Bill shrugged. "She's more than a secretary, and hell hath no fury like a woman double-crossed. And that phone call was a sticker. She might have chipped in." He gazed calmly at Matthew Fern. "All nice and straight now, little one?"

"Thanks, yes," Fern said, smiling.

"For a guy that's gonna burn," Jay O'Brien frowned, "you seem almighty happy. You're a wise guy, huh?"

"Sure," Fern said. "I'm a wise guy. I just came from Jules Valliers' house. I found Valliers and my wife together. If you don't think I'm a wise guy, go and look."

●　●　●　●　●

# DEAD DOG

BY THE TIME THIS STORY ABOUT POOCH HANLEY AND MR. BUTTONS APPEARED IN
*BLACK MASK* IN MARCH 1937, CAP SHAW HAD BEEN REPLACED AS EDITOR BY FANNY
ELLSWORTH. OTHER TALES OF MINE APPEARED ABOUT THAT TIME IN *ADVENTURE, CLUES
DETECTIVE STORIES, DETECTIVE FICTION WEEKLY, FEDERAL AGENT, THE FEDS, POPU-
LAR DETECTIVE, THRILLING MYSTERY,* AND, UNDER MY JOKEY PEN-NAME JUSTIN CASE,
IN THE *SPICY* MAGAZINES (WHICH, INCIDENTALLY, BY TODAY'S FREEDOM-OF-SPEECH
STANDARDS WOULDN'T RAISE AN EYEBROW). AS FOR THE MR. BUTTONS CHARACTER
IN THIS STORY, I'VE HAD DOG AND CAT FRIENDS SINCE I WAS A KID, AND HAVE TURNED
OUT DOZENS OF STORIES ABOUT THESE FOUR-FOOTED FRIENDS. IF YOU'RE INTERESTED
IN CATS, YOU MIGHT WANT TO CHECK THE INTERNET OR CERTAIN BOOKSTORES FOR A
COLLECTION OF MINE CALLED *THE LADY WORE BLACK AND OTHER CAT TAILS,*
PUBLISHED THIS YEAR BY ASH-TREE PRESS.

HBC

*Mr. Button buys a life with his death.*

EVERYBODY was always giving Pooch Hanley dogs, and when he left
the Palace Bar that evening and strolled homeward he had no intention of picking up a dog *en route*. He had dogs enough at home already.

But the mongrel mutt came sniffing along the sidewalk in front of the Corsair Club, and got tangled up in the legs of a drunken young man who was
being steered to a taxi by Louis Zapelli, the Corsair's head thief.

The mutt was pathetically frail and certainly meant no harm. But the young
man pushed Zapelli aside, shouted drunkenly, "Punt formation, hip!" and
punted the dog with sickening accuracy into a No Parking sign. And when
that happened, something exploded in Pooch Hanley's brain.

Hanley strode forward. With one hand he swung the young man around
and with the other he sent the fellow staggering against the open door of
the taxi.

It was a hard punch, loosening several teeth. Blood trickled down the young man's chin.

Pooch Hanley said to Louis Zapelli: "When he sobers up, tell him why I did it and who I am. If he wants to make something of it, all right."

The dog had not moved after dropping to the curb. Hanley picked it up. "Hip broken," he muttered, and glared at the man who had broken it.

He took the mutt home with him.

There were dogs galore at the Hanley homestead. There were kennels in the back yard, near the fringe of woods sloping down into Pine Pond, and countless cartons of canned dog food in the cellar. Pooch Hanley liked dogs, all kinds of dogs. Being a bachelor, he could give them his undivided attention and affection.

Even before he got the front door open, Mr. Buttons was violently assaulting the barrier from within. Mr. Buttons, a red-haired cocker spaniel, was two years old and uncontrollable. His adoration for Hanley was a form of St. Vitus's dance.

Tonight, after launching himself at Hanley's legs, he retreated amid ominous growls of suspicion. Hanley grinned at him.

"It's the uniform you don't like, is it?"

Some weeks ago, Mr. Buttons had been severely kicked by a short-tempered mail carrier. Since then, the mere sight of a uniform had been sufficient to arouse his anger.

Hanley was wearing part of a uniform. "This," he said to Mr. Buttons, "is a motorman's coat and nothing more, so don't be losing my temper. I borrowed it from an old-timer at the Palace Bar. I had no yen to be walking home naked after losing my shirt in a poker game."

That settled, he spent the next hour setting the broken hip of the mutt he had brought home with him. Then he went to bed.

FIVE MINUTES after he entered Police Headquarters the next morning, Pooch Hanley was summoned to the sanctum of Inspector John Murray. Murray greeted him coolly and said, "Sit down, Hanley," and then said, "I hear you were at the Palace last night. That right?"

"Yes, sir. I was checking on this White case."

The White case involved Mr. Louis Zapelli of the Corsair Club and Mr. Jake Doonan, proprietor of the Palace. It was a queer tangle. Paul White silent partner of Louis Zapelli, had been found dead in an alley, shot through the hip and the head. It was quite likely that Jake Doonan had done the shooting.

It was likely because White and Doonan had hated each other intensely. White had claimed vehemently that the Palace Bar was an eye-sore and had threatened to put Doonan out of business. Doonan had sworn publicly to commit murder or mayhem if White came within reach.

White was dead now, and good riddance of a politically-minded knave with underworld connections. But it was a crying shame that Jake Doonan, whom everybody liked, would probably pay the extreme penalty for doing the good deed.

"So you were working on the White case," said Inspector Murray.

"I was, sir," said Hanley. "Yesterday afternoon I spent four hours snooping around the Corsair Club, talking to the hired hands there, and then I dropped over to the Palace. I had a few beers and played some poker with the boys."

"And what did you learn?"

"Well, I —"

"Don't say it, Hanley. I know all the excuses. You apparently think more of your dogs than of your job."

Hanley sighed softly. "Now listen, Inspector," he said.

"On your way home from the Palace you assaulted a man."

"Yes, sir."

"That, Hanley, was conduct unbecoming an officer."

"Well, sir, he —"

"Kicked a dog. I know all about it. The District Attorney paid me a visit."

Hanley sat very still. "The District Attorney?"

"The young man you assaulted," said Murray curtly, "was the D. A.'s son. You, Hanley, are now without a job. You may appeal the suspension if you like, but I'd advise against it. When the D.A. has cooled down a bit, I'll see what I can do."

Pooch Hanley's face paled and he pushed himself erect.

"It's a good thing," he said slowly, " the young squirt didn't kick one of my dogs. I'd have killed him."

Without waiting for Murray's reply, he slammed the door furiously behind him.

A N HOUR LATER, Pooch Hanley sat on a stool at the Palace Bar, despondently drinking beer. The beer wouldn't help, he knew, but the business of drinking it would keep his mind off the fact that he had been suspended. Besides, it was soothingly quiet here at the Palace. Since Jake Doonan's incarceration, customers had kept away. Doonan's daughter was officially in charge. Her boy friend was tending bar.

Molly Doonan was young. She had a slim, trim little figure, black hair and dark eyes. The eyes were circled now from lack of sleep, and when she put a hand on Hanley's shoulder he stared and felt sorry for her.

"Pooch, when are they going to let father go?"

"It's hard telling, Molly."

"But why are they holding him? They can't prove anything, can they, Pooch?"

No, they couldn't prove anything. Doonan was merely being held on suspicion. The hell of it was, Paul White had left the Corsair Club that night and come here, via the alley, to lay down the law to Molly's father. That, at least, was Zapelli's story. White had talked it over with Zapelli at the club and then barged out. Zapelli, having a mess of trouble with a new floor show, had thought no more of it until informed that White's body had been found in the alley, midway between the Corsair and the Palace.

Jake Doonan had an alibi, of course. Half a dozen customers were willing to swear that he hadn't left the Palace between ten and midnight. The Medical Examiner placed the time of White's death at about eleven. But Doonan *had* sworn to lay White among the daisies, and it looked bad, because even without leaving the Palace, he could have stood in the back doorway and fired the fatal shots.

"Now listen, Molly," Hanley said softly, holding the girl's slim wrist. "You and I both know Jake didn't do it. Jake had a temper and might have gone to work on White with his fists if given the opportunity, but he'd never have used a gun. The police took this place apart looking for the gun that killed White, and didn't find it. So, they've got nothing on Jake."

"Then why are they holding him?"

"I guess they've just got to hold someone, Molly."

Tears gleamed in her eyes as she sat on the stool next to him. "Pooch, you've got to help us. You've got to. I — I'm scared."

"I guess I'm out of it, Molly. I'm fired."

"You were fired! *You?*"

"Well, suspended. An hour ago." He reached for a beer glass, made rings on the bar. "Of course, if you want me to work on the case, I can be hired as a private dick. It won't cost you anything . . . ."

She was silent a moment, staring at him. "Won't that get you in trouble with the department?"

"Might. I'll risk it."

"Then you're hired, Pooch."

"That," Hanley said, pushing the beer glass away, " makes me feel a whole lot better. Thanks, Molly."

TWO DAYS LATER, Pooch Hanley hiked into the news-room of the *Herald* and pulled a chair up to the desk of City Editor Bill Howard.

"In the past," he said gently, "I've done you favors, Bill. Now it's your turn."

Howard, editing copy, looked up, said, "Shoot, Pooch," and went right on penciling.

"It's about that White murder."

Howard dropped the pencil, pulled up his head and stared. He looked surprised. "Yeah? I would like the lowdown on that!"

He was a short, pudgy man with big hands and almost no nose. A story was meat and drink to him, and the smell of one made him ravenous.

"I want a front page story," Hanley said. "Something like this: Detective working on White killing suspended for striking District Attorney's son. Retained privately by daughter of suspected slayer, is ready now to present sensational evidence to convict real murderer. That sort of stuff, Bill. Big type."

"And then what?"

"When it breaks, I'll save it for you."

"Why not give it to me now?"

"There's nothing to give," Pooch admitted. "I want the man who killed White, Bill. I can't go to him because I don't know him. So he's got to come to me."

"And you think a story like that will bring him?"

"It might."

"It might send you to the morgue," Howard said calmly. "But I'll run it. As you said, I owe you the favor."

Pooch Hanley said, "Thanks."

"What about that second bullet?" Howard demanded. "Did they find it yet?"

"No."

"There's something queer in that, Bill. The guy was shot twice, once through the left hip, once through the head. The bullet in the head killed him, and they dug it out of his skull. But that other bullet went right through and is still missing. It wasn't in that alley. That fatal slug was from a thirty-eight, and they haven't found the gun yet. You any idea where the gun might be?"

"No."

"Well, I'll run the story, Pooch, and if it sends you to the morgue —"

"You can put my picture on page one," Hanley said quietly.

T HE STORY, emblazoned with a three-column portrait of the D. A.'s son, was a good one. It had news value because the D.A. himself was in the midst of a buzzsaw political scrap, and because people were still wondering who had murdered Paul White and what the police proposed to do about it.

The papers were on the street at 3 P.M. At five, Pooch Hanley walked into the D. A.'s office, closed the door behind him and said politely: "Well, well, this is a surprise."

The D.A. and the D. A.'s son were waiting for him. They were a strange pair. Kenneth Innman, the District Attorney, was big enough to be startling, had thin gray hair showing streaks of pink scalp, and owned a championship belt for heavyweight wrestling in amateur ranks. Strong as a horse, he was well over fifty and showed no signs of flabbiness.

His son, Russell, had been kicked out of Harvard two years ago for doing more sousing than studying. He'd had affairs with torch singers, been refused admission to a nudist colony, warbled smutty tunes in a night club, and invented a cocktail containing three ounces of absinthe for a base.

Both men stared as Hanley sank into a chair. The D.A. did the talking.

"I suppose you rather expected this, Hanley."

"Being sent for by you?" Hanley murmured. "To tell you the truth, no, I didn't."

"You went to a lot of trouble getting my son's picture in the *Herald*."

Hanley glanced at the son and thought it too bad that the younger Innman could not do some picture-posing right now. Decked out in a khaki and blue uniform, with many buttons, he looked like an anemic monkey on parade. There was to be a political display this evening, and Russell was attired for the occasion. Hanley recalled vaguely that the fellow played in some sort of band.

"Well, yes, I did go to some trouble about that picture," he admitted. "But not to make *you* dance."

"I'm not dancing, Hanley," the D.A. said coldly. "I merely think, Hanley, it's bad for everyone concerned when a former police detective, like you, becomes vindictive against the department. You were a good detective. One of the best. And we — well, we can't have you making faces at us, Hanley. It gives the newspapers too much lurid frontpage copy. You see?"

"I'm listening."

"Well, I think the entire thing was a misunderstanding in the first place, Hanley. Your suspension, I mean. When I talked to Murray about you, I didn't expect him to be so drastic. Now, I'd like to make amends."

Hanley was silent, anticipating what was coming. It was simple, of course. The D.A. was ear-deep in politics and at this particular time could not stand too much of the wrong sort of publicity. His son's picture in the paper, with talk of drunkenness and late hours at night clubs . . . .

"You'd like your job back, Hanley?"

"On what terms?"

"That you drop the newspaper campaign, of course, and, if I may suggest it, that you more or less forget the White case."

Hanley grew an inch. A scowl pulled his thick brows together. "Forget the White case? Why?"

"The case has petered out. Jake Doonan is still being held but will undoubtedly be released for lack of evidence. White's dead. You can't bring him back to life, and the public seems to think it's a good idea that he was murdered. So, why clean out the sewer when the taxpayers care nothing about it?"

"Someone," Hanley said slowly, "murdered that guy."

"Of course, of course."

"My job is — or was — to bring murderers to justice."

"You talk," said Russell Innman, "like a boy scout reciting his lessons."

Hanley ignored that. He centered his gaze on the D. A.

"So," Hanley said, "if I agree to lay off the White case, I get my job back. If not, what?"

"Why be so concerned over Paul White? I've told you, Hanley, that Jake Doonan will be released. Isn't that enough?"

"That doesn't answer my question."

"You insist on an answer?"

"I want to know where I'm at."

The D.A. shrugged his big shoulders, glanced wearily at his son. "It's my way, Hanley, or not at all. I'm sorry."

Pooch Hanley said, "Well, it's not mine."

A T NINE O'CLOCK that evening Hanley rang the bell of a Back Bay apartment, climbed a flight of stairs, and was greeted by a genial, bald-headed man wearing a bathrobe. The man was Medical Examiner Andrew Edson.

"It's like this, Mr. Edson," he said. "I'm working on this case and think I've got something. But I want to be sure of the fundamentals."

Edson had examined the body of Paul White at Headquarters, shortly after it had been brought in. "You know, of course," he said, "that the body was discovered by some chap who was on his way home from a theater and used the alley as a short cut. He notified the police.

"Well, he'd been shot twice. One bullet passed through the left hip and was not found. The other lodged in his brain, killing him. He died in agony, Hanley. The body was found face down, on cobblestones. The toes of White's shoes were practically worn through; and most of his fingernails were broken. He'd clawed up a lot of dirt, and one hand was wedged so hard between the cobblestones it had to be pried loose. Evidently the first shot — the one through the hip dropped him, and he writhed about for some time before being put out of his misery. The second bullet killed him instantly."

"That second bullet entered the back of his head and lodged in his brain?"

"Right."

"And this happened about eleven o'clock, did it?"

"About eleven, Hanley."

RAIN WAS DRIZZLING out of a midnight sky when Hanley got home. Pushing his key into the lock, he wondered why the house was so silent and why Mr. Buttons was not throwing fits against the door.

The door creaked shut behind him, and the only light in the room was the red end of Hanley's cigarette. Mr. Buttons was evidently asleep and that was queer because Mr. Buttons usually heard his master's footsteps and came to offer vociferous welcome

In the darkness of an adjoining room something moved. Pooch Hanley stiffened on the balls of his feet, with one hand outthrust toward a light switch.

It happened abruptly. The floor creaked, and a gun belched flame and thunder. A slug tore through space and buried itself in Hauley's arm. Hanley slewed backward, staggered against the wall and dropped.

He was reaching for his own gun even then, and it was in his fist, ready for business, before he slapped the floor. He didn't use it, didn't have to. No second blast came from the killer's weapon.

Instead, heavy shoes rapped out a tattoo across the floor in the other room, and a door shattered shut as a man fled.

Hanley squirmed to his knees and swayed erect, his left arm hanging limp. Blood seeped out of it and warmed his shoulder. While he stood there, drops of blood made soft whispering sound on the carpet. The house was eerily quiet.

Without touching the light switch, Hanley walked into the adjoining room and opened the door leading to the kitchen. The door on the far side of the kitchen, leading to the back porch and the back yard, was open. He closed it.

"So now," he said softly. "I'm a candidate for the morgue. Maybe the guy thinks he killed me."

He waited five minutes before showing a light. Five minutes would give the fellow time to cover a lot of distance, and it might be a good idea to let him go right on thinking Pooch Hanley was dead. Seeing a light, he might return to finish the job.

In the bathroom, Hanley examined his shoulder, cleaned the wound and bandaged it. The bullet had gone through flesh. He found it imbedded in the living-room wall, dug it out with his door key, and pocketed it.

Then, making a tour of inspection, he found Mr. Buttons.

The dog was dead. Blood and matted hair on the floor indicated that he'd been slain near the front door. Red saliva covered his mouth, and a gray film dimmed the big brown eyes. Near-by lay a metal ash-stand with which Mr. Buttons had been viciously clubbed.

Hanley placed Mr. Buttons on a chair and stared down at him. Hanley was trembling, his face was white and stiff, and his eyes smouldered. His hands curled convulsively.

"Dead," he whispered.

It was like losing an arm or a leg. The pain was not the same sort, but was equally unbearable. It began in the region of his lungs and crawled through him, reaching every nerve-end.

Mr. Buttons — dead! But Mr. Buttons had never in his short span of life done harm to anyone. He'd been a cheerful, affectionate ball of fluff, bouncing around and spilling sunshine. Now he was dead, and he had died the hard way, in torment.

"I guess," Hanley muttered, "you tried to keep the guy out. I guess that's what happened."

He sat and thought about it, and the thoughts were ugly, twisting his face and hands. About ten minutes passed before the real meat of the thing exploded in his laboring brain. Then he telescoped out of his chair, strode across the room and picked up the ash-stand.

The fingerprints on that ash-stand were good ones. He caught them with powder, lifted them on celluloid and transferred them to a stiff sheet of white paper. With the paper safely cached in his wallet, he hurried out of the house and drove downtown to Headquarters.

**H**ALF AN HOUR later he parked his car in front of the Corsair Club. It was close to eleven o'clock then, and the Corsair's early floor show was in full swing. A dozen scantily clad girls danced on the rectangle of gleaming floor, and the band brewed music. Hanley, feeling queerly undressed in streetclothes, followed a roundabout route to Louis Zapelli's office.

The door was closed, locked. A waiter, passing, indifferently, listened to Hanley's question and supposed Zapelli was upstairs.

Pooch Hanley found Zapelli at a crap table. "Like to talk to you," he said, and Zapelli nodded.

Zapelli's private talk-chamber was at the end of a short hall, where the noise from the gaming-room did not penetrate. He closed the door, stared unsmilingly at Hanley, and said, "Well?"

"The night Paul White was murdered, Zapelli, he had a talk with you and told you he was going over to the Palace to lay down the law to Jake Doonan. Is that right?"

"That is right."

"He went out about ten o'clock, and you thought no more of it. You were busy around here. In fact, you forgot about him until you heard he'd been killed."

"That," Zapelli said quietly, easing himself into the chair behind the desk, "is correct."

"Zapelli, you're holding out on me!"

"You mean I'm lying?"

"I mean this, Zapelli: Just as soon as I began to get warm on this case, the D.A. pulled me off it. He suspended me. He figured the suspension would keep me out of circulation, and when he found out I'd been hired privately to continue the investigation, he offered me my job back — on condition that I drop the case. I turned him down, Zapelli. And do you know what happened then?"

"No," Zapelli said.

"The D.A.'s son tried to gun me."

Motionless behind the desk, Zapelli allowed his face to register amazement. "Gun you?" he whispered.

"So," declared Hanley, still on his feet despite the pain in his shoulder, "the D.A.'s son holds cards in this game somewhere. He didn't gun me for target practice. There are two ends to this alley, Zapelli — Doonan's place and the Corsair Club. Russell Innman never hung his hat in Doonan's place. He was here that night. So . . . ."

Zapelli leaned forward, put his elbows on the desk and pushed his pink lips apart with the tip of his tongue. "I like you, Hanley," he said. "You're a fine fellow — sometimes. Take a tip and forget all this foolishness. Take your job back on Innman's terms, and I'll see that the kid apologizes for trying to gun you."

Hanley's laugh was low and ugly. He was thinking of Mr. Buttons.

"You see, it's this way," Zapelli said, leaning back again. "The kid is a pretty good friend of mine, and —"

Pooch Hanley had been expecting it and was ready for it. When Zapelli's right hand slid down below the level of the desk top, Hanley's own right hand streaked to a coat pocket.

"Sure you like me," Hanley said. Sarcasm dripped from his voice.

Zapelli shrugged, put his hands on the desk again. His gaze remained glued on Hanley's pocket, and Hanley's fist stayed in the pocket.

"You've got me wrong, Hanley."

"I've got you," Hanley said acidly, "right where I want you, louse."

"You think I killed White?"

"You'll make a lot of money out of this joint, running it alone."

"You're in the wrong booth, Hanley. I didn't kill White. The D.A.'s son did."

Hanley took a step sidewise, leaned against the wall because his throbbing shoulder needed support, and said, "I'd like to hear about it, Zapelli."

"The three of us," Zapelli said, shrugging, "were right here in this room. The kid was a regular customer of ours; he owed us a big chunk of money and White was demanding payment. The kid was tight, so tight he could hardly stand. He got sore. He pulled a gun. He shot White twice. The first bullet went through White's hip and gouged a chunk out of the desk here. The second stuck in his brain and killed him."

"Well?"

"Well, I done some fast thinking, Hanley. With White dead, this joint was all mine. I didn't have the political drag White had, and here was a chance to get a nice big load of it. With a stranglehold on the D.A.'s son, I could make the D.A. clean my shoes. See?"

Hanley saw and nodded. The gun in his hand was getting heavy, but he wanted to hear the whole story before escorting Zapelli to Headquarters. It was not going to be easy to walk Zapelli out of his fortress here, either.

"The kid," Zapelli said, "was scared stiff when he realized what he'd done. I took the gun away from him and hustled him out of here and made arrangements to have him driven home. Then I hung around about half an hour until the coast was clear, and lugged White's body out the back way. I dumped it in the alley and cooked up a story about how he went over to the Palace to see Doonan.

"And that's how it all happened, hey?"

"That's on the level. You can see now why the D.A. tried to haul you off the case, and why his son tried to gun you when you refused to take the hint."

Hanley nodded. The story appeared to be solid and reasonable. It might have a gap or two, but apparently Zapelli knew all the answers.

"O.K.," Hanley said. "Let's go."

Zapelli was grinning. It was an ugly, crooked grin. "Don't be a sap," he said. " You're not taking me anywhere."

Behind Hanley, the door was creaking open.

Pooch Hanley didn't make the mistake of whirling. He had a gun in his hand and lifted it, aiming the muzzle at Zapelli's face. Without shifting his gaze from that face, he said quietly, "No matter what happens, boys, I'll still have enough left to take Louis with me. Louis wants to go on living — so take it easy."

Zapelli turned pale. The gun frightened him and he cringed from it. Hanley took two steps forward and said grimly, "Get out of that chair!"

The fact that he knew what to do and did it swiftly probably saved Hanley from annihilation. Zapelli obeyed orders without realizing their significance. His henchmen were held back by bewilderment.

They could have murdered Hanley, but Hanley, before dying, would murder their boss.

Zapelli got out of the chair. Menaced by Hanley's gun, he squirmed around the desk. Before he knew what had happened, he was standing between Hanley and the men who had entered.

Hanley, entrenched behind the desk, said softly, "Now order your gorillas out of here!"

Zapelli shot frantic glances to right and left, as if estimating his chances of escaping by lunging. A sidewise lunge might give his gorillas a chance to mow Hanley down. Evidently he considered the risk too great.

"Get out, boys," he bleated. "Wait outside."

"And close the door," Hanley ordered.

There were four of them, all dressed in evening clothes. Apparently when not needed by Zapelli, they earned their keep by running the gambling devices. Zapelli had summoned them by pressing a bell-button under the desk.

Obeying orders, they filed out. The door clicked shut. Hanley said to Zapelli: "Come here!"

Zapelli swayed forward, pale and trembling.

"Seems to me you're taking some mighty big risks to help out Russell Innman," Hanley said.

"I need the kid on my side," Zapelli mumbled. "With a hold on the D.A. I can turn this place into a gold mine."

Hanley's glance strayed to the door. It was the only door. In the corridor outside, Zapelli's gunmen were undoubtedly cooking up a scheme to turn Pooch Hanley into a corpse. Time was short.

"We're leaving, Zapelli."

"But —"

Hanley's fist swung from the hip and made crunching contact with Zapelli's jaw. The jaw was brittle. A bone cracked, and a look of surprise ballooned over Zapelli's features. Twice more the fist drove to its target. Zapelli collapsed.

A moment later Pooch Hanley opened the door and stepped into the corridor. Zapelli's gunmen let him through because Zapelli's unconscious body hung over Hanley's right shoulder, his head drooping against the detective's chest. The gun in Hanley's right hand was jammed hard against the back of the gambler's head, where the hair grew short. Hanley's trigger finger was curled, ready to send a bullet crashing into the unconscious man's skull.

Zapelli's henchmen were helpless. If they opened fire, it meant certain death for Zapelli. When Hanley growled, "One side, muggs!" they fell back and kept their distance.

Straight through the gaming-room Hanley strode, and downstairs, and out the back way to the alley. By the time he got that far, his underclothes were sticky with sweat and his tongue was a thick, dry lump in his mouth.

His car was parked in front of the club. He left it there, walked to the Palace Bar and rapped on the rear door. A customer opened the door.

"Tell Molly Doonan to hustle out here. Tell her Pooch Hanley wants her."

The fellow took one look at the gun and hastened to obey. In a moment, Molly was on the threshold, her eyes wide with questions.

"Your car here, Molly?" Hanley asked her.

She stared at Zapelli, got over her amazement and nodded. "It's by the fence," she said.

"Give me the keys," Hanley said.

He dumped Zapelli on the front seat, slid behind the wheel and backed the machine into the alley.

Twenty minutes later, with Zapelli half-conscious and leaning against him, he stood on the veranda of the District Attorney's house and thumbed the bell.

INNMAN'S house had been in darkness. A light glowed now behind the frosted glass of the door, and the door opened. "I'd like to see Mr. Innman," Hanley said to the woman who stared at him

"Which Mr. Innman?" the housekeeper demanded.

"Both."

Apparently thinking Zapelli was drunk, she cast a contemptuous glance his way and went to wake the Innmans. Hanley said, "This way, mugg," and assisted the staggering gambler into the living-room.

Russell and Kenneth Innman came over the threshold, both wearing bathrobes over bright-hued pajamas. Both gaped at Zapelli.

"What's the meaning of this, Hanley?" the D.A. demanded tartly.

"Zapelli has something to tell you."

The D.A. scowled. He had looked sleepy at first; now he was wide awake and bewildered. Pooch Hanley took charge of the situation, pushed Zapelli into a chair, and said softly, "O.K., Zapelli. Talk."

"I got nothing to say," the gambler muttered.

"You had plenty to say back there in your office, when you were stalling for a break. It was all about Paul White and Russell Innman and a murder. I'm sure the District Attorney would like to hear it. Talk!"

Zapelli took a long look at the D.A.'s son and shrugged his shoulders. The D.A.'s son watched him and turned pale.

Zapelli talked. There'd been an argument The D.A.'s son, drunk, had pulled a gun and shot Paul White, killing him instantly. Zapelli had the gun and the first bullet — the bullet which had passed through White's hip and lodged in the desk — to prove it. Frankly, he'd been holding those bits of evidence because later they might come in handy. Later, if the cops got nasty about the way the Corsair Club was being run, Zapelli could wave those bits of death-chair evidence in front of the D.A. and the cops would get their orders to go elsewhere.

"The gun," Zapelli said, " is wrapped up in a handkerchief and locked in my safe. There'll be fingerprints on it. The bullet won't mean much, probably, but I guess the cops have the other bullet — the one that went into White's brain — and I guess they can prove it came out of that gun, all right. Any ballistics expert can prove that. And with this kid's fingerprints on the gun . . . ."

The District Attorney's face was a gray mask. Almost without breathing, he turned to gaze at his son.

The son hadn't moved. Erect, he was gripping the back of an overstuffed chair. His skin was yellow. His eyes were bright and loaded with terror.

The D.A. said almost inaudibly: "Is this true?"

The kid nodded.

Pooch Hanley felt rotten. He had thought, before coming here, that the D.A. knew; that the kid had confessed and that father and son were working together to keep the thing hushed up. He knew better now. The D.A. was learning the truth for the first time, and it was like a rusty saw biting into the man's heart.

Whimpering, the son took two faltering steps backward and collapsed on the arm of a chair. "I didn't mean to do it," he moaned; "So help me, I didn't mean to! I was drunk, and there was an argument, and . . . ."

Zapelli, calmly sucking on his cigarette, was again smiling his crooked smile. The D.A. looked at Hanley and said, "I owe you an apology, Hanley. I tried to keep you off this case. My son begged me to. He said Zapelli was a friend of his and would suffer from the publicity. I'm sorry."

Hanley said gently, "You'll owe me more than that in a minute," and stepped toward Louis Zapelli. Standing wide-legged, he glared down into the gambler's face.

"You had a lot to gain through White's death, Zapelli."

"Sure," Zapelli said. "Could I help that?"

"No, I don't suppose you could. There's one point I'm not clear on, though. You say White was dead when you lugged him into the alley."

"Sure he was dead. That bullet in the brain killed him on the spot."

"That, Zapelli, is what the Medical Examiner says, too."

The gambler spread his hands palms up. "So what?"

"So he wasn't dead when you lugged him out to the alley, Zapelli. He wasn't even dying. The kid shot him, and the bullet went through his hip. Undoubtedly it knocked him cold, but broken hips don't kill a man."

Zapelli straightened a bit in his chair and put his hands on his knees. The grin faded.

"The kid didn't fire that second shot, Zapelli. You did."

"You're off your nut!"

"The kid fired one shot all right. You can prove that, Zapelli. You've got the gun, and the gun has fingerprints on it., But the second shot, Zapelli, was fired in the alley, after you carried Paul White out there. He was alive before that second shot. Dead men don't grab handfuls of dirt and break their fingernails clawing at cobblestones. Dead men don't scuff the toes of their shoes out, having convulsions. White was hurt, all right — he was in agony — but he was alive in that alley until you killed him, Zapelli!"

Zapelli pushed himself erect and made fists of his hands. "You're a liar!" he bellowed. "You can't frame me like that!" His face was the color of chalk and from the knees up he was trembling in every muscle. The explosion of words came with a spray of spittle.

The spray made Hanley step back. The door was only ten feet distant. Zapelli was a gambler.

Zapelli's left hand sent the table crashing against Hanley's legs. His right hand, clenched, split the side of the D.A.'s face and sent him reeling. Like a racing greyhound Zapelli sped toward the door.

Pooch Hanley raked a gun from his pocket and fired twice at the spot where the bullets would do the most good. Pooch Hanley was a marksman. Both slugs caught the fleeing murderer in the right knee, and Zapelli's howl of agony was smothered by the crash of his hurtling body.

He was trying to get up when Hanley reached him. Blood from his shattered knee-cap was reddening the carpet.

Without compassion, Hanley jerked his wrists together and snapped cuffs on them.

The D.A. was pawing at Hanley's shoulder. There were tears in the D.A.'s eyes. He was saying brokenly: "I'll be indebted all my life, Hanley, all my life."

Hanley led him back into the living-room where the son stood gaping, and said grimly: "There's a little matter we can clear up right now, Mr. Innman. All this about Zapelli is just part of my job, but there's something else."

"Something else?"

"This son of yours tried to gun me. We'll overlook that, because he didn't succeed. But when he let himself into my house, a pal of mine named Mr. Buttons didn't like his looks because he was wearing a uniform. Your son clubbed my pal to death with an ash-stand. There were fingerprints on the ashstand, and your son's prints are in the volunteer file at Headquarters, so I checked up to make certain."

Innman's face was gray again. "My son killed someone?"

"He butchered my dog. What he's going to get now won't hurt him any, and it may help to straighten out his morals. If you'll just leave us alone for a moment . . . ."

The District Attorney's gaze traveled from Hanley to Russell Innman and back again. He nodded slowly, turned on his heel and walked out. He closed the door behind him.

A few moments later, when Hanley opened the door, the District Attorney was waiting in the hall. He said simply: "If your knuckles aren't too sore, Mr. Hanley, I want to shake hands with you."

Pooch Hanley winced at the pressure of his grip.

● ● ● ● ●

# SHADOW

THIS LITTLE STORY APPEARED IN *BLACK MASK* ONLY A MONTH AFTER "DEAD DOG." IT PROBABLY ISN'T THE BEST TALE IN THIS COLLECTION, BUT I BELIEVE YOU'LL LIKE THE FORMER KID BOXER CALLED "THE NUT" AND WILL WANT TO SEE THE VILLAIN BROUGHT TO JUSTICE.

HBC

**H**is name was Weinbaum, but of course by the time he reached the goofy stage his name and most of his past were forgotten. The lads who hung around Johnson's Gym knew him as "The Nut" and dimly remembered that he had once fought under the tag of Tiny Tim Winters. Anyhow, he was harmless.

Detective Carney knew it because Carney was an old hand. Patrolman Steve Dougherty, still green enough to be gazing at his reflection in store windows, hadn't encountered The Nut prior to that night or heard about The Shadow.

Steve had been a patrolman just twelve days and was doing his night shift for the first time. And of course he hadn't been told about Tiny Tim Winters. Rookies were never told about The Nut. Ready to laugh themselves sick, the wise boys just hung back and waited for the first encounter.

Almost always, after Johnson's Gym closed up for the night, Tiny Tim staggered down Harrison Street, then along Rigney to the subway entrance. That night, Steve Dougherty was all alone on Rigney. A clock uptown had just struck one A.M. and around the corner, as usual, weaved Tiny Tim.

Drunk, guessed Steve.

Waddling like a duck, The Nut approached. He seemed to be hurrying, as always, but made little progress.

When within arm's reach of the patrolman, he suddenly struck up a fighting pose, went through some fancy footwork, and took a few lusty jabs at the night air in front of Steve Dougherty's face.

"Got ya!" The Nut wheezed.

Utterly amazed, Dougherty gaped at him. "What the devil! Get on about your business, you crazy drunk, or I'll run you in!"

The Nut struck an attitude and sidled closer to paw at Steve's sleeve. "Listen," he whispered confidentially. "I'm bein' followed!"

"Huh?"

"I'm bein' followed, I tell ya!"

Dougherty's handsome, boyish face lost its shape in a black scowl. "By who?" he demanded.

"I dunno. Only I'm bein' shadowed. I been hearin' footsteps behind me. Ya gotta do somethin' about it. I gotta have protection!"

"You're drunk!" Dougherty growled. He didn't know The Nut never touched alcohol.

"I ain't!"

"Well, get on about your business. Be off with you!"

The Nut grinned. His shoes scuffed the sidewalk as he delivered a knockout punch to an imaginary opponent. "Got ya!" he yelped triumphantly and then, waddling like a duck again, continued on his way.

Steve Dougherty scowled after him and did some pondering. "Followed, huh?" he mused. "Now I wonder what . . ."

But Dougherty was a rookie. How could he know that Tiny Tim was always being followed — that for years The Nut had been hearing footsteps and demanding protection from invisible pursuers.

Dougherty discovered the theft about fifteen minutes later when, hiking down Harrison Street, he saw that the door of Angelo DiConti's store was open. It had been locked the last time he walked past it.

Using his flashlight, he entered to look around and instantly spotted the safe in the corner, behind the counter. The safe door had been hacked off its hinges. Watches, jeweler's tools and cheap junk of every description lay strewn about on the floor.

Dougherty remembered something. A while ago, when he had come on to relieve Bill Gilson, Gilson had said, "Keep an eye on DiConti's Jewelry Store tonight. He says he's got some valuable rings in the safe."

There were no rings in the junk on the floor. Apparently the thief had pulled the junk out in order to get at the rings.

Dougherty shut the store door behind him and hurried to the nearest callbox. He was just finishing his call when Joe Lenehan, the lad who cleaned up the Eagle Pool Room after hours, came skidding around the corner from Rigney Street and began yowling at him.

"It's The Nut! He fell down the subway stairs! I think he's croaked!"

Dougherty hesitated. By rights he should stay where he was and keep an eye on the looted store until men from Headquarters arrived. But the subway wasn't far distant.

"All right," Dougherty said, and followed him.

Tiny Tim Winters would be pursued no more. His pitifully frail body lay in a crumpled heap in the gloom of the subway entrance, at the foot of the first flight of steps. Dougherty saw that he was dead.

Apparently he had fallen down the steps.

There was blood at the corners of his mouth, and both of his spindle legs seemed to be broken, and he was dead. Dougherty carried him up the steps and around the corner to DiConti's store, where a police car at the curb was disgorging men.

One of the men was Matt Carney, of the Detective Division, who knew all about Tiny Tim. To him Dougherty told the whole of it.

"Followed?" Carney said, with hands on hips and a grin spreading. "The Nut — followed? Sure, sure. You want to look into that, mister. That may be the key to the whole situation."

The others laughed, and Dougherty didn't understand their laughter. He flushed a little because he was sensitive. But being more bewildered than sensitive, he kept his peace.

Carney and the others trooped into the store and looked the place over, but it was Dougherty who picked up one of the watches on the floor and said, "It happened at ten minutes to one."

"Huh?" said Carney.

There was a tag attached to the watch, and Dougherty read it aloud. " 'Clean. Adjust stem. Mrs. Haggerty. Two dollars.' And look," Dougherty said. "It's marked O.K. That means it was running. It stopped when the thief dropped it."

He turned to peer out at the sidewalk, where lay the body of The Nut. Ten minutes to one, eh? After that, the thief had looted the safe, which must have used up five or ten minutes more. And then Tiny Tim had come weaving around the corner just after talking to Steve Dougherty at one o'clock.

"Maybe he saw the thief," Dougherty said, pointing.

Carney and the others laughed. "Now that is a possibility," Carney said, grinning. "Too bad he can't tell us. Tiny Tim was a real smart character."

Dougherty felt a little foolish and resented the jeers of his companions, but again kept his peace. After the others had finished their investigating and gone away, though, he did some heavy thinking.

MATT CARNEY made the DiConti case very interesting by accusing DiConti himself. It was open and shut, said Matt. "Listen. Weeks go by and there ain't a thing in that store worth stealing. Then DiConti buys a fistful of diamond rings from a pawnbroker uptown who needs money, and what happens? Thieves break into the store."

DiConti wailed his protests. To be sure, the stuff in his store was insured against theft. He admitted that. But why would be steal it? Was he not an honest man?

"Listen," said Carney. "No one else but you even knew the rings were in the store."

"That is not true! Solly Minkler, who sold me the rings, he knew I had them. And so did Officer Gilson, to whom I said, 'Please keep a careful watch over my store tonight!' "

Without tangible evidence Carney could make no arrests. He concentrated on the task of locating the stolen jewelry.

About that time, Steve Dougherty, who did not know that The Nut had always been followed, arrived at certain grave conclusions and went to work. He first asked questions concerning the reputation of Officer Gilson and learned that Gilson's record was of the finest. Then one afternoon when off duty and out of uniform, he strolled to the pawn shop of Solly Minkler.

It was a grimy little store and Solly Minkler was a grimy little character with small, wide-awake eyes and a shrill voice. Dougherty took some long looks at Minkler and bought a second-hand camera.

"My name's Anderson. I got something maybe you'd like to buy," said Steve Dougherty.

"Yeah? Like what?"

"Well, I got a friend who knows the fight game, see? Me, I ain't interested in the fights much, but this friend of mine, he owns a collection of pictures that's supposed to be worth real dough. Maybe you'd be interested?"

It was not a blind stab in the dark. A number of old-time fight pictures hung on the walls of the shop, and dozens of dog-eared, sporty lithographs were stacked in a corner.

"Whatta ya mean, real dough?" Minkler demanded suspiciously.

"Well, they ain't junk like these. They're real."

Minkler hesitated, rubbing his chin. "We-e-ll, sometimes I buy stuff like that. You bring 'em in Friday when Jake's here. I wouldn't buy no fight pictures without Jake's approval."

Having no friend who owned a collection of fight pictures, Steve spent the rest of the afternoon in second-hand bookstores acquiring a collection, and went that evening to Johnson's Gymnasium.

"You remember Tiny Tim Winters?"

"The Nut? Sure I do!" said Johnson.

"He was pretty good once, wasn't he?"

"Sure. He fought some good fights in his day."

"Well," Dougherty said, "I want to get a picture of him in his fightin' clothes. You know — for a collection."

Amused, Johnson took a dusty one from the wall and gave it to Steve.

Friday morning Steve strolled again into Solly Minkler's hock shop. "I brought the prints," he said.

"Yeah?" said Solly dubiously. "Let's have a look at 'em."

Dougherty spread a dozen large, good prints on the counter. There were lithographs of famous fights and fighters — Cribbs, Sayers, Mace of the old-timers, John L., Jeffries, Jack Johnson and others. "Worth dough, eh?" he said hopefully.

Solly Minkler examined them, then walked to the rear of the store and opened a door. "Jake!" he called. "I want you should look at some fight pictures for me!"

A large individual with cauliflower ears came and looked at the pictures. He seemed impressed until he bent closer to examine one marked Kid McCoy. Then he frowned at Dougherty and expelled a prodigious guffaw.

"McCoy!" he bellowed. "Would you look at who the sap thinks is McCoy!"

"What's the matter?" Dougherty mumbled.

"What the matter? This here ain't Kid McCoy, sap! This is Goofy Tim Winters. Who in hell wants a picture of him?"

"There must be some mistake," Dougherty faltered.

"McCoy!" Jake choked. "Tryin' to pass The Nut off as McCoy! G'wan, scram!"

Dougherty looked scared. He meant to look scared. Hastily snatching the bundle of prints, he hurried to the door.

Half an hour later, when the man named Jake came out of Solly Minkler's store, a shadow straightened in a doorway across the street and moved along in stride with him. The shadow was Steve Dougherty and the rookie, despite his size, shadowed well.

"I TELL YOU," Carney declared, "DiConti is guilty as hell. Look. He buys those rings and puts 'em in his safe. He tells Gilson to keep an eye on the place, when he knows Gilson won't be walking that tour after six P.M. Then what? The thief got into the store without any trouble because he had a key. As for bustin' the safe open, of course he busted it open! He had to, to make the job look real. We didn't find any fingerprints on that safe, though, did we? None but DiConti's!"

It looked very bad for Mr. DiConti, but DiConti himself was still wailing his innocence. And Carney still had no proof.

Meanwhile, Matt Carney heard something. Heard it first from Murray Saunders, who ran the Eagle Pool Room, and later from others along Harrison Street.

"Sa-a-ay, Carney. What do you know about that new cop, Dougherty?"

Carney grinned. "Dougherty? Ha! The dumb rookie is still tryin' to find out who was shadowin' The Nut that night!"

"Yeah, but listen. He's no sap. He may be drawin' a rookie's pay but he knows how to get more."

It seemed inconceivable, of course, but Carney discreetly checked around and discovered it was true. Despite his faults, Carney was honest. It grieved him to learn that Steve Dougherty, for a price, was willing to overlook some of the things that went on around Harrison Street.

"Listen, kid," and the frown on Carney's face had roots that ran deep, "what's this I hear about you drawin' extra pay? Are they kiddin' me or is it true?"

Dougherty shrugged his shoulders. "Sure it's true. All cops do it, don't they?"

"Not in this department they don't!"

"Well, I'm gettin' what I can."

Carney could have gone to those higher up, but didn't. The kid was up to something, he told himself.

He wasn't there, though, when Steve Dougherty put through the important phone call. Steve was off duty that afternoon when he telephoned the pawn-shop of Solly Minkler. Minkler's high voice answered.

"Listen, Solly," Dougherty said, his mouth close to the phone and his voice pitched low. "This is Whitey."

It had taken many days of cautious inquiry to unearth the fact that a Mr. Whitey Reynolds and the man named Jake — whose other name was Bartell — were Solly Minkler's two closest associates. Such things are not easily learned.

This afternoon, more than two hours ago, Whitey Reynolds had boarded a train for Albany. Dougherty had watched him depart.

It was now or never.

"This is Whitey," Dougherty mumbled. "Listen. I ain't left town yet. By accident I heard something and I been checkin' up—and what I heard is true."

Solly Minkler listened most attentively.

STEVE DOUGHERTY stayed at home that evening. Home was a small, tidy two-room apartment on Beecher Street, just around the corner from Police Headquarters. Dougherty did a lot of other things while staying home, but when the phone rang he was at ease in his shirt-sleeves, stockinged feet propped on a chair, and a newspaper in his lap. Without disturbing himself he reached for the phone.

"Is this Steve Dougherty?" It was the voice of Jake Bartell.

"Yeah."

"Well, I'd like to have a talk with you. In person, I mean. You gonna be home this evening?"

"Yeah."

"Then I'll drop around. The name's Bartell. O.K.?"

"O.K.," Dougherty said.

Bartell arrived about twenty minutes later, alone. He knocked, and Dougherty shouted, "Come in. Door's unlocked. I figured you'd be around eventually."

Bartell didn't take a chair right away. He looked around first and seemed to think he might find something to justify the suspicions that were obviously gnawing him. He glanced through the open door to the bedroom and said, "I just gotta make sure, buddy." His right hand stayed in his pocket all that time, and when he came back to the table Dougherty said, "Take it easy. I don't bite."

"This joint is too near Police Headquarters to suit me," Bartell muttered. "Anyhow, I guess you know why I got the jitters. I only found out today that —" His eyes widened. "Sa—a-ay! Ain't you the guy that brought in the pictures?"

"Yes."

"Then there's somethin' screwy here! I was a sap to come here!"

"Take it easy," Dougherty said softly. "You'll be a bigger sap if you walk out. The pictures were just an idea, see? Just to find out what you and Solly Minkler knew about the fight game."

Bartell sat down, but kept a hand in his pocket. Sweat glistened on his face and the corners of his mouth twitched. "What do you know?" he muttered.

"I know it all."

"Yeah?" Bartell's voice was not much more than a whisper. "Well, listen. You ain't no sap, Dougherty. I been around, checkin' up to find out what kind of a guy you are, and you ain't no dumb cop. Anyhow, it wasn't murder. The Nut was goofy, wasn't he? He woulda croaked anyhow in a little while. It was an act of mercy, almost."

"Oh, sure."

"Now look, Dougherty. I ain't no millionaire, but I got a little dough, see? I inquired around before I come up here, and the wise boys tell me you're a regular guy. Even if you are a cop."

"I might listen to reason," Dougherty said quietly.

Bartell relaxed a little and seemed to gain confidence. Then with a crafty gleam in his narrowed eyes he said, "What makes you so sure I done it, anyway?"

"You were seen," Steve Dougherty lied.

"Who seen it?"

"That's my business."

"Well, look. It coulda been an accident, that's how easy I shoved him. So help me, I practically only slapped him on the back!"

"But the stairs were steep, Bartell, and that made it murder."

"You can't prove that!"

"You had the motive."

"You can't prove that, either!"

"No? You're forgetting that the police know exactly what time DiConti's store was robbed. Between ten of one and one. And at one o'clock, or a few seconds after, Tim came walking around the corner, Bartell. So . . ."

"I could twist that around to prove The Nut stole the stuff himself!"

"He wasn't the type, Bartell. It proves only one thing: The Nut happened along and recognized you. You were scared. You knew he'd talk."

Bartell's lips were twitching again. "All right, all right. I said I'd pay you off, didn't I? How much?"

"I been wondering. Why should you dig down for the whole of it?"

Bartell's eyes narrowed. Apparently it hadn't occurred to him that he might pass part of the buck to someone else. "Yeah, why should I? Minkler thought up the idea. I done the job alone, but he gimme my instructions. Why should I take the rap?"

"Who's got the loot now?"

"He has! All I got was a measly five hundred for doin' the job!"

"Well, how you handle Minkler is your own business," Dougherty said. "I've got my end figured out, and I'll give it to you straight." His glance roved to Bartell's hands, which were now in the open. "See this?" he said softly, standing up.

Pushing the newspaper from his lap, he exposed a small electric switch in his hand. A cord snaked from it down behind the couch and under the carpet to a large wastebasket under the table. Dougherty pointed to the wastebasket.

"There's a dictaphone in that. I paid out ten dollars to rent it, so Police Headquarters could listen to you later."

Most coppers would have told Bartell about the dictaphone after closing a cell door on him. Dougherty said later that he kept looking at Bartell's big hands and kept remembering Tiny Tim Wnters and, well, the desire to mangle that smug, fat face was just too much.

Bartell gaped at the cord. The color ran from his smug, fat face like paint from a cracked cup. It took about five seconds for the truth to seep home. Then he reached for his gun.

Steve Dougherty's head and right shoulder caught him square in the chest at the end of a flying tackle. Bartell's contorted body broke through the back of the chair and crashed to the floor.

The gun stayed in Bartell's pocket. He couldn't get to it, so he used his fists instead, and they weren't good enough.

He knew the fight game from first-hand experience in the ring, and out-weighed Steve Dougherty by thirty pounds. He used his knees, feet and elbows and even tried to get a grip with his teeth. But although he threw all he had into every effort, fair and foul, it wasn't enough.

Dougherty said later he just kept thinking he was Tiny Tim Winters getting even. He kept remembering that small, broken body at the foot of the subway steps.

He rid himself of that memory with blows that put Jake Bartell on ice. Then in his boyish exuberance he yelled at the unconscious Jake while he waited for Carney to answer his call to Headquarters.

"They think I'm a crook down at Headquarters, see? First they called me crazy for not believin' DiConti was guilty. Then they found out I was acceptin' bribes. Well, I had to. It was the only way to get you. I'm new at this game and I had to plug along slow and easy, the hard way, with no mistakes.

"That money goes back now, Bartell. Back to the guys who gave it to me. But DiConti goes free and you and Minkler go up for murder, so it was all worth it."

It was all over when Carney and the lads from Headquarters arrived on the scene. Bartell was still out cold on the floor and Dougherty was sitting near him, kind of groggy and dazed but making gestures and elaborately explaining the business of the dictaphone—as if Bartell cared!

"Thought you were smart, huh, when you looked the place over? Well, I didn't think you'd be smart enough to look in a wastebasket. I wasn't takin' no chances with you."

Carney and the others took Bartell to Headquarters, and it wasn't long before Solly Minkler was brought in to keep him company. They poured a lot of hot coffee into Steve Dougherty, and after a while the kid stopped talking to himself.

"Well," Carney said admiringly, "I guess the booby prize goes to me."

Dougherty shrugged. "It had to be Solly Minkler," he said, still a bit dazed. "You see, it couldn't have been Gilson because policemen are honest. And it couldn't have been Mr. DiConti because he wouldn't have thrown all that stuff around and broken Mrs. Haggerty's watch — not after he'd just finished repairing it. So it had to be Minkler or someone working for Minkler, and he had to know Tiny Tim, because if Tim hadn't recognized him . . .

"Don't you see?" the kid rambled on. "When I told you what Tim said about being followed, you just laughed at me. And now, you see, he was followed."

"Kid," Carney declared humbly, "you're all right. You're gonna be a first-class cop."

●  ●  ●  ●  ●

# CURTAIN CALL

THIS ONE APPEARED IN *BLACK MASK* IN NOVEMBER 1938, A MONTH IN WHICH I HAD OTHER STORIES IN PULP MAGAZINES *ACE G-MAN STORIES*, *DETECTIVE FICTION WEEKLY*, *THRILLING MYSTERY*, AND SOMETHING CALLED *TEN STORY GANG*. BUT I WAS AIMING SOME OF MY STORIES AT THIS SLICKS, AND BY THIS TIME I HAD BEEN PUBLISHED IN A NON-PULP CALLED *HOUSEHOLD MAGAZINE*, AND 15 TIMES IN THREE CANADIAN SLICK-PAPER MAGAZINES, *THE CANADIAN*, *CHATELAINE*, AND *NATIONAL HOME MONTHLY*. *THE SATURDAY EVENING POST* AND OTHER BIG SLICKS WERE JUST OVER THE HORIZON.

HBC

*Suicide or Murder? This cop plays out his strange hunch mercilessly*

"THE TROUBLE with you," I said, glaring at Jojo Evans, "you think everything connected with the detecting business is funny. You're like a lot of guys that write these dumb detective stories. Murder is just something to crack wise about."

I felt that way. It could have been the rain, and most likely part of it was but, whatever the reason or the excuse I was in a mood that morning to bite the head off a rattlesnake. And it didn't help to have Percy Joseph Evans sitting there with his feet on my desk, kidding me about my attentions to a corpse.

I'm dumb. I admit it. Any other dick on the force would have taken one look at that corpse and scribbled "suicide" down in his hip-pocket notebook; but yours truly Thompson the Trouble Seeker, had to stand right up in public and call it murder.

Why? Because it should have been murder. This guy Vanetti had been begging for it.

Only it wasn't. Or was it?

I walked into the private sanctum of W. J. Reynolds, my boss, and said morbidly: "You sent for me, Chief?" He scowled at me.

"Close the door, Thompson."

"Sure." I closed it.

"Sit down."

"Sure." I sat. Two other men were sitting, too, and both gave me a good looking-at. One was Detective Inspector Bill Donahue; the other was Mr. Nick Lomac. Putting those two together in the same room was like parking St. Peter alongside the devil's number one furnace stoker. Bill Donahue was big, gray at the temples, middle-aged and honest. Nick Lomac was small, slick, black-haired and vicious. A politician.

The Chief narrowed his gray eyes at me and pulled a scowl across his mouth. He was a good man, Reynolds. He'd been around a long time and without him Kolb City would have been a heap crookeder than it was.

He said, "The papers have printed statement by you, Thompson, about the death of Leon Vanetti. An unauthorized statement and a most embarrassing one. Perhaps you can explain."

"You know these newspaper reporters as well as I do," I muttered.

"Meaning?"

"I spoke out of turn and some squirt scribbled it down."

"Then you don't actually believe Vanetti was murdered?"

"Listen," I said, hauling in a breath because it was going to take a bit of time. "I'll tell you exactly what happened. I was around here last night with Joe Evans, waiting for curfew, when this call came in from the joint where Vanetti had a room. I took the call myself. It was Vanetti's landlady.

"She was in a lather about something but she talks with a spaghetti accent and it took me at least five minutes to unravel the spaghetti. What she was trying to tell me was this: Some woman telephoned and wanted to speak with Vanetti. So Mrs. Fretas the landlady hoffed upstairs to Vanetti's room and knocked and got no answer. She figured he must be asleep because she herself'd been sitting out on the front steps when he came in an hour ago and he hadn't gone out again since. So she knocked again."

I was deliberately dragging it out, not to hear myself talk but to see what the story would do to Nick Lomac. Apparently it did nothing. Lomac sat there with indifference warped all over his swarthy face and listened to me. The way you'd listen to a Sunday morning sermon after being out on a binge the night before.

"So Mrs. Fretas," I said, "put an eye to the keyhole, to see if Vanetti *was* in, and she saw him hanging there."

"You and Evans went over there?" the Chief said.

He knew we'd gone over there. He was just pulling it out of me for the benefit of Nick Lomac. It didn't take a swami to size this thing up. Nick Lomac was sore because of my murder talk, and he wanted a complete, detailed explanation, and he was influential enough to get it.

"When we got there," I said, "we had to bust in the door. Mrs. Fretas didn't have an extra key because, so she says, she gave her spare to Vanetti, a couple of days ago. He lost his and asked for another. So we broke in and found him hanging there."

Nick Lomac opened his mouth for the first time. "What was he hung with Thompson?"

"Fishline."

"Fishline?"

"Yeh. The kind you catch cod on. Heavy stuff, tarred. It seems Vanetti did a lot of fishing in his spare time and had a couple of tackle boxes under his bed."

Nick Lomac had an imagination. He put his fingers up to his throat and rubbed them around the edge of his starched collar, and winced. I didn't blame him. That line had almost sawed Vanetti's head off.

"So you and Evans walked in," the Chief said, "and found him hanging there. The door was locked. The windows were locked. On the floor you found the chair on which Vanetti stood while adjusting the noose. That's right, isn't it?"

I nodded.

"You cut him down?"

"We cut him down."

"Then what?"

"Nothing," I said. "Just police routine."

"But when the reporters arrived, you told them it was murder."

"That's not so," I insisted. "I just warned them to leave things alone because it *might* be murder."

"But damn it, Thompson they quoted you as saying it *was* murder!"

"That was their mistake."

The Chief glared at me then let me have it. He possessed a nice vocabulary most of which he picked up while handling mules in the War. Ordinarily I'd have grinned at him but with Nick Lomac there I didn't. Because the lacing I was getting was solely for Lomac's benefit and I knew it.

When it was over I muttered under my breath and got up and walked out pretending to be sore.

Jojo Evans still had his dogs on my desk. He grinned at me. "Way out here," he said "I heard the biggest part of it. There's one word he uses that really gets me. That 'scurrilousness.' Some day I'm gonna look that up. What's it mean?"

PIPPO'S LUNCH CART has the best coffee you ever tasted, and he deals it to you by way of his black-eyed daughter Anna who stands five-three and has a smile that wide.

I slupped the coffee and thought things over. This wasn't an ordinary case of detecting. There are standard jobs and there are crazy quilts. In the former you smell along a given trail knowing more or less what ought to be at the end of it. You just keep on smelling until you uncover the source of the stench. But in this particular job there were too many possible angles. Smells emanated from it the way tentacles curl out from an octopus.

First-off the world was never going to miss Vanetti. The air would be cleaner with him underground. And I could name at least ten persons to whom his demise would bring a great big belly laugh. So without any deep thinking at all you could practically fill a phone book with the names of suspects.

And then again maybe Vanetti'd really hung himself.

I drank a second mug of coffee just to see Anna Pippo smile at me. Jojo Evans slid onto the stool beside me.

"There's going to be hell to pay," he said.

I glared. "Why?"

"Nick Lomac didn't ask to have you fired. I eavesdropped."

"Why should he ask to have me fired?"

"He's sore."

I said, "That guy is always sore. He just hops from one sore spell to another. Last week he burned up because a right guy got elected to fill that vacancy on the school committee. The week before that he had pups because Mitchell Brothers got the contract for that high school."

"Only this time," Evans said, "he didn't blow up. He didn't shoot off his mouth." He gave me a fishy stare. "I'm only the police photog man but I know this time, Thompson, that it goes a lot deeper. The Lomac guy actually told the Chief to lay off you. Said you only did what you thought was your duty."

"Real nice of him," I snapped.

Evans reached across me for the sugar. "You keep out of dark alleys, cop. You watch your step."

I didn't think much about it. There was too much else on my mind. "You get those pictures finished yet?" I asked.

He shook his head. I dropped my check into his coffee and walked out and drove up to Ancell Street, to the rooming house where Mr. Leon Vanetti had committed suicide — perhaps.

It was a crummy dive, as you'd expect in a neighborhood like that. The name of Ancell Street got to be so bad at one time that respectable residents at the cleaner end of it petitioned the city fathers to change its label. Mrs. Fretas' rooming house offered its high class tenants a nice respectable view of a dump on one side and an abandoned brewery on the other.

The downstairs door was open and I walked in. The door of the landlady's apartment was open, too. Mr. Fretas was parked in a rocking chair in his shirtsleeves, reading a paper, and the missus was jammed into another chair, the whole two hundred and fifty pounds of her, peeling spuds.

I told her I was going upstairs to have another look around.

"Sure," she said. Her old man didn't even look up.

Vanetti's room was second floor front, and when I got into it I just stood there looking around, wondering why I'd come. It wasn't anything I could put a finger on, but that room fascinated me, just the way certain scenes in a movie do things to you. As a room it was worth just about what Vanetti'd paid for it — four bucks a week. The bed was up against one wall, a seedy green carpet covered the floor, and the furniture was heavy old-fashioned stuff salvaged from a junk store somewhere.

I felt dumb, gaping there. Something in that room was getting me down. I walked around it slowly, poking at the bed, the bureau. I hefted the chair which Jojo and I'd found overturned on the floor. I decided what the hell, maybe I was crazy. But still I couldn't shake that feeling.

I hiked downstairs again, and Mrs. Fretas was still peeling potatoes. I sat down, envying her old man because he looked so all-fired comfortable. A spud dropped with a noisy plop into Mrs. Fretas' bucket of water and I asked:

"Did Vanetti have many phone calls?"

She blinked her eyes at me. She had a face like an inflated basketball and her eyes were like imperfections in the leather. "Phone calls?" she echoed. "Why, no, I don't think so, officer."

"Who was the girl called him last night? Know?"

She shook her head, very solemn. "No, I don't think so."

"Did she ever call before?"

"No. No girl ever call him before, which I know of."

"And she didn't give her name, hey?"

"She just say, 'Please, I wish to speak with Mr. Vanetti. You call him to the phone, please.' "

I was wasting time. Still, that phone call could have been important. I wondered if by any streak of long-shot luck I'd be able to trace it.

There was another angle, though, which might prove to be more valuable at the moment. I lit a cigarette, watched the skin curl off a potato for a moment, then said: "You have keys to most of your rooms, don't you, Mrs. Fretas?"

She said, "Yes," and labored around to point to a row of hooks on the wall. Each hook held a couple of keys and the keys were tagged.

"Did Vanetti lose his keys very often?"

"Oh, no. Just once."

"You remember exactly when that was?"

I didn't think she would, but after scowling at a potato for a couple of minutes, she surprised me. "Today," she said, "is Thursday. Now let me see. Mr. Vanetti, he kill himself yesterday, which is Wednesday. The day before that I go to the movies with Mrs. Molinoff. That is Tuesday. So it is Monday Mr. Vanetti lose his key."

"Monday, hey?"

"Monday. I am sitting here reading the noosepaper. My husband, he is go out for some beer. It is maybe ten o'clock when Mr. Vanetti comes in. He goes straight up the stairs. Then he comes down again and he says, 'Mrs. Fretas, I lose my key I am afraid. You give me another, please, and tomorrow I get a new one made for myself and give your key back to you.' So I give him my key and he goes upstairs again."

"Ten o'clock Monday night, eh?" I said. "I don't suppose you'd have any idea where he went that night."

She shook her head. "No-o. He go to the doctor that afternoon, I remember, because his leg trouble him. But where he go at night . . . ." She shrugged her shoulders.

I almost had it then. The reason for my queer ideas about that upstairs room, I mean. The doctor. Vanetti'd been to a doctor because his leg troubled him. A couple of years ago Vanetti'd been banged up in an automobile accident which had left him with a limp.

I almost had it. It came up to me like a wave on a beach whispering closer, closer, and then suddenly receding without having washed out the cobwebs in my brain. Like a name you almost but can't quite remember. Like a strain of music or a voice on the telephone. Close but not quite.

I closed my eyes and conjured up a mental picture of Vanetti as I remembered him: Small, thin, ratty in face and figure, dipping along like a two-wheeled cart with one wheel off center. I made fists of my hands and tried to force my brain to think through that last thin layer of mist. But it was no go.

I sat there, struggling, then gave it up. You can put yourself in a chuckle college that way. I stood up and said good night to Mrs. Fretas and her old man and walked out of there, my face so full of scowl that it ached.

I T WAS ALL over town of course that Vanetti'd committed suicide and that didn't help me a bit. When I asked my questions I got a flock of negative head-shakes for replies and I put those questions to citizens who couldn't possibly have been so void of information. I asked bartenders in joints where Vanetti had hung out. I asked men who had palled around with him. They just didn't want to remember. Had any of those mugs seen Vanetti Monday night? Hell no!

I made a nuisance of myself for two days. I covered the town like an epidemic, visiting every possible place the guy could have been to. But he hadn't been anywhere. So far as Monday night was concerned Vanetti could have hung himself Monday morning.

I had a talk with Bill Donahue who'd sat in on my little conference with Nick Lomac and my Chief. Bill didn't get around much lately. A seige of the flu had taken plenty out of him, and the doctors had warned him to ease up. But he still had the best brain in the department. Put that guy flat on his back, lop off his arms and legs, and with his brain alone he could solve more cases than most of the healthy lads who do their thinking on the hoof. Including me.

He heard me out and then spent a long time looking at me, with a solemn frown on his rugged face. Finally said, "Why don't you drop this business, Thompson? After all, Vanetti was just a heel. No one misses him."

"And besides," I said, "I have no proof he was murdered. I can't even convince myself."

"Huh?"

"You're telling me," I said, "what Joe Evans told me. Keep out of dark alleys. Pull in my horns before someone breaks them off and rams them down my throat. Okay, Bill. You want me to go on living, and I like you for it. On the other hand I'm single — no wife, no kids — and I'm an insatiable glutton for punishment. And this thing has me goofy."

He did his best to dissuade me, and he failed. I'm a sap. I'm a dope. I'm always going into barrooms and gulping down some screwy concoction the barkeep claims will knock your hat off.

So Bill said, "Well, if you must find out where Vanetti was Monday night, try number 10 Casavant Street. And be careful."

I thanked him. On my way I bumped into Jojo Evans. "Listen, you," I snorted. "When do we get a look at those pictures of the room and body?"

"I'm gonna do them up tonight," he informed me.

I told him he'd better. Then I drove out to Casavant Street.

You wouldn't expect to run into a mugg like Vanetti at Number Ten Casavant. We have a Social Register in our town, and a lot of those lads with too much money and nothing to do like to play around; and Number Ten Casavant is where they do it.

What I mean, you have to be properly dressed, properly named and quite properly heeled; otherwise your ambitions are deflated at the front door and you are reminded that for ordinary bums like you there are beer joints, bowling alleys and backroom crap games.

The police shut both eyes when looking in that direction. It would have been voluntary suicide for any mere cop to get tough with that glittering collection of money-changers.

I spoke to Paul, the gate-keeper. I said, "How's everything tonight, Paul?" and he said, "Oh, so-so. Quiet." I'd been there before. Venny Hamlin was always very nice to cops, provided the cops were nice to Venny.

"Mr. Hamlin around, Paul?" I asked.

Paul nodded.

I strolled in, and at that hour the place was a morgue. A couple of blue book laddies were sipping cocktails at the fancy bar, and off in a corner four well dressed men were silently playing with a deck of cards, and that was all. I hiked along a soft red carpet, went down the hall to Venny Hamlin's office and knocked.

Venny was a bit surprised when I entered. He arched his eyebrows and said, "Well I! My friend, Detective Thompson!" He pushed a box of cigars toward me, leaned back in his chair and frowned. "Sight-seeing or what?"

"Sleuthing," I said.

"Here?"

"I'm as surprised as you are. The tip almost floored me."

He hung onto his scowl. It didn't mean anything. Venny Hamlin was really a good egg when you got to know him. No gangster background, no gutter up-bringing. Out of college four years ago, he'd chauffeured for some old gal with a heap of bank books. This Number Ten Casavant Street was a natural outgrowth of a dawning realization that the money-money people didn't mind losing a few dollars if they could be entertained while parting with them.

I said, "Strictly off the record, Venny, I'm checking the activities of one Leon Vanetti. He was here Monday night."

"Leon Vanetti? That the Vanetti who hung himself?"

I nodded.

"I don't think I know him."

"You might not, by name," I told him. "But he was here Monday night. Bill Donahue says he was here, and Bill's never wrong."

Venny shrugged.

"Listen," I said, and described Vanetti. Described the face, the form, the limp. The limp did it.

"Right," Venny admitted. "He was here."

"Who brought him?"

"Why?"

"Just curious."

He hesitated, looking very thoughtful. "Thompson," he said finally, "you don't want to know the answer to that."

"Why don't I?" I snapped.

"Look. This Vanetti is gone, forgotten. From what I've read in the papers, he won't be missed any more than a case of smallpox. You, Thompson, you're a good guy, a smart dick. You've got a future. You take my advice and drop this. There's nothing in it for you except trouble some night in a dark alley."

It was funny, and I don't mean humorous. Joe Evans had handed me that same line; now I was getting it from the sachem of a gambling casino. Lay off.

I didn't press him for more. I knew one thing, anyway, and it was big enough to chew on for a while. I said, "Well, thanks, pal," and walked out.

Business, I noticed, was picking up. There were three more cars outside now than when I'd entered.

I piled into my own jalopy and drove back to town, slowly, thinking about Leon Vanetti and his limp, and that room at Mrs. Fretas' place. I had a lot to think about, and I must have driven three miles before I waked up to the fact that someone in a machine behind was more than a little interested in me.

I slowed to a nice smooth twenty on a four-lane highway. By rights the fellow should have whizzed past. He didn't. I reached up, tipped the rearview mirror to a better angle and hoofed the jalopy up to forty. He came right along.

One of Venny Hamlin's men? I didn't think so. True, Venny had gently tried to nudge me off this job, and perhaps he had other reasons than an interest in the future state of my health, but this particular bit of play was crude. Venny Hamlin was never crude.

I did my level best for a mile to make that lad go by me, so I could get a look at his face, but it didn't work. When I slowed, he slowed. When I stopped — just once, as an experiment — the louse pulled off into one of those shady glens built by WPA to accommodate neckers and picnic hounds.

Disgusted, I said to hell with him and gave my jalopy the gun. He wasn't behind me when I turned into Mitchell Street, where I live.

And yet, I wasn't alone.

I'm a quiet guy with few bad habits, and I selected that Mitchell Street apartment house three years ago because in more ways than one it's soothing to jaded nerves. You don't hear street cars. You don't have kids yawping on the sidewalks before breakfast. I'm harmless, I like to be left alone; and now, damn it, I was being watched. Not only followed, but waited for.

Because when I parked my crate at the curb and got out of it, a lad across the street ducked quickly for the shelter of a doorway. And on Mitchell Street people don't move that fast unless they have guilty consciences.

I stood there and stared holes in the doorway, my mind half made up to go over there and yank him out and demand of him how-come. Nothing makes me sorer than to be spied on. But I let it go, knowing the guy would most likely have vanished by the time I crossed over. And besides, from the window of my front room upstairs, I'd probably get a better look at him.

I walked up and let myself in, and my phone was ringing. I scooped it up. "Thompson speaking."

It was Jojo Evans. He was excited. "Listen," he said. "You remember those pictures I took?" And before I could reply, to tell him I not only remembered them but was wornout with waiting for them, he rushed on: "I developed 'em tonight, Tommy, and they're hot. They're dynamite! You get over here quick!"

"Right over," I said, and hung up.

I went right out. The guy across the street could wait, I told myself, until I saw those pictures. If he wanted a look at me hard enough, he'd be there again, some other time. I breezed downstairs and pushed my jalopy across town with my heart pounding and fire in my nostrils.

Those pictures taken of Vanetti's body and the room in which he died were going to tell me something. They were going to explain the queer feeling I had. Otherwise I was going to be the sorest Homicide dick this side of the place where detectives go when they decompose.

EVANS LIVED in a swank little apartment house overlooking the park lake. I scraped a fender getting the car parked, and near pulverized a lady with a poodle when I barged into the place. My thumb went to the bell and stayed there. I'd been twenty minutes getting over from Mitchell Street, I figured, and that was nineteen minutes too long when you smelled the end of a trail.

No answer.

"Damn it," I stormed, "that's like him, to go out for a beer at a time like this!"

I stepped out, looked for his car. It was down the line a short way, snugly parked. He couldn't have gone far on foot, I told myself, so I sat on the white steps in the lobby and waited for him.

Five minutes, ten, fifteen. Twice I rang the bell again. And he didn't come.

I buzzed the janitor. I snapped, "Detective Thompson, Police Department!" at him, and in a couple of minutes he came wobbling up from his basement suite, fat and anxious and out of breath.

He let me into Jojo's apartment, and the place was empty.

I looked around. I barged from bedroom to living-room and back again; into the kitchenette, the bathroom.

There was a faint smell of chemicals around the joint, and in the bathroom on a shelf were some wet white enamel trays. But no Jojo, no pictures.

I glared at the janitor. "I suppose you've been down cellar. You wouldn't know if Mr. Evans had any visitors in the past half-hour."

He wagged his head. "I wouldn't know."

It looked bad. After calling me, he wouldn't have gone out alone on the trail of any clue furnished by those pictures. He'd have waited. Unless, maybe, he'd rushed over to Headquarters.

I phoned Headquarters. They hadn't seen him. I was worried as hell.

I was a lot more worried when I got through shuffling around and began to think the thing out. You look. Jojo'd phoned me to hustle over and see those pictures. Hot pictures. He'd been expecting me. Those pictures were going to prove that I was right about Vanetti's suicide being no suicide.

Vanetti'd been murdered. His murderers were wise to the fact that I was smelling along and getting warmer. They'd had me watched. More than likely they'd had Joe Evans watched, too, because the photographer was with me when we first laid eyes on the corpse.

Suppose that telephone conversation was overheard? Suppose the wire was tapped?

I was at Headquarters before I got things straightened out to my own satisfaction, and by that time I had the jitters. It wouldn't have been so bad if I'd found the pictures; but their absence meant that whoever walked Jojo out of that apartment had confiscated the pictures also. That was bad. Those pictures were hot. They'd burn 'em. And unless we worked fast, lightning fast, they'd take steps to put Jojo out of the way, too.

I boiled into Headquarters and spilled it, the whole of it, because this was no time to play lone wolf. I threw it at the Chief in one big chunk and he turned pale. Then I demanded Bill Donahue, because if ever we needed a man with brains, with uncanny ability to see through fog, this was it. But the Detective Inspector wasn't there. He wouldn't be, the Chief informed me.

"They took him to the hospital this afternoon, on a stretcher. His heart again."

I could have cried. It wasn't fair to put a mastermind like Donahue in hospital when the life of a swell guy might depend on him. "You send someone over there!" I croaked. "Send someone to tell him what's happened!"

Then I barged out.

I didn't use my own jalopy. It was too slow. I used a police car that would do eighty, and I was out at Number Ten Casavant before the engine warmed. There were two ways, I figured, to get Jojo Evans back. One was to comb the city, dig into every possible hide-out in search of him. It wouldn't work in time. He'd be dead before we found him.

The other way was to smash the Vanetti business wide open and put a finger on the man or men responsible. They were the ones who had Joe Evans.

It began to rain when I drove driveway of Number Ten. I didn't park the car. The yard was crowded and there was no room. I bailed out, ducked up the steps, and when Paul tried to block me off, not recognizing me, I shouldered him aside and barked, "Hamlin."

Venny Hamlin was talking to a nice genteel group of blue-bloods near one of the gaming tables. I just shoved in and grabbed his arm.

"See you alone!" I snapped. "Important."

He was smart. He took one look at the sweat on my face, the fire in my eyes, and knew better than to cross me. He didn't even excuse himself, just nodded, jerked around and strode down the hall to his private office. I yanked the door shut behind me.

"All right," I rapped out. "Who was he with?"

"What the hell's eating you, Thompson?

"Time's precious! Who was Vanetti with when he came here Monday night?"

He took a deep breath, then shook his head. "I can't tell you."

I damn near lost my temper. My arms went up in the air, waving, and I yodelled: "Get me, Hamlin, this isn't a game any more! It's life or death! *Who was he with?*"

Hamlin's right hand was in his pocket and he said softly: "I think you'd better go away and cool off, feller." That iced me.

I was cooler at that moment than I'd been since leaving Joe Evan's apartment. I looked at Hamlin's pocket and said, "Listen. Get this straight. I came here to find out who Vanetti was with and I'm not leaving till I know. The guy was a big shot; otherwise you wouldn't be so reluctant to spill his name. Big shot or not, you talk or I'll tear the joint apart. And you with it!"

I walked straight toward him. It sounds dumb, maybe, but it wasn't. He had nothing to gain by blasting me, except maybe a kind word from the big shot whose name, as a mere matter of ethics, he was holding back. Nothing to gain and the world to lose, because if he shot down a cop it would be the end of him.

He didn't shoot. He showed me both his hands, heaved a sigh and said, "You win, Thompson. It was Dane Moeller."

"Thanks," I said. Dane Moeller was the right-hand man of Mr. Nick Lomac, and his name on Venny's lips bore out what I had known from the beginning: that Venny would not be protecting small fry, but someone high up in the political or financial parade.

I said, "Why'd you hold back?"

He shrugged. "Moeller is one of my best customers."

"And Nick Lomac, too?"

He nodded. "Lomac, too."

I said gently: "O. K., Venny, I'll play ball. My mouth stays shut provided you keep away from telephones for a while. Whatever happens, no one knows you opened your trap."

I hiked out. The Thompson brain was beginning to click on all cylinders by then, and I had a pretty fair idea of what lay ahead. If I made mistakes, it would be lights out. Even if I didn't make mistakes it would probably be fatal to my career as a detective, but anyhow, I knew what had to be done.

I drove back to town and headed for the palatial residence of Mr. Nick Lomac, without wasting any time at all.

LOMAC HAD A big joint on the boulevard, something like a transplanted Spanish castle. You and I, if we pooled every cent we could get our hands on, wouldn't be able to buy a foot of land in that district, because our names aren't in the Blue Book. Mine isn't, anyway. But little things like that never bothered Nick Lomac. He bought himself an acre and built himself house. The citizens paid for most of it, thinking they were buying bricks for a new airport. And the citizens paid for most of the upkeep. Nick Lomac knew all the angles.

I rang, and a servant opened the door to me. I asked if Mr. Lomac was in, and told who I was.

When I paced into the parlor, Nick Lomac stared at me without smiling, put down the highball he was sipping, and said, "Sit down, Thompson." The servant vanished.

I didn't sit. I hadn't come to do any sitting.

"Where is he, Lomac?" I said.

He blew smoke from his nostrils. Despite his lack of size, you'd never make the mistake of underestimating Nick Lomac. You'd never make it twice, anyway. He was little, but so was Napoleon, so's your wife, probably.

"What's the trouble, Thompson?" he said softly.

I would have enjoyed fooling around him, but there was no time for it. A glance told me we were alone in the room, and that was enough. I said, "Where's Joe Evans?"

"Who?"

I snapped, "You want to hear me talk?"

"Well," he said, shrugging, "I certainly would like to have an explanation of some sort, Thompson."

"All right, you'll get it. But, first, let me tell you something. If Joe Evans dies, Lomac, you burn for it. So it might be a good idea if you went to a phone right now and told your gorillas to lay off. If I were you I wouldn't take any chances."

I watched him when I said that, but might as well have been watching the outside of an egg. His face didn't change. His eyes didn't blink. "I don't know what you're getting at," he said.

I threw my guesses at him. "Vanetti was murdered. Moeller, your right-hand man, stole the key to his room Monday night; then later you sent some boys up to get rid of Vanetti and fake the suicide. Joe Evans and I were wise when we saw the set-up. You had us watched. When Evans phoned me about those photographs he'd taken, those hot pictures, you snatched him. Where is he?"

It didn't even jar him. He smiled that oily smile of his and said, "You've been seeing too many movies, Thompson."

I said, "I hope you've seen a few. Then you'll know what this is."

I showed him my gun. Muzzle first. He took a quick backward step. A lot of tough lads get the jitters when you aim guns at them.

"Where is he, Lomac?" I said.

"Thompson, you're crazy."

"Where is he?"

He dragged in a deep breath. The kind you need when you get a hollow feeling in your mid-section. "Well," he said, "it so happens I do know where Evans is. But I didn't have a thing to do with him being there."

"Where is he?"

"Over on Dexter Street. The Dexter Social Club. You go over there and you'll find him."

"And you're not responsible," I said sarcastically, "for his being there."

"No."

"Of course not," I agreed. "Okay, Lomac, you're coming with me."

"Me?"

"If you think I'd let you out of my sight, you're crazy."

He threw out a sigh and shrugged his shoulders. "I'll order the car," he said.

I let him pick up the phone. What the hell, I had a gun on his back, and wouldn't he be the world's biggest fool if he tried any stunts? Besides, I couldn't use my own car unless I forced him to drive it. You can't drive and hold a gun on a man at the same time.

He said into the phone: "Tell Andy to bring the car around front right away." Then he forked the phone and looked at me and said nothing.

I should have been tipped off right then. If he'd been really scared, he would have done a lot of talking. About how he wasn't responsible for what had happened, and so forth. But he just stood there, looking at me. Looking at the gun in my fist.

In a couple of minutes a horn tooted outside. I put the gun in my pocket and kept my hand on it. "You first," I said.

We walked out and down the hall and out the front door into the darkness, Lomac first, me a couple of steps behind. Everything was in order, I told myself. The guy was scared and he was going to take me to the joint where Joe

Evans was imprisoned. When he got me there, his gorillas might make a play to keep me there, but that was a bridge we hadn't yet reached. The point was, we were on our way.

Yeah . . . .

So he walked down the steps toward the waiting car, and I started after him. And suddenly I was a slice of cheese between two thick slices of bread. Because while I centered my attention on Lomac's chauffeur, reasoning that a certain amount of trouble might emanate in that direction, two lusty lads folded in on me from the flanks and laid hold of me.

They took me under the arms, where it hurts, and both of them shoved guns into my ribs. When Lomac heard my grunt, he turned. The oily smile was back on his face. I couldn't see it because of the darkness, but I could see the gleam of his white teeth and knew he was smiling, and knew the smile was oily.

"Nice work, boys," he said. "Nice timing."

I felt mean, but there was nothing I could do about it. Nothing at all. One of Lomac's lads relieved me of my gun, thumbed out the clip and put the empty weapon back in my pocket.

Lomac said, "Take him over to the club."

They shoved me down the steps, and Lomac stepped aside as we went by. He was grinning. He said something about the average mentality of detectives and I had no comeback. He was right. If I was any example, the average mentality of detectives was low as hell.

The car door was open and they marched me up to it. Lomac tagged along so as not to miss any of the fun. He said, "Maybe you hadn't better take him to the club after all, boys. Just chauffeur him out into the sticks some place and — lose him. You know."

They nodded. One of them climbed into the car. The other pushed me in beside him. Then something happened.

He'd been waiting, I suppose, for me to get into the machine, where I wouldn't be in the way if fireworks developed. At any rate, I was no sooner ensconced in the back seat when the guy stepped out from behind a clump of Lomac's elegant shrubbery and snapped in a voice you could hear for ten miles: "That'll be all of that! You're pinched!"

I T WAS LIKE a thunderclap at a funeral. Lomac jerked around scared stiff. The gorilla standing beside him acted the way most of those guys do — by instinct. He went for his gun, which, like a damn fool, he'd dropped back into his pocket.

Bill Donahue — it was Bill Donahue — blasted him from a distance of ten yards, and didn't miss. The mugg folded.

Lomac was too scared to move. But the two dogs in the car, the one beside me and the one at the wheel, had no intention of being taken that easily. The one at the wheel said, "Get him, Frankie," and jabbed a foot at the starter button. Frankie shifted sideways and whipped his gun up to the rear window.

Bill Donahue was doing a foolish thing. He was striding toward the car and making a target of himself.

It was up to me. I still had my gun. It was empty but still useful. I grabbed it, and before my pal Frankie knew that I was up to any mischief, he had a face full of gunbutt. I didn't aim. I didn't have time for any aiming. All I did was swing.

Frankie's gun exploded and the bullet went into the upholstery. Frankie sagged. I swung clear of him, in time to toss up my left arm and slap a gun out of the hand of the driver, who whirled to blast me.

We mixed it, hands and elbows doing the work. The car shot across the street, bounced up on the curb and kissed a lamp post. Bill Donahue came running.

But I didn't need Donahue. I may have been born without brains, but the Lord granted me a fair pair of dukes, and at in-fighting I'm remarkable. In a phone booth I could probably lick Joe Louis.

When Bill Donahue got the door open I was still throwing punches, but the guy wasn't aware of it. He was out, cold. I untangled him and shoved him away from me, and got out.

"Lomac!" I muttered. "He'll get away, Bill!"

Bill shook his head, and I looked across the street and understood. Lomac was sprawled out on his elegant lawn. I hadn't seen Bill bop him, but he certainly wouldn't do any running for a while. I blinked at Bill and said warmly: "You got here just in time." Then I added: "What's the matter?"

He didn't look so good. His face was sort of yellow, as if he were seasick, and he swayed a little on his feet. I remembered that he'd been in a hospital. His heart again.

I grabbed him, but he shook his head, told me he was all right. "It'll pass," he mumbled. "Can't be sick now, Thompson. Too much to do."

I shot a glance at the two guys in the car, to see if they'd be apt to give us any trouble. They wouldn't. Not for quite a time yet. I steered Bill across the street and sat him on the steps of Lomac's mansion. "What brought you here?" I asked.

"The Chief came over to the hospital. Told me what'd happened. I skipped and came over here quick as I could."

"Why? Why here?" I said. "You seem to know a lot about this mess."

He gave me a queer look. "You better find Evans," was all he said.

He was right. I went into the house and used Lomac's phone, called Head-quarters. The Chief answered and I told him what was up, where we were at. "You send some men over here to pick up Lomac's gorillas," I begged, "and send a raid gang over to the Dexter Social Club on Dexter Strect. I'll be there with Lomac."

He said he would. I went outside and Bill Donahue was bending over the mugg he'd blasted. I got Lomac into my car, but Bill wouldn't come. "I'll stay here and wait for the boys," he said. He still had that queer look on his face, like he was going to be sick, awful sick, and was fighting to stay on his feet until the bell rang.

So with Lomac slumped on the seat beside me, I drove over to Dexter Street, parked at the corner and waited. In a little while the boys arrived.

The Dexter Social Club is a basement joint on the south side of the street, under a hotel. The Dexter Hotel. One is a hangout for thugs, big and small, and the other is a flop-house of the lowest order. I had half a hunch, even when we paraded down the steps and into the club, that we'd wind up in one of the frowsy rooms in the hotel.

As it turned out, I was right. The club was practically deserted. A couple of guys were shooting pool. A couple more were drinking beer out of bottles and watching them. They were all plenty scared when they saw so many uniforms.

We rounded them up and went through the place in search of others, but it was wasted effort. So then we hiked up into the hotel.

A thin little guy at a desk turned white as a sheet when he saw us. He shriveled up and his teeth chattered. I grabbed his necktie. "You know what we want," I said.

"I — I don't!" he wailed.

"No? Well, maybe you don't Maybe you don't. Who's living here right now?

He didn't shove the register at me. He had one, but it was a laugh; a guy would be a sap to scribble his name in a dump like that. No. He just let his teeth chatter for a while and then said, "We — we got a guy on the top floor, a sailor, I think he is. And a couple of girls that — that —"

"Work here?" I snapped.

He nodded. "Yes. Work here, sort of. And then there's two men in 419. That's all."

WE HIKED UP the stairs to 419, and went the last few yards along the corridor on the soles of our shoes, making no noise to warn the occu-pants of that room of our arrival. I had a gun in my right hand and knocked with my left.

A voice said: "Who is it?"

"Lomac," I said.

The door opened. Before the guy even had time to widen his eyes, my foot crunched against his shin. He bent double and ran his chin straight into my fist. The fist knocked him back into the room and he fell with a crash. Even if I do say so myself, that was nice timing.

I barged in, and a flock of uniforms barged in behind me. "Move," I snapped, "and you get it!" They didn't move. It would have been suicide.

There were three of them, and I knew them all. Knew them by name. Shorty Macrae was a greasy, sawed-off monkey with a face as grimy as his record. Tony Partucci was tall, built like a wrestler, and reputed to be dangerous as hell with a gun. The third one, Buddy Carter, was just a tough kid doing his best to graduate into major crime. Three bad babies.

They were reaching for the ceiling, and I motioned a cop forward to frisk them. He did. Then I stood in front of Tony Partucci and snarled, "O. K., where is he?"

He must have known it wouldn't help him any to stall. Or maybe he didn't like the looks of the fist I held ready to tag him with. He jerked his head toward a door on the other side of the room and said, "In there."

I crossed over and jerked the door open. Jojo Evans was inside, bound to the end of an iron bed.

He didn't say anything. Couldn't. His mouth was smothered under layers of tape. He stared, though, and don't ever let anyone tell you a man can't talk with his eyes. I was as welcome as sunshine after three weeks of rain.

I got him untied and he pulled the tape off his mouth. I would have done that for him, too, but my hands were twitching so hard I probably would have torn away his teeth.

I said, "Lomac's responsible for this. Just wait until I get my hands on that rat!"

Jojo slumped down on the bed and sat there, sucking his lips. He was a sight. His clothes were covered with floor dirt and torn half off him, and his face was a mass of bruises. They'd tossed him around, slugged him, doused him with water to bring him to again. He'd been through hell.

"How'd they get you out of your apartment?" I demanded.

"I thought it was you," Jojo said. "Like a sap I just opened the door."

"They took the pictures?"

He shook his head. "Couldn't find them. That's why I'm not dead yet. They been beating hell out of me, trying to make me tell where to look."

I said, "Where are those pictures?"

"There aren't any."

"What?"

"I mean there aren't any prints. All I did was develop the roll. It's hanging up to dry in the apartment house airshaft."

I gave him the fish stare he deserved, and walked into the other room. The boys had cuffs on Lomac's three rats and were ready to herd them out.

"Take 'em to Headquarters," I said. "I'll be over later with Evans and Lomac."

I almost had to carry Jojo down the stairs. He needed a doctor, but I had something else in mind that would do him a lot more good. Mentally, anyway. We piled into my car and I dismissed the cop who was waiting there, guarding Lomac. Lomac was coming to.

I took a roundabout way to Headquarters, a route that led through a couple of nice dark alleys. We spent some time in one of those alleys. When we did reach Headquarters, Jojo felt better. So did I. I slung Lomac over my shoulder and lugged him up the steps, took him into the Chief's private sanctum and dumped him down on a chair. He slid off it and lay in a heap on the floor.

"What the devil happened?" the Chief demanded, looking at him.

"He resisted arrest," I explained.

The Chief said, "Oh."

Later, Jojo and I went over to Jojo's apartment and picked up the roll of film. I held it to a light and looked at it, while Evans stared at me. They were pictures he'd taken in Leon Vanetti's room, with his camera. They showed the corpse hanging there, the fishline, the overturned chair.

It was the chair, of course. I'd been in that room enough times to know it, but sometimes when you're that close to a thing you don't see it. The pictures gave me the proper perspective.

The chair was a mighty long way from the dangling feet of Mr. Leon Vanetti. And it was a heavy hunk of furniture; I knew because I'd hefted it. And no guy with a game leg could ever have kicked it so far out from under him.

I said, "Lomac hangs for this, Jojo. At least he rots in jail for a time. They planned this thing beautifully. Moeller swiped Vanetti's door-key out at Vemmy Hasnlin's place, Monday night. The rest was easy. They just laid for Vanetti and strung him up. Maybe Lomac wasn't on the scene, but he engineered it, and when we put the pressure on those rats who kept you company at the Dexter Hotel, something'll break wide open."

"It would be easier," Jojo declared, if we knew *why* they hung Vanetti."

"I think maybe we'll find that out."

"How?"

"From Bill Donahue. He seems to know plenty about all this."

Bill Donahue wasn't at Headquarters when we got back with the film. He'd stayed on his feet long enough to superintend the cleaning up at Lomac's house; then he'd collapsed.

Jojo and I drove over to the hospital to see him.

He was in bed and he didn't look too good. We parked beside the bed, and when the nurse went out I said, "Mister, we want to know why Lomac saw fit to rub out Vanetti."

Bill scowled. "Any reason will be good enough for a jury," he said.

"I know that, but just between us we'd like to know the truth. And where you fit into this thing."

Bill handed me a long, quiet stare. "I suppose you know I'm through," he said.

"Hooey! You'll be up and around —"

"Not a chance," Bill declared calmly. "As long as a month ago I knew I was through. I went to a flock of doctors, Thompson, and they all told me the same thing. Bum ticker. Lights out any time. A month at the most."

"You mean it?" I said, feeling queer.

He nodded. "So I decided to raise a little private hell before I turned in my checks. I've been a dick a long time, and I've taken more than my share from crooked politicians and plain rats like Lomac. So I snooped around, Thompson. I snooped and came across a pretty chunk of crime in which Lomac was sunk up to big greasy neck. You remember that Mason Street underpass?"

I said I remembered it. Why wouldn't I? When the Mason Street underpass caved in — by accident — three workmen died.

"Lomac was the lad who arranged that cave-in," Bill Donahue said quietly, "because he was sore about not getting the contract in the first place. He arranged it, and Vanetti did the dirty work. I dug up positive proof. Not the kind of proof that would convince a jury, but more than enough to convince me. So . . . I planned a curtain call for him. Me, too, I guess."

He hooked his mouth into a smile. To this day, when I go past the cemetery where Bill is buried, I can still see that smile. "So . . . I decided to scare the wits out of Lomac, just for the hell of it, Thompson. I made a few cagey phone calls. I tipped him off that the cops were wise about that underpass cave-in. I figured it would do me a lot of good to see that rat shake in his shoes for a while."

I stared at him. After a while I said, "So he figured he'd be safer with Vanetti out of the way."

"And that," Bill declared, "was the mistake he made."

● ● ● ● ●

# LONG LIVE
# THE DEAD

BLACK MASK USED TWO OF MY TALES IN THE DECEMBER 1938 ISSUE, AND RAN THIS
ONE UNDER THE NAME OF ALLEN BECK. "THE FAMOUS MAGICIAN PULLS A MANIACAL
KILLER OUT OF HIS HAT," SAYS THE COME-ON. THE MAGICIAN HAS LOST THE USE OF HIS
HANDS AND LIVES ALONE BY A LAKE IN THE WOODS. THERE IS A MURDER, AND THE
MAGICIAN IS FRAMED FOR IT BY THE KILLER. TAKE IT FROM THERE, PLEASE.

HBC

*Twisted hands and a twisted mind break a killer's alibi*

THEY CALLED HIM a nut and avoided him, but some of those same
people, had they known his real name, would have strained their necks
for a glimpse of him and driven him mad with their morbid curiosity.

Nothing about Mr. Dennis, however, pointed back through the shadows of
the past to the amazing exploits of the renowned Malkar. He was simply Mr.
Dennis, a thin, silent man who lived alone in a gray cottage near the lake. A
recluse, whose past — or future — no one cared about.

He was not old. About thirty-five, his neighbors said. But queer.

"For three years he's lived there in that gloomy old cottage. And never a
visitor!"

They were wrong about that, of course, but the error was proof of the fact
that they cared not even enough about him to spy on him. Because he did
have visitors. The great Cameron called to see him once, and so did the world-
famous Nicholas Mitchell. And once a week, regularly, *she* called.

He was expecting her the night of Brandon's escape from the asylum. He
sat there alone in the dim light of that gloomy living-room, watching the door
and listening for her step on the walk outside. Sat there with his lifeless eyes
wide and unblinking, his gloved hands on his bony knees. Waiting. And hoping she would not come, because of the danger.

"It's a lonely road," he thought, "and in the dark, anything might happen."

Three times in the past hour the musical program emanating from his small radio had been interrupted by reports of the search for the escaped madman. "Brandon is five feet eleven inches tall, weighs about one hundred sixty pounds. He has brown hair, brown eyes, dark skin. He is wearing a heavy brown overcoat over white cotton pajamas and is without shoes or stockings. This man is dangerous. He is cunning and clever. Residents of the Logan Lake district are warned to be extremely careful."

Mr. Dennis frowned at the door. "She shouldn't come," he thought. "She shouldn't come anyway. People will begin to talk." The clock on the table said nine-thirty.

At ten, convinced that she was not coming, he walked wearily into the bathroom and took a large bottle of oil from the cupboard. He carried the bottle into the kitchen and poured three inches of oil into an enameled pan and put the pan on the stove. And removed his gloves and looked at his hands.

They were not pretty. Eternities ago they had been famous; now they were stiff, yellowish claws — ugly bony claws covered with a paper-thin layer of scarred skin-tissue.

He looked at them and closed his eyes and groaned. "Three years," he muttered bitterly. "Three endless, useless years. Dear God, can't a man *ever* die?"

Three years ago those withered claws had amazed the world with their magical cunning. Now, cursing them, he dipped one gnarled finger into the warm oil to test its temperature, and then slowly, laboriously began the massage which the doctors had told him might some day restore life to shrivelled muscles and warped tendons.

He had no hope. That had died long ago. But every night, as a kind of ritual, he went through the motions.

The kitchen door was closed, and he did not hear the front door open, nor did he hear the footsteps. His mind, choked with bitterness, was focused on events buried under three years of shadow. When the kitchen door creaked open, he turned with a startled intake of breath.

She stood there, staring at him. "I'm late," she said.

He stared back at her, his thin face convulsed. Abruptly he turned his back to her and groped with his twisted hands for the long black gloves which lay on the chair.

When he faced her again, his hands were hidden.

"You shouldn't have come at all," he said bitterly.

The girl said softly, "But I did. I always will."

FOUR MILES from Mr. Dennis's cottage, in the living-room of another cottage on a lonely back road, an old man with white hair played solitaire with a worn, grimy deck of cards. Papa Nickson they called him. "He's a grand old man, Papa Nickson. A bit feeble, of course, but always friendly, and quite a philosopher, too."

Everyone knew Papa Nickson.

He peered through thick lenses at the cards and played the game with grave deliberation, now and then cocking his head to hear some bit of music on the radio. He had begun that particular game of solitaire four hours ago, but there was no hurry. "People who hurry," Papa Nickson always said, "never get nowhere. That's a fact."

A voice interrupted the radio music and said: "Residents of the Logan Lake region are warned again to be on the lookout for John Brandon, dangerous madman who escaped a few hours ago from the Logan Lake Asylum. Brandon is still at large."

"Still at large," Papa Nickson said, frowning. "That's bad. Still, I don't believe he'd harm anyone. I'm safe enough here, I reckon, even if I am all alone."

He put another card down, thumbing his chin over it, and then suddenly turned his head to look at the door, because someone or something had made a noise outside, on the veranda.

"Who's there?" Nickson asked anxiously.

For answer, someone knocked.

"Who's there?" Nickson asked again.

"It's me. Andy Slade."

"Oh."

He went to the door and opened it, and a gust of cold wind, off the lake, came in with the lean, long-limbed youth who entered. Papa Nickson closed the door quickly and shivered, and then frowned at his visitor and said, "Well! What brings you around, Andy?"

"I was just passing by."

"Oh. Sit down, then. Sit down. I've been playing solitaire."

Andy Slade slouched over to a chair and seated himself. For his age — eighteen — he was big and powerful, with big, heavy hands. It was a shame, Papa Nickson thought, that the boy's mind was so far behind his body. Of course Andy wasn't really a halfwit, as some people believed, but he wasn't normal.

He sometimes had queer ideas.

"How's business, Andy?"

"What business?"

"Why, the last I talked to you, you were fixin' to be a guide. You know, to take people out fishin' and things like that."

The boy snorted. "Hell, there ain't no money in that."

"But you said —"

"Who cares what I said? What I want is real money, and I got an idea for gettin' it."

"That's fine, Andy."

"Sure it's fine. You ought to know. You got plenty of money."

"Have I?"

"Everyone says you have, don't they? You got it hidden around here; that's what they say. You been hoardin' it."

Papa Nickson leaned back in his chair and chuckled for a long time. "You believe that, Andy?"

"What do you think?"

"What — what's that you say?"

"I said what do you think? Why do *you* think I come here tonight?"

Papa Nickson narrowed his eyes and peered long and hard at his visitor. He didn't like what he saw. He didn't like the ugly smile that clung to the boy's moist lips. He said anxiously, "Why — why did you come here, Andy?"

"For money."

"I haven't any money. You know that."

"You got money all right. And I'm fixin' to take it. Money ain't no good to an old man like you." Andy jerked his head around sharply. He thought he heard a scraping noise at the black window, but his single-track, childish mind forgot it almost instantly.

"Andy, believe me, I haven't any," the old man said.

Andy Slade got out of his chair and took a step forward, clenching his fists. There was a strange, warped expression on his face, half snarl, half grin. He thrust out his hands and seized the old man's shoulders.

"I want that money," he yelled suddenly. "I want it and I'm gonna get it. See?"

He lifted Papa Nickson out of the chair and shook him. "I'm gonna get it! *See*?"

"I — I haven't any money, Andy!"

"You're lyin'!"

"No, Andy, *no*!"

"Then I'm gonna kill you," the boy said. "And after I kill you, I'll find the money myself. I was gonna kill you anyway."

He took hold of Papa Nickson's neck, and the old man clawed at him, trying to scream. The old man's voice made a few scratchy sounds that died against the four walls of the room. Andy Slade laughed at him — and squeezed.

He had huge hands. Powerful hands. When he squeezed and twisted, holding the old man's squirming body against his own, something snapped. The bone in the old man's voice box cracked, cut into an artery. Blood spurted from Papa Nickson's gaping mouth.

Andy Slade let go and the old man slumped to the floor. Andy looked at him, grinning. "No one will ever know I done it. Now I got to find that money."

He looked for it. For one solid hour he looked, emptying out drawers, turning up rugs, tearing down pictures. It was a small house but it had many potential hiding places. Once he thought he heard a noise outside but he couldn't see anything or anyone in the black night.

At first he was confident. Then sullen. Then violently angry. And then, after walking around Papa Nickson's dead body and stepping over it and looking at it time and again, he got scared.

"I can't look no longer," he muttered. "I got to get out of here. I got to get out before someone comes!"

He didn't forget, though, that he had planned the crime so that no one would ever point a finger at him. He stooped and gripped the old man under the arms and dragged him. Dragged him off the carpet, toward the door, leaving a trail of blood which would make people think the old man had crawled that distance after being assaulted.

There by the door Andy Slade took hold of Papa Nickson's right wrist and dipped the index finger of that hand in the dead man's own blood, and scrawled on the painted hardwood floor:

"Dennis did it. My money —"

That would help, but it wasn't enough. Even though everyone said that Mr. Dennis was a nut, it wasn't enough.

He fished in the dead man's pocket and found a handkerchief, and looked at the handkerchief to make sure there were no marks or initials on it. Wetting his hands in the blood, he used the handkerchief to dry them. Then he tucked the blood-stained handkerchief into his belt and went out.

He didn't hurry. It was four miles to Mr. Dennis's cottage and the road was lonely, winding through the dark along the lake shore. He walked slowly, cursing Papa Nickson for not having any money. Maybe later, he told himself, he would go back and look again. Anyway, no one would ever know he did it — because, Andy laughed to himself, he was going to be smart and make 'em all think Mr. Dennis. . . .

The wind was strong off the lake and the waves beat against the shore, but he paid no attention. The darkness didn't bother him, nor did the occasional shrill cry of a catbird. Over across, lights winked in the asylum.

"Some feller escaped from there today," Andy mused. "Maybe they'll blame *him* for killin' Papa Nickson. Him or Mr. Dennis, I don't care, long as they don't say *I* done it."

After a while he saw another light, and it was a light in the living-room of Mr. Dennis's place.

He approached cautiously. He crept up to the front door and took the bloody handkerchief from his belt and dropped it. Dropped it beside Mr. Dennis's steps. Then Andy backed away, and turned, and ran. He made a noise, running, but apparently no one heard it.

NO ONE did. Mr. Dennis sat in the living room behind drawn shades, and *she* was there, and they were talking.

"You can't give up like this," she said. "You're too young."

"I'm old," Mr. Dennis muttered. "When a man ceases to be useful, he's old. Old enough to die."

"Nonsense!"

He raised his gloved hands and looked at them. Even though covered, they seemed thin and crooked in the dim light of the lamp beside his chair. "I've done everything possible," he said bitterly. "I've been to the best doctors; I've done what they've told me to do. And it's no good. It's hopeless."

"But there is an improvement," she said in a low, pleading voice. "I've seen it, Andre."

"You've imagined it."

"No, no! Six months ago you were as helpless as a man with no hands at all. Now you can use your hands."

He laughed, but there was no mirth in it. "Yes, I can use them. I can open doors now. I can dress myself in half an hour, where before it took me all morning. I can even shave, if I'm careful. Oh yes, there's improvement."

"You see," she said triumphantly, "you admit it!"

He glared at her with smouldering eyes that frightened her. "Admit it?" he snarled. "I admit nothing — except that I'm beaten! Beaten, do you hear? Twenty years of my life I slaved to make these hands of mine worth something. For years they made me a living on every stage in the world. Now it's all been taken from me, and what am I? A pitiful parasite, useless, practically penniless, a miserable ghost of one who could have been great. Friendless —"

"Not friendless, Andre. You have me."

"I have you because you are mad! Mad enough to go on loving a wretch who will warp your life with bitterness."

"I love you. I have faith."

"*You* have faith. I should laugh at that. Are they *your* hands?"

"I wish they were," she said simply. "I wish I could trade with you."

"Trade with me! So you could sit here night after night cursing them, struggling to make them obey you. Sometimes, Marie, I think you *are* mad to keep on caring. I am sure of it. And so — we must end it. Tonight, when that door closes behind you, it sees the last of you. I won't have you spoil your life. You must not come here again."

"But I shall," she whispered.

"You shall not."

"You no longer love me, Andre?"

"Love you? No! What right have I to drag a beautiful woman down into the depths of my own darkness? My love for you died when these died." Raising. his gloved hands from his knees, he glared at them.

She went to him and put a hand on his shoulder, "You're a lovely liar. You're not yourself tonight, my darling," she said softly.

"Then leave me."

"No. I shall stay. You need me."

"And if people talk?"

"Let them."

He shrugged. "Do as you like. I'm going to bed."

She helped him out of his chair and went with him to the door of the bedroom. There she held his arms, forced him to look at her. "Kiss me," she said.

He shook his head, freed himself and closed the door behind him, leaving her there. She turned and went slowly back to her chair, her eyes wet with tears.

The clock on the table said two A. M. and the radio, turned low, sent out a voice to smother the sound of the girl's sobbing.

"Station WPSO signing off . . . . Attention, please. Police have requested all radio stations in the state to issue a final warning to residents of the Logan Lake region. John Brandon, dangerous madman who escaped yesterday from the Logan Lake Asylum, is still at large. Shortly after midnight this man attacked and critically injured a member of a searching party and escaped with the man's gun. He is now armed and is therefore doubly dangerous. Local and State Police, aided by hundreds of private citizens, are combing the lake district in search of him. This man is cunning and desperate. A description of him —"

She shut the radio off and returned to her chair and sat there in the dim yellow glow of the lamp, sobbing. There was no sound anywhere but the sound of her sobbing. Once or twice she glanced at the door of the bedroom, but it did not open.

About an hour later she fell asleep.

MATTHEW KARKIN, known affectionately as Matt, was Chief of Police in Lakeville. He said he would do it alone, and he did. He was a brave man. He said, "I been the law in these parts for seventeen years without no help, and I can handle this without help. The feller may be a nut, but even so I reckon I can handle him."

His men and the townspeople didn't argue. They knew better.

He arrived at Mr. Dennis's cottage at seven-thirty that morning, and it was raining. Not raining hard, but drizzling enough to make the morning gray, the sky heavy, the lake ugly.

Scowling to himself and feeling vaguely uneasy, Karkin approached the front steps — and stopped. And picked up a bloody handkerchief.

He looked at the handkerchief for a moment, then wrapped it in his own clean one and thrust it into his pocket. He drew his gun and knocked.

He had to knock several times because the girl, asleep in the chair, waked slowly and was bewildered by the knocking when she did wake. Rubbing the sleep out of her eyes, she stood up, her body a vast ache from being curled so long in an awkward position.

She glanced at the closed bedroom door and then she said anxiously: "Who — who is it?"

"The law," Karkin said.

She opened the door and he entered, staring at her. Her presence confused him. He had been given to understand that Mr. Dennis lived alone and never had visitors.

"Who're you?" he demanded gruffly. And added: "Where's Dennis?"

She ignored the first question and answered the second. "He's asleep."

"Oh. Well, I want to talk to him."

"Who are you?"

"Chief of Police."

She said, frowning: "Can't I answer your questions? Mr. Dennis needs his sleep so badly."

"Sorry," Karkin told her, "but my business is with Dennis."

She turned to walk to the bedroom door, but it wasn't necessary. The door opened before she reached it. Mr. Dennis, with a dressing gown over his wrinkled black pajamas, stood there staring.

"What is it?" he demanded.

Karkin, his gun back in its holster with his right hand resting on it, scowled and said, "You're Dennis?"

"Yes."

"Like to have a talk with you, then."

"Who are you?"

"Chief of Police. Matt Karkin."

Mr. Dennis thought he understood, and nodded. It would be about the escaped madman. The police were combing the region, and this was a routine visit. He paced forward, motioned Karkin to a chair and sat down himself. The girl sat, too, and stared uneasily at both of them.

"You ever hear of Papa Nickson, Mr. Dennis?" Karkin asked.

"Papa Nickson? No."

"You sure of that?"

"Quite sure. I know very few of my neighbors, Mr. Karkin."

"Who said he was one of your neighbors?"

"Well," Dennis said with a vague smile, "I assumed from the question —"

"Papa Nickson," Karkin declared gravely, "was murdered last night."

"Murdered?"

"Murdered," repeated Karkin slowly, his gaze falling to the long black gloves which covered the other man's hands and wrists, "by someone with mighty strong hands."

"I'm afraid I don't understand."

"It's rumored around here," Karkin said, "that Papa Nickson was what you might call a miser. Folks were of the opinion he had money hidden away. Last night or some time yesterday, someone tried to get that money."

"I see. And just how does this concern me?"

"It was a brutal murder," Karkin said. "Like I just told you, someone with mighty strong hands did it."

"Mr. Nickson was strangled, you mean?"

"Worse. His neck was broke. Matter of fact, his neck was near twisted off."

Dennis glanced at the girl. Her face was pale, her eyes very wide.

"It sounds," Dennis declared, "like the work of that escaped madman."

"It wasn't. We might've thought so, but Papa Nickson lived long enough to tell us the name of the man who did it."

"Oh. And his name?"

"Dennis."

Mr. Dennis sat quite still, staring at his accuser. His lean face seemed to dry up a little, but his other reactions were entirely internal. The girl was different. She stiffened spasmodically in her chair, leaned forward and said shrilly: "But that's ridiculous!"

"Is it?" Karkin said grimly. "Then maybe Mr. Dennis can explain this. I found it out by the steps, on my way in." With his left hand he fumbled the bloody handkerchief from his pocket, unwrapped it and held it up. His right hand remained on the butt of his gun.

"So I'm — accused of murder," Dennis said wearily.

"That's right; you're accused of murder. Maybe you'd have got away, but it so happened we stopped at Papa Nickson's early this morning for coffee, after searching for that crazy guy all night."

"You realize, of course," Dennis said, "that I didn't do it. That I couldn't have done it."

"Why couldn't you?"

"He couldn't," the girl said quickly, "because —"

A glance from Dennis silenced her.

"You say Mr. Nickson was murdered by a man with unusually strong hands?" Dennis asked.

"That's right."

"You think my hands are strong, Mr. Karkin? You think I wear these gloves to conceal the fact that my hands are scratched, perhaps — or bruised, or bloody?"

Confused by both the question and the tone of voice in which it was put, Karkin scowled, said nothing.

"I'll show you," Dennis said quietly.

He held his hands out, and Marie gently removed the gloves. Rising then, he took a step forward and showed the Chief of Police his hands. Karkin gaped at them, stupefied.

"They've been like that," Dennis said wearily, "for three years. Once they were strong; I admit it. But a piece of apparatus exploded with my hands inside it — and now these fingers are not flexible enough, Mr. Karkin, to break a match, let alone a man's neck."

Chief of Police Karkin stared at the withered hands and shook his head, frowning. "Before Nickson died, he wrote on the floor — in blood — that you did it. Why would he do that if you're not the man who killed him?"

"Perhaps he was mistaken."

"Then what about this bloody handkerchief I picked up outside the house here?"

"That I can't explain."

"Well, neither can I," Karkin mumbled. "Those hands of yours sure couldn't break a man's neck; I admit that. But still . . . ." He stood up, shaking his head. "You'll have to come along with me, Mr. Dennis. Even if you ain't guilty you'll have to come along, because if you didn't do it — who *did*?"

"I'll get dressed," Mr. Dennis said wearily.

He went to the bedroom and Karkin followed him to the threshold, stood there and waited for him. Marie remained seated, her face still pale, her eyes wide and staring.

It took Mr. Dennis a long time to dress himself. Watching him, Karkin felt sorry for him. Certainly Mr. Dennis had not murdered Papa Nickson with those pitifully weak hands.

"I don't like to be doin' this," Karkin said, "but if I didn't, it would go hard with me. You won't have no trouble proving you ain't guilty, Mr. Dennis."

Mr. Dennis came out of the bedroom and said: "I'm ready, Karkin."

Marie closed her eyes to hide the tears in them.

**I**T WAS KARKIN who opened the door. He did it because Mr. Dennis was slowly and painfully pulling on those long black gloves. And when he opened it, he drew a quick, sharp breath and stood stiff.

A face stared at him. A bearded, gaunt face with abnormally wide eyes hung there in the gray of the morning, atop a muscular body as big as Karkin's own.

The face snarled, and Karkin reached quickly for his gun. That was a mistake. Flame spurted from a weapon in the visitor's left hand, and the Chief of Police bent double with a guttural exhalation of breath. Bent double in agony, and stumbled back, dropping his gun. And crumpled to the floor.

The report ran back and forth across the room in small, weird echoes. Karkin clawed at the floor, groaning. Marie clung rigidly to the arms of her chair. Mr. Dennis stood quite still, staring from Karkin to Karkin's assailant.

"John Brandon," the radio had said, "is five feet eleven inches tall, weighs about one hundred sixty pounds. He has brown hair, brown eyes, dark skin. He is wearing a heavy brown overcoat over white cotton pajamas and is without shoes or stockings."

This man wore shoes and trousers, but otherwise the description was accurate. This man was John Brandon.

Mr. Dennis backed slowly away from him as the madman entered and pushed the door shut. The radio reports, Dennis decided, had not been exaggerated; this man was both mad and dangerous. Color ebbed from Dennis's face and a queer numbness crept through him. Then abruptly he regained control of himself and said calmly: "You've hurt him. You shouldn't have done that." And went to his knees beside Karkin.

It was not serious. The bullet had shattered Karkin's collarbone and deflected out through his shoulder muscles. It was a nasty wound. He would suffer, but he would live.

Brandon, snarled, "Leave him alone."

"But he's hurt."

"I said leave him alone! Go sit down."

Mr. Dennis retreated slowly to a chair and sat down. The madman glared at him. A moment later Karkin groaned and the madman stepped forward, reached down with one hand and yanked the Chief of Police to a sitting position. When he did that, something at Karkin's belt, under his coat, clinked.

Brandon reached under the coat and pulled loose a pair of handcuffs.

He looked at them and grunted. Kneeling, he placed his gun on the floor for an instant, jerked Karkin's wrists together and snapped the cuffs into place. Then he rose, gun in hand, and stared at the girl. And licked his lips.

Mr. Dennis said quietly, with a calm he did not feel: "You mustn't stay here, Brandon. The police are looking for you."

"Are they? Let 'em look."

"They'll come here after you."

"Let 'em come," Brandon snarled.

You couldn't reason with the man, Dennis realized. A soft voice, gentle persuasion, an outward appearance of calm — all the artful devices supposed to be effective when dealing with a deranged mind — were useless here, because Brandon's gaze was on the girl, and that gaze was hungry.

Frightened by it, Marie shrank back in her chair and turned a white, pleading face to Dennis. The madman saw and was amused.

He paced behind the girl's chair and lifted an ornamental coil of rope from its place on the wall. Strong rope, new rope. Testing it, Brandon approached Mr. Dennis from the rear.

"Put your hands behind you," he said.

"Why?"

"Why? So I can tie you up the way they tied me!"

"But I don't wish to be tied up, Brandon."

"Shut up and do like I say!"

He made a thorough job of it. Marie, watching with fear-widened eyes, shuddered at his diabolical cleverness. Evidently at the asylum he himself had been bound many times, and had learned the secrets of twisting a rope.

Mr. Dennis did not resist. With his eyes closed and a queer, detached expression on his face, Dennis patiently endured the torture. His thin frame was almost limp.

The madman bound his arms and elbows to the chair and tugged on the rope until the detached expression on Dennis's white face changed to a look of intense pain. While he worked, his gun lay on the floor beside him and he raised his head continually to look at Marie, who sat facing him.

Finished, he said grimly, "You won't ever get loose from that, mister," and then pushed a chair close to the girl and sat down, staring at her.

Just sat there, staring, as if her beauty troubled him.

A strange silence crept through the room. The girl, cringing, tried to look away from the bearded face so close to her own, and was unable to. Behind Brandon, Mr. Dennis sat motionless. On the floor behind Dennis lay the Chief of Police, conscious now but too weak from loss of blood and too sick with pain to inch himself across the few feet of floor that would have brought him close enough to Mr. Dennis to reach the twisted ropes with his teeth.

"You're pretty," the madman said. "What's your name?"

"M-Marie."

"Marie. They didn't have girls like you in the place I escaped from. No, they didn't." He scowled at her. "But you don't like me, do you?"

"I — I don't know you," she whispered.

"You'd like me if you knew me?"

"I — might."

"It don't make any difference," he said. "I'd have to kill you anyway, after a while, same as I got to kill those two." His head jerked in the general direction of Mr. Dennis and the Chief of Police, but he did not turn to look at them.

"Why?" Marie whispered.

"They sent me to that asylum."

"But they didn't! They never saw you before today!"

"All the same I was sent there, and I got to kill people for it. I got to get even. Only first I'm gonna look at you for a while. You're pretty."

He inched his chair closer and his breath was hot on the girl's face. Grinning at her, he put out a hand and touched her arm.

"It's a long time since I was this close to a woman," he said.

DENNIS sat in his chair and stared at the madman's back. He breathed hard and his face was white, strained, his eyes glittered with a strange kind of desperation. Swelling his chest with a prodigious breath, he tested the strength of the rope that held his wrists.

Agony crawled down his arms to the tips of his withered fingers.

He turned his head and tried to see how the rope was tied, but though the cords of his neck stood out in hard white lines, he could not move his head far enough. But his gaze did meet that of the Chief of Police.

The madman had leaned closer and was stroking Marie's hair. And saying: "You're pretty. It's too bad I got to kill you, ain't it?"

Mr. Dennis rolled his wrists, his emaciated useless wrists, in a desperate attempt to create slack in the rope. The agony came again, this time bringing beads of perspiration to his face. Only two men in the world could have escaped from a rope so cunningly knotted — Houdini, the great Houdini, and a magician named Malkar.

Both were — dead.

Mr. Dennis exerted all his strength, defying the agony. It was not enough. Despair darkened his eyes and again a slow, creeping numbness moved through him. It was ironical, this. The dead could not return to life, even to save the living. And if by some monstrous miracle the dead did return to life — if by some amazing power of mind over matter those withered hands of his could be endowed with a strength and dexterity lost three years ago — those same crooked fingers would sign their master's death warrant. For Karkin was watching. Karkin would know then that the puny hands of Mr. Dennis were not too puny to twist a man's neck until it snapped.

The madman caressed Marie's face and said softly: "It's a shame I got to kill you. I ought to make love to you a while first. But I can't do that. I got to get out of here."

Ghastly pale, she looked past him and her gaze met that of Mr. Dennis.

The soul of Mr. Dennis groaned. He clenched his teeth. For three years he had tried in vain to make those withered hands work. Now he tried again, knowing the fate that lay in wait for him if he failed — and if he succeeded.

Perspiration poured from his face. Agony filled it. But he closed his eyes, sunk his teeth into his lower lip and reached back through three years of shadow to a flickering light which still glowed. A strand of rope snapped.

"I got to get out of here and I got to kill you first," the madman said.

Mr. Dennis's contorted face was black with agony, but he refused to give up. A second strand snapped, and a third. The madman didn't seem to hear. He was encompassed with furious passion. He got out of his chair and gripped the girl's white neck with both his hands.

She tried to scream, but his hands held the scream back. She clawed at him, raked his face with her nails. Her feet beat a tattoo on his legs. Angry, he cursed her and dragged her from the chair to the floor.

Mr. Dennis broke the rope. He jerked his hands around in front of him and stared at them, and his eyes were afire with a kind of madness. Then he hurled himself out of his chair and gained possession of the gun which had fallen from the hands of Chief of Police Karkin a long while ago.

"Stop it!" Mr. Dennis hoarsely shouted. "Stop it, Brandon! By God, I'll kill you!"

The madman turned, releasing Marie. In a half crouch he blinked his eyes at Dennis, who stood wide-legged, holding the gun.

A snarl curled Brandon's lips. He reached out with both hands and lurched forward to drag Mr. Dennis down.

Dennis shot him twice and stepped aside as the man fell sprawling.

The silence came back.

For some time Mr. Dennis looked down at the gun in his hands; then he placed it on the table and lifted Marie into a chair. He looked tired. His face wore an expression of misery.

The girl stared at him and her eyes were wide. "You did it, Andre!" she whispered. "You did it! Your hands —"

"Yes," he said, "I did it."

He turned then and said to the Chief of Police: "Have you a key to these cuffs?"

"No," Karkin said.

"It doesn't matter." Mr. Dennis removed his gloves and quietly stripped a lace from one of his shoes. On his knees, he formed a loop with the lace and deftly worked the loop over the end of the screw. A quick tug snapped the bolt back and the cuffs were open.

Karkin rose to his knees. "You told me," he said slowly, "those hands of yours were weak."

"Yes."

"After what I just saw, I know you lied. You'll have to come with me, Dennis."

"Yes, I know. For murdering Papa Nickson."

Karkin nodded. Sliding his gun from the table, he holstered it but kept his hand over it. "I hate to do this," he muttered, "after you saved our lives, but the law is the law. Maybe you had a good reason for killin' Papa Nickson, but it ain't up to me to ask you."

Mr. Dennis lifted Karkin to his feet. Lurchingly, the officer put a hand on Mr. Dennis's arm. "You gotta come with me."

Mr. Dennis said, as if to himself: "The dead live — and the dead die again."

"What's that?"

"Nothing," said Mr. Dennis, and stopped. "Wait a minute, Karkin. This madman isn't dead."

Karkin scowled and looked down at John Brandon, and Brandon reached out to clutch at his leg. Blood trickled from a corner of his mouth, but the mouth was grinning.

"You're makin' a mistake," Brandon laughed. "You're crazy like they said I was. He didn't do it."

"Didn't do what?"

"Kill that old man. A man he called Andy done it. I was right there, lookin' in a window. That's how smart I am! I heard them talkin' and I seen it happen, I did." He laughed insanely and blood came. "If you think this man done it, you belong where I come from. Andy done it. But I won't tell. I won't tell and they'll put *you* away!"

"Andy Slade?" Karkin breathed.

"That's right. Andy Slade." The blood came faster. "I was right there and I seen it, and I followed him here through the woods, and . . . ." Brandon howled horribly in glee. "Hell, are you dumb! I seen it from the window, I heard it all. But I ain't telling you that I seen that kid kill the old fellow."

Karkin looked at Mr. Dennis. "I'm glad," he said. "I'm real glad, Mr. Dennis." He put out his hand and Dennis gripped it. Gripped it hard. "I'll go get Slade," Karkin said. "Get me help — from town."

Mr. Dennis started out to go to the village, and in a moment Marie joined him.

"The great Malkar is alive again," she said softly.

• • • • •

# SMOKE GETS IN YOUR EYES

THIS IS A LONG YARN WITH A RATHER COMPLICATED PLOT ON SEVERAL LEVELS. THE LONGEST, IN FACT, THAT I HAD WRITTEN FOR *BLACK MASK* UP TO THAT TIME, DECEMBER 1938. WHEN I BEGAN SELLING TO THE PULPS I DIDN'T HAVE AN AGENT, BUT AFTER A WHILE ROGERS TERRILL OF POPULAR PUBLICATIONS PUT ME IN TOUCH WITH AGENT LURTON BLASSINGAME (WHOM EVERYONE CALLED 'COUNT'), AFTER WHICH I MAILED EVERY STORY TO LURTON INSTEAD OF TO EDITORS OF MAGAZINES, SO I DIDN'T DEAL DIRECTLY WITH EITHER CAP SHAW OR FANNY ELLSWORTH. EVENTUALLY, BY THE WAY, LURTON BECAME A CLOSE FRIEND. FOR YEARS WE WENT FISHING EVERY SPRING AND FALL TOGETHER, OFTEN WITH EDITOR KEN WHITE OF *DIME DETECTIVE* (AND LATER OF *BLACK MASK*). ONE SUMMER WE EXPLORED THE CANADIAN WILDERNESS BETWEEN LAKE HURON AND HUDSON BAY BY CANOE — A GRAND ADVENTURE WHICH, IF YOU LIKE, YOU CAN READ ABOUT IN MY FIRST NOVEL, *FISHERMEN FOUR*, OR MY 39TH BOOK, *THE DAWNING*, PUBLISHED IN JULY 2000 BY LEISURE BOOKS.

HBC

*The girl in a red cape pursues trouble and stumbles
onto a plot where life means little.*

JOHN SMITH gazed with exaggerated tolerance at his fair companion. Of course it was not difficult to exercise patience with a young lady so scandalously lovely. He was, in fact, used to it.

"Ever so many men, Angel," he declared, "smoke long black cigarettes. Even I do at times."

"The heat, Mr. Edgerson, has made you lazy. Otherwise you'd jump at a thing like this."

Smith's other name was Philip Edgerson. He hated it because it brought to mind too many memories of birthdays, Christmases and people sick in bed. He was head of a greeting card company. Now he put down his cocktail and leaned back.

They were dining in Polinoff's, and it had not been a good idea. Polinoff's on an August afternoon was far too hot, too stuffy, for the enjoyment of pig knuckles and spiced red cabbage.

"I'm thinking of abandoning Trouble, Incorporated, Angel."

"Said he, lying," she retorted.

"No, I mean it. Look. I've paid rent on that ninth floor cell for eleven months now, and not a customer. Not a single client. A man's hobby, as I see it, should be more productive than that."

"It has been," Angelina said simply.

"Not financially."

"Mr. Philip Edgerson," she said, "makes quite enough money to support the hobby of John Smith. It's the heat, that's all."

"I suppose it is."

He reached out then and picked up the letter she had read to him. It was a neat little thing, written delicately in green ink on ten-cent-store paper which bore the gilt initials, M.A.B. It read:

Dear Miss Kaye,

This is the third time I have tried to write to you, but on each previous occasion my courage has left me before I could finish. This time, however, I am determined to go through with it. You see, I am really desperate.

Please do not be angry with me if this is a long letter. I know that you urge those who write to you to be brief, but I have so much to tell.

I am nineteen years old, Miss Kaye, and was married just a little over a year ago to the dearest boy in all the world. Teddy was so loving then and so considerate. We saved money and planned for the future and were just as happy as two birds in a nest. And now all that is changed.

I am not really sure when the trouble began. Now that I look back on it, I realize that Teddy acted queerly for days, even weeks, before he actually began staying out nights and leaving me alone. During that period he was awfully quiet and seemed always to be wrapped up in his thoughts. I thought he was worried about his job, and I tried to be tender with him, but he refused to confide in me. He even told me once that it was none of my business.

Then, Miss Kaye, he began staying out late at night, sometimes until two or three o'clock in the morning, and I was sick with worry. When I spoke to him about it he told me to leave him alone and stop nagging him, but I wasn't nagging him, I was just frantic that our love would die and he would drift away from me.

It went on this way for almost a month, Miss Kaye, and then he began bringing these men to the house. Three or four times a week they came, and they were nice enough, I suppose. At least they always said hello to me, but instead of sitting in the parlor like ordinary friends, they and Teddy would go upstairs to Teddy's den and close the door and stay up there until all hours. Sometimes there would be three of them, sometimes more.

Well, Miss Kaye, I do not pretend to be any judge of character, but I am positive in my own heart that these men are not good for Teddy. They are not his kind. They are older, for one thing, and they seem very wise in the ways of the world. One of them, whom the others seem to look upon as a sort of leader, is a foreigner, at least twenty years older than my husband, and he smokes long black cigarettes continually, and the house reeks from it. And furthermore, if these men were proper companions for Teddy, he would introduce me to them, wouldn't he? But he hasn't. He just said, "Boys, meet the wife." Which hurt me terribly.

Please, Miss Kaye, tell me what to do to win my husband away from these men. I am worried to desperation for fear I will lose him, and for fear he is getting mixed up in something that will bring trouble to us both.

Anxiously yours,

Margaret Arnold Burdick.

P.S. If you print this letter in your column, please sign it "Worried Wife" because if you used my real name Teddy would be angry, I'm sure.

M.A.B.

John Smith, president of Trouble, Inc., carefully folded the letter and passed it back. "Do you get many like that, Miss Kaye?" She frowned at him. Her name was not Katherine Kaye any more than his was John Smith. Her name, when she was not opening letters from love-sick wives at her desk in the *Star* office, was Angelina Copeland. Angel to her friends.

"You think it's a rib, Philip?"

"As phony, Angel, as some of the sentiments I'm guilty of perpetrating."

"I don't. I think it's on the level. I'm going out there. After all, Philip, you've bored me to death for months about that fool professor who smoked black cigarettes and here we have a guy who — "

"You know the address?"

She took from her purse an envelope which matched the letter. "Spencer Street, 154. You *could* drive me out there," she said. "Otherwise I'll have to go by trolley."

Edgerson heaved an elaborate sigh. It was a hot, sticky afternoon. From nine to twelve he had faithfully perspired through his duties as president of the Edgerson Greeting Card Company, watching the clock and looking forward to a long, cool drive into the country with Angel, a dip in some shady lake, dinner and dancing at some quiet roadhouse far from the city's heat.

Now he was to be John Smith again. It was inevitable. He disliked this silly Margaret Arnold Burdick intensely. He resented the fact that she had found it necessary to mention a large foreign person who incessantly smoked long black cigarettes. Because, after all, the thing was ridiculous. Dubitsky was dead. Dubitsky had been dead for at least four months. The Dubitsky whose strange death had intrigued him was gone forever. Margaret Burdick's foreigner would turn out to be a wrestler or a man selling carpets. Or a myth.

"I'll drive you," he said sourly, "but you'll regret it. Mark my words, Angel, you'll regret it."

AT LEAST half a dozen times since the birth of Trouble, Inc., Edgerson had been on the verge of closing the tiny office in the Mason Building and chucking the whole thing to the dogs. On each and every one of those occasions, Angelina had popped up with something "hot." It was she, not he, who kept his hobby, Trouble, Inc., going. He half suspected that the Trouble idea had been hers in the first place anyway.

When they reached Spencer Street on the outskirts of town, and found the house, he was relentlessly gleeful. He pointed to the sign in the window and said: "You see? I told you so." The sign said "For Rent."

Angel frowned at it. The frown was most becoming to her beauty. Edgerson gently patted her shoulders. "We still have time for the ride into the country, the swim, the — "

"Apply at 27 Brook Street," Angel said.

"What?"

"That's what it says. 'For rent. Apply 27 Brook.' That's the next street over, Philip." He said nothing, merely groaned and put the car in gear. Angel was silent, too, until he stopped the machine in front of a small brown cottage on Brook Street. "The trouble with you, Mr. Smith," she said then, sweetly, "is that you give up too easily."

He followed her up the walk, between beds of marigolds. She rang the bell. In a moment the door was opened by a plump female in flowered apron.

"How do you do?" Angel said in her nicest Sunday voice. "I'm Mrs. Smith. This is my husband."

The woman said, "How do you do?" wonderingly, and glanced at Edgerson and stared at Angel. Women usually stared at Angel. And envied her slimness, her remarkable blond hair and her more than pretty face.

"We noticed a house over on Spencer Street, for rent," Angel said.

"Oh, yes."

"Is it occupied at present?"

"No." The woman shook her head. "We had a nice young couple living there, but they've moved out."

Edgerson, recovering from his shock at so casually being called "my hus-band," smiled slyly. He was John Smith now, and John Smith was at times a pretty fair detective. Angel, fishing for information about the nice young couple on Spencer Street, was going to encounter difficulties. The plump lady in the flowered-apron was obviously not a talker.

"We've looked so long for a house," Angel said, "that I really don't know *what* I want. You know how it is, I'm sure. You go from one place to another and simply get all worn out."

The woman nodded sympathetically. There were chairs on the porch and she moved toward them. "Won't you sit down, Mrs. Smith?"

"Thank you," Angel breathed. "Thank you so much!"

"It's really a very nice house," the woman said. "My husband and I built it ourselves and lived in it four years. Then last year Mr. and Mrs. Burdick, the nice young couple I mentioned to you, moved in."

Angel looked thoughtfully at the tips of her fingers. "They didn't stay very long, did they?"

"No, they didn't. It wasn't because of the house, though. Mr. Burdick worked for the Glickman Company and lost his job. He had to go to another city to find work."

"Oh," Angel said. "That's too bad. And they'd only been married a year?"

"Only a year."

Angel widened her large brown eyes and looked soulfully at Edgerson. "You know, dear," she said, sadly shaking her head, "when you hear of the misfortunes that beset other married people, it makes you realize how terri-bly fortunate we've been." She turned the soulful eyes on the woman again. "Married only a year, and so in love with each other! I just know they were!"

"Well," the woman said dubiously, "well, yes, I guess they were."

"And are they coming back some day? To visit you?"

"Well, I don't know. Theodore, that's Mr. Burdick, said they were moving to some place near Boston. Margaret went last Wednesday to put things in order, and he went Saturday, with the furniture truck. They may come back, but of course I couldn't hold the house for them. Now if you'd like to look at it, Mrs. Smith . . . ."

But Angel was looking at her "husband" again. "You know, darling, per-haps Mrs. — er — " She glanced helplessly at the woman who said, "My name is Crandall."

"Perhaps Mrs. Crandall could recommend someone to move our furni-ture. Those last people we had were simply unbearable. I'll just never forgive them for ruining our twin beds." Edgerson gulped.

"Could you recommend someone, Mrs. Crandall?" Angel cooed.

"Well, we like the Hartley people ourselves. If you're just moving a short distance, that is. The Burdicks used the McCullen Warehouse people."

"You saved her a lot of trouble," Edgerson thought. "She was going to ask you that in a minute. Twin beds! Of all things, twin beds!" Angel stood up. "Would you like to look at the house now, dear, or come back tomorrow? It's quite late, and we did promise to meet the Burrs."

"Tomorrow," Edgerson said.

"Will that be all right with you, Mrs. Crandall?"

"Well, yes," Mrs. Crandall agreed.

"Then we'll see you tomorrow. . . . Come, darling. I really think we've accomplished something!"

In the car, Edgerson drew a slow deep breath and said, "You little hellion!"

She grinned. "It worked, didn't it?"

"It worked, but I've a mind to put you across those mythical twin beds and spank you." Gnomes and pixies would have danced to her laughter. But then she was suddenly sober.

"This thing sounds ugly to me, Philip."

"Why?"

"First, that letter. I received it Wednesday, the day she left. She must have written and mailed it Tuesday. Then, more important, why the sudden departure? If she'd known that they were leaving the city, she wouldn't have written the letter at all. I never answer letters personally. When people write to my lovelorn column they expect to see the replies in print."

Edgerson, silent for a moment, said, "Would it be all right with you, Angel, if I did a little detecting myself for a change? After all, I'm president of Trouble, Inc."

"You're not a very ambitious president."

"I might surprise you." He turned the car onto a main street. "The McCullen Warehouse is on Canal Street, isn't it?"

"Yes. Why?"

"We're going there. Between your nutty curiosity and my interest in any guy who smokes black cigs like Dubitsky did . . . . I'll never believe that guy's really dead."

It was a huge red-brick building growing out of the damp, sticky smells of the waterfront. Smith went in alone and was gone a half-hour. Returning, he had a triumphant smirk on his angular face.

"They didn't move out of town," he said. "Their furniture is in storage, most of it. A studio couch, two easy chairs, a table and a large double bed — not twin beds, Angel — were trucked over to this address as soon as the van reached the warehouse." He passed her a slip of paper. She peered at it. "Gayland Avenue. That's an apartment house district. Very snooty."

"You know," Smith said, putting the car in gear, "this is beginning to show signs of promise. Maybe your lovelorn wife was in trouble."

GAYLAND STREET was in a district of fancy dress shops, delicatessens and pomeranians, and the figure on the slip of paper was the number of an imposing structure housing a nest of apartments. This time Angel refused to sit in the car while he investigated. She went with him up the gleaming steps into the hallway with its glittering brass mail-boxes, and she looked with him at the long list of names beside the long row of bells.

Bell number 17 had no name beside it, but Smith pushed it anyway. The studio couch, chairs, table and bed had been delivered to Suite 17.

He pushed again and frowned. "They don't answer."

"I've been wondering something," Angel said.

"Yes? What?"

"If you were a young man fresh out of a job, Philip, would you feel able to afford an apartment in this neighborhood?"

Smith shrugged. "If we wondered at all the queer things people do, we'd wind up in a chuckle college."

"I'm serious, Philip."

"So am I. They don't answer." Angel looked annoyed. She walked up two white steps and tried the door and it was locked. She said, "Damn!" and stood there glaring at it. All at once her eyes widened; she turned quickly, beckoned with an outstretched hand and said,

"C'm'ere, quick!"

At her side, Smith peered through the thick clear glass of the door and saw a man backing out of an apartment at the end of the hall. A suitcase lay beside the open door and the man was lugging out another. He closed the door and picked up both pieces of luggage and plodded down the corridor with them, staggering a little because they were heavy and he was a small, thin-legged, bald little lad without much strength.

"Plouffe, by gosh! Plouffe, of all private dicks."

The little dick kept his head down until he reached the door, and by that time Smith had faded back on one side, Angel on the other. Plouffe put down his burdens, opened the door, held it open with a foot and picked up the suitcases. He squirmed out and the door clicked shut behind him. Then he saw Smith. He dropped the suitcases again and said, "Well, my, my! Look who is here!" Smith looked at the luggage. It was expensive but old. It was initialed.

"So you're demoted to bellhop," Smith said.

"Huh?"

"You make a very handsome bellhop, don't you, Mr. Plouffe?" said Angel sweetly.

Nick Plouffe pulled a large moist handkerchief from his pocket and mopped his brow. He frowned, using his whole face, and said sourly: "At least I don't have to give myself no fancy name like Trouble, Incorporated to get business."

"Of course you don't," Angel said.

"And I ain't a bellhop, see?"

"Of course you're not. You live here."

"Me? Live here? Say, are you nuts?"

"We're looking," Angel declared solemnly, "for my Aunt Agatha. Apartment eighteen. We have a key to Aunt Agatha's apartment — she's in Bermuda, you know — but no key to the door you're leaning against. Could you let us in, maybe?"

Nick Plouffe blinked, registering suspicion. It was hard for him to register suspicion, or anything else, because his moist little face was small and V-shaped and not very elastic. He did his best, though, and then grumbled: "Well, all right." He fumbled for a key and unlocked the door.

"Thank you so much," Angel cooed. "Come, John."

She and John Smith paced down the hall without a backward glance at the suspicious Plouffe, and Smith said dryly, "There, my dear, is a scraping from the lowest stratum of the private detecting profession. Dumb but dangerous. A mouse, but a mean mouse. I met up with him on another case and caught him pretending to be a G-man. He asked me to promise not to tell on him. Did you note the initials on the two suitcases?"

"I did. M.A.B. and T.L.B."

"The Burdicks."

"Or a monstrous coincidence, because Plouffe came out of this apartment," Angel declared, stopping beside a door, "and it happens to be suite 17."

Smith glanced back, then, to make certain

Plouffe had departed. Satisfied, he knocked. After a moment's wait he knocked again.

"They don't answer."

"Perhaps we should tail Mr. Plouffe," Angel suggested. "Or is it too late?"

Smith leaned against the door of apartment 17 and scowled at her. Scowled fiercely, because he knew from past experience that Miss Angelina Copeland — she had once been his secretary and had since become both the bane and the beacon of his existence — would talk him out of it unless he were savagely stubborn. "It's too late," he said firmly, "for absolutely everything except that drive into the country, that swim, and — "

"But tomorrow we start in again. Promise?"

"No!"

She rolled her eyes at the ceiling and tapped a toe on the tile floor. "No promise, no ride. It's for your own good, darling. If I didn't keep jabbing you, you'd turn into a Christmas card, and that would be such a waste of talent." She took his arm. Smith sighed and went with her, muttering under his breath.

M ISS MIGGSBY, who wore large rimless glasses, placed a sheaf of papers on Edgerson's desk and said, beaming: "We think, Mr. Edgerson, that these are simply delightful!"

Miss Miggsby had been Edgerson's private secretary since the departure of Angel. She possessed some of Angel's brains, none of Angel's disturbing physical attraction, and was very, very easy on the nerves.

Edgerson gravely accepted the papers, glanced at them. The door of his private sanctum opened at that moment and he looked up. Looked up and groaned. He could tell by the grim little smile on Angelina's lips that something had happened.

Miss Miggsby fled. Angel, radiant in something ultra modern and startlingly yellow, came around the desk and looked over Edgerson's shoulder.

"Christmas?" she asked innocently. "Or just happy birthday to my ex-wife?"

He made sure that the door between Miss Miggsby's office and his own was closed before he answered. Then he said firmly, "Whatever you've found out, it's no go. I'm busy. I got in this morning with a prize hangover, thanks to your mania for daiquiris last night, and found enough work piled on my desk to keep three men busy for a week."

"Oh."

"Don't *you* ever work?"

"Uh-huh. I just finished my column. Look, Philip. I've discovered the whereabouts of Margaret Burdick."

"I'm not interested."

"You've got to be. It's terribly important." She cleared a space for herself on his desk and sat down, swinging a most attractive leg.

"First I went over to the Glickman Company where Mr. Burdick — Teddy, that is — used to work. I smiled my prettiest and found out that Teddy wasn't fired; he quit. He told them he had a better job offered to him in Boston. I deserve credit for that. The Glickman outfit is a big concern. They make chemicals and do a lot of work for the government. It took talent to go in there stone cold and come out with information."

"I'm still very busy," Edgerson muttered.

"So then," she continued, "I went over to that little dumpy hotel where your little Plouffe lives. The clerk told me he was in, so I slipped into a phone booth and called him and talked the way you'd expect Margaret Arnold Burdick to talk — after reading that letter she wrote me — and I told Plouffe to come right over because I needed him. And he fell for it."

Edgerson was not sufficiently surprised to show it.

"He fell for it," Angel declared, "and when he left the hotel I followed him. He didn't go far. He went to another grimy little hotel, the Lester, and that, Philip, is where Mrs. Burdick is hiding out."

"You saw her?"

"No, but — "

"What about her husband? Is he living there, too?"

"After all," she said, "I'm not the president of Trouble, Inc. I'm just an underpaid hireling. Don't expect too much."

"I can't see that you've done too much."

"But I haven't confessed all. Not yet. I've been to the morgue," she said.

That got him. His mouth sagged and he gaped at her.

"The newspaper morgue," she explained softly, "to check on Dubitsky. Do you know why I did that?"

He said nothing.

"Because," she went on, "I discovered over at the chemical company that young Mr. Burdick is a graduate of our nice big university here where Dubitsky taught. And when I found that out, I got to thinking about the foreigner who smoked the long black cigarettes, and so I went over to the university and did some snooping. Guess what I found."

"If you don't stop beating around the mulberry bush," Edgerson said, "I'll fire you!"

"Young Mr. Burdick was a student in some of Dubitsky's classes."

"You mean it?"

"It's the truth. He was an honor student. One of Dubitsky's pets."

"I'm not," Edgerson said, "as busy as I thought. Go ahead."

"You mean it?"

"Go right ahead. I've always been intrigued with Dubitsky. The Christmas ditties can wait."

"Well," she said, "I've brought you some of the newspaper accounts of Dubitsky's death."

"I don't need them. I know the details by heart."

"Do you? Lead on, MacDuff."

"The great Dubitsky," Edgerson said, "left his bachelor apartment about six-thirty that night, intending to drive to a little camp he owned on Loon Cry Lake, sixty miles north of here. It was a miserable night, and he was alone. He stopped in Midville for gas, and the attendant warned him not to try the Loon Lake road because it was inundated and dangerous, and an electrical storm was coming up over the mountains.

"He went, and was caught in the storm. His car went over a cliff and caught fire, probably struck by lightning before it went over. The charred remains of Dubitsky were identified by a watch and a couple of rings."

"And I'll wager my next year's salary as nonpaid vice president of Trouble, Inc.," said Angel calmly, "that you believe Professor Dubitsky is still very much alive. Now don't you, Mr. Smith?"

Edgerson scowled at a tiny image of Santa Claus which sat on his desk. It was a birthday gift from Miss Miggsby. "Now why," he insisted, "should a self-respecting professor of foreign languages, including the Malaysian, wish to plunge himself into oblivion?"

"What nationality is Dubitsky?"

"Darned if I know. German, Czeck, Russian, Polish — he might be most anything."

"The point is," she said, "he's not American. He came to this country six or seven years ago, to take up his duties at the university. No one knows much about him, except that he's a mental giant. Put two and two together, Philip. Dubitsky. A mysterious accident. The Glickman Chemical Company. Young Burdick. It's positively sinister; that's what it is!"

"What," Edgerson said, "do you propose to do about it?"

"Have a talk with Burdick's wife. And you're coming with me. This, Mr. Smith, is the biggest thing that ever fell into the lap of our little organization, or I'm a monkey's uncle."

"I think a better move," Smith declared thoughtfully, "would be to call on Plouffe."

"Plouffe?"

"The girl might be a bit difficult. Plouffe, on the other hand, would hardly dare to be. I know too much about him. I might still talk about him impersonating himself as a G-man." He smiled, pushing himself out of his chair. "Trouble, Incorporated, is at work again," he said.

NICK PLOUFFE, when not at his hotel, could generally be found between bottles of beer in his office or between martinis at the Andolf Tap. He was in his office this time, suffering from the heat. A cheap fan sent the hot air surging about the room and Plouffe's handkerchief was sodden from face-mopping.

He peered suspiciously at his visitors and said: "Well, my, my! Look who is here!"

"You're surprised," Smith said.

"I am pop-eyed!"

Smith shut off the fan and eyed the half-empty bottle of beer on the detective's desk. He sat down without awaiting an invitation. Angel followed suit. Nick Plouffe stood beside the desk, mopped his pleasant, little face again and registered uneasiness.

"So what can I do for you?"

"You're not going to like this, Nick."

"I feel it in my bones."

"What we'd like to know, Nick," Smith said, "is how you got mixed up in this Burdick business."

Plouffe sat down. His tie was askew and his striped shirt was open down to the third button, revealing a moist undershirt and a few chest hairs. He said plaintively: "On a hot day like this you should come here to ask questions! What did I ever do to you?"

"Give, Nick."

"Give! Do I ask you to hand out professional secrets? Do I come barging into Trouble, Incorporated, and act like I was a partner?"

"You wouldn't want to be a partner," Angel said sweetly. "There's no money in it."

"Give," Smith said.

"So why should I?"

"Must we go through all that again? About how unhealthy our local jails are, and how bad the food is? Nick, you surprise me."

Nick Plouffe slumped lower in his chair. The desk hid most of him but his eyes were little gray bugs just visible over the rim.

"The Burdick girl is a client of mine," he mumbled.

"How come?"

"You would not be interested. So help me it would bore you, I swear it."

"I'll risk it. Go right ahead."

"Well, it is like this. It is very ordinary. The Burdick girl comes up here and says she sees the name of my agency in the phone book. Then she spills a sob story into my ears, and so help me, Mr. Smith, it is nothing that would interest you. It is like every other sob story you ever heard."

"I'll hear it again," Smith said.

"But it will bore you stiff!"

"The food," Angel chimed in gently, "is really atrocious, Mr. Plouffe. They feed you bread and mush three times a day, and sometimes the mush is maggoty. If it isn't, I'm sure Mr. Smith can arrange to have them inject a few maggots, just for your benefit."

Plouffe mopped his face. "She has a husband, see? And he stays out late at night, and sometimes he doesn't come home at all. She says to me, he is keeping bad company and will I look into it? So help me that's the whole story."

"The bell-hopping was just your own idea, eh?" Smith said.

"Huh?"

"If that's all there is to it, Plouffe, why'd you move her from a swank apartment house to a frowsy dump of a hotel?"

"She — she couldn't pay the rent them vultures was asking."

"Maggots, Plouffe, are apt to make you hellishly sick."

"Well," Plouffe muttered, avoiding Smith's steady gaze, "I had to get some dough out of this business somehow, didn't I?"

"Meaning what?"

"She pays me to tail her husband. There wouldn't be no dough in that even if I could locate the husband, which I can't. So I have to tell the dame something, don't I? Would you want me to let her down and have her get a wrong idea about the private detective business?"

"The light begins to dawn," Angel murmured.

Plouffe looked at her gratefully and forced a grin. "Sure. She wanted service, so I gave it to her. There wasn't no harm in that, was there? All I told her, I checked up on her husband and found out he was mixed up with some tough mobsters, and things looked pretty bad, and her own life could easy be in danger unless she put herself in my care for a few days until I got things straightened out."

"And she believed you?" Smith asked.

"Sure she believed me."

"And to make it more realistic, you moved her out of the apartment and obtained a room for her at the Lester."

"Yeah. Hell, if these dumb dames want adventure, Nick Plouffe sells it to 'em. Why not?"

Smith stood up. "I'm hiring you, Plouffe."

The gray little eyes grew to twice their normal size. "Huh?"

"You say you tried to locate Burdick and failed. Is that right?"

"Sure I tried."

"Hard?"

"I done all I could," Plouffe insisted. "I checked every lead the dame gave me."

"And you couldn't find him. Very well, Plouffe, he's missing. Something has happened to him. And if we're not careful, something may happen to the girl. Therefore, I'm hiring you to keep an eye on her."

"Listen," Plouffe said. "This don't make sense."

"It might, later. You're to watch the girl and keep in touch with me, report to me every move she makes. I'd do it myself, Plouffe, but I'm going to be busy. Very busy. So is Miss Copeland. And our staff at Trouble, Inc., is limited."

"Say, what's back of all this?"

"A certain crack someone once made," Angel replied quickly, flashing a smile, "about twin beds."

"Huh?"

"You wouldn't understand, Plouffe. Don't worry about it. Some day Mr. Smith is going to write a treatise on it. Then you'll know."

Smith turned to open the door. "You can get in touch with me, Plouffe, at Trouble, Inc. If I'm not there, Miss Copeland will be. And I'll expect your first report about an hour from now."

Outside, Angel said sweetly: "What I like about you, Mr. Smith, is your uncanny faculty for persuading people to work for you — for nothing. Including," she added, taking his arm, "me."

SMITH WAS BUSY the next day. Visiting the university, he spent two hours investigating the history of Professor Benedetto Dubitsky and another hour on the records of Mrs. Burdick's Teddy. To his work as president of Trouble, Inc., he applied the same tenacity which had made him president of a prosperous greeting-card concern.

He then visited the Glickman Company's huge chemical plant and learned that Mr. Theodore Burdick, formerly employed there, had been hired in the first place because of flattering recommendations tendered by the university.

It dovetailed nicely. Just what it meant, Smith was not sure.

With Angel, in the tiny office of Trouble, Inc., he had a dinner which consisted of cold lobster and ginger ale, purchased at a delicatessen.

Angel was dressed, Smith thought, more like a devil. She had on a handsome evening dress that gleamed under a brilliant red opera cape. Its tiny hood was made to be drawn over her sleek hair.

"Why the fancy set up?" he asked.

"I thought you were going to buy me a dinner and dance. Instead I get this and a ride, I guess."

About that time Nick Plouffe, who had been calling every hour to make his report, phoned in again.

Nick Plouffe was excited. "Only two minutes ago," he wailed, "she give me the slip! I was watchin' the Lester, see? Like I been doin' right along. I'm standin' there earnin' the salary you don't promise me, and all of a sudden she comes out with a couple of guys, and they get into a car.

"This car is parked in front of the Lester ever since around eight o'clock, and there's a ticket on it. I myself see the cop put the ticket on it. So they get into it, Mrs. Burdick and these two guys, and I pile into a taxi and tail them. And I lose them. On account of the taxi driver is dumb as all get-out, I lose then. Up around Mitchell Street and the Avenue is where I last see them."

"You get the number of that car?" Smith snapped.

"Yeah, sure. C-3145."

"Where are you now?"

"In a drug store on Mitchell."

"Get into your cab," Smith ordered, "and come over here as fast as you can. You may be needed." He cradled the phone and gazed solemnly at Angel. "C-3145, Angel. Think you can find out to whom that car is registered?"

"I can try."

She called her newspaper and four minutes later reported: "The car belongs to Alvin McKenna, 92 Follett Street, vice-president of the Glickman Company. Something?"

Smith, at his desk, wrote the name and address on a pad and stared at them clicking the pencil along his teeth as a small boy would rattle a stick along a picket fence.

"McKenna — the Glickman Company — a ticket for parking," he mused. "And two men. Not one man, Angel, but two. Dammit, what's keeping Plouffe?"

There was a knock at the door. Angel opened it and Plouffe entered, out of breath.

"I got here quick like you told me, Mr. Smith."

"Now let's have it all, Plouffe. Slowly. Begin with the car. Did you see it pull up?"

"Sure I seen it."

"Two men in it?"

"Now that's funny," Plouffe said. "When the car drove up there was only one guy in it. I was standin' right there and I couldn't've made no mistake. The guy parks the car in a one-hour space and goes into the Lester."

"What kind of a car?"

"A Packard coupe."

"A man as wealthy as McKenna," Angel declared, "would have more than one car, Mr. Smith."

"I realize that. Now, Plouffe, how long was that car there?"

"More'n two hours."

"And when the two men came out, with Mrs. Burdick, there was a ticket on it?"

"That's right."

"One of those men was the driver?"

"Yep. One was the guy who parked it there."

"Did you get a good look at Mrs. Burdick? Did she look scared?"

"Without bein' no authority on women's looks, I would say she did. Definitely I would say she was at least uneasy."

Smith stared into space and drew meaningless circles and triangles on a desk calendar. The Smith brain was hard at work; you could tell by the roadmap of wrinkles that spread away from his eye-corners. He reached suddenly for the phone book, ran a finger down the long line of McKennas and impulsively snatched up the phone. Then slowly replaced it, shaking his head.

"If you want my opinion," Plouffe ventured timidly, "I'd say — "

"Quiet," snapped Angel. "He's thinking."

"Oh."

Smith seized the phone, dialed a number. Angel relaxed. "McKenna?" she asked softly. He nodded, waiting for the connection.

"I still think," Plouffe insisted, "that — "

"Quiet."

Smith registered impatience while waiting. He looked worried. Finally he slapped the phone down and stood up. "They don't answer," he said curtly. "Let's go."

"Out there?" Angel asked.

"Yes! Don't you see through it? McKenna's car — first one man, then two — and a deliberate ticket? It's plain as day!"

"Not to me it isn't," Plouffe complained.

Smith favored him with a scornful glance and went past him, grabbing at Angel's hand as he jerked open the door. Plouffe followed, not knowing what else to do.

"If you're thinking what I'm thinking you're thinking," Angel said on the way down the corridor, "I'll bet my year's pay that you're wrong. It's just your evil mind at work."

"You mean it's yours," Smith retorted.

"Mine's away ahead of you. Come on, you two."

McKENNA'S HOUSE was a twenty-room affair with an acre of lawn cut by a driveway and a colored fountain out front. Alvin McKenna, forty-nine, was a widower worth plenty.

The house was in darkness. The car crunched up the drive and stopped, and Smith jumped out. Before ringing the bell he tried the front door. It was locked. After ringing the bell he waited only a moment, then broad-jumped a flower-bed and hurried around the side. Every window he tried was locked.

He paused, baffled, and Angel caught up with him. "Sometimes," she said pleasantly, "you surprise me, Philip. So athletic!"

He ignored her. To Plouffe he snapped: "How do we get in here?"

"You want to get arrested?" Plouffe gasped.

"I want to get in!"

"Well, it could be done easy enough, but —"

"Do it!"

Plouffe looked around, shaking his head, and then sidled to a window. It wasn't easy but in a few minutes with a penknife he managed it. With a boost he was over the sill.

"I still don't like this," he complained.

Ignoring him, Smith leaned out and gave a hand to Angel. She climbed. Half-way over the sill she said, "Oh!" and when inside she looked down at her legs and said: "I'll send you a bill for that. My best stockings!" Then she said soberly: "What do you expect to find here, Mr. Smith?"

"I don't know. I'm just full of premonitions." He produced a flash-light, drilling the darkness with a thin sliver of illumination. "I hope," he said grimly, pacing forward, "I'm at least half wrong."

It was a bedroom. With Plouffe and Angel trailing, he went down a long hall to the front of the house, through two huge living-rooms, along another hall to a library. The house was a tomb.

Its owner was in the library.

Smith's light missed him at first. It played over the walls, yellowing rows of books, a small wall safe, a few large portraits. There was no need to illuminate the floor until he began to pace forward. Then he almost stepped on the thing because it lay just a few feet from the threshold.

He looked down, holding the light on McKenna's face, and behind him Plouffe said explosively: "Hey!" Angel put a trembling hand on Smith's arm and was silent. McKenna gazed at the ceiling.

He was a big man, wearing an expensive blue dressing gown over white flannel trousers and a white sport shirt. The white sport shirt was now a Jap flag, with its red moon of blood.

Smith stared a moment, then bent over him. "Shot," he said softly. Then he straightened and focused the light on the wall to his left.

The tiny beam came to rest on the wall safe. Smith strode forward, looked at the safe, looked down at McKenna again.

"Have you a finger-print outfit at your office, Plouffe?"

Plouffe nodded solemnly.

"Take the car and go get it," Smith directed. "Come back as fast as you can and don't say a word about this to anyone."

"But the cops oughta know about it! We'll get in trouble!"

"They'll know in due time. You do as I say." Smith glared at him and he went out wagging his head, mumbling protests. Smith and Angel heard him fumbling along the hall in the dark.

"Who did it, Philip?"

"I don't know."

"But you know something, or you wouldn't have come here."

"I think I know who'll be blamed for doing it. That's all."

"Who?"

"Burdick."

She stood there in the dark, scowling at him. "But why?"

"It wasn't McKenna who visited the Lester Hotel tonight," Smith declared softly. "It could have been, of course, but it probably wasn't. That's where you had me wrong when you tried to read my mind, Angel. This isn't any ten-cent clandestine love affair. Can't be. Too many angles."

"You think someone borrowed McKenna's car?"

"And deliberately got a ticket."

"Why?"

"Look. Burdick is missing. His wife goes to Plouffe for assistance. Guided by Plouffe, she takes a room at the Lester. Meanwhile this other thing — what ever it is — is moving on relentlessly to some kind of climax. Part of that climax is the planned murder of McKenna here. And McKenna's murderers are clever, clever enough to plan the alibi before the crime. They swipe McKenna's car, take it to the Lester, leave it parked where it's bound to catch a ticket. No one can deny now that McKenna's car was parked in front of Mrs. Burdick's hotel; the proof is down in black and white. You see? McKenna visits Mrs. Burdick at hotel with bad reputation. McKenna is found dead. Angry young husband is arrested for murder."

"You're guessing."

"It's the best I can do. We'll know more when Plouffe gets back."

She was silent a moment, and the silence of the big house crept in to take possession. Then she said, "Why the finger-print outfit, Philip?"

"Why is McKenna dead?" he countered.

"You mean the safe?"

"It's possible."

"A man as brainy as McKenna wouldn't keep any big amount of money in a house like this."

"Maybe not, Angel. But money isn't the only thing worth stealing. You're forgetting that McKenna was vice president of a chemical company."

Angel voiced a little snort. "You'll be telling me next that you're a G-man tracking down scurrilous agents of a mysterious foreign power!"

"I'm not, really. I'm waiting for a street car."

Very shortly Plouffe returned, with a small black case wedged under his arm and a flash-light gripped in his left hand.

"You have any trouble?" Smith asked.

"Me? Oh, no."

"Get to work then. What I want to know is this: Has anyone recently opened that safe, and if so, who?"

Plouffe opened his finger-print case and timidly stepped up to the safe. While he worked, Smith held the light for him, cupping it carefully to keep the glow from striking the room's only window.

Plouffe was good at this sort of thing. In a few moments he said definitely: "It's been opened all right. There's fresh oil from the hinge" smeared down the side. Not long ago, either."

"I thought so."

"You see, Plouffe," Angel said sweetly. "Mr. Smith is really very smart. He sees all, knows all, tells nothing."

"This here," Plouffe declared, ignoring her and handing Smith a thin sheet of celluloid, "is a pretty fair thumbprint."

"Good. Can you get a print of McKenna's thumb?"

"I guess so."

"Be careful," Smith warned, "where you leave your own prints around here."

"You're damn right I'll be careful!"

Finished with the safe, Plouffe knelt beside the dead man. In a moment he rose, handed over a slip of paper. As an afterthought he stooped again and with a handkerchief carefully wiped a smudge of ink from the dead man's thumb.

"Looks the same to me," he said, "though I ain't no expert."

"So it was McKenna who opened the safe. Probably forced to and then killed so he could never identify the thief. We can go now, Angel. We've a job to do. A most important job, and one that may take a long time. We've got to find Mrs. Burdick. And her husband."

Angel twisted her lovely mouth into a scowl. "All we have to go on," she said, "is that car. The one Plouffe trailed."

Smith shook his head. "No go. It's probably right here in McKenna's garage by now."

"It is," Plouffe said. "I seen it when I come back. I was meaning to tell you."

"Then," said Angel, "we're stymied. Unless," she added, glancing suspiciously at Smith, "that brain of yours is working overtime again. Sometimes that brain amazes me."

**E**DGERSON did some serious thinking as he drove away from the elaborate home of the slain McKenna. It was high time, he realized, to do some thinking. Up til now this affair had been little more than a pleasant diversion, a relief from the monotony of being president of a greeting card concern. A hobby, like amateur theatrics or peephole photography. Now it was murder.

He scowled at the windshield and mentally fitted together the pieces of the puzzle as he saw them. The pattern was a bit startling.

"You know, Angel," he said, "the safest thing we could do right now would be to go straight to the police, tell them all we know and then go for a nice long ride into the country."

"Nonsense!" she said scornfully.

He sighed. "We'll do the next best thing. Plouffe, we'll leave it to you to phone the police and report McKenna's death. You can do it from a booth somewhere without leaving a trail."

"And what'll you two be doing?" Plouffe demanded.

"Pushing our noses deeper into affairs that don't concern us."

"Well," Plouffe said, "I don't like it."

"Neither do I."

Smith stopped the car at a restaurant. "There should be a phone inside," he said. "Use it, then go home. If we need you again, I'll call you."

"I still don't like it," Plouffe muttered, but he got out.

"And now," said Angel, when the car was under way again, "just what *do* we do?"

"What time is it?"

She looked at her watch. "Four-ten. Fine time of night to keep your best girl out."

"We drive to Warren Avenue now," Smith declared calmly, "and get out of bed a young man named Timothy Kenson. I don't believe you know Timmy."

"Who is he?"

"He works at the office. But for the past several hours he's been working at the Krashna Tobacco Store, downtown."

"Why?"

"You'll see," Smith said, "in due time."

She didn't like that. She glared at him. "He knows all, sees all, tells nothing." Smith ignored her and she adjusted her red cape about her angrily.

He drove in silence. The streets were deserted, and it was difficult to realize that on so calm and peaceful a night murder had been done. But Smith's mind, agile now, was ahead of the murder and groping for the motive.

He knew, or thought he knew, the elaborate steps leading up to McKenna's death, and the probable aftermath. But the motive still evaded him. Unless, of course, the answer lay at the Glickman Company.

He turned the car into Warren Avenue and stopped. "You wait here," he told Angel. Climbing the steps of a brown cottage, he put his thumb against the doorbell. In a moment a light winked on and the door opened. A young, red-haired man in wrinkled pajamas blinked at Smith and said, "Oh, it's you, Mr. Edgerson."

"Any luck, Timmy?"

"Sure thing. He came in late this afternoon. I been trying to get you ever since."

"A tall, dark man, Jimmy? With a beard?"

"Nope. He was a little runt. Crummy looking."

"Oh. You followed him?"

"Sure thing. He walked down the street a ways and got into a taxicab. So I did like you said. I jumped into another taxicab and told the driver to keep him in sight. He went into a house on Canal Street, down near the river. Wait a minute and I'll get you the number. I wrote it down."

He was back in a minute or two with a slip of paper which he thrust into Smith's hand. "Here it is, Mr. Edgerson. Number 23 Canal. Just a couple of doors down from the McCullen Warehouse, if you know where that is."

"Timmy," John Smith said, "you're a genius!"

"It was easy," Timmy said.

"It was masterful. Tomorrow you get a raise in pay."

Smith hurried back to the car, stuffing the slip of paper into his pocket. He said nothing to Angel, but the triumphant smirk on his face gave him away.

"You look," she said, "as if you just ate the goldfish. What's up? Where are we going now?"

"To the hideout of the dark foreigner who smokes long black cigarettes."

"What?"

"It was really quite simple. While you were holding down the fort I visited the only two tobacco stores in the city where a man can buy long black cigarettes. They're Cuban, you know. I discreetly asked questions. The man in the place on Fernald Street told me he used to carry them because he had a customer who came regularly, twice a week, for a large supply. The customer was Professor Dubitsky, and the fellow had sold no Cuban cigarettes since Dubitsky's death. But in the second store I had better luck, Angel. The man there informed me that he did carry them. He hadn't used to, he said, but about three months ago a customer placed a standing order with him, and the customer called twice a week to pick up his supply."

"The original Sherlock Holmes!" Angel gasped. "And all this time I thought you were just plain Philip Edgerson!"

"I got quite chummy with the man," Smith informed her, "and enlisted his aid. He agreed to let Timmy work for him. Timmy did so, and when the buyer of the Cuban cigarettes came in, Timmy followed him. That's all there was to it. Quite simple, you see."

"You mean Timmy followed Professor Dubitsky?"

"No. Dubitsky himself wouldn't come out in the open like that. But if we fail to find him at the address to which we're going, I'll be a most crestfallen sleuth."

She gave him a sidelong glance from beneath the red hood and then looked out the car window, noting the sinister section of town into which he was taking her.

"Are you armed, Philip?"

"I don't own a gun. You know that."

"Philip," she said in a manner of confession, "I have one. I borrowed it from my office."

He frowned. "Keep it," he said bluntly.

The car had entered the waterfront warehouse district, and at this time of night the streets were black, deserted, ominous. A short-lived downpour had beaten to life sour smells of fish and fruit, and the dampness held those unsavory odors in suspension. You smelled trouble. Danger.

Smith pulled the machine to the curb. "For you, Angel," he said firmly, "this is as far as the car goes. I may be a willing slave to my hobby, but I drag no hapless woman with me."

"It's not your hobby. It's ours."

"Nevertheless, you wait here — you and your silly popgun."

"That," she said, "is what you think."

"It's what I know," he said. Then, suddenly serious: "Look here, darling. We've not even the vaguest idea of what we're getting into. It may be as mean and dirty as the district it's in. I'd be scared stiff if you came along."

"So I'm to sit here and be scared stiff until you get back?"

"Or else," he threatened, "we go straight to the police. Although any self-respecting cop would arrest you in that devil's cape."

She was angry. He looked at her and saw that she was staring straight ahead, her lips tight-pressed, her chin rigid. He patted her knee and got out, walked away.

Just once, as he went past the warehouse a hundred yards or so distant, he turned his head to look back. The car's headlights owlishly stared at him. Uneasy about leaving Angel alone too long on a street so dark and unsavory, he quickened his step.

Number 23 was one of a row of tenements, all of which looked alike in the dark. A battered ashcan filled with refuse stood on the concrete stoop beside the door. The door opened when Smith pressed it.

He stepped over the threshold into a black, smelly hall. Stopped there, scowling, and realized that the house had three floors and he had no idea on which level to concentrate.

His flash-light winked, threading a narrow beam through the gloom of the lower hall. A baby carriage stood there. He went past it, past the door of the first floor tenement, to the stairs. The building was a tomb, cold and damp and dark.

With the light cupped in his hand he climbed slowly, testing each ancient step before trusting it with his weight. The second floor landing came level with his eyes and he stopped again. The light showed him a small and black cigarette stub lying by a door. He smiled a tight, twisted little smile and knew that the door was his destination.

He stepped beside it, scowled, and snapped out the light. There was no sound anywhere. The fact that he was unarmed did not greatly worry him. It never had before. The day he began to carry a gun, he told himself, Trouble Incorporated would cease to be a hobby. Besides, he had no permit.

He tipped his hat back on his head and loosened his tie. He opened his coat, rubbed a hand over the floor and transferred the dirt thus collected to the front of his shirt, blackening it. For good measure he pulled off two buttons, to make the shirt sag.

He dirtied his face and rumpled his hair, and put on a pair of horn-rimmed spectacles, the lenses of which were clear glass.

Then he seized the doorknob and rattled it, and then he banged on the door and cursed it and began talking to himself.

Results were not long coming. A couch squeaked inside and a voice said sharply, "Who's there? Who's out there?"

"It'sh Percy," Smith slobbered. "Lemme in."

"Who? Who is it?"

"It'sh Percy! You lemme in or sho help me I'll busht the door down!"

A key turned in the lock and the door opened. It didn't open far. Just far enough to frame a short, thickset man whose swarthy face was all scowl.

"Listen, buddy," the swarthy man said. "You're in the wrong place. Beat it."

"Who're you?"

"Never mind who I am. It's the middle of the night, see? And you're in the wrong alley. Scram!"

"Thish ish where I live," Smith snorted. "Don' you tell me I don' belong here. I know different."

The dark fellow was in no mood to argue with a drunk. He came a step closer, put his right hand flat against Smith's chest, and pushed. He slammed the door as Smith staggered away from it.

Smith smiled that tight little smile again and resumed his assault. If he made enough noise, the occupants of the tenement would do one of two things: Either slug him or try to reason with him. He didn't think they would slug him. This was a hideout. They would want to avoid trouble.

And they most certainly would open the door if he hammered on it long enough.

It opened. The swarthy man said savagely, "Listen, buddy, will you for Gawd's sake go away and leave us get some sleep? Or do I have to get rough with you?"

Smith's eyes glowered at him out of a slack, stupid face. "You lishen to me," he said. "My name'sh Percy Smith an' I live here. An' nobody'sh gonna keep me out!"

Behind the swarthy man an impatient voice said, "Let him in, Max."

"Oke, buddy," Max sighed. "Come on in."

"That'sh better," Smith said. "That'sh much better."

He walked in, weaving a little. Max closed the door.

"Now take a good look around, Percy," Max said, "and you'll see this ain't the place you thought it was. You're drunk and you're in the wrong house."

"Who saysh I am?"

"Look around. See for yourself."

Smith looked around. The room in which he stood was a living-room, furnished with table, chairs and a couch. The swarthy man, Max, had evidently been sleeping on the couch, in his clothes. His clothes were wrinkled and he wore no shoes.

The other man was bigger. He wore gray pajamas which hung loosely from his lank frame, revealing a generous expanse of hairy chest. His hair was in his eyes and he stood with his hands hipped, feet spread wide, just back of the table. A door behind him led to what appeared to be a bedroom.

"I — I guessh I was mistaken," Smith mumbled apologetically.

"Convinced, are you?"

"I musht've got mixed up somehow."

"Well, if you're convinced," Max said, "just scram like a nice guy and don't make any more noise'n you have to."

Smith stood where he was. "I — I don' feel sho good," he said.

"O.K., O.K.," the other man said tartly. "Beat it! Be sick outside!"

"I wanna shtay here. I wanna lie down somewheres . . . ."

The two men exchanged glances. The man named Max took his right hand out of his pocket, where it had rested since Smith's entrance. They stepped forward. "Sure," Max said. "We'll help you lay down, buddy. We wouldn't think of puttin' a nice guy like you out in the street at this time o' night. No-o-o. Would we, Vick?"

"Of course not," Vick said.

They took hold of Smith's arms. That was their mistake. He had been waiting for it. Waiting to get them both together, both in reach at the same time. Any other way would have been fatal, because undoubtedly both men were armed.

Smith's heel came down hard, piston-fast, on a shoeless foot that belonged to Max. At the same time he twisted, stabbed an arm out and caught the other man's wrist. He was suddenly not drunk any more, and before his adversaries were over their amazement, Smith had the situation in hand.

You didn't need a gun. All you needed was a slight knowledge of the fine art of Oriental wrestling, plus a fair to middling physique and a nickel's worth of nerve.

Max yelped, bent double at the waist as pain streaked up from his tortured foot. He bent into an upthrust knee that smacked his chin and snapped his teeth together. He staggered against the table, dazed, and had sense enough left to reach gropingly for the pocket where his gun lay. But he was too slow.

Smith had hold of Vick's wrist. He yanked Vick off balance, stooped, caught the arm above the wrist and pulled it. Not hard. Really not hard at all. But fast.

Vick's feet left the floor. He lost his breath in an explosive grunt as his big frame looped through space. His hundred and eighty pounds crashed into Max and Max was finished. Vick sprawled to the floor, stunned, and Max fell over him.

Smith waded in. What little fight remained in Vick was dissipated quickly by a hard, clean punch to the button. For his trouble, Smith had nothing to show except a few minor beads of moisture on his face and forehead.

He stepped back and surveyed the wreckage, highly elated. Luck, he realized, had been with him. He turned then and strode into the bedroom. It was empty.

Scowling, he walked through the bedroom into a kitchen. That was empty, too. . .

He went back to Vick and Max, sorry now that he had knocked them so thoroughly out. There were questions he wanted to ask. Questions concerning the whereabouts of Mr. and Mrs. Teddy Burdick.

He stared at them for a moment, undecided what to do; then, stooping, he went through their pockets. Both men were armed. He removed the weapons and placed them on the table, careful not to blur any finger-prints that might be on them. One of those guns, Smith was reasonably certain, had murdered McKenna.

In Vick's pocket he found a slip of paper. Penciled words, written in a stiff, marching hand, said: "Fix up the girl tomorrow night, provided the papers are in our possession by that time. The following night take care of the husband. Carefully now — suicide."

Smith read it twice, then pocketed it. An ugly fear took hold of him. Fear that he might have come too late. That the thing had already been done. He went into the kitchen, found an empty tin can and filled it with cold water. Returning, he knelt beside Vick and poured the water over his face.

Behind him a voice said quietly: "We will omit that, please. We will stand up and put our hands high and turn around very slowly."

IT WAS A familiar voice. Quite a famous voice, in fact. Smith had heard it several times on the radio, had heard it also at university lectures. He knew, therefore, even before he obeyed the command, that at long last he had come face to face with the supposedly dead Dubitsky.

It was not a pleasant sensation. He turned, raised his hands, and stared glumly at Dubitsky's face. The hall door was open and the professor stood just inside it, tall and stoop-shouldered and grim. The automatic in his hand was small but deadly.

"Your name, please?" Dubitsky said curtly.

"It'sh Percy Smith, mishter." It was worth a try, anyway, Smith figured. "These two men shaid I didn' live here an' I had a dishcussion."

"We will omit that, also," Dubitsky snapped. "You were not drunk when you came from the kitchen!"

Smith sighed. "I'm not drunk now, either," he said, hunching his shoulders.

"Why are you here?"

"Vick's an old friend of mine."

"Explain, please."

"Sure. Back in the old days, Vick and I used to work together. So when I met him on the street a while ago, he invited me up here, just to talk over old times. Me and him and this other guy here, we got into an argument. That's all."

"You are lying," Dubitsky said.

"So help me, it's the truth!"

"Is it? Suppose, then, you tell me Vick's full name."

"Huh?"

"I thought so," Dubitsky said. "You are an agent of the government." He came a step closer, his eyes flashing. "Well, my meddling friend, you are too late. Most of the papers are already on their way to an agent of my government. Except for minor details, my work is finished. And you, my friend, will not interfere with those minor details, I assure you."

Smith did not answer. His gaze was on the door and he was frightened. His upraised hands trembled and perspiration gleamed on his face.

Dubitsky misunderstood. He smiled. "You have good reason to be afraid of me, my friend," he said.

Out in the hall, Miss Angelina Copeland placed on the floor the shoes she was carrying. They were her own shoes. She had removed them before ascending the stairs. She looked like little Red Riding Hood, except Red didn't pack a gun. She measured the distance now between her outthrust hands and Dubitsky's broad back, and still in a crouch, she set herself. They she lunged.

The threshold creaked as she went over it, and Dubitsky whirled. He whirled too late. Angel threw herself at his knees and bucked him off balance. Smith closed in and caught him.

Smith's hands closed over Dubitsky's wrist and twisted. He hadn't used that particular twist before. It was dangerous. In the gymnasium where he worked out, it was outlawed. You could break a man's arm with it.

Smith put all he had into it, and the arm snapped. He stopped then and threw Dubitsky over his head, and when the professor crashed into the door frame something else snapped.

Dubitsky shuddered to the floor and lay in a sprawled, unlovely heap. Smith straightened, gasping for breath.

"Lord!" he said. "That was close! Angel, you were marvelous! Why didn't you shoot, though?"

"I was scared to," she declared, picking herself up and still clinging to the gun.

"I told you to keep out of here!"

"I know you did. So I drove the car up and parked it just across the street. You didn't expect me to stay in the bleachers when the ringside was vacant, did you? Then I saw Dubitsky walk in here, and my woman's intuition told me I'd be needed."

Dubitsky had not moved. Scowling a little, Smith knelt beside him.

"Is it bad?" Angel asked.

"Bad enough," he said, holding a hand over the professor's heart. "I suppose he'll live, though. They usually do." Then he turned to her. "Put that silly gun away."

"You'll be answering a flock of awfully embarrassing questions, darling, if he doesn't live," Angel said, letting the gun swing loose in her hand.

He stood up, glancing at Vick and Max. "Speaking of questions, I still want to ask a few." Vick, he saw, was coming to. The cold water had begun to take effect.

He put a hand on Vick's neck, groped for a moment with one finger and then pressed.

"Hey!" Vick choked.

"Nice, isn't it?" Smith said quietly. "Hurts a little." He pressed harder.

Vick jerked clear of the floor and fell flat again with a spongy thud. There was a nerve back there that was really sensitive.

"You're killin' me!"

"I will, too," Smith promised solemnly, "unless you cooperate. Tell me now — what have you done with the Burdicks."

"I never heard of no Burdicks."

Smith tickled the nerve. Not gently this time, but strenuously.

"They're upstairs!" Vick gasped. "For Gawd's sake, cut it out!"

"See if you can find some rope around here, Angel," Smith said. "If not, rip up a bedsheet. Now, Vick, it's my turn. I'll tell you what I know, or guess, and you can supply the rest."

"The place for that," Angel said, "is not here. Too much might happen. Let's take him with us. First thing you know, someone will walk in here with a machine gun, and then where will you be with your Chinese wrestling?"

"It worked, didn't it?"

"Yes, but even Steve Brodie didn't try it twice, darling. I'm going upstairs and collect the Burdicks."

She walked out. Smith glared at Vick and said grimly, "One thing I do want to know. What's so all-fired important about those papers?"

"You go to hell," Vick snarled.

Smith found the nerve again. Vick shuddered to the tips of his fingers.

"It — it's a formula," he gasped. "It's some screwy formula for a new high explosive. That's all I know. I swear it!"

"I think," Smith said slowly, "I get it. At least, I begin to. Our friend Dubitsky was sent here by a foreign government. He took his time. He planned things carefully. Through him, Burdick and one or two other students obtained jobs at the Glickman Company. Through Burdick, the learned professor obtained information on the whereabouts of the formula. But things were hot. He decided to vanish. As Professor Dubitsky he did vanish. How right am I, Vick?"

"I wouldn't know," Vick mumbled. "Lay off of me, will you?"

"He found out," Smith said, "that the custodian of the secret was McKenna. With that to work on, he planned to rob McKenna's safe, and also, very cleverly, figured out an alibi because he knew he'd have to kill McKenna after he got him to open his safe. To cover up the murder Dubitsky planned that the police would discover after a while that McKenna was paying attention to Burdick's wife, and that Burdick himself, soon after McKenna's murder, had committed suicide. It would appear to be the usual sordid triangle. leaving Dubitsky and the real motive thoroughly obscured. I like to reason these things out, Vick. It's half the fun."

Angel, appearing in the doorway, said impatiently: "Mr. and Mrs. Burdick are now in your car, Mr. Smith. Could you cut it short, perhaps?"

"One more thing, Vick."

"Huh?"

"Who murdered McKenna?"

"You go to hell!"

Smith caressed the nerve again.

"He did," Vick groaned. "So help me, I ain't lyin'. Dubitsky did it. After gettin' McKenna to open the safe with them papers in it Dubitsky had to kill him to keep him from ever identifying him."

Smith sighed. "It really doesn't matter who shot him because I'm going to tie the three of you up, Vick, and as soon as I'm out of here I'm going to phone the police. You won't escape before they get here, Vick. Doing tricks with ropes is another of my little accomplishments, and you won't even wiggle when I'm through with you. So the police will come and find you, Vick, and find those two guns on the table; and if either of those guns fired the bullet that killed McKenna, the police will know it. Ballistics, you know."

"Here," Angel said, "are your ropes. Mr. and Mrs. Burdick were wrapped up in them, upstairs."

Smith went to work tying them up while Angel stood by with her gun trained on them. Finished, he stepped back and surveyed the results of his efforts, and grinned.

He took Angel's arm. "Let's go, darling," he said.

"THAT'S right," Mrs. Burdick's Teddy said timidly. "I got the job through Dubitsky and then a couple of months later he died. And then he came to life again, and came to see me."

"And told you he was a Federal agent?"

"That's right, Mr. Smith. He told me he was a Federal agent, working to break down a spy ring. And I believed him. I guess I'd been reading too many stories."

They sat, the four of them, in the tiny office of Trouble, Inc. Teddy Burdick, Mrs. Burdick, Angel and Smith. Burdick was limp with gratitude. Mrs. Burdick was exactly like her letter — small, scared, not too gifted with brains.

"Dubitsky asked you then to help him. He told you the officials of the Glickman Company were under suspicion, and asked you to find out which of them had been entrusted with the safe-keeping of the formula. That it?" Smith asked.

"That's right. And when I did find out that Mr. McKenna kept it at home, he advised me to quit my job. He gave me a thousand dollars and told me to move to a small apartment somewhere and keep very quiet until the thing came to a head."

"What happened then?" Smith asked.

"Well, at the last minute, just when we were all set to move, he sent for me. He called me on the phone and told me to come to that address on Canal Street. When I got there, those two men, Vick and Max, jumped on me."

Smith leaned back in his chair, smiling. "You see it now, Angel?" he asked gently.

"There's one thing," Angel declared, " that still bothers me."

"Yes?"

"Look, now. Dubitsky planned this business very nicely, but right smack in the middle of it he 'died.' There must have been, at that time, a fear in his mind that he was being watched. In other words, government agents were closing in on him." She drew a deep breath and stared at the floor, marshaling her thoughts.

"Well," she continued, "he came to life again and went through with his plans. He got the formula. If Trouble, Incorporated, hadn't landed right kersmack on the back of his neck, he and his buddies would have disposed of Mrs. Burdick, to keep her quiet, and then murdered Teddy, making it look like a suicide to give the police an answer to the McKenna kill and steer the investigation away from Dubitsky and his pals. You follow me?"

There was a knock on the door. Smith got up to answer it. "So far, yes," he said. "Go ahead."

He opened the door and Plouffe stood there.

"Well," Angel said, scowling, "what I want to know is why the G-men, after getting close enough to scare Dubitsky into temporary oblivion, didn't see through his phony death and ultimately get their hands on him."

Plouffe, blinking his gray eyes at her, said: "So help me, Miss Copeland, you're clairvoyant. Meet my friend here, Mr. Toomey."

He stepped aside and a man walked past him. "Mr. Toomey," Plouffe said, "is a G-man. It seems he's been keeping an eye on me ever since Mrs. Burdick come to me for advice."

"On all of you," Toomey said quietly. He was a tall, gray-haired man with a pleasant smile. "You see, Mr. Smith, we were just warming up to this case when you stepped into it."

Smith stood up, his face sheepish.

"What Dubitsky was after," Toomey said, "was the formula for a new explosive being manufactured for the government by the Glickman Company."

"And thanks to us," Smith admitted, "he got it."

"No. He never would have got it. What he took from McKenna was the original formula, long ago proved to be worthless. I doubt if Dubitsky even knew that the original has twice been revised, and that the only existing copy of the approved, final formula has never been out of government hands. What you did do, Mr. Smith, was save the lives of Mr. and Mrs. Burdick and save us a lot of work."

"Oh," said Smith.

"He's really very smart," Angel cooed.

"Thanks to you, Mr. Smith," Toomey said, "the dangerous Dubitsky and his two associates are in custody. I'm here simply to offer congratulations."

He thrust out his band. Smith took it. Angel beamed.

"You know," Plouffe said, "he's really a pretty good guy. Maybe we should ought to tell him the truth, Toomey."

"Truth?" Smith said.

"You owe me some money," Plouffe declared, pacing forward to the desk behind which Smith stood. "I'll match you to see whether I get it or not."

He took a coin from his pocket and flipped it. Slightly bewildered, Smith did likewise.

"Heads," Smith said.

Plouffe thrust out his hand with the coin on the back of it. It wasn't a coin. Not exactly. It was a gold identification disc of the Federal Bureau of Investigation.

Smith gaped at it.

"A lot of things," Plouffe said softly, with a smile, "are not what they seem. Believe it or not, when I let you hire me I thought you were after that formula, too. I deliberately let you believe I was impersonating an F. B. I. man so you'd feel you had something on me. That way I might get onto a lot of things. Sorry, pal." He turned to Toomey. "Well, Toomey," he said, "let's go. And you and your wife, Mr. Burdick, if you'll come along too and answer a few questions, you can go home afterward."

They went out. Smith looked solemnly at Angel. "I," he declared slowly, "will be damned."

She said, "Nothing surprises me any more."

"I've another surprise for you," Smith told her, smiling.

"Really?"

"I'm going to pay you for all the work you've done."

"No! You don't mean it!"

"But I do." He put his arms around her.

"Like this," he said, and kissed her.

•  •  •  •  •

# LOST – AND FOUND

WE JUMP TO APRIL 1940 WITH THIS LONG STORY. I HAD SPENT TWO WINTERS IN FLORIDA
AND WAS USING FLORIDA SETTINGS IN STORIES FOR SEVERAL MAGAZINES. THIS ONE IS
LAID MORE OR LESS IN THE FLORIDA KEYS AND I THINK YOU'LL AGREE IT'S ONE OF THE
BETTER YARNS IN THIS COLLECTION — A FAST-MOVING TALE WITH AN ENDING THAT,
ALTHOUGH PERHAPS NO LONGER POLITICALLY CORRECT, MAY STILL BRING A SMILE.
INCIDENTALLY, I HAD 11 STORIES IN *DETECTIVE FICTION WEEKLY* THAT YEAR, ALSO
STORIES IN *DOUBLE DETECTIVE, DETECTIVE SHORT STORIES, DETECTIVE TALES, DIME
DETECTIVE,* AND *RED STAR DETECTIVE.* BUT THOUGH I SEEMED TO HAVE BECOME A
WRITER OF CRIME STORIES ONLY, ABOUT EVERY FIFTH STORY I ATTEMPTED WAS AIMED AT
THE BIG SLICK MAGAZINES, AND THEIR DOORS WERE ABOUT TO OPEN.

HBC

*Who was the girl in the crashed plane? Whose brain
plotted to wreck a tycoon's empire? How does a dick find
a girl who won't be found?*

KIMM swung himself out of the chartered plane almost before it stopped
rolling. With an upward fling of his hand and a "Nice work, buddy!"
to the pilot, he began running across the field, his heavy tweed overcoat sailing in the breeze behind him.

Kimm did everything that way. Small and wiry, with a body thinned by
too much srnoking, he moved, when he moved at all, with an impetuous rush
that kept the dust flying. When thinking, he preferred to be flat on his back
with his shoes off, smokes and a drink handy, a little soft slow music teasing
his ears. But the same shoes, when attached to his feet, were forever taking
him somewhere in a hurry.

He was in a hurry now, and mouthed a snort of disgust when he got to the
waiting car and found it empty. He put a hand on the horn and the hot, sleepy
afternoon shivered to the blast. Kimm didn't know the afternoon was hot. He
wore a brown felt hat slapped shapeless by New York wind and sleet; he
wore rubbers and the overcoat, and he was not warm. This was Florida but he
had not been in it long enough to thaw out.

He smacked the horn again and a big man, loose with fat, came waddling in no hurry from a tin-roofed building near-by. Wearing slacks and sneakers and a polo shirt, the fellow looked askance at Kimm's overcoat, scowled and rubbed a chin black with stubble "You Mr. Kimm? Mr. Abel Kimm?" Sunlight, dancing on the hangar's tin roof, frolicked no less wonderfully on the big man's hairless head.

Kimm nodded.

"I'm Henry Crahan," the man said.

Kimm said, "Good," and stepped into the car. He was tired but taut. After his talk with Julius Macomber in the latter's Park Avenue apartment, he had hurried at once to Newark Airport, hired the plane and proceeded to put miles behind him. He was hungry. He was thirsty.

Crahan carefully eased his hulk behind the wheel and put the car in motion. "You have a nice trip down, Mr. Kimm?"

"Mmn."

"Been in Florida before, have you?"

"Twice."

The car rolled out to the Dixie and proceeded south. It crawled, and Kimm said impatiently, "Can't you make this crate go a little faster?"

"I don't reckon there's a whole lot of hurry," Crahan shrugged.

"Why?"

The big man shrugged again and let it go at that. He didn't have to talk. He was a cop, Kimm supposed. A town constable or local hick cop. In some parts of Florida — those parts not dependent on tourist trade for sustenance — strangers were looked upon as unwanted outsiders.

The car made a right turn off the main highway and Henry Crahan said matter-of-factly, "This here is Kelver City."

Kimm didn't see any city.

He saw a widish road flanked by leaning palms and weedgrown sidewalks. He saw a few big houses, most of them for sale, and a large ugly brick building evidently designed to be a town hall. Farther on he saw a handful of mangy stores and a gas pump or two, but the whole thing looked like an old movie set long since abandoned to the elements.

Kelver City was a ghost town, a relic of the boom. It depressed Kimm.

The car stopped in front of a stucco house a little less seedy than some of its neighbors, and Crahan said, "Doc Wardley's house. They brought the girl here right after she crashed."

"Don't you have a hospital?"

"In West Palm Beach, sure. But she couldn't be moved to no hospital."

Kimm got out. He hated things blue and Doc Wardley's house was a washed-out shade of blue that made him wince. He trotted to the steps and went up them into a screened porch. A brown lizard the length of his middle finger streaked off the sill and shot between his legs and vanished. The air reeked of jasmine.

Crahan came up behind him and opened the door. "Go on in."

Wardley was an odd duck, Kimm thought. Thin as a straw, pasty-pale behind dark horn-rimmed spectacles that belonged on a man fifty pounds heavier, he had a trick of holding his eyes wide open that made him appear startled. He wasn't startled. He said gently, "Ah, yes. Mr. Macomber's representative, ah, yes. I — er, I'm afraid Mr. Macomber will be shocked."

He turned gravely and walked down the hall to a closed door and turned again to say, "This way, please." He had another trick of walking on his toes, soundlessly. The whole house was soundless, Kimm thought. The silence came at you in a wave, the moment you stepped inside. It was as tangible as the stink of jasmine on the porch, and as unpleasant.

Wardley stood aside, waiting, and Kimm went past him into a small blue room that reeked of medicines and antiseptics. Except for a couch and a couple of chairs, the room was empty. Kimm paced to the couch and stared without blinking at a pair of upturned toes. Bare toes. A sheet covered the rest of the body, but, even so, the outlines were attractive.

"I — ah, I am sorry about this," Wardley said. He had come up soundlessly and his voice was so close to Kimm's ear that it created a draft. An ordinary man would have jumped. Kimm merely turned his head, focused his gaze on the wide eyes behind the spectacles.

"How long has she been dead?"

"She died at exactly four-seventeen, Mr. Kimm. I — ah, have witnesses, of course. Mrs. Wardley, my wife, and some of our neighbors. Mr. Crahan was not here, unfortunately. He had gone to meet you."

Kimm glanced at heavy Henry Crahan. "You a cop?"

"Chief of Police," Crahan said listlessly, "in Kelver City." He inhaled wetly through his nose, swallowed. "I'm all the police we have in this town. She's really dead, Doc?"

"I — ah, am afraid so. Yes."

Kimm raised an end of the sheet and looked at the girl's face. He did this without wanting to, but with the knowledge that he owed it to Julius Macomber, who was paying the bills. He stared hard. He stared a lot longer than was necessary. The face he saw was young, reasonably attractive. It was nothing to set the male hearts of a nation to twittering, but it was above average. What troubled him was something else again.

He lowered the sheet, said, "Let's go over this." Trailed by Wardley and Crahan, he went down the hall to the living-room.

It was a big room full of sunlight and potted cacti. Crahan lifted a bottle of whiskey from what looked like an old Victrola cabinet, glanced at Kimm and poured three drinks. Kimm sipped his and felt warm for the first time in weeks. He shed his overcoat. He sat.

"The plane crashed," Wardley said, "about six o'clock last evening. We heard it, you understand. We heard it in the air and knew by the sound of the motor that something was wrong. I was in Fred Meaton's store at the time; Fred and I saw the plane come down and, of course, distinctly heard the crash. Others did, too. How many of us drove out there I'm sure I don't know, but Fred and I were there, Henry was there," he looked at Crahan, "and at least half a dozen others."

"Just where did she crash?" Kimm asked.

"On the old Furgusson bean farm," Henry Crahan said, "out on the edge of the 'Glades. If she'd landed in the 'Glades proper, we'd have been a week gettin' to her. It was tough enough as it was."

"You knew who she was when you saw the plane?"

"Her name's on it. Spirit of 1940. Fern Macomber. Besides — hell, we get newspapers here, even if this is the end of the world."

Kimm finished his drink. "I'll have to know what killed her."

"That — ah, is rather hard to say, Mr. Kimm. I did all that was possible, of course, and when I wired Mr. Macomber I believed the young lady had a fair chance for recovery. There were immediate complications, however. Internal injuries . . . ."

Kimm nodded, reaching for his coat. "You'll arrange to send her to New York, of course. Macomber will foot the bills." He moved to the door. "I may want to see the plane, Crahan. Later, not now. Can I rent a car anywhere in this town?"

The big Chief of Police looked at Doc Wardley, shrugged, and said to the whiskey bottle in his fat fist, "I reckon Fred Meaton'd lend you his, if he ain't usin' it."

Kimm hurried out.

O N HIS WAY south to West Palm Beach in a jallopy rented from the Kelver City storekeeper, Kimm's thoughts buzzed like blowflies around a mental picture of Julius Macomber. The Wall Street tycoon was not going to like this mess. For several important reasons, it was essential for Julius that his daughter Fern arrive in New York, alive and healthy, within a week.

Hearing the latest, Julius would probably tear out what few thin gray hairs remained on his head. His bellow would rock the Empire State Building.

Working for Julius was a lucrative pastime but hard, damned hard, on the nerves. Kimm parked in front of the George Washington Hotel, signed for a room and slid into the bar.

He drank rum and soda, changed a five-spot into smaller bills and silver. With a second rum and soda in his hand, he ensconced himself in a phone booth and called New York.

Abel Kimm would have been the last man on earth to admit that in every human being lurks something of the sadist. Yet after getting his party and establishing his identity, he said, "The girl is dead, Macomber." And sipped his drink.

The answer came slowly, was so thin, so fragile, it almost didn't come at all. "She's — dead?"

"Yes. But she's not your daughter! Who she is I don't know, and I don't believe the Kelver City people know, either, or they'd have made something of it. They think she is your daughter. I know she's not. Now what?"

Julius Macomber, a smart man, took time out for thinking. When he came in again his voice had lost its quiver, was low and ugly. "She's pulled a fast one on me, Kimm. She and that greasy louse of hers! Where are you?"

"West Palm."

"Go down to that damned island of his, that Angel's Acre. Find out where she is! She's got to be in New York by Wednesday! Got to, do you hear?"

"I'll do what I can," Kimm sighed, and hung up.

Lovely, he thought. You work hard and go to night school and do your good deed daily, and in time you get to be decently successful. That is to say, you reach a station in life where it is no longer part of your job to cover social gatherings, report court proceedings and write obituaries. You become — ah, vanity! — an astute and capable city editor, with a purely avocational flair for solving crimes. At which time your esteemed newspaper has a minor argument with certain Chambers of Commerce, is blackballed by a moneyed group of advertisers, goes broke and is snatched up, butt and barrel, by Mr. Julius Macomber, who thinks it a sin and a shame for one of your remarkable talents to decompose at an editorial desk.

You therefore become the private trouble-shooter of a financial genius whose empire reaches to the far-flung corners of the civilized world. Lovely, Kimm thought, snorting. Where the hell was this private island of Miguel Reurto, anyway?

He had another rum and soda while trying, not too hard, to remember where Angel's Acre was. He felt better then and decided to go by road. A plane would get him there faster, no doubt, but Reurto's Island was somewhere in the Keys, closer to Key West than to the Florida mainland. In Key West a man could eat genuine *arroz con pollo* and wash it down with real rum . . . .

It was a long ride. There was a lot of swamp, a lot of sea, to look at. Kimm broke the monotony by reviewing his repertoire of music. He liked music, all kinds of music. His favorite compositions were the "Honkytonk Train Blues" and the Tschaikowsky Symphony No. 6 in B Minor.

Long before he reached Key West, darkness descended upon the earth and a fog rolled in.

He had his *arroz con pollo* in a place called Sadie's, then drifted out and learned that no one owning a boat would even consider taking him to Miguel Reurto's private island in such weather. The run to the island was dangerous, he was told, even in good weather. Kimm did not argue. He took his low spirits to a bar and proceeded to revive them.

It was a joint. A man could get rolling drunk on cold water, merely by staring at the murals on the walls. Kimm sought a remote table and thought darkly of Julius Macomber. He'd been doing this about half an hour when three men squeezed past him and took a corner table.

Kimm caught a fragment of conversation. "But in this weather, Mr. Reurto . . . if she hold out!" It was accompanied by a shrug of huge shoulders, a spread of unwashed hands. Kimm crinkled his nose to shut out a smell of sweat.

The three sat down and a bow-legged waiter took their orders. Their heads came together over low talk. Kimm's excellent ears were not good enough; he had to depend on his eyes.

So this was Miguel Reurto, the six-footer wearing dampish tropical worsted, a brown shirt, livid yellow tie. A handsome mug, Kimm thought, if you were partial to flat black hair, sharp and angular features, a ghostly wisp of hirsute growth above a mouth much too small. This was the dashing South American with whom Macomber's million-dollar daughter was oh so veddy much in love.

The other two were more his type. Their villainy was out in the open, where you could see it. They were dirty, they needed shaving, they stunk. Their nationality was anyone's guess, but they were tough hombres, salty and barnacled.

They talked for an hour. When they got up to go, Kimm tailed along. Outside the joint they separated, Reurto and one roughneck to the right, the other one, short, stocky and not too sober now, to the left. It was raining.

Warm enough internally to be indifferent to the weather, Kimm scuffed along after Reurto and his pal, followed them to the waterfront. The two engaged in a final five minutes of talk there. The big South American took a wallet from his pocket, carefully counted and handed over some bills. He lit a cigarette, studied the burning match for a moment, then turned abruptly with no audible farewell and went aboard a cruiser made fast to the pier. A twenty-six footer, Kimm guessed. Built for speed.

Riding lights winked on. The craft's engine sputtered, steadied to a purr. The big bruiser on the pier watched the receding lights for a mile, then shoved his money into his pants and walked away. Kimm eased after him.

It wasn't far this time, and the hulk that took shape in the rain and darkness was a whole lot bigger than Miguel Reurto's put-boat. It was a schooner, a fifty-footer, not too young or too trim, but rugged enough, from the looks of her, to ride a hurricane.

Kimm hung back and watched and he learned plenty in the next hour. The schooner was the *Milly Mae*, her home port Key West, her skipper the big bearded man who had taken money from Reurto. She had a crew of the hardest looking thugs Kimm had ever seen outside a waterfront flop house, and they spoke a language not English.

The big man not only gave orders, he pitched in and did two-thirds of the work. Most of the work, done under a flock of gasoline lanterns, appeared to be a general job of cleaning up. It was probably the first time in years, Kimm mused, that the *Milly Mae* had been so sissified.

For a woman, perhaps?

The conviction grew on him and he edged closer to seek an answer. It wasn't that easy. Growing impatient, as usual, Kimm pushed himself out of hiding, strode forward with no further attempt at concealment. He got in the way of a man carrying a length of hose and a hand-pump. "Hey," Kimm said. "You!"

The fellow stopped and glared.

"Mr. Reurto sent me over," Kimm stabbed. "He wants to know if you got a full-length mirror on board for the lady." Devils danced in Kimm's eyes and a grin worked its way to his face.

The fellow dropped what he was toting and slapped his hands to his hips. He cursed fluently in bad Spanish, then said in explosive English, "So now it's a mirror! What the hell else does the dame desire? A perfumed bathtub, maybe?"

"She's a very special dame," Kimm said. "You want to remember that."

A shape came out of the rain and grabbed Kimm's arm. Kimm resented the intrusion; it spoiled a beautiful string of invectives from the man with the hose. He turned, scowling, and the grip on his arm tightened. He was face to face with the *Milly Mae's* skipper. In the big man's other hand lay a length of two-by-four.

"Who sent you?"

Kimm measured him with a glance. "Reurto."

The skipper looked squintingly at him and said, "You're a liar. Reurto left for his island an hour ago What's your game?"

"You only think he left," Kimm said.

"What?"

"This whole business smells. All you'll get out of it is trouble."

The big man withdrew his hand, wiped it on his thigh and would have shifted the two-by-four into it. That was his mistake. With both arms free, Kimm thrust forward a foot and pushed him over it. Pushed him hard, with clenched fists, in the stomach.

The skipper wallowed back off balance and went down in a heap, cursing. The man with the hose and hand-pump took a step toward Kimm, with ominous intent, and caught a beautiful right to the chin, a blow that clipped his mouth shut and sent him sprawling, stern first, into the skipper's flailing legs. Kimm wheeled and ran. He could run like an antelope. Being a smallish man and cautious, he often did.

He came out on the town's main street, wet and winded and wondering if the *Milly Mae's* crew would waste any time looking for him. They probably would. The thought was not comforting, nor was the realization that in order to upset Reurto's plans and lay hands on Miss Fern Macomber, he would have to get to Angel's Acre before the *Milly Mae's* skipper, by phone or otherwise, got word to Reurto that something smelled in Denmark.

Cursing his job, Kimm ventured into a bar and asked questions, then visited two other bars and a hotel, asked more questions and finally got an answer. A man named Gleeson, it seemed, might brave the elements tonight, despite wind and weather, if shown enough money.

Kimm located the man's home, a waterfront shack half a size larger than a phone booth. Standing ankle-deep in mud, he knocked, got no answer, pushed open the door. The darkness baffled him but it shivered with the wheeze of a man snoring. He struck a match.

The shack contained an iron bed, an oil stove and an upturned soap box. The thing on the box was a quart whiskey bottle, empty. The thing on the bed was a sprawled, vaguely human shape with a week's growth of beard and a bad breath.

Kimm squeamishly entered, touched the match to a stump of candle. He grabbed the man's shoulders and shook them. When that failed, he pulled aside a filthy rag of blanket, baring the man's feet, picked up the candle and held it close to a leathery lump of heel.

The fellow groaned. Kimm shook him again and his eyes opened. They were small, swollen eyes, marvelously ornate with fine red whorls. He blinked them and sat up. "What the hell?" he bellowed.

"You Gleeson?" Kimm said.

The fellow rubbed his eyes, blew breath into his cupped hands and sniffed it and made a face. "The stuff they sell you for liquor in this man's town!" He leaned far over and pulled a pair of mud-caked boots from under the bed, began to pull them on. "What d'you want? Who are you, anyway?"

"The name's Kimm. I want transportation to an island."

"Huh?"

Kimm repeated it. Gleeson scratched his head and looked around him, as though wondering what time — or perhaps what day of the week — it was. "What island?"

"A place called Angel's Acre."

Gleeson got unsteadily to his feet and went to the door. He looked out. "Hell of a night for it," he said pleasantly enough. "Cost you money, mister." He scowled at Kimm and, despite the red whorls, his eyes were shrewd. "Forty bucks. Thirty, anyway. That's a hell of a stretch of water, full of shoals. You got a drink?"

Kimm had been tipped off by the clerk at the hotel. He produced a pint, quietly unscrewed the cap and passed it over. Without making an issue of it, Gleeson killed half the pint before needing a breath, then took another swig, rinsed his mouth out and spat. "Thirty bucks O. K.?"

Kimm gave him three tens. Gleeson pulled on a torn blue sweater, covered that with a heavy leather jacket that smelled of fish, and they went out together into the rain. Kimm marveling at the man's ability to walk without staggering.

G LEESON'S BOAT was a commercial fisherman. You could smell her fifty yards away, and the smell got worse as you approached. It wormed its way into Kimm's stomach and he desperately wanted a drink but knew better than to risk one.

You got used to the smell, though. After a while, with the cough of the engine in his ears and the keel rolling under him, with the few winking lights of Key West smothered by a veil of rain and only empty gurgling blackness around him, Kimm became acclimated. He sucked a cigarette, shielding it with his hand.

Gleeson sat with one arm looped over the tiller. He consulted no chart; the boat had no compass. Every now and then he raised his head, peered into the dark and gave the tiller a pull or a shove. This appeared to be an event in his life. After each such operation, he calmly tipped the pint to his lips and took a nip out of it.

Kimm said, "What kind of guy is this Miguel Reurto? You know?"

"I never met him."

"This quite an island he has?"

"Small. Damned hard to get to. House on it, big house, couple of smaller buildings and a place for planes to land. Every now and then he throws a party, and, boy, they're rip-snorters. You can hear 'em clear to Bimini."

"He come to Key West often?"

Gleeson shrugged. "I wouldn't know him if I saw him."

Kimm sat in silence for a while. "Who's on the island now?"

"Search me," Gleeson said.

It began to rain harder. Kimm wished he were in a warm bed somewhere, with a hot-water bottle between his feet and some hot toddies in his stomach. He risked a nip at the bottle and regretted it instantaneously. He stood up to get rid of it and the boat lurched under him, with a grinding sound like crushed stone under a steam-roller. The boat shuddered, lost its headway. The sea turned it around and began to slap at it.

"Done it," Gleeson said. "We're a-ground." He began to curse. He had a nice vocabulary.

Kimm stared at him for a while and sat down again. He said, "So what do we do now? Sit?"

Gleeson did a lot of things, all of which indicated that he had no love for the boat and cared little what happened to it. He did everything but tear its bottom out. Finally he gave up and turned his attention whole-heartedly to what was left of the pint.

"Maybe the tide will help us," he said.

Kimm stooped and went into the cabin. He found a heavy, odorous blanket, lay down and pulled it over him. After a while he dozed off . . . . When daylight came he was chilled to the bone and his teeth were rattling.

He put aside the blanket and looked out. The sea was like an inland pond, mirror-still and shedding a thin gray mist. Gleeson was asleep and the boat was drifting. "Hey!" Kimm croaked.

Half an hour later he got his first view of Angel's Acre.

It was a ghostly place at that hour, with crooked cocoanut palms leaning against the mist, the house a white blur struggling to take shape. Gleeson ran his boat against the pier and Kimm glumly noted that no other boat was tied there. He looked around, scowling, and saw no other craft anywhere.

He clambered up on the pier and said, "Stick around. If I'm too long gone, we'll up the ante." Having trouble with his legs, he headed for the house. The mist licked at him.

It was as modern as tomorrow, that house, and when Kimm pushed the bell button, chimes inside played a melody that sounded like the first four notes of Beethoven's Fifth. He recalled uneasily that those particular notes, in Beethoven, were supposed to represent Fate Knocking at the Portals. He didn't feel like Fate. He had an idea Fate had outmaneuvered him and was now in Key West, putting Fern Macomber aboard the *Milly Mae*. This would raise the blood pressure of Julius Macomber considerably.

The door opened noiselessly and Kimm looked into an aged, cadaverous face that wore no expression. He said, "Mr. Reurto in?"

The eyes of the face widened. "Who are you, sir?"

"Abel Kimm. It's important as hell that I —".

"I see, sir. Please come in, sir."

The cadaver led Kimm down a broad white hall into a room that was all fireplace. You could have your modern furnishings, Kimm thought, scowling around. You could have your tipsy ceilings and pink walls, your inlaid floors and plate-glass windows. This room had them and it gave him the willies. He sat down.

The cadaver said, "It is my belief, sir, that Mr. Reurto is not at home. I shall attempt to find out." He didn't risk a smile; it might have caused his face to crumble and fall away in a mist of powder. He went away.

Kimm heard a man singing.

The sound came closer. It was not good singing. It came through the door and its maker stopped short, blinked at Kimm and said, "Well, well, well!"

P. K. Esterhood didn't look like a money-money man at that moment, but he was one. One of the biggest and best. Right now his stock form was encased in a dressing-gown of robin's-egg blue and his round, good-natured, pug-nosed face hid behind a mask of shaving cream. He had a blue-bordered towel over his arm and a safety razor in his hand. His sandy hair hung wetly.

He said, "Well!" again, and added, "Of all people, you!"

"So you're in this, too," Kimm said.

Esterhood dabbed at his face with the towel, hung the towel on a lamp and sat down, showing his hairy legs. His smile was beautiful to behold, but he had smiled that way for years, while crushing all opposition. He had the build of a fullback, the face of a curious boy, the voice of a female soprano, and the heart of a steam-roller.

His presence on Angel's Acre meant no good for Julius Macomber. He and Macomber had been storming each other's money-bag fortresses for years.

"I take it," Kimm said grimly, "you're cutting a throat or two. You wouldn't be here, else."

"I like it here. The fishing is grand."

"The fishing is grand in Lauderdale, and off Block Island. Maybe you can tell me what's up, Esterhood."

"But of course."

"Reurto, for instance. And Macomber's daughter."

"They're in love," Esterhood beamed.

"With what?"

"Why, with each other, of course. Don't tell me Julius is angry!"

"Julius," Kimm said, lapping the end of a cigarette, "is having kittens. Striped kittens. No doubt that delights you."

Esterhood chuckled. "Julius was having a little trouble with the government's Foreign Trade Committee when I left. I had a talk with him, you know, and he was worried. And how he was worried! They had him on the carpet for selling all kinds of contraband to a couple of firms in South America. He asked me to go to bat for him."

"Like hell he did. When a hurricane threatens, you don't barricade the door with a keg of dynamite."

"Well," Esterhood said, "no, you don't. But Julius really was desperate. He didn't have the slightest idea where these wild charges came from, but the government lads believed them, apparently, and it was up to Julius to prove them false. He said something about needing his daughter for a witness . . . but I suppose everything's patched up now, eh?"

"You know better."

"I do, at that."

"I wouldn't be surprised," Kimm said, "if you were the little man in the wood pile. Would you?"

"Nothing ever surprises me," Esterhood beamed.

"One thing I like about you, you're honest. You —"

The cadaver came into the room and Kimm was silent. The cadaver bowed, and said with all the emotion at his command, "It grieves me, sir, to say that Mr. Reurto is not at home. I have no idea when to expect him."

"He left early this morning," Esterhood said, "in the cruiser."

"With Fern?"

"I wasn't up."

Kimm looked at the cadaver and said, "Is Miss Fern Macomber here?"

"No, sir."

Kimm thought it over and stood up.

He decided the cadaver was telling the truth. He thought probably Reurto and Macomber's star witness were already aboard the *Milly Mae*, bound for a destination unknown. P. K. Esterhood was probably behind the move, or a part of it, but there was nothing whatever to be gained by tossing accusations at the man. Nor was there any point in a further sojourn on Angel's Acre.

"O. K.," Kimm said. "I'm the worm under the eight ball." Deep in thought, he paraded out. He made for the pier.

Gleeson, the Great Unwashed, blinked at him with red-veined eyes and said, "Where to now?"

"Back."

"Good," Gleeson said. "It's after breakfast time and there ain't a drop on board."

THE *MILLY MAE* was gone. Kimm disconsolately gazed at the vacant pier to which she'd been made fast, then walked over to Sadie's and put away a paltry breakfast of ham, eggs, hot cakes and coffee. His appetite would return, he told himself, if he could dope out some way of getting Fern Macomber off the *Milly Mae* and transporting her to New York. Because, obviously, this whole business was a gigantic frame calculated to wreck the empire of Fern's father, with more than one jackal ready and waiting to profit thereby. And Julius Macomber, when you got to know him, wasn't such a bad sort at all. He didn't deserve such a fate.

Kimm pondered all the angles. About ten o'clock he knocked again on the door of Gleeson's waterfront shack. "Got a proposition for you," he bluntly told the fisherman.

Gleeson, his breakfast finished and the empty bottle parked on the soap box, grinned pleasantly without disturbing himself. He was at ease on the bed.

"This morning," Kimm said, seeking a place to sit, "the *Milly Mae*, with Captain Bayha, left Key West, destination unknown. Think we could catch up with her?"

"How?"

"I'm asking you."

"That boat," Gleeson grunted, "has been clear to the Azores. How in hell would I know where to look for her?"

"I don't believe she'll head for the Azores this time. If we could cruise around . . . ."

The Great Unwashed spat derisively. "Hell, what you need is a plane, mister. But if you want to hire my boat, O. K." He stood up, reached for his boots. Kimm waved him down again.

"Wait a minute. That's an idea."

"What is?"

"A plane," Kimm said. "Maybe I won't need you after all." He rose gingerly from the soap box and opened the door.

"You get a plane," Gleeson said, "and I'll pilot it for you. Versatile, that's me." He grinned. "I raised plenty hell with a flying coffin in the war. The last war. And I can even play an accordion."

Kimm hired a battered cab with a Cuban driver to take him along the waterfront, past sponge fishermen and turtle-crawls, to the plane basin. He liked Key West, wished he were in a better mood to appreciate its unique attractions. A big silver ship dipped out of the sky and glided overhead, settled down on the water as the cab stopped. Kimm gave it only a glance.

He gave it more than a glance a few moments later. Out on a pier, he was dickering with the tow-headed owner of a small red seaplane when the silver ship's passengers came ashore in a launch. Kimm stared at the tall, stoop-shouldered man climbing the ladder. Abruptly he turned his back. The fellow strode past without a glance.

With a grunt of apology to the towhead, Kimm about-faced and gave pursuit.

He kept his distance, though. When the tall man approached the cab, Kimm hung back. The cab rattled off with its passenger. Kimm found another.

Half an hour later, with the second cabby's assistance, he located the first cabby and asked pertinent questions. The tall man had gone to the Colonial. Kimm went there and registered.

Mr. Paul Bibeault, the book told him, had taken room 217. Kimm took 219. His luggage, he explained, would be along later. He found a phone booth, called New York, and got Julius Macomber.

"Things," Kimm said, "are happening. You know Bibeault is down here?"

"Down where?"

"Key West. And P. K. Esterhood is whiling away his time on Reurto's island. I don't like it, Macomber. Unless something big were in the air, those two vultures would be in New York, sipping weak tea and letting underlings do their footwork. What's up?"

Macomber had a trick of hissing through his teeth while thinking over the phone. He hissed now and the hiss was ugly. "Damn it, Kimm! If only I could get my teeth into this! But I'm stuck here. If I made a move to leave New York, I'd be jumped on."

"What about Bibeault and Esterhood?"

"Those two," Macomber growled, "stand to make a fortune if I'm cleaned out. Vultures, just as you called them. The difference is, Esterhood cuts throats with a smile, Bibeault does it furtively, in the dark. If that's any difference. Damn it, where's my daughter?"

Kimm hesitated before answering that one. If he told what appeared to be the truth — that Fern and Reurto had carried out their threat to elope and were now honeymooning aboard the *Milly Mae* — Julius might go off the deep end, defy the gods, and make a desperate attempt to reach Key West. That would do no good and might cause a distinct upheaval.

"I can't find your daughter," Kimm said.

"You've got to find her! Man, think of what I'm up against! They're accusing me of secret dealings with a foreign government, of selling contraband, of half a dozen other things! Their whole case rests on some letters they've got, letters supposedly written by my daughter! If she isn't here to deny those letters, I'm sunk! You hear me, I'm sunk!" He paused to gulp a breath. "Where *is* my daughter? Where is she, Kimm?"

Kimm explained patiently that Fern Macomber was on a boat somewhere; that he, Kimm, was doing his best to locate the boat and hoped to succeed. He talked for some time, hung up and was damp with perspiration. He went up to his room.

Paul Bibeault's room was next door, and judging by the sounds that seeped through the wall, Bibeault was in it. Kimm sat.

It stood to reason that Bibeault had not journeyed all the way from New York merely to view the beauties of Key West. The man had come to attend to some business, probably to meet someone.

After the night aboard Gleeson's boat, Kimm longed to stretch out, turn his face to the wall and snooze. He didn't. He thought Bibeault would probably be going out; then there would be a job of tailing to do.

Bibeault went out. Kimm slipped from the room and followed him. The tall man went downstairs to the hotel dining-room, sat alone at a table for two and ordered lunch. He ordered turtle steak.

Kimm took a near-by table, ordered chicken, and pretended to read a folder he had picked up at the desk. The folder said that Captain James L. Pink, South Street, had boats and expert guides for hire, and would show you the world's finest tarpon fishing. Kimm wished he had time for it. His gaze slid sideways to a young woman who was dining alone.

He wished he were ten years younger.

The girl was expensively and gorgeously dressed in Fifth Avenue clothes, but was not an American. Her hair-do was Spanish, her hair and eyes were black as polished ebony. She was small, slim. She should be on a moonlit balcony, Kimm thought, with some handsome bull-fighter strumming a guitar down below. She seemed unusually interested in Paul Bibeault.

Suddenly there were two men, not one, at Bibeault's table. Kimm blinked. The newcomer was Miguel Reurto!

Kimm thought he was dreaming.

The two men talked, and it was obvious they had a lot of talking to do. Kimm caught none of it. Once, just once, the voice of Miguel Reurto, sharply argumentative, reached him with a few words, but a waiter chose that moment to begin clearing off a table.

After a while Bibeault rose, went out. His face was stormy.

Reurto had cognac and coffee after that, leisurely smoked a long black cigarette, then carefully napkinned his mouth and mustache, and stood up. He turned to leave the dining-room and caught for the first time the steady gaze of the girl at the other table. He stopped as if stabbed.

The girl rose. She was not smiling, Kimm noted. Her face was a mask, and the only barometer of her emotions was the hand that held her purse. The hand was trembling, its knuckles white and bloodless.

She stepped up to Reurto and spoke to him. He nodded. They went out together and Kimm followed.

They went into the lobby and sank onto a divan which, from Kimm's viewpoint, was the worst in the place. He could not get near them without betraying his intentions. He sat and smoked and watched them. They talked.

Reurto did most of the talking. The girl's face remained a mask.

After a while the girl stood up and walked to the stairs. She went up them. Reurto savagely crushed out a cigarette and strode away in another direction. Kimm elected not to follow him, strolled instead to the desk and said softly to the clerk, "The young lady. Does she come here often?"

The clerk had a good-natured boyish face and red hair. He grinned. "Never saw her before, sir."

"Know her name?"

The clerk looked it up. "*Señorita* Carmen Molina. From Bogota."

Kimm made a low whistling sound. He wondered if the *señorita* would talk to him . . . if he went quietly to her room and knocked on her door and told her who he was. He lit a cigarette and thought about it, and thought probably it might be a mistake to show his cards without first sizing up the situation.

There was nothing much he could do, he reasoned, until some of the seeds he had planted began to sprout. Still, this was no time for sleeping. He found a comfortable club chair near the stairs and sprawled into it, one eye shut, the other half open.

Dozing, he wondered about the dead girl in Kelver City. It didn't seem very important.

THE TOWHEAD from the plane basin walked into the hotel at eight-thirty that evening, stepped up to the desk and asked for Abel Kimm. The clerk sent him up to Kimm's room and he knocked, got no answer, came down again. He looked around the lobby, peered into the dining-room. Finally he went back to the desk, scribbled a message. "See that Mr. Kimm gets this, will you?"

The clerk slid the message into Kimm's box and the tow-head walked away, scowling.

At that particular time, Kimm was busy.

He had hung around the hotel all afternoon waiting for something to happen. Nothing had. At eight o'clock, however, *Señ        orita* Carmen Molina of Bogota, Colombia, had appeared. On the barest of hunches, Kimm had tailed her from the hotel.

He was prowling now along a dusky street near the extreme end of town. The street lights were dim blurs in gathering darkness; old-world houses with mahogany spindles and iron lace frowned over him. A hot, humid smell of subtropic vegetation hung in the listless air.

Just ahead, the beautiful visitor from South America strolled along with no apparent destination, and in no particular hurry.

Kimm wished he were back in bed. But all at once he stopped short and caught a breath.

There had been nothing human in sight a second ago — except, of course, the girl from Bogota. Now, between him and her, two crouching shapes had materialized, moving with silent, predatory swiftness toward the girl. They could have come from any of a dozen dark doorways or back yards. It didn't matter. What did matter was that the girl had whirled, was facing them, and was screaming.

Kimm darted forward, one hand fumbling with a harness under his left arm.

The girl's scream ended abruptly, smothered under a heavy paw that covered her mouth. She struggled. Kimm was mildly surprised that a creature of such delicate beauty could so suddenly be transformed into a clawing wildcat. He had an idea, as he ploughed into the mess, that he really wasn't needed, that Carmen Molina could hold her own, if necessary, in a cage full of gorillas.

Nevertheless, Kimm grabbed a handful of soiled shirt, yanked one of the girl's assailants back and clubbed him Breathing hard, his nose whistling like a peanut roaster, he laid about him with the gun from his shoulder harness. He was a little man but he could be tough at times. Exceeding tough. And this was a time for it.

The clubbed thug stumbled against a black iron fence, hung there a moment, and sagged. The other released the girl and aimed a fist at Kimm's head. Kimm ducked.

In the dim light a knife glittered. Kimm went under it, it swept down, slicing his outthrust arm, and he rolled under it, rose with his shoulder jammed against the man's armpit. He thrust a foot forward for leverage, caught the man's knife-arm and heaved. It gave him a lot of satisfaction to feel a human hulk, twice his own weight, go hurtling over his shoulder.

The fellow landed on all fours, in a cat-crouch. He picked himself up and ran. Kimm scowled after him, retrieved his gun and the knife, and turned his attention to the girl.

She was on the ground, straightening her skirt. She caught his proffered arm and pulled herself up, swayed a little. Kimm put an arm around her and eased her against the iron fence. With her hair mussed, a smudge across her mouth, her clothes twisted, she was even lovelier, he thought, than before. He stared rudely and said, "That was nice work."

She stared back at him, frowning.

"Have you any idea," Kimm asked, "what these thugs wanted?"

She shook her head.

"Well," Kimm said, "perhaps we can find out."

He stepped away from her and looked down at the fallen thug. Out cold, the fellow lay on his back with one leg drawn under him, his head cocked at a queer angle. Kimm scowled and said softly, "Oh-oh. It's you."

It was one of Captain Joe Bayha's men from the *Milly Mae*. More precisely, it was the one with whom Kimm had held a conversation on the pier.

Kimm tugged him to his feet, propped him against the fence. The girl came closer. The thug opened his eyes and blinked into Kimm's face.

"What's the big idea, buddy?" Kimm said.

The man licked his lips and stared. Kimm cocked a fist and showed it to him. "What the big idea?"

The fellow mumbled something in Spanish.

"Now in English!" Kimm snapped. "We've met before."

The man said in muddy English, "We was supposed to grab the lady here and take her to Munson's Key. That's all I know."

"Whose orders?"

"I don't know."

Kimm studied the man and saw a stubborn, thin-lipped mouth, hard eyes. He saw a creased, swarthy face which, from the looks of it, had been pounded more than once by hostile fists. He didn't think a mere barrage of words would break down the man's defenses.

Shrewdly he said, "Would you remember for fifty bucks?"

The fellow smiled crookedly. "I would if I could, mister."

"Where's the *Milly Mae*?"

The man shrugged. "Joe Bayha took her out this morning, early. I dunno where."

Kimm sighed. "Who was your pal here tonight?"

"Dutchy Schmidt. He works for Bayha. He give me ten bucks to help him with this job. It's a cinch if I could earn fifty more from you, just for information, I'd earn it."

"What's your name?" Kimm snapped.

The fellow clamped his mouth shut and looked away.

Kimm said wearily, "All right, all right," and gave the man a shove that sent him sprawling. He turned then and took the girl's arm, walked her away. She limped a little, but she had straightened her clothing, wiped her face with a postage-stamp of lace handkerchief, and looked trim again.

Kimm walked her back to the hotel. Crossing the lobby, he was stopped by a word from the clerk, who waved an envelope at him. He took the envelope in passing and shoved it into his pocket. When they reached the girl's room, she took out a key and opened the door.

Kimm went in with her. She seemed surprised.

He sat down, lit a cigarette and stared at her. He said, "Your father is a Colombian merchant, Miss Molina."

She widened her dark, lustrous eyes at him. "How do you know that?"

"My name's Kimm. Abel Kimm. I work for Julius Macomber."

Carmen Molina sat down. After a moment of silence, she too lit a cigarette, waving Kimm back as he politely leaned forward to hold a match for it. "Well?" she said then.

"It's all rather complicated," Kimm said. "In New York, Julius Macomber is under investigation by a government committee which has accused him of selling contraband, secretly monkeying with prices, *et cetera*. Basis of their claim is a hatful of letters supposedly written by Macomber's daughter, who's done a lot of traveling in S. A.

"Fern — that's her name — wouldn't come to New York when Julius sent for her. She said the whole thing was ridiculous. Julius applied pressure, threatened her. No go. She tried to bargain with him. Told him she was madly in love with one Miguel Reurto, whom you seem to know, and if he'd give his consent to the marriage, she'd show up in New York in time to deny the letters.

"This burned the old boy up. He informed her she could be dragged back as a witness, bodily, if he pulled strings. She melted under this barrage and promised to fly her own plane home.

"Well, she didn't fly it. She stayed on Reurto's island. I got here in time to prevent her elopement with Reurto on the *Milly Mae*, a schooner owned by Captain Bayha, but I muffed it. I got to the island and found one of Macomber's bitterest rivals camping there. Got back to Key West and ran into another one. And now Reurto is back — if he ever went away — and you're here, and a couple of Bayha's thugs make a pass at you.

"What, may I ask," Kimm concluded, getting his breath after the harangue, "is the answer?"

The girl said quietly, "I don't know."

"But you're here."

"My father and Julius Macomber are good friends. They have done business together for years."

Kimm said, scowling, "Reurto works for your father."

"He is my father's right-hand man."

"You came here to see him?"

She hesitated. Kimm wished the business at hand were less pressing. He would have enjoyed sending down for a pot of tea, moving a little closer to the girl and turning the talk into more friendly channels.

"I can't answer that," she said. "I'm sorry, too, after what you've done for me."

Kimm fumbled for another cigarette and pulled out of his pocket the envelope handed him by the clerk. He scowled at it, excused himself and opened it. He inhaled slowly and stood up.

"I hope," he said, "we'll meet again."

Carmen Molina said nothing.

Kimm opened the door, turned. "Joe Bayha's thugs may try it again," he warned her. "I'd be careful."

Kimm closed the door and went out.

I T WAS A dark night. A stiff breeze off the Gulf brought sea-smells and gull cries; you could peer into the dark, and see dim pin-points of light on ships riding at anchor. Or, with Abel Kimm's vivid imagination, you could see the predatory ghosts of ancient pirate craft, smugglers; you could hear in the gull cries the screams of seamen on old-time traders snared by the treacherous Florida reef.

Kimm prowled along the waterfront to the shack of Gleeson, the Great Unwashed, and thumped on the door. There was no answer. He pushed the door open, struck a match and found Gleeson asleep on the bed, cocooned in a nest of blankets that reeked of fish. He shook him awake.

"You told me," Kimm said, "you were a pilot in the war. That a fact?"

"I told you I could play an accordian, too," Gleeson said, grinning. "You want to hear me?"

"I want you to fly me to the Dry Tortugas."

"Tonight?"

"Now," Kimm said.

Gleeson swung himself off the bed and, as usual, reached for his boots. Tugging them on, he said, "You got a plane?"

"I can get one."

"I wouldn't do this for everyone," Gleeson grinned. "But you're all right, Kimm. I'm getting to like you."

They went out together, and, on the way to the plane basin, Kimm did some explaining.

"The *Milly Mae*," he said, "is at anchor off the Tortugas. Young fellow named Hale located her for me with his plane, and left a note for me at the hotel. There's a girl on the *Milly Mae*, Gleeson — held aboard against her will, perhaps — and my job is to get her off. I'll need help because Joe Bayha knows me."

Gleeson merely grunted.

It took Kimm some time to locate the tow-head. He had grown tired of waiting, had drifted off to a barroom for a few drinks. He and Kimm talked; money changed hands. Kimm hurried back to the pier, where Gleeson was looking over the plane.

"She's a beauty," Gleeson said. "All set?"

"All set."

It was the second time in his life Kimm had been in the air. He didn't say so. He took his place, hung on, and closed his eyes as the ship raced over the water. All the wind in the world, it seemed, tugged at Kimm's shuddering frame in an effort to pluck him loose. He opened his eyes and looked down.

The lights of Key West traced a delicate pattern far down in darkness. The plane roared west.

Sixty-five miles later Kimm peered down at the velvet waters of a lagoon surrounded by a ring of small islands.

There was a moon for a moment, slipping between clouds. It showed him the shadowed hulk of old Fort Jefferson, complete with courtyard and moat. It limned native homes under palm trees, whitened the rigging of a score or more ships of the kingfish fleet. He spotted the *Milly Mae*.

Gleeson set the plane down lightly. He turned. "Now what?" he said, grinning.

"Does Joe Bayha know you?"

"Sure."

"Tell him," Kimm said grimly, "Miguel Reurto sent you to fly Miss Fern Macomber back to Key West."

"You think he'll believe me? That guy would suspect his own mother."

Kimm was thoughtful for a moment, then produced from his pocket a small gold cigarette lighter. It was not an ordinary lighter, and it had not cost an ordinary amount of money. Engraved upon it, neatly, was the legend: "To Miguel, with love, from Fern."

Kimm had palmed it from a table in the living-room of the island home of Miguel Reurto, in the belief that it might somehow come in handy. He thought probably it would come in mighty handy right now.

"Show Bayha this." He passed it over. "Reurto gave it to you for identification."

"What about you?" Gleeson scowled.

Kimm hunched himself into as small a space as possible and made himself invisible except from a line of vision directly above the cockpit. "I'm not here."

The Great Unwashed gave him an approving grin, gunned the motor and sent the plane forward. He guided the ship neatly to the frowning stern of the *Milly Mae*, waved a flash-light and sent up a shout. He got an answer. A search-light on the schooner's deck swept the plane.

After that it was remarkably simple.

A boat was lowered, and Gleeson went aboard. He was gone about ten minutes, during which time Kimm kept under cover. When he returned, he politely handed Miss Fern Macomber into the rear cockpit, while the boat stood by.

The girl lost her balance, stepped on Kimm and screamed. Kimm grabbed her. He sat her down abruptly, scrambled over her and barked an order at the pilot. A yell went up from the schooner's boat, and the search-light caught Kimm full in the face.

The plane leaped under Kimm and dumped him. He caught himself. A gun spat at him from the schooner's deck and the booming, cannon-like voice of big Joe Bayha hurled curses.

Kimm slipped his own gun from its harness and threw a shot at the searchlight. The fact that he hit it — from a moving plane — forever after amazed him. The light went out. The plane soared into darkness. Miss Fern Macomber came out of her trance, flung herself at Kimm and began clawing him.

He sat on her. A little out of patience by this time, he said gruffly, "Lady, you be good! Or else!"

She wasn't good; Kimm clipped her.

FERN MACOMBER shrilled, "I'm warning you for the last time, you'll spend the rest of your life in prison for this!" She had a terrible voice. It rose in a high shriek above the drone of the plane's motor and raised hell with Kimm's eardrums.

She was a little thing, but she had a temper. What a temper! It went, Kimm supposed, with her pert, pug-nosed face, her reddish hair. Her eyes shed sparks at him. She was the only daughter of Julius Macomber and as such, had too much money. She was a spoiled brat but, in a way, Kimm liked her.

He said quietly, "Now, now, honey, you'll thank me later."

"I won't thank you later! And I don't believe Miguel is in Key West! He's sick on board the *Milly Mae*, and you know it." If glares could kill, hers would have left only a dark red smear where Kimm was sitting. "Now you listen to me!" she screamed. "Miguel was taken ill just before we left Key West. Mr. Bayha called a doctor, and the doctor said he had to have absolute quiet. The doctor said no-one could see him, not even me. And now you — you have the nerve to tell me . . . ." She whipped her hands up to claw Kimm's face again. Kimm grabbed them.

"So that's it," Kimm said. "I wondered about that, honey. Smart, this Miguel of yours."

"You —!"

"Shut up," Kimm growled, "and listen. If Reurto played sick, it was a fake, the idea being to get you out of Key West without arousing your suspicions. There was nothing sick about Miguel Reurto when I saw him in Key West a few hours ago. You'll find out. If you think he sailed with you aboard the *Milly Mae*, locked up in his cabin with a doctor, you're plumb crazy." He looked down at the approaching lights of Key West and was glad the journey was about over. It had been a turbulent one. "If he'd really been on board, why'd Bayha let you leave?"

The girl was silent, biting her lip. When she spoke again, her voice dripped acid. "What are you planning to do with me?"

"Daddy wants you," Kimm said.

"I won't go to New York!"

"Your father," Kimm said firmly, "is in a jam. You're his only out."

"It's ridiculous! Miguel says —"

"Miguel," Kimm said, "is anxious to keep you *out* of New York. You can discount what he says. You're going to New York — with Abel Kimm." A thought suddenly occurred to Kimm and he gazed soberly into the girl's face. Her lips curled. "By the way," he said, "you might straighten me out about that plane of yours. The one that crashed. Or don't you know it crashed?"

The lights of Key West were closer. The girl's face was suddenly stiff, her mouth quivering. "C — crashed?" she gasped.

"In Kelver City, on the edge of the 'Glades."

It hurt. He could see it hurt, because the hate went out of her eyes and she clenched her hands, hard. She said uncertainly, "Was — was Carmen hurt?"

"Carmen?"

"Carmen Molina. She came up from Bogota with me and stayed a few days at Miguel's place. I — I lent her the plane to fly to New York."

Kimm's face did not betray him. It could be a poker face when the need arose and he sensed an ice-cold necessity, now, for concealing his emotions. Carmen Molina! Then the South American beauty at the hotel . . . the one he had saved from Bayha's thugs . . . .

"I wouldn't know," he shrugged, "whether Carmen was hurt or not. How long have you known Carmen Molina, anyway?"

"Ages."

"Pretty good at handling a plane, is she?"

"She's the best woman pilot in South America."

"You gals sure do get around," Kimm murmured. But he didn't feel facetious. Under the mask he felt mean. His thoughts were storm-clouds.

Gleeson set the ship down and brought it to a stop while Kimm was struggling with those same storm-clouds. The girl balked, then. Stubborn, she shook Kimm's hand off her arm and told the surrounding darkness, in a shrill howl, that she did not intend to go to New York with Abel Kimm or anyone else. Furthermore, Kimm was a blackguard and a liar and she would have him arrested, tried, convicted and hung for abduction and persecution.

Kimm put a hand over her mouth, gathered her in his arms and gingerly stepped into the dinghy. He had his troubles with her while Gleeson rowed them ashore. Gleeson thought it very funny. He grinned and made sarcastic remarks. The pier, Kimm noted, was deserted and damned dark.

He clambered out of the boat and set the girl on her feet, removed his hand from her mouth and let her get a breath. He needed a breath himself and would have liked a drink to go with it. He wondered how best to get Fern

Macomber, temper and all, from Key West to New York, which seemed a million miles away; and then abruptly he stopped wondering about this and made a dive for his gun.

He was too late for it, but not too late to shove the girl aside and blast a fist into the teeth of the first man who rushed him.

They were strong teeth. They ripped his knuckles to the bone. A lunging shape dived for Kimm's legs and upset him; then the crowding darkness was alive with legs, arms and ambitious mutterings.

Kimm battled to his feet again and laid about him. He couldn't see much. A slashing heel had gouged his forehead, opened a gash, and warm blood trickled down into one eye. He heard the girl yelling at full lung capacity and wished she would shut up. Then, with his hands full, he saw Gleeson clambering up from the dinghy.

Gleeson brought an oar with him and used it. For a man who subsisted on bottled nourishment and appeared to get most of his exercise with his feet up, he was good. With the oar gripped in both hands, he let out a roar and ploughed to Kimm's side.

He almost made it. He caused as much damage, anyway, as a minor hurricane before the butt of a gun smashed him and sent him reeling. Then another gun bored into the small of Kimm's back, and a noisy, familiar voice snarled in his ear, "Hold it, you damn octopus!" The "or else" wasn't added, but was present in implication.

Kimm reluctantly released a handful of human face and heaved a sigh. He'd been enjoying himself. He lowered his hands and was grabbed from behind, yanked over an outstretched foot. He looked up into the scowling face of a Joe Bayha thug — the one he had tossed over his shoulder in the presence of the girl who called herself Carmen Molina. His name, Kimm remembered, was Dutchy Schmidt.

"For a little guy," Dutchy growled, "you do right well. Get up."

Kimm stretched his aching frame erect. He wondered at the sudden soothing silence around him, and realized Miss Fern Macomber had stopped shrieking. For that he was grateful. All the same, a couple of Dutchy's pals were having their hands full with the girl. She was a lot like her father, Kimm thought. A fighter.

They quieted her, and Dutchy said matter-of-factly, "O. K., let's go." He removed Kimm's gun and shoved him forward. No one appeared to be interested any more in Gleeson, who lay sprawled on the pier.

Kimm sucked his bleeding knuckles and walked no faster than he had to. He felt low. He thought probably the world was full of violent persons bent on preventing him from getting Fern Macomber to New York. What he needed, he decided, was a drink.

"You got a drink?" he asked Dutchy. "I could use one."

Dutchy, behind him, said darkly, "You'll get a drink, and then some."

Kimm decided it was no use. He walked the rest of the way in sullen silence.

It was not far. The way led along the waterfront a short distance, through abysmal darkness, then along a short, inky lane to a house. The house was old. It smelled old and it smelled empty. One of Dutchy's pals held open a heavy door, and the others filed past, Kimm and Dutchy ending the procession. The door clicked shut, and someone touched a match to the wick of an oil lamp.

The room was big, big as a barn, its windows shuttered. A dozen lamps would not have rid its corners of shadows. What little furniture it contained was a weird mixture of French, Spanish and English. The high dark walls were hand-planed boards, shiplapped and unplastered.

Kimm wished he were at liberty to look the place over. He tried it and was yanked back. Dutchy shoved him into a chair and stood over him, watched him with one eye while barking crisp orders to the others, in Spanish.

The big pistol in Dutchy's fist was as old, almost, as the house. One of its slugs would have blown a hole in a brick wall. Kimm eyed it in silence, weighed his chances of revolt and decided to wait.

He watched while Dutchy's pals backed Fern Macomber into a chair and made her fast with ropes. She didn't protest. She couldn't. A bright red bandanna, not too clean, had been knotted around her mouth.

This done, the gentlemen of Joe Bayha took their departure, and Kimm wondered what was next on the program. He scowled at Dutchy. The latter sat down, aimed his gun at Kimm's stomach and said unpleasantly, "I don't want no trouble from you, Kimm. Just keep quiet."

Kimm was quiet. The whole house was quiet, except for the occasional creaking of a loose shutter somewhere high up in darkness. Fern Macomber glared at Kimm, her eyes laden with hate. She blamed him, he supposed, for what had happened. She was probably right.

"Would you mind explaining —" Kimm said, and was silent because the gun in Dutchy's fist warned him silence was safer. He sighed, stretched his legs out and tried to get comfortable. His head ached.

About half an hour passed; then a knock on the door broke it up. Dutchy went to the door and said through it, "Yeah?" and got an answer which to Kimm was inaudible. He opened the door.

Miguel Reurto walked in.

Fern gasped through her gag.

REURTO closed the door behind him and looked at Kimm. He bared his teeth in a mirthless smile, nodded to Dutchy and said briefly, "Good." Then he saw Fern Macomber.

It seemed to Kimm, who was watching the South American's face, that Miguel Reurto did some rapid thinking in the next few seconds. It seemed to Kimm that the man's eyes clouded, he sucked the situation up in one noisy breath and made a snap decision concerning it. Because Reurto, face to face with Fern Macomber, hesitated just long enough to label his next act a phony; then he lurched forward, tore the red bandanna from the girl's mouth and set her free. And then, whirling on Dutchy, he loosed a torrent of abuse.

"I didn't order this!" he raved. "You stupid, blundering fool, I told you to protect Miss Macomber, not abuse her! What's the meaning of this?"

Had the girl been watching, Dutchy's look of utter astonishment would have given the play away. But she wasn't watching Dutchy. Her gaze was all for Reurto. Her hero!

Kimm groaned.

Dutchy muttered, "What the hell, boss, you said —"

"You know very well what I said! I told you to explain all this to Miss Macomber!" Reurto turned again, darkly scowling, and took the girl in his arms. His scowl softened. So did his voice. "I'm sorry, darling," he murmured. "Terribly, terribly sorry. I do owe you an explanation, don't I?"

Kimm felt terribly, terribly sick. He said crookedly, "You might explain the *Milly Mae* business first, Fancy Face." And that was a mistake.

Reurto released the girl and walked over to Kimm. He did this slowly, with a glance at Dutchy to make sure he was not putting himself between Kimm and Dutchy's gun. Maintaining this advantage, he lifted Kimm from the chair and planted a fist squarely in Kimm's face. Kimm struck the wall with a thud and fell against a chair. He could have got up, but didn't. He liked it there. The light was less revealing.

Reurto said to Fern Macomber, "It is true, my dear, that I deceived you on board Bayha's schooner. I had to make you believe I was aboard, sick. Your life was in danger here, and I had to get you away while removing the menace. Brave heart that you are, you wouldn't have gone if you had known the truth." His voice was a caress. It made Kimm sick, but Fern seemed to like it.

Julius Macomber's daughter clung to him, sobbing a little. She said, "It isn't true that you're plotting against my father. It isn't true, is it?"

"But of course not, my sweet!"

"I knew it wasn't."

Kimm was glad that his thoughts could not get up and walk around the room. The smell of them would have been unbearable. He eyed the gun in Dutchy's fist. He was wondering if, with luck, he could get to it. He decided to try it and, as a preliminary, inched his left hand along the floor and gripped the leg of a chair. And then the door opened.

Dutchy whirled to look at the door, and Miguel Reurto cried shrilly, in a voice not at all masculine, "Look out!"

For a moment Reurto's warning was the only sound in the room except the noisy rasp of a breath drawn by Dutchy. Obviously, Dutchy did not quite know what to do about the person who stood in the doorway. The intruder was a woman.

She was the beautiful woman who had called herself Carmen Molina.

Kimm plucked the chair off the floor and went into action.

He was magnificent. He thought later it was a crying shame that no one in the neighborhood had turned a motion-picture camera on him, in order to record for posterity the events of the next few moments. Diminutive but ambitious, Kimm swung the chair at Dutchy Schmidt's head and scored with it. The blow pitched Dutchy into the woman who called herself Carmen Molina, and both went down.

Kimm leaped for Reurto. Reurto, suddenly white of face, stepped behind Fern Macomber and went for a gun. The gun was under his coat, in a specially designed pocket close to the snug waist-band of his trousers, and he had trouble getting it out. He had so much trouble that Kimm was on him, having shouldered the girl aside, before the gun came clear.

Kimm blasted a fist to the South American's face and followed through with another, then hurled himself bodily at the man's legs and knocked him sprawling. He ducked, then, because someone was shooting from the doorway. He crabbed sideways, came up with Reurto's gun, aimed at a pair of silk clad legs, and squeezed the trigger — and discovered the safety catch was still on: He cursed Reurto for being so damn careless, threw the gun and watched it bounce off the chin of the woman who called herself Carmen Molina.

She dropped her own gun, with which she'd been frantically trying to hit something. She made a noise like a kicked cat and turned to run.

Gleeson, the Great Unwashed, came over the threshold at that moment and caught her in his arms. He seemed surprised. His wide-eyed expression said plain as day, "Well, think of this! Pennies from heaven!"

"Hold her," Kimm snapped.

The big, barny room was quiet again. Well, almost. Reurto moaned on the floor, pawing at his face. Carmen Molina struggled in Gleeson's grasp and tried to bite him. The air reeked of smoke.

Kimm said, "Well, well."

He wondered if things like this happened often in Key West, and if so, why the Chamber of Commerce didn't advertise them. Scowling a little, he stepped past the petrified form of Fern Macomber and looked down at Reurto. "Oh-oh," Kimm said. "She hit you."

"Get a doctor!" Fancy Face wailed. "For Gawd's sake, get me a doctor!"

Kimm looked at the wound and decided it was nothing to worry about, even if he felt like worrying. He worked his hands under Reurto's arms and wrestled the man into a chair. "A lawyer would do you more good," Kimm said. "That's what you'll be needing, fella. A smart lawyer. One of the slick, crooked kind who take pity on slick, crooked birds like you — for a price." He hipped his hands and struck an attitude. "On the other hand, a murder rap is hard to beat," he finished.

Reurto flinched. Fern Macomber took a faltering step toward Kimm and stopped. The girl in Gleeson's arms shrilled, "I hope they do pin a murder rap on you, you heel!"

"Oh," Kimm said softly. "You *meant* to hit him?"

"I meant to hit *you*."

"I'm having the damnedest time," Kimm said, "trying to dope you out." He scowled at her and still thought she was beautiful, but her beauty now was a little too violent for his liking. "The boy friend was crossing you, hey?"

"I'll tear his eyes out!"

"That," Kimm said severely to Reurto, "is what you get for crossing a woman. Rather, it's what you get for letting her *know* you're crossing her — by setting thugs on her. You weren't smart. Two or three times in this game, fella, you weren't smart. Now look at you."

Reurto showed his teeth in a snarl. "You'll regret this, Kimm!"

"As I get it," Kimm said, "you and your girl friend here planned this together. Your part of it was to play up to Miss Macomber and get her to write some letters — or maybe you wrote them for her. The letters went Washington and put Julius Macomber in a hole. All you had to do, then, was keep Macomber's daughter under your thumb until the explosion." He wagged a finger under Reurto's nose. "Was this your own idea, Handsome, or did it spring from the fertile brain of P. K. Esterhood?"

"I wish you'd tell me," Gleeson said, "what the hell to do with this dame. She's got more wiggles than a snake."

"Sock her," Kimm grunted. "Well, Reurto?"

"But you are insane! You are mad!"

"With a phony accent," Kimm nodded. "Which proves I'm close to home. All right, P. K. Esterhood doped out the play and you pulled it off. But you ran into trouble. Carmen Molina, the real Carmen Molina, was on your island chumming with Fern. She got wind of what you were up to, tried to get to New York to tell Julius where the smell was coming from. Her father and Julius are friends. More than friends. If Julius folded, her father would fold with him, and she meant to prevent it. But you monkeyed with that plane, fella, and she crashed."

This, Kimm realized, was a guess. It made sense and it slid neatly into its proper niche, but he had nothing with which to hammer it home. The effect of it, therefore, surprised him. Miguel Reurto's face turned the color of a sheet not washed in Fels Naptha and began twitching.

"All you had to do then," Kimm said, satisfied, "was get Fern to a place where her father wouldn't find her. You used Joe Bayha's boat. You fooled her into thinking you were on board, while you stayed in Key West to meet another vulture, Paul Bibeault. I don't get that, entirely, unless at this stage of the game you figured to play both ends against the middle and double the take. Esterhood planned the job and no doubt paid a fancy price. So maybe you thought Bibeault would pay, too. No?"

"Look," Gleeson complained. "She won't stay socked." He grinned at Kimm, put the palm of his right hand over the face of the girl who called herself Carmen Molina, and gave her a shove. The shove dumped her into a chair and she cursed him. Kimm turned again to Reurto.

"Which brings us," Kimm said, "up to the present, to your girl friend here. Is she in this?"

"No!" the girl shrilled. She popped out of the chair despite Gleeson's unambitious attempt to stop her. Confronting Kimm, she thrust out her chin, which was black and blue now. "I came here," she snapped, "because I heard he was too damn interested in other women. I used the name Carmen Molina because I'd heard of her and it was the first name came to my mind when I registered, and I didn't want to use my own. If this slick-haired Romeo is going to jail, count me out!"

"Cute, ain't she?" Gleeson said. He slouched forward and stroked the girl's arm. "I could use someone like you to pour my meals for me. I'm right easy to get along with, honey, and —"

She bit his hand.

"Well," Kimm said with a glance at Dutchy Schmidt, who was still out, "let's go." He leaned over Reurto.

Fern Macomber said, "You leave him alone!"

She had a gun. Dutchy Schmidt's gun. It looked like a cannon in her small brown hand, but she held it in front of her and managed somehow to keep it pointed in the general direction of Kimm's stomach. Kimm stood very still and broke out in sweat, because a gun in the unsteady hand of a rank amateur is bad, very bad. A gun in the hand of a professional goes off when the professional wishes it to go off, but a gun in the hand of an amateur is apt to go off any time.

"Now, listen," Kimm said.

Fern Macomber was being stubborn. Her colorless face was stiff and her lips were curled hard against her teeth and her heart was pounding. She said,

"I don't care! It can't *all* be true, what you've said about him. And you're not going to ruin my life just for a lot of filthy money!"

"*Your* life?" Kimm said.

"We're going to be married, and you can't stop us!"

Kimm opened and closed his hands convulsively and longed to shake the little fool's teeth loose. He opened his mouth to say this and heard laughter. Loud, shrill laughter. It was like nothing human and he wondered if by some chance the pelicans of Key West were cousins to the loons of Canada. He turned, scowling, and Miguel Reurto's beautiful girl friend brushed past him.

She was practically doubled up with the mirth that poured out of her. Oblivious to the gun, she walked up to Fern Macomber and thrust her left hand under Fern's face. A ring winked on the third finger and she wiggled the finger to make it more prominent.

"See it?" she said. "It's probably made of tin, but he gave it to me, honest he did. He gave it to me two years ago when I was sap enough to marry him."

"W-what?" Fern said.

"He's my husband, dearie. You can have him if you want him, but you'll be awful surprised." She wagged the finger again, took the ring off it. She threw the ring and it rolled to Reurto's feet, stopped there, and he pulled his feet back as though it were a snake about to bite him.

Mrs. Reurto said to Kimm, "I'm on my way and don't anybody try to stop me." She went out.

Fern Macomber looked down at the gun in her hand, shuddered and dropped it. Inwardly grinning, Kimm said to Gleeson, "Run out, fella, and hunt up the cops."

K IMM drove leisurely over the highway from Key West to Miami, the night air cool off the Atlantic, strange and interesting sounds rising from the cypress swamps on both sides. It was one A.M., the day was Wednesday, and after he got to Miami and called Fred Meaton, the Kelver City storekeeper, to come and get the car, a plane would take him to New York in time for Fern Macomber to speak her little piece in defense of her father. Kimm was at peace with the world.

The girl beside him stirred a little and opened her eyes. She had been sleeping. She said, "I suppose you think I'm an awful fool."

"Mmn," Kimm said.

The stars were very bright.

"It's just that I'm so darned romantic," Fern declared gravely. "I wouldn't have married him, really. I mean I don't think I would. He *was* handsome, though."

"Mmn."

"You're kind of handsome yourself."

"Mmn."

"And brave, too. Awfully brave. Why, the way you sailed into that man Dutchy. . . ." She snuggled closer. "I'm a fool about strong, brave men. I guess I need someone to take care of me."

"I'll tell you what," Kimm said.

"What?"

"There's something I ought to do, just to make this night complete."

Her wide eyes looked up at him under long lashes and she whispered, "Yes? What?"

"This," Kimm said.

He stopped the car. Then the bright stars looked down in solitude on a strange sight. They saw Abel Kimm, grimly chewing an unlighted cigarette, shift himself out from under the wheel, turn the daughter of Julius Macomber over a knee and spank her. Soundly.

• • • • •

# THE MISSING MR. LEE

THIS IS ANOTHER 1940 TALE PUBLISHED IN *BLACK MASK*, APPEARING IN THE MAGAZINE'S NOVEMBER NUMBER. FOR ME, AT LEAST, IT'S A ONE-OF-A-KIND STORY. I DON'T BELIEVE I EVER WROTE ANOTHER SUCH, WITH EACH OF FIVE OR SIX CHARACTERS COMING FORWARD TO TELL WHAT HE OR SHE THINKS HAPPENED. IT'S A FAVORITE TALE OF MINE, AND I HOPE IT WILL RATE HIGH WITH YOU AS WELL.

HBC

*He was wanted for murder and troopers, city cops, reporters, and mere citizens combed New England for him. How could they tell he had evaporated in a cloud of alcohol fumes? Of course they might have guessed, for wasn't Mr. Lee a liquor salesman after all?*

## 1. NORA ABBOTT

IN MY OWN WORDS? Well now, that's what I'm trying to do — if you'll just be good enough to *let* me. After all, I have my rights, don't I? There's no law says I have to sit here and be insulted. Some of you policemen think . . . Oh, all right, all *right*! Shut up then, and listen.

This Mr. Lee was an odd sort of person, right from the beginning. I said so to Judith, the day he rang the doorbell and asked if I had any rooms to rent. He knew right well I had rooms to rent. I keep a sign on the front door all the time. But he asked me in that little pipsqueak voice of his, and I said yes, and then I took him upstairs and showed him the perfectly elegant front bedroom, but he didn't like it.

"No," he said, "I don't want anything so pretentious, Mrs. Abbott. It isn't the price I object to," he said. "It's just that I like to be off by myself. There are too many windows in this room, for one thing," he said.

So I showed him my other rooms and the one he liked, mind you, was that little back bedroom, the smallest and gloomiest room in the house. I hadn't rented that room in six months! But he liked it, so I cleaned it up for him and he moved in.

What's that? Oh, yes, he paid his rent promptly enough. I never had any complaints on that score, the whole nine weeks he was with me. For that matter I don't suppose I had *any* complaints. He was quiet enough, and he never bothered anyone. But I tell you I just couldn't bring myself to *like* him.

Why? Well, his looks, for one thing. He was only half a man for size, and bald as a doorknob. It gave me the creeps to look at him, sometimes. And I swear he used rouge, his cheeks were so pink. I always said, "If that's what they're passing off for a specimen of manhood these days, I'll go right on being a widow."

He used to read a lot, Mr. Lee did. Every other night or so he'd go over to the branch library on Elmwood Street and get more books. He spent most of his time reading, and it wasn't until the last week that he began going out nights. But when he did begin going out, he certainly did it up brown! Every single night, until two and three o'clock in the morning! And never a word to the rest of us where he'd been. Oh no! He was a sly one. It was always, "Good morning, Mrs. Abbott," nice as you please, or, "You're looking bright and cheerful today, Miss Whitson," but never a word about himself. Why, he'd been with us nearly two whole weeks before I even knew what his business was.

Yes, he was a liquor salesman. Can you imagine it — a liquor salesman! But I never saw a sign of liquor in his room — not even a bottle of beer. If you ask me, I think a good stiff drink of anything stronger than water would have killed him!

Well, I *am* telling you. I'm coming to that. For heaven's sake, don't rush me.

The night you're asking about — the night he and poor Mr. Paine had their argument — I was playing Chinese checkers with Judith and Mrs. Baylis. She's the lady across the street. We were playing in Judith's room and listening to some silly drama on the radio, and we heard Mr. Paine shouting.

It's a funny thing, but we thought it was part of the radio play at first. But the man on the radio began talking about face powder, and of course Mr. Paine wasn't shouting about any face powder. So we listened, and I distinctly heard him say what I've told you.

What's that? Well, if I must repeat it, I suppose I must. It doesn't seem to occur to you people that I'm a lady. What he said was, "It's a filthy rotten way to make a living, that's what it is, and you ought to be ashamed of yourself!" It's very evident he was talking about Mr. Lee's job, because Mr. Paine was always dead set against liquor in any form. Why I've even seen him throw away a bottle of expensive medicine because it contained alcohol.

Yes, I suppose he *was* an eccentric sort of person, though that isn't exactly the word I would have used myself. He was with us almost five years and I was used to his ways.

But he *was* queer. There's no denying that.

I beg your pardon? Well, for one thing, he used to be on the stage, and he was forever quoting Shakespeare and such nonsense. And another thing. Mr. Paine was awfully clever at imitating people. Why, he'd sit down by the radio and listen to some of those performers and he'd take them off so smart you couldn't tell the difference. You absolutely couldn't tell . . . . I beg *your* pardon, Captain. Unless I'm sadly mistaken, you asked me to tell this story *my* way. What? Well, I *am* offended. I think I have every right to be offended.

Well . . . all right. I was coming to that, anyway. You see; there was bad feeling between Mr. Lee and Mr. Paine, and while we never did wholly understand it, I'm morally certain it was about the liquor. At any rate, Mr. Paine made some very cutting remarks about liquor, in Mr. Lee's presence. And I think *that* was the cause of what finally happened.

No, I wasn't at home when it happened. I've already told you I was across the street, helping Mrs. Baylis shorten a dress. When I opened the door and walked in, there was Mr. Paine lying in the hall outside the door of Mr. Lee's room, and Miss Whitson at the telephone, calling you people. And I want to tell you right here and now, I was never so frightened in all my life! After all, you could *see* the man was dead. I mean, you could see the — the instrument sticking right out of him.

Well, it was and it wasn't. I mean — well — we used to have a nice old gentleman named Mr. Freelove, who was retired from the Arnold Silver Company. He was a jewelry designer and he had all these tools up in his room, and he used to make little brooches and pendants and things, just as a hobby.

It was about a year ago he died, and his son came on from Ohio I think it was, by plane, to bury him. The son said he had no use for any of the old man's things — heaven knows they weren't worth anything, anyway — so *I* took them. I kept the box of jewelry tools on a shelf in the kitchen. Once in a while I'd find a use for some of them, such as —

What? Yes, he asked me for it. I was getting supper and he came into the kitchen with a belt in his hand. "Mrs. Abbott," he said, "have you an ice-pick around, or something sharp? I want to punch a hole in this belt," he said.

I fished around in the box and found that particular tool, whatever it is, and gave it to him . . . . It's what? An engraving tool? Well, I wouldn't know. I only know it was long and sharp, like an ice-pick, and had a good solid handle you could get your hand around. I gave it to him and he said, "I must be getting thin, when my belts won't fit me any more, Mrs. Abbott. Maybe you're not feeding me enough." He was always making pointed remarks like that.

It was about five thirty, I think. Of course if I'd known he was going to murder poor Mr. Paine a few hours later, I would have paid more attention to the time. But good heavens, how was I to know? It seemed harmless enough, him asking me for . . . .

No, he didn't. He went straight to his room after supper, and he was there when I went across the street to Mrs. Baylis's. I heard his radio going. That was about half past eight.

Close to ten o'clock, I think. You can figure it out easily enough, I expect. Miss Whitson was telephoning you when I came in, and it seems to me you were at the house almost before she hung up.

No, I didn't touch him. For one thing, I had my hands full with Miss Whitson. She was just about out of her mind, poor thing, and why wouldn't she be, with *that* happening right under her nose. Nobody touched him. Nobody even laid a hand on him.

No. I've already told you that. His door was open, but he wasn't in his room. I *did* look. After all, the body was lying right there within a few feet of the open door. But he wasn't around. What *I* think happened — he rushed out right after killing Mr. Paine It's only a cat-jump to the back stairway, and I think he ran down the back stairs and made his escape *that* way. He could have done that without being seen by anyone.

Well, I'm not so sure. If you ask me, I think he's a whole lot smarter than you realize. Naturally, I hope you do catch him, but I have my doubts. Meanwhile, if you're finished with me . . . After all, I'm a very busy woman, Captain.


## 2. MISS WHITSON

THANK YOU, Captain. I *am* a little upset, naturally, after what has hap pened. If you care to tell me how much of the ground Mrs. Abbott has covered, perhaps I can go on from there.

I see. Yes, I understand. Please don't think that I am attempting to run your business for you. It's just that I have very little knowledge of police procedure.

Yes, a teacher. In a small private school for children who are not too gifted. In these difficult days one takes what one is able to get, and the teaching profession is sorely overcrowded.

Twenty-eight, Captain.

I'll do my best. You realize, of course, that I have been living with Mrs. Abbott only about a month. I came here from New York, and frankly was forced to look for an inexpensive place to live, not too far from the school. Mrs. Abbott's house is not exactly what one might prefer, but it was recommended to me as being inexpensive and quite respectable. I find Mrs. Abbott herself rather trying at times — she's so garrulous, you know — but one mustn't be too particular.

Mr. Paine? I hardly knew him, Captain. He was a late riser and seldom had breakfast with us. Then of course I was away at the school all day, and was often too tired to bother with supper. In the evenings I usually confined myself to my room. A teacher's work does not end in the classroom, you know.

He *was* eccentric. Old people so often are, aren't they? Well . . . no, I can't give you any concrete examples. He just impressed me as being rather a queer, childish old man. He'd been on the stage, I understand. His superficial knowledge of Shakespeare was truly amazing. At the oddest moments he would break out in a positive rash of quotation.

I think I did, once. It was Bing Crosby, I believe. For myself, I didn't think much of the imitation, but Mrs. Abbott was immensely impressed by it. He had a knack, of course — there's no denying that — but I seldom enjoy imitations. Especially of Bing Crosby. Oh, you do? Well, tastes do differ, Captain.

Yes, I remember that particular evening well. We were playing Chinese checkers, I think it was — or some equally childish game — Nora and myself and that atrocious creature, Mrs. Baylis, who lives across the street. I hadn't wanted to play, but Nora is sometimes so insistent. Orson Welles was doing *Lost Horizon* — a beautiful interpretation! — and all at once we were disturbed by a violent argument from Mr. Paine's room. Mr. Lee and Mr. Paine, you know, simply did *not* get along.

It was something about liquor. Mr. Lee is a liquor salesman, and Mr. Paine had definite ideas about the evils of alcohol.

Have I? Well, I do hold an opinion, of course, but on the other hand I believe in respecting other people's rights. After all, the eighteenth amendment was repealed, and if foolish people wish to ruin their health and lose the respect of their friends, it is legally their privilege to do so. I firmly believe —

I quite agree with you, Captain. On the other hand, murders are frequently committed with even *less* reason, are they not? To me it is quite conceivable that Mr. Lee turned on Mr. Paine in the heat of argument . . . .

No, I didn't. On the other hand, I was in my room with the door shut, and there are times, Captain, when I become so engrossed in my work that I hear absolutely nothing of what is going on around me. People speak to me on the street, sometimes, and I walk past without noticing them. Many a time I've had to apologize . . . . But don't misunderstand me, please! I'm not expressing *any* opinion. After all, it's *your* duty to find out who killed Mr. Paine, not mine.

I realize that. But on the other hand, what I think and what I saw with my own eyes are two utterly different things, Captain. I really saw nothing.

Why, he screamed. I heard the scream and rushed out of my room and there he was, on the floor in the corridor.

I don't know. Obviously he came from Mr. Lee's room. He most certainly was not murdered in *my* room, and there are no other rooms at that end of the hall. I suppose the murderer must have been there when I rushed out. The hall itself was empty except for Mr. Paine.

Yes, right away. Or at least, within a very few minutes. I don't remember exactly what I did, because I was so upset, but it seems to me I ran toward him and then realized he was dead, and then I believe I just stood there for a moment, too stunned to think or act. But I ran to the telephone as soon as the first shock passed, and —

Yes. Yes, he could have slipped out of the room while I was telephoning. I hadn't thought of that. He could have fled down the rear stairs, without my seeing him. Still . . . .

May I have a glass of water, please? Thank you.

Well, I hardly know just how to answer that question, Captain. One really should know a person a lot longer than I have known Mrs. Abbott before attempting to form an opinion. I don't believe in snap judgments. She is, how-ever, a rather quick-tempered woman. That much I do know. And of course not what you and I would call exactly literate, certainly not cultured. She talks entirely too much, not only about herself but about everyone with whom she comes in contact. She —

No, I wouldn't say she had many friends. Most of the neighbors avoid her because she is such a gossip. Mrs. Baylis is a close friend, of course, but Mrs. Baylis is not the sort to be choosey, and for that matter is an inveterate gossip herself. As for friends of the other sex, I don't believe Nora Abbott has even looked at a man since her husband passed away.

You're entirely welcome, Captain. If I can be of any further help . . . .

### 3. MRS. BAYLIS

GOOD AFTERNOON, Lieutenant What's that? Well, I'm sure it don't make a bit of difference to me whether you're a captain or even a corporal. I'm not here because I want to be here, I can tell you that, and the quicker I'm out, the better.

Go right ahead. Them I can answer, I'll answer. Them I can't, you'll have to plague someone else with.

Sure I knew Mr. Paine, and it's a dirty shame, I'm telling you, that he's gone to the land of his fathers. A positive scream the man was, when he got going with his imitations. Listen to some of them big shots on the radio, he would, and come out with stuff of his own that put them to shame. Why, only the other night —

Eh? Sure he had a temper! Let fall a word about alcohol and he'd turn red with rage to the roots of his hair. A crank he was on that subject, a downright crank. I always said to myself, I said, "The trouble with that man, he's had his fling and it was a rip-snorter, and now with his head subject to aches and his liver out of order, he's forgotten all the fun he had and remembers only the mornings after." Lord, the arguments him and Mr. Lee got into over liquor!

When? Well, there was one night Nora and Miss Whitson and myself was playing checkers, and . . . . Oh, you do? Well, if you know all about these things, why ask me? No, I can't remember any other times. I didn't know Mr. Lee so good. The only time I ever saw *him* close up was when I'd drop over there around supper time. He didn't hang around much of an evening. Off he'd go to the library or to a movie, as if he never could find time to be sociable. He wasn't much of a man anyway.

Miss Whitson? Well, now, she's not my type, and I'm frank to say I never could make head nor tail of her. I always get suspicious of girls that act too goody-goody, Captain. Miss Whitson, now, you'd think to look at her and hear her talk, she was just too good to live. But I know better.

Eh? Well . . . maybe I didn't mean just that. Maybe I can't prove nothing. But I'm entitled to my own opinions, I guess. For one thing I know she's not so death on liquor as she pretends to be. Oh, I know, I know she has a lot of lordly opinions on the subject. I've heard her shooting off. "Liquor," says she, "is all right in its place, but its place is not in the home." Well, maybe, but I can tell you I've seen her come home with a skinful!

About a week ago, it was. This car pulled up at the corner of the street, just a little ways down from my house, and she was in it with a man. I didn't get a look at the man. I wouldn't know him again if he walked in here right now. But I was sitting there at my front window, and with my own eyes I seen Miss Goody-goody Whitson get out of that car and walk along to the house — if you can call it walking when a person stumbles over her own feet every other step and just about gets there.

I was over there the next morning and I sort of let fall a remark. "Where was Miss Whitson last night?" I said. "Why," said Nora, "she went to a concert with some of the teachers from the school where she works."

"Did she get home late?" I said. "Why," said Nora, "I guess she did. I was in bed and I guess everyone else was. I didn't hear her come in."

So there you are, Captain. You can't always judge a person by the fancy front they put on. But as for this murder, I'd say Mr. Lee done it. I'd say there was no question about that. He always impressed *me* as a sneaky sort, and I never did like him.

Why certainly, Captain. Any time at all. My telephone number is —

Oh, you do? Well — he-he! — I'm surprised at you, Captain. You're a lot faster than you look!

### Interstate Police Teletype, February 7

ATTENTION POLICE DEPARTMENTS ALL NEW ENGLAND CITIES STOP NEW HAYDON MASS HQ REQUESTS COOPERATION IN APPREHENDING GEORGE ALDEN LEE WANTED FOR QUESTIONING IN KILLING OF ALVIN PAINE STOP LAST SEEN TEN PM FEBRUARY SIXTH IN VICTIMS RESIDENCE THIS CITY STOP AGE ABOUT THIRTY HEIGHT FIVE FOUR WEIGHT ABOUT ONE THIRTY BLUE EYES LIGHT BLOND HAIR SMALL MOLE UNDER LEFT EYE STOP IS PROBABLY WEARING LIGHT BROWN HERRINGBONE WEAVE SUIT DARK BROWN HARRIS TWEED OCOAT BROWN HAT STOP ALSO WEARS HEAVY YELLOW GOLD SIGNET RING LEFT HAND STOP IS LIQUOR SALESMAN STOP IS PROBABLY DRIVING MAROON CHEVROLET TOWN SEDAN MASS C4042 STOP NHPD

### *The New Haydon Times*, February 9

#### HUNT FOR LEE CONTINUES!

#### NEW ENGLAND COMBED FOR LIQUOR SALESMAN SOUGHT IN BOARDING HOUSE SLAYING

#### POLICE HINT NEW ANGLE

The New England wide search for George Alden Lee, missing liquor salesman, continued today with local and state police feverishly running down rumors from more than a score of widely separated communities.

While admitting that most of the clues are undoubtedly the work of cranks or mistaken well-wishers, police insist that all leads, no matter how seemingly worthless, are assiduously being followed in an attempt to locate the man who, they believe, holds the answer to the Paine stabbing.

Meanwhile, reliable sources hint that there may be other angles to the case.

### 4. THE COCKEREL CLUB

HELLO, JOE. You look pretty swell this evening. Ha! Who, me? Well, you know how it is, Joe. Monday nights are pretty dull out here. I think sometimes I do better if I sell this place and buy a place in town. Out here, when you figure it all up, Saturday night is the only night I make the money. Plenty of times I say to myself, "Salvatore," I say, "this is tough life. Everybody is sit at home saving the money so they can eat. Over there in Europe a war goes on. Nobody here feels like dancing and drinking and having good time any more.

"Well," I say to myself, "Don't you worry. If Salvatore Puleo's night club is not make the money, nobody else is make it either." I see in the papers you have a murder, Joe. I shake my head when I see that. I say to myself, "This job of being a cop is fine till people start killing somebody." Plenty of times I envy you, Joe. I say, "Maybe I should give up the night club business and be a cop like Joe Gleeson." But I don' know. I don' like murders. You think you will catch this feller?

Is funny thing, this murder, Joe. Last night I look in the paper and I see a picture of this girl who live in the house where the guy was killed. I look at the picture a long time and I say to myself, "Salvatore, you know this girl. She is out here not so long ago, stinko drunk."

Eh? Sure she was out here! So what if she is a nice girl — plenty of times I see nice girls take one drink too many out here, and then they are like every one else — stinko. You want to know something? When the nice girls get drunk they are worse than the others. They make more noise. They cause more trouble. Most of the time they get sick all over the place.

Well now, let me think. When she first comes in I do not pay any special attention to her, because she is not drunk then — or anyhow she is not so drunk I have to be watching her. She is with some feller. They sit in booth over there. Bye and bye a lot of noise begins to come from over there, and I walk over, easy like, and the girl is having a high old time for herself.

This time I do not say nothing. After all, is it for me to hush up the customers just because they enjoy themselves? That way I would lose all my business sure!

But this girl, the first thing I know she is sick, and I have to help Nicky clean up the mess she make. Then the man she is with, he begins to take her out of the place right in the middle of the floor show when Antonina is dancing. And the girl fall down, and everybody say "Ooooh!" and Antonina gets mad because nobody pay attention to *her* any more. Well, it is a fine mess, I tell you. I am glad when I get rid of them. I say to myself . . . .

Hey? No, I do not think so. I think that is the first time I ever see them here.

Him? No, I do not know who he is, Joe. I tell you how you can find out who he is, though. Wait a minute.

Here, Joe. You see this number? M-8991. When they get into the car to go away from here that night, I say to myself, "A man so drunk as he is should not be driving an automobile. Maybe there will be a smash-up. Maybe the cops, who are all the time doing favors for Salvatore Puleo, will come around looking for information. So I write down his number.

This time I do *you* a favor? That makes me very happy, Joe. Me, Salvatore Puleo, I hope you catch this killer.

*The New Haydon Times,* **February 10**

### LEE TRACED TO PITTSFIELD!

### TRUCK DRIVER SAYS HE GAVE HUNTED MAN A LIFT

*The New Haydon Times,* **February 11**

### LEE SOUGHT IN HARTFORD

### LUNCH CART EMPLOYEE SAYS MIDNIGHT
### CUSTOMER WAS LIQUOR SALESMAN

## 5. RODNEY TILLSON

ARE YOU THE guy I talk to about the feller that was killed over to Mrs. Abbott's house? Yeah? Well, I'm Rodney Tillson. I live acrost the street, under Mrs. Baylis, and I know somethin' about that murder. My mom said I'd have to come over here to the police station and tell you about it, so here I am.

Huh? I'm thirteen. What difference does that make?

Well, it's like this. I'm always runnin' errands for old lady Baylis, see. Mom says I got to be nice to her because she's old and kinda feeble. So the night Mr. Paine was killed, I was in the back room workin' on my airplanes, and Mrs. Baylis banged on the floor, like she always does when she wants me. So I went up the back stairs and she was in the kitchen, talkin' to Mrs. Abbott.

She says to me, "Be a good boy, Rodney, and run across to Mrs. Abbott's house and get the pair of scissors out of the sewin' machine." And Mrs. Abbott, she says, "You know where the sewin' machine is, don't you?" And I says, "Sure. It's in the kitchen."

"Well," Mrs. Abbott says, "just pull out the drawer and you'll find the scissors. Hurry now." She's always in a hurry, that dame is.

So she give me a key to the front door, and I went acrost the street. But I didn't get no scissors, see? I was just about to go up the front stairs, when I heard someone talkin' in a loud voice, in the hall up there.

Now get this, and don't be tellin' me I'm crazy. *The person I heerd talkin' was Mrs. Baylis!*

Huh? Of course I was just talkin' to her in her own kitchen! That's what's so queer about it. A person can't be in two different places at the same time, can they? Nope, I'm positive. Gee, I live under her, don't I? I been runnin' errands for her ever since I was big enough to walk, I guess. I ought to know her voice, if anyone does.

Well, I ain't exactly sure what she was sayin'. It sounded sarcastic-like. Awful sarcastic. "So you despise people who get drunk, do you? Well, well, well. *You* wouldn't touch the stuff, would you now?" It was somethin' like that she was sayin'. I couldn't make nothin' out of it, honest.

Why didn't I go upstairs? Because I was scared, that's why! Who wouldn't be scared? Gee, I don't believe in ghosts and stuff like that, but I *knew* Mrs. Baylis wasn't up there, not really. How could she be? So I beat it out of there, fast as I could go.

Yeah, I went back to Mrs. Baylis's house and there she was, big as life, just like I'd left her. She could see I was scared, I guess. She and Mrs. Abbott asked me what the trouble was, and I told 'em. Then Mrs. Abbott went over to her house — maybe she thought I was lyin', but gee, what would be the point of lyin' about a thing like that?

Anyhow, the next thing I knew there was a police car outside Mrs. Abbott's house and Mrs. Baylis was tellin' me not to breathe a word of all this to anyone. And I didn't, except today I told my mom, and Mom sent me straight over here.

Captain Lovett? Who's he?

Shucks, do I have to talk to him? Can't you tell him?

Well . . . aw right, if I got to. But I got a date to play hockey with the kids. I can't be wastin' too much time.

### Memo to Detective Macomber, New Haydon P. D.

HERE'S THE LATEST ON THAT SCREWY PAINE KILLING — A STATEMENT FROM A NEIGHBORHOOD KID WHO BELIEVES IN GHOSTS. MAYBE YOU CAN MAKE SENSE OUT OF IT. I ADMIT I CAN'T.

THE CASE SHAPES UP AS FOLLOWS: PAINE AND LEE HATED EACH OTHER AND WERE OFTEN CLOSE TO BLOWS. BOTH MRS. ABBOTT AND MISS WHITSON AGREE ON THAT. AT THE TIME OF THE KILL, MRS. ABBOTT WAS ACROSS THE STREET WITH

MRS. BAYLIS, UNLESS YOU CAN BELIEVE THIS KID'S STATEMENT, WHICH PUTS MRS.
BAYLIS IN TWO PLACES AT ONCE. MISS WHITSON WAS IN HER ROOM, WORKING. SHE
DIDN'T HEAR ANY ARGUMENT, BUT HEARD PAINE SCREAM, RAN OUT INTO THE HALL
AND FOUND HIM LYING THERE IN FRONT OF LEE'S ROOM. NO ONE SEEMS TO HAVE
SEEN LEE MAKE HIS GETAWAY, BUT HE CERTAINLY DID VANISH.

AS FOR SIDELIGHTS ON THE CASE, WE HAVE THE FOLLOWING: MISS WHITSON
PRETENDS TO BE A SNOOTY DAME BUT JOE GLEESON LEARNED SHE WAS DRUNK TO
THE EYES AT SALVATORE PULEO'S COCKEREL CLUB ONE NIGHT RECENTLY, WITH A
GUY NAMED ANDERSON, ASSISTANT PRINCIPAL AT THE SCHOOL WHERE SHE WORKS.
MRS. BAYLIS WAS DOING SOME NEIGHBORHOOD SNOOPING THAT NIGHT AND SAW
WHITSON COME HOME. ANDERSON IS OUT OF TOWN.

SEE WHAT YOU CAN DO. THE NEWSPAPERS ARE DRIVING US CRAZY.

LOVETT.

"Captain Lovett? Macomber speaking. Listen, Fred. About that memo you
sent over. Do I have free sailing on this job, or do I have to answer for my
methods? Good. Why sure, sure, it's open and shut. I'll have your killer before you can get a cell ready for him. 'Bye."

## 6. DETECTIVE MACOMBER

GOOD evening to *you*, madam. I am Detective Macomber, of the police
department. Is Miss Whitson at home? Good.

Ah, Miss Whitson! Delighted. The name is Macomber — Detective
Macomber. Perhaps Captain Lovett has mentioned my name. Now, if I may
have a word or two with you in private . . . . This is your room? Now if I may
just shut the door . . . . I beg your *pardon,* Mrs. Abbott, but privacy is essential
to one of my — er — profession. Really? But I assure you, dear Mrs. Ahbott, I
have no designs on the young lady. None at all. My dear Mrs. Abbott, I don't
give a damn what the rules of the house are! Miss Whitson and I are going to
talk behind a closed door! Go away, Mrs. Abbott. Sit down somewhere and
knit a sweater for some freezing Finn.

Now, Miss Whitson. Thank you, I will. Cigarette?

The purpose of my visit, Miss Whitson, is to acquaint you with a few new
developments in the murder of Mr. Paine, and to ask one or two rather pertinent questions. First, I must ask that none of this be repeated.

Thank you. I am sure of it.

Mr. Lee, Miss Whitson, has been found. He is at present in custody. He
insists, Miss Whitson, that he is not guilty of the murder of Mr. Paine.

You think he is lying? Perhaps he is. Let me tell you the story as he tells it.

On the night of the murder, Miss Whitson, Mr. Lee left the house sometime
between nine thirty and ten o'clock. He is not sure of the time, but he insists that

he was out of the house before anything happened. As a matter of fact, he swears that he knew nothing of the murder until he read about it in the newspaper.

A logical question, Miss Whitson. I expected it. If Mr. Lee departed before the murder, who *did* kill Paine? As I understand it, you and Lee and Paine were the only occupants of the house. Mrs. Abbott was across the street. So . . . if Lee went out before the murder, only you and Paine were left. And discarding the vague possibility that Paine killed himself . . . . You see, Miss Whitson, you're in rather a spot.

H'm. That *is* a poser. Of course, if I were an ordinary run-of-the-mill detective, I might suggest that you and Mr. Paine were in love, or something like that, and that you quarreled . . . but that would be a tabloid murder, Miss Whitson, and I am not a tabloid detective. Ah, no. We have a different motive here, I think. But first, about the engraving tool. You borrowed that from Mr. Lee's room, I suppose.

Oh, come now, Miss Whitson. Surely the time for stubborn denials is past. You must have borrowed the tool. I don't say you borrowed it with the intention of killing someone with it — but let's say you wanted to punch some holes in a sheet of paper with it. Shall we say that? No? Well, some other time, perhaps.

As for the murder itself, I believe it was quite impromptu. I'm going to sketch a picture of it for you.

Here you are, Miss Whitson, in this very room, working on some papers. I see you have a desk here. We'll assume, then, that you are sitting at the desk, with the lamp turned on and the rest of the room more or less in shadow. The house is very quiet. Mr. Lee has gone out. You are engrossed in your work.

Suddenly you hear a voice — the voice of — now wait a moment, Miss Whitson. Let me continue, please! The voice you hear is not that of Mr. Paine. Oh, no. It is the voice of a woman who hates you, who has tormented you with sarcastic innuendoes ever since a certain night, not long ago, when she happened to see you come in drunk.

Perhaps she has done more than torment you, Miss Whitson. Perhaps she has threatened to write a letter to the school where you are employed. She knows, and you know, that such a letter would result not only in your dismissal, but in the dismissal of the young man with whom you got drunk that night. The assistant principal, I believe.

And now, suddenly, you hear the voice. Her voice. The voice of Mrs. Baylis. "So you despise people who get drunk, do you?" she says. "Well, well well. *You* wouldn't touch the stuff, would you now?"

What happens, Miss Whitson? You stiffen on your chair. This is more than you can bear. It is the last straw. You lurch to your feet as the door opens. You snatch up the first thing that comes handy and rush toward the person who stands there. You *think* you are striking Mrs. Baylis.

But when this unfortunate person stumbles back, his face twisted with agony, his hands clutching at the engraving tool which you have plunged into his breast, you realize your mistake. You have not killed Mrs. Baylis. No. You have slain poor old Mr. Paine, who was a positive whiz at imitating people, and who probably thought it would be a fine joke to announce himself in the voice of Mrs. Baylis, using certain words he had overheard on some previous occasion.

Well?

O.K., lady. Let's go. And by the way . . . that story of mine about Lee. A little white lie. We don't know *where* Lee is.

*The New Haydon Times,* **February 16**

## NOTES IN THE NIGHT
### By J. C. OWLE

THE BOARDING HOUSE MURDER OF ALVIN PAINE, PUT ON ICE TWO DAYS AGO WITH A FULL CONFESSION FROM THE GUILTY PARTY, SPAWNED A STRANGE AFTERMATH THIS FINE FEBRUARY AFTERNOON. MR. GEORGE ALDEN LEE, NEW CLAIMANT TO THE TITLE OF VANISHING AMERICAN, HAS BEEN FOUND!

"FOUND" IS HARDLY THE WORD, AT THAT. WHAT MR. GEORGE ALDEN LEE DID WAS "EMERGE" — EVEN AS THE GROUNDHOG.

IT APPEARS THAT MR. GEORGE ALDEN LEE TAKES HIS ANNUAL VACATION IN WINTER, BECAUSE, BEING A FLORIDIAN BY BIRTH, MR. LEE FINDS OUR NEW ENGLAND WINTERS JUST TOO, TOO ARDUOUS. AND MR. LEE, WHEN HE VACATIONS, TAKES A PAGE FROM THE BOOK OF THE GROUNDHOG.

MR. LEE HIBERNATES. HE HIBERNATES WITH A QUANTITY OF FESTIVE BEVERAGES SUFFICIENT TO LAST HIM A FULL TWO WEEKS. IN A COMFORTABLE LITTLE CAMP ON HIDDEN LAKE, LESS THAN EIGHT MILES FROM THE HEART OF DOWNTOWN NEW HAYDON, MR. LEE SECLUDES HIMSELF FROM TELEPHONES, RADIOS, AND ALL THE SORDID TROUBLES OF THE WORLD WITHOUT.

THIS AFTERNOON MR. LEE EMPTIED HIS LAST BOTTLE, CLOSED THE DOOR OF HIS SANCTUARY BEHIND HIM, STEPPED INTO HIS CAR AND DROVE TO TOWN. HE WAS SLIGHTLY BEWILDERED BY HIS RECEPTION.

"ME, A MURDERER?" MR. LEE GASPED. "WELL, GOOD GOSH, I DIDN'T THINK I WAS *THAT* DRUNK!"

AIN'T MURDER WONDERFUL?

• • • • •

# FRONT-PAGE FRAME-UP

THIS STORY, PUBLISHED IN THE FEBRUARY 1941 *BLACK MASK*, IS TOLD IN THE FIRST PERSON, IN A SOMETIMES HUMOROUS FASHION, BY DETECTIVE JEFF CARDIN. I SEEM TO REMEMBER THAT I WROTE SEVERAL STORIES ABOUT JEFF CARDIN, AND HE WAS A POPULAR CHARACTER WITH PULP-TALE READERS. THIS COULD BE ONE OF THE BETTER STORIES IN THE BOOK YOU ARE NOW READING. HERE'S HOPING.

HBC

*The lecher and the lady — that was the way the papers and the public regarded Jeff Cardin and the Anderson girl. The mere fact that it was the other way around — that she happened to be a tart and he a gentleman didn't cut any ice with the cops who needed a fall-guy to preserve their "untarnished reputation."*

## CHAPTER ONE
### A Matter of Morals

IN CASE you are one of those who saw my name and picture in the papers about two months ago, and sadistically added your scornful voice to the weight of public opinion that put the skids under me, let me put you straight on a thing or two.

First of all, I'm not lecherous. That was a word applied to me in the *Tribune*, by some hop-head who probably came across it while thumbing the pages of a dictionary. I can't be called a respectable married man, I'll admit, because I'm not and never have been married. But unless I'm a somnambulist and do strange things in my sleep, I've never, to my knowledge, gone out of my way to make passes at young ladies on street corners.

They know this down at Headquarters. The commissioner knows it, too. But what they know and what they have to do to please the public — meaning you and you and you — are two different things.

The truth is, I was driving to Bayview at the time, to have another talk with Jerry Simms, the smart young Bayview cop who first smelled the stench of this blackmail business. Jerry had phoned to say he had uncovered still another victim of the squeeze, and if I'd come up there he would introduce me to the fellow — a break for me, it seemed, because after six weeks of tiresome plugging on the case I had got practically nowhere.

It was a nasty night. The roads were still lumpy and treacherous with the remains of last week's blizzard, and the rain was so heavy you couldn't see ten feet in front of the windshield.

So when the girl flagged me, just this side of the state line, I stopped to give her a lift.

Maybe that's being lecherous. I wouldn't know. All I know is that the poor kid looked drenched and frozen, and she thumbed me for a lift, and on that kind of night I'd have gone out of my way to pick up Frankenstein's monster.

She climbed into the car and I asked her where she was going. Bayview, she said, when her teeth stopped chattering We talked about the weather, as one does, and I guessed she was about nineteen or twenty — a sweet young thing and probably pretty, though for all I could see, under the enormous coat she was wearing she might be as fat as your Aunt Emma.

About half a mile over the state line, when we stopped for a red light at the Four Corners, she staged her act.

It stunned me, and I'm a city dick who has seen a lot of phoney business in my day. There we were, waiting for the light to turn green. A rotary traffic circle confronted us, and on both sides of us were big gas stations, brilliantly lit-up in the downpour. And she began screaming.

She turned on me like a crazy person and began clawing at me. .She had nails for clawing, too. They raked my face and drew blood, ripped my collar, damn near tore my tie off, and pulled a couple of buttons off my coat.

She got the door open, hut she didn't get out right away — she kept clawing at me, and screaming for help.

That sort of thing would draw attention anywhere, and my sweet companion had picked a spot where there was an abundance of attention handy. A couple of fellows tore over from the nearest gas station, just as she shoved herself clear of me and sprawled out over the running-board. They laid hold of me.

You know the rest, if you read the papers: *Cardin fought viciously to escape* — Get that? To "escape" — *but was overpowered by men who rushed to the young woman's assistance. The girl herself managed to stumble across the highway to a gasoline station, where she hysterically sobbed out her story of what had happened.*

Her story. It was a beauty. I, Jeff Cardin, had offered her a ride to Bayview, and though she was not the sort of girl to accept such offers from strangers, she had welcomed the offer this time because of the weather. She had been on her way to visit friends in Bayview, and I had — looked like a decent, respectable sort of man — and so forth.

Probably I had been drinking. At any rate, after leading off with a most embarrassing line of talk, I had attempted to force my attentions upon her, and when repulsed had grown violently angry. Then I had assaulted her.

She didn't endeavor to explain why I had picked the Four Corners, of all places, to do my assaulting. That was a minor point that Percy P. Public, meaning you and you and you, overlooked. You were more interested in devouring the descriptions of her disheveled clothing, and of how Jeff Cardin, The Beast, was given a thorough going-over by the lads from the gas station, which served him right.

A ND NO DOUBT you thought her little speech to the police a generous and beautiful thing when she said angelically: "I do not wish to take this man into court and be the means of costing him his job. No doubt he had been drinking and was not himself. He has learned his lesson. I want to drop the whole thing and forget it."

Nice of her.

But if any of you had taken the trouble to go deeper into the matter — to check, for instance, on the young lady's name — you might have shouted less vehemently for Jeff Cardin's hide. Mary Anderson, she said her name was. From out of town, way out of town — Wheeling, West Virginia. Living in a respectable rooming-house on Norton Street, and looking for a job.

We checked all that, and it was phoney. No Mary Anderson had ever been known at the Wheeling address she gave us. And as for the Norton Street rooming-house, she had resided there just four days, and was listed among the alumni when a couple of the boys went down, the day after the fracas, to ask her a few more pertinent questions.

In short, she pulled her little stunt and then flew the coop. But public indignation is a peculiar thing. Once aroused, it goes thundering along like a steamroller, and is as difficult to stop as a bull elephant with a bad temper.

Most of you didn't read the follow-ups in the papers. Most of the papers, for that matter, didn't lean very far over backward to print them, there being sensational war news on the front pages at the time. So, with an ear to the ground and an eye on the political horizon, the commissioner sent for me.

A fine man, the commissioner. Oh yes. The papers tell you so, and the papers never play politics. Oh my, no! We should all be thankful for having such an upright man at the head of our police department.

He fired a cigar and folded his hands over the balloon he calls a stomach. He cleared his throat. "Er — Cardin," he said to me.

"Yes, sir," I said.

"Er — about this business in the papers, Cardin. They've made a lot of it. It's ridiculous, of course. We on the inside know that the whole thing was a put-up job. But — er — public opinion has to be handled with kid gloves, Cardin."

I said: "I'm going to get that girl, commissioner, and when the papers print my picture again, the musical accompaniment will be in a different key."

He cleared his throat. "Er — quite right, Cardin. Quite right, of course. But for the present — that is to say — you know, with elections in the offing — I suggest a short vacation."

I said: "The quickest way to get rid of a bad smell, commissioner, is to throw open the windows. I don't want any vacation. I want to clear this up."

"Later, Cardin," he said.

"But it's my reputation you're sending on a vacation! I've been a dick for ten years, commissioner. My rep is clean. I can't let this thing drag on!"

"I'm sorry, Cardin," he said, frowning at his cigar, "but I advise a vacation." He cleared his throat for the third time. "The — er — the papers will call it a suspension, of course, but we on the inside will know what it really is, and that's all that matters. I know best, Cardin."

"This," I said, "is final?"

"That's right, Cardin."

"Well," I said, on my feet and glaring at him, my temper climbing like the mercury in a hot thermometer, "it isn't. You're not throwing Jeff Cardin to the wolves, not for politics or any other cheap reason!"

"Now, now, Cardin," he said. "There are times when —"

"There are times when the stink in this department is more than a decent man can stand!" I snarled. "My resignation goes into effect right now. Goodday to you, commissioner, and to hell with you!"

I walked out.

They didn't call it a resignation in the papers. They informed the general public, meaning you and you, that Detective Cardin had been relieved of further duty with the police department. The commissioner, sore with me, spread a layer of smelly ointment to the effect that the department must at all cost be kept free of any smudge of suspicion. "We have one of the finest police departments in the world," he wrote. "Nothing ever has tarnished, or ever will be permitted to tarnish, its splendid reputation."

"It serves him right, the heel," said you and you and you.

Now you know the truth.

I DIDN'T expect any business, except perhaps some shady business, until the hue and cry died down. The thought occurred to me that maybe I should change the name, shedding my now odorous reputation along with it, but something else in me rebelled, and I'd be damned if I would.

So there it was on the door of my dingy office on the eighth floor of the Baker Building — *JEFF CARDIN, INVESTIGATIONS*. And there I was, cooling my heels and nursing my hate.

With only a paltry hundred dollars to my name, I couldn't very well go combing the country for Mary Anderson, much as I wanted to, and I'd already exhausted all local leads that pointed even a flimsy finger in her direction. So that would have to wait.

My first visitor was a charming little old lady who wanted to know if this was the eighth floor or the ninth. I told her it was the eighth. She looked annoyed and asked where the stairs were. I walked her down to the elevators, put her on a car, received a nice "Thank you, young man," for my trouble and went back to my brooding.

My second was a loud-mouthed egg peddling something. He stayed twelve seconds.

My third, fourth, fifth and sixth were the same.

My seventh — a client.

He was a good-looking chap, well-dressed, perfectly at ease. I thought he was a college boy until he sat down and gave me a chance to look at his face — then I saw that he was older. Not much older, but older. His name, he said matter-of-factly, was Standish. Edgar Standish. "I've not stolen anything or murdered anyone, " he said with a pleasant smile, "so I don't suppose you've heard of me, Lieutenant."

I said darkly: "Why the 'Lieutenant'?"

"You are, aren't you?"

"I was."

"I don't believe all I read in the papers," he shrugged. "If I did, I wouldn't be here."

I sort of liked him.

"As a matter of fact," he said, "if I believed that hokum about your lecherous nature, I'd be the last man in the world to come here. Because, you see, I want you to take care of a young lady for me. At least, to keep an eye on her."

So it was one of those things. But it wasn't.

"I live out of town a little distance," he said, "in Green Hill. I'm married — have a youngster, in fact — and the young lady in question, Miss Grace Marvin, is a guest of ours. Not a very willing guest, I'm afraid," he added, shaking his head.

I paid attention.

"She has been ill, Lieutenant, and is mentally not just right. Encephalitis sometimes does that, you know — leaves the patient somewhat unbalanced. Miss Marvin isn't at all dangerous, you understand. In fact, most of the time she is quite normal. But at times she suffers from the delusion that she's being held prisoner."

"Is she?" I asked.

"Frankly, yes, until her doctor feels safe in giving her free rein. The situation is somewhat peculiar, in that the girl's folks are in Europe somewhere, and she must either stay with us or go to a nursing-home. Doctor Truett is convinced that the atmosphere of a nursing-home would do her more harm than good. We like her and want to do all we can to help her, but frankly, Lieutenant, she's quite a problem."

"And you want me to play watchdog?"

"That's right."

"For how long?"

"As long as necessary. When the girl's parents return, she can go to them, of course. But so far we've had no luck in trying to make contact with them. This war, you know."

"Well," I said, matching his frankness with some of my own, "I could use the job."

H E SEEMED pleased and grateful, gave me a check for one hundred dollars and said he would stop at my apartment, on his way home from work, to pick me up. When he'd gone, I went down to the third floor, to the office of the building-superintendent, and paid my rent.

I had plenty of time that afternoon to look up the past and present of my client, but the job was not an easy one The Green Hill directory, or rather the directory of the town of Greenwood, of which Green Hill is a handsome suburb, listed him as a home-owner, all right, and from the same source I learned that his wife's name was Caroline.

The telephone book listed both a home and office phone, the former in Green Hill, which checked, and the latter at 32 Waverley Building, downtown. He was an architect.

If you know a man's profession and are trained in the business of snooping, you can generally get a pretty good line on him. The line on Edgar Standish made him thirty-four years old, a graduate of M. I. T. and the son of a former Tech professor. It's nice to know these things.

I was ready at five fifteen and he was there on the dot. We drove out to Green Hill.

He had quite a place, even for Green Hill. The road climbed a bluff and Standish's house was at the top of it, overlooking the colony of expensive residences on one side, the bay on the other. The air was different out here. There was a stiff, clean breeze that appeared to be permanently a part of the location. The sea looked cold and gray, and the cliff fell into it with an abruptness calculated to make timid men steer clear of the brink. The house itself was a modern affair surrounded by lawn and gardens.

He introduced me to his wife, and I was impressed. My opinion of the other sex had been lower than the commissioner's conscience since my set-to with Miss Mary Anderson, but now it took an upward turn. Caroline Standish gave me an honest hand and hoped I would make myself quite at home. "I'm afraid," she said with a smile, "you'll just have to make yourself one of the family. We have no servants except Mrs. Meade, the housekeeper, and it's every man for himself down here."

She was slim and pretty, with honest blue eyes. I liked her.

Standish himself toted my bag upstairs and showed me my room, and while I was wrestling into a clean shirt a little while later, I heard the youngster cutting up. He came tearing up the stairs, charged into my room, stared at me and said: "Hi!" A cute little guy about four years old, with his mother's blond hair.

"Hi, yourself," I said.

He said: "You're an old friend of Daddy's, aren't you? You're going to live with us for a while?"

"That's right."

"We'll have lots of fun," he declared.

He was right — but not the way he meant.

## CHAPTER TWO
### Footfalls After Midnight

A T DINNER I met Mrs. Meade, a comfortably plump woman on the verge of fifty, and was introduced to the strange cause of my being there — Grace Marvin.

She surprised me. Friends of genteel people are usually genteel themselves, and this girl wasn't, or at least didn't give that impression. She wore bright yellow slacks and a form-fitting sweater. Her mouth was reddened to look larger and more sensual than it was, her thick black hair was rakishly drawn back and bound with a red handkerchief, and the shadows that made her eyes so dark and wistful were as phoney as bootleg bond.

Standish introduced me as a very old friend of his, and the girl cooed: "How very nice!" That kind of goo, from her, was like *Traumerei* from a danceband fiddle.

I pigeonholed these first impressions, though, for future study and alterations. First impressions can be treacherous.

We spent a quiet evening, played bridge for a while and quit to listen to a symphony concert on the radio. I like that sort of thing myself. Maybe it's old age creeping in, but my fondness for jazz went winging when the boogie-woogie boys began to slug out the sub-dominants. Miss Marvin, however, was plainly bored.

"Give me," she said, "Benny Goodman any time."

She excused herself with a yawn and went up to bed, giving the Standishes a chance to talk to me.

"Well," Edgar said, "what do you think of her?"

"Seems perfectly normal to me," I declared.

"She is, tonight. That doesn't mean she will be an hour from now." He gave me a peculiar stare. "I'm afraid you won't get much sleep around here, Lieutenant."

"You mean she prowls at night?"

"We never know when she'll act up. That's what makes it so difficult."

I shrugged. "It won't be the first time I've survived on cat-naps. Ten years of being a cop, and you're —" I didn't finish it. It wasn't important anyway. What was important was a furtive footfall over my head.

I looked up. The room above that end of the living-room was the bedchamber assigned to me. I got out of my chair and toed into the hall, stopped with one hand on the stair-rail.

It was dark up there. I shed my shoes and went up as quietly as was humanly possible. They were good stairs and they didn't creak, which is something when a man weighs close to two hundred pounds.

The door of my room was closed. I'd closed it myself, before going down to dinner. I steadied myself outside it, listening for more of those furtive footfalls. I put a hand on the knob, turned it slowly and straight-armed the door open.

A voice in the darkness of the corridor, not ten feet from me, lifted me out of my socks by saying sweetly: "You don't have to be *that* quiet, Lieutenant. He's awake anyway."

There she was, just her face and hands visible in the dark. I blinked at her, feeling like a ten-year-old caught in the act of swiping cookies. I fumbled the light on and she came toward me from the door of the youngster's room, those too-red lips mocking me with a smile.

She was quite a girl in that snaky black negligee. Quite a girl.

"I thought he was crying," she said, "but he isn't. Just gurgling to himself." The odor of her perfume hung like a mist in the hall as she glided by me. "Good night, Lieutenant."

I closed my door. Maybe she had come down the hall to investigate sounds from the youngster's room. The youngster's room was not over the living-room though. I looked around.

There was nothing much she could have snooped through, except my suit-case. I'd unpacked a toothbrush, a few odds and ends and a clean shirt, nothing else. But the perfume gave her away.

Dumb of her, I thought. Even if I'd stayed downstairs until midnight, that heady smell would have-tipped me off. It was strongest near the bureau, but I hadn't stored anything in the bureau yet.

I pulled the drawers out. They were empty.

Just snooping, I figured. Just trying to get a line on me. I went downstairs again, put my shoes back on and walked into the living-room. Standish gave me a questioning stare.

"She was in my room, " I said, "prowling."

He sighed, shaking his head. "I hope this isn't going to be one of her nights, Lieutenant."

"You think I ought to be up there, keeping a weather-eye open?"

"I don't like the signs," he said.

I said good-night to both of them and went upstairs. This time I left my door open, figuring that if Grace the Goofy took a notion to do any more prowling, she might hesitate before passing my doorway on her way to the stairs. That, at least, would restrict her range to the corridor.

I went to bed.

It was about one thirty by my watch when I heard the door open at her end of the hall. I had been dozing but not sleeping and with the house quiet as a tomb, the click of the door sounded like a pistol-shot. Then I heard footsteps.

S HE MUST BE partially deaf, I told myself, or she would know that she was making a lot of noise. Her idea of stealth was to scuff along, stirring up little whispers with her feet. I slipped out of bed, toed over to the door and looked through the crack.

She stopped when she saw my door was open. Stopped and stared straight at me, and I wondered if she could see the whites of my eyes. Then she began to back up.

The footsteps receded. I heard the door of her room click shut. For about five minutes the house was a tomb again. Then I heard a window open.

I crossed the room and opened my own window, making a lot less noise than she had — but then, windows are temperamental things, no two alike. A cold, steady breeze swept in off the Atlantic, toying with the curtains. A cloud thinned to let the moon through, and for a moment the house and grounds were touched with silver.

She threw a rope out of her window first. As it fell, it uncoiled like one of those rolls of colored paper you throw at New Year's Eve parties. I heard it smack the ground. Then I saw a shapely leg emerge, and another. She slid down that rope like a born athlete, pedaling the wall with her feet.

At the bottom she hesitated, furtively looked around her but did not look up. Her hair streamed out in the wind and with a quick flip of her hand she snapped it out of her eyes. Then she prowled across the lawn.

There was a bird-house over near the high stone wall that bordered Standish's property — a cute little replica of the house itself, set on a pyramid of metal balls. That was her destination. From the folds of her negligee, she whipped out an envelope, or something that looked like an envelope, and jabbed it into the birdies' doorway. Then she ran back to the rope and went up it like a deepwater man climbing the shrouds of a windjammer.

Quite an athlete, that young lady! But not smart enough to glance even once at the window of my room and realize she was being watched.

The rope snaked up and out of sight, slap-slapping the side of the house as the wind played with it. She closed her window. The silence came back. I closed my window, drew on a pair of trousers over my pajamas and slipped into the hall.

I went downstairs and out, but the expanse of lawn between the house and and the birdies' domicile was too open for comfort. In a crouch I followed the outer face of the stone wall — then I waited a full ten minutes, plagued by the wind, for a cloud to smudge the moon.

When that happened, I went over the wall, snatched the envelope out of the bird-house and ducked back again.

That was quite a letter. With my door closed and the dim light over the bed turned on, I studied it and wondered which of us was crazy:

> He is here, and there are three moons tonight. I sing your hated song in my sleep and the beat is one-two-one-two-four-two. Never mind Hamlet. Three mornings from tomorrow the crow will croak again, despite him and his soliloquy. Nothing happens till then. Be careful, all of you. He is no fool.

I ask you. I ask you twice — how could there be any sense to prattle like that?

I read the thing through at least a dozen times. I applied to it all I know about ciphers, trick codes and hieroglyphic acrobatics, which is considerable.

I even culled from my memory the major portion of Hamlet's soliloquy. And got nowhere.

There was one thing I could do, though, and I did it. With a clean sheet of paper and a fountain-pen I sat down and wrote a letter of my own, aping the girl's hand to the best of my ability. It read:

> Meet me at the foot of the cliff, tomorrow midnight. Important.

This I sealed in the envelope — then I made another trip to the manor of our feathered friends and left it there for collection.

*Someone* was supposed to call around for that letter, I figured. You don't write mysterious missives and sneak them into bird-houses just for exercise, or to annoy the birdies.

So when I got back to my room I pulled a chair close to the window, parked myself and prepared to wait for development number two.

I had it doped out this way. He — or she — would arrive sometime before daylight, gather up my substitute letter and read it. Unless it lacked some secret identifying line or phrase, the handwriting was sufficiently like Grace Marvin's to pass inspection.

Tomorrow night at midnight, then, this person would journey to the foot of the cliff, as requested, and from what I'd seen of the bottom of the cliff, it was a mighty difficult place from which to exit in a hurry.

When I pounced out of hiding at midnight tomorrow night, I'd catch my mouse. If I tried it tonight, I might miss and scare the mouse into permanent hiding.

Moreover, the intervening hours would give me a chance to work on Miss Marvin's letter.

So I sat by the window and waited.

And waited.

And nothing came but the dawn.

It was a miserable dawn, in more ways than one. A sticky fog rolled in off the Atlantic. The fog turned to a slow, dreary, drizzling rain. Thoroughly disgusted, I shed my pajamas, got dressed and went down to breakfast in a black mood.

THAT WAS NOT a very cheerful breakfast. Mrs. Meade, the housekeeper, had a long face and wore an expression you could have used in the making of quince jam. This sort of weather, she explained, brought on her rheumatism.

Caroline Standish was put out because she had planned on a trip to the city but couldn't go. "With Mrs. Meade feeling so miserable," she said, "somehow I don't like to leave her in charge of Junior."

Edgar Standish offered no explanation of his misery, but his eyes told a story. His eyes said he'd been drinking and was deep in the toils of a hangover. I wondered about that. He hadn't done any drinking before going to bed last night — so when?

The object of my professional attentions, Miss Marvin, didn't show up for breakfast at all. I was told that she frequently didn't. "Doctor Truett told us," Caroline said, "to let her sleep as long as she wished. She often sleeps until noon."

I thought it might be a good idea to go out and remove my letter from the bird-house. No one, in broad daylight, was going to hop the wall to collect it, and Miss Marvin might just take a notion to go exploring.

"While she's asleep," I announced, "I believe I'll go for a walk. I need a bit of exercise."

Edgar lent me his raincoat, and off I went.

The envelope was still in the birdhouse. I slipped it into my pocket, feeling somewhat ashamed of myself, and then I saw the footprints. That is to say, shoe-prints.

The grass was worn pretty thin in the immediate neighborhood of the birdhouse, and in patches of dark bare ground the prints were plainly visible. My own, some of them. My own where I'd jumped the wall, prowled over to the home of our feathered friends and prowled back again. The others were hers.

They were sneaker-prints, and I distinctly recalled that she had worn sneakers.

Here was proof, anyway, that she had put that goofy missive in the birdhouse, and that I, Jefferson Cardin, had not merely dreamed it up out of a nightmare.

I went for a walk.

It was a nice place Mr. Edgar Standish had. Being an architect, he had probably designed it himself, and while I have no particular fondness for so much ocean, with its clammy rains and fogs, I had to admit the joint was no dump.

What stopped me, and stumped me, was a sudden discovery of more of those sneaker prints.

They were on the sheltered side of the house, where the sweep of the rain had not yet been able to blur them. They ran from a very cute little doorway under what I suppose you'd call a sun-deck, to a gate about sixty feet distant — and back again. I don't mean in a straight, unbroken line, mind you, like footprints in snow — but they were there for the finding.

I snooped around the gate. The road ran past it. There was no sidewalk other than a strip of bare ground, now soggy, between the road and Edgar Standish's stone wall.

She had leaned on that gate for some time. No deerslayer instincts were needed for the observance of that little fact, since the marks of her sneakers were deep and definite. Furthermore, she'd been conversing with someone of the opposite sex. *His* shoe-prints were now half-filled with rain.

I wondered about that goofy letter. I wondered about me, and did some mumbling.

The cute little door under the sun-deck was unlocked. I opened it and went snooping. The snooping took me through Standish's study, which he democratically called a workshop, into the main entrance hall.

The door-chimes were ringing. Caroline Standish came down the stairs without seeing me, opened the front door and said, "Why, how do you do, Doctor Truett!"

Just for something else to do, I'd been wondering about him, too.

He was a short, stubby male with a paunch. He had a round, red face with a bristle of mustache, and you guessed, looking at him, that when he removed his hat he would have more hair than a man his age ought to have.

He removed his hat and had it.

"Nasty weather, Mrs. Standish," he said. His voice was a bedside caress, and the smile that accompanied it was as mechanical as Charlie McCarthy's. "Miss Marvin is expecting me, I hope."

"She's in her room, Doctor. I'll call her."

"Excellent. And — er — Mrs. Standish."

"Yes, Doctor?"

"I think it might be better if I saw her privately."

"Certainly, Doctor."

Mrs. Standish went upstairs. The good doctor shed his raincoat, draped it carefully over the hand-rail and sighed prodigiously, as though that, in itself, were a day's work accomplished. He adjusted his sleeves, his lapels and his tie with grave deliberation, as though about to wade into a major operation.

I wondered how far off the floor he would jump if I coughed to advertise my presence.

I didn't cough.

Dr. Truett walked into the living-room and passed out of my line of vision.

I STEPPED OUT of hiding and edged closer, hoping for better luck. At that moment Mrs. Standish came down the stairs with Junior.

"Hi, there!" Junior yipped.

"We're going to have our morning study period," Caroline informed me with a smile.

"Mr. Cardin," the youngster shrilled, "was listening at the keyhole. That isn't polite, is it, mother?"

"Hush, Junior!"

"But it *isn't*, is it?"

The S. P. C. C. could have prosecuted me for my thoughts, at that instant, and won a unanimous verdict of guilty. I tried to laugh it off. "Matter of fact," I said lamely, with a grin equally lame, "I was pulling up my socks. When you grow up, Junior, always wear garters and keep out of trouble." Something told me that Dr. Truett and Miss Grace Marvin were listening to every word.

With a feeble grin at Caroline, I went up the stairs and slunk into my room. Maybe, with an ear to the floor, I'd be able to accomplish my purpose.

It didn't work. Either Grace or Dr. Truett was smart enough to turn on the radio down there. All I got for my backache was the hundred-and-eighth instalment *of Dolly Dawson's Diary* and a lecture on the unsurpassed qualities of Snappy Soap Suds, after which Mrs. Meade burst into the room with some clean bed-linen draped over her arm.

She evidently thought it somewhat strange for a grown man to be down on his hands and knees, smelling the floor. I told her I'd lost a quarter. She said that was too bad. I said it didn't matter, and slunk out.

For a sleuth with ten years of experience, I was doing fine. Still, with Grace Marvin out of her room, Caroline busy with Junior downstairs and Mrs. Meade in the throes of bed-making, here was an opportunity not to be sneered at.

I slipped into Grace Marvin's room, shut the door behind me and went exploring.

There should have been something of importance in that room. By all rights and logic, after all I'd been through, there should have been something to clear up at least one of the mysteries that were crawling around this place.

If there was, I overlooked it. Or did I? For after snooping in vain through a closet full of clothes, opening in vain a couple of suitcases that proved to be empty, and poking in vain through an assortment of junk in and on the vanity — if that's what you call those ultrafeminine bureaus — I found a scarf.

It was a soft, silky thing with more colors than the map of Europe. It smelled, but the perfume of which it smelled was not a perfume heretofore encountered by the Cardin nostrils — at least, not in this household.

I worried about that scarf. It plagued me. I would have wagered my hundred-dollar retainer that I'd seen it before, or seen one exactly like it. But my brain, if any, was cluttered up with so many other things.

I slipped out of the room and went quietly down the hall. Mrs. Meade was pushing a broom in my room, in a manner that indicated she hoped to find my mythical quarter. The radio was still churning in the living-room. With no other place to go, I eased into Edgar Standish's study and sat to do some thinking.

The good doctor departed half an hour later, shutting the door with what appeared to be more noise than was necessary. Grace Marvin went upstairs.

About an hour later the rain stopped, and about an hour after that, Edgar arrived home.

We sat and talked. I didn't show him the goofy letter. I didn't tell him what a remarkable athlete Miss Marvin had turned out to be. He said: "I'm afraid, Lieutenant, for a man of your experience this is a rather boring iob."

And I said: "Well, it has possibilities."

He said: "Selfishly speaking, I hope it hasn't."

"How long have you known Miss Marvin?" I asked.

"Years."

"And Doctor Truett?"

"Went to school with him."

"I'd like to make a little experiment this evening," I said. "Are you game?"

"I don't understand."

"Miss Marvin is up to something. I saw signs of it last night, heard her prowling around. She saw me and gave it up, whatever it was, but if we could find out what's on her mind, it might save us some headaches. An ounce of prevention, you know."

"What do you want me to do?"

"I'll tell you. Miss Marvin seems to think —"

The phone rang. We were both sitting within arm's reach of it, there in the study. Standish picked it up. I walked to a window.

"Why — hello," he said. "Evidently I just missed —"

I couldn't hear the voice in the receiver. I did, however, sneak a look at Standish, and saw that his face wore a scowl as he listened. Presently he said: "It was an absolute necessity. I'm perfectly willing to do all I can for her — I've told you that — but good Lord, man, it's been damned awkward around here for both Caroline and myself, and there's the youngster to consider. I felt that we needed some sort of protection . . . What's that? . . . I know you did . . . ."

His fingers beat out a nervous rhythm on the desk as he listened. He was breathing hard, and I had an idea that he was not entirely happy about this particular phone call.

Finally he said with some force: "I'm sorry, Frank, but he stays. I've got to consider Caroline and the boy and — well, he stays. That's final."

He hung up, stared sullenly at his fingernails for a moment and said under his breath: "No matter how decent you try to be —" Then he exhaled noisily, looked up and said with a mechanical smile: "Well, Cardin? This scheme of yours?"

I explained it, being extremely careful in explaining my reasons for suggesting it.

"It sounds fantastic," he said.

I shrugged and said: "Maybe it is." But I didn't think it was fantastic. I thought it would work.

## CHAPTER THREE
### Mr. Smith of Flodin Street

T HAT WAS A beautiful night — damn it! The rain and the fog had dissappeared entirely, and the sky was so full of moon and stars that it looked like the ceiling of a planetarium. About nine o'clock I snared a symphony concert out of the maze of junk on the radio, and Miss Marvin rewarded me by yawning, rising, and saying: "Well, if we must have our culture, I'd much rather take mine in bed."

She went upstairs. I glanced at Standish and he said with a dubious shake of his head: "Well, all right, Cardin, but I think it's fantastic."

He really looked a lot like me when he put my coat and hat on. My clothes always look a lot like me, which is no compliment to my tailor. Standish turned the coat collar up and the hat brim down, shoved his hands into his pockets and hunched his shoulders to give them the Cardin slouch, and I nodded my approval.

"I give you fair warning," he said, "a little of this sort of thing goes a long way with me. If nothing happens in an hour or so, to the devil with it!"

That was a chance I'd have to take — that it might not happen before he grew disgusted. The rub was, it might not happen at all. It might have happened last night.

He went out, and I watched him from the living-room window. Caroline, reading a book, frowned at me and said: "What in the world are you two up to?"

"An experiment, Mrs. Standish."

Good girl — she let it go at that and went back to her reading.

Standish played his part well. He left by the front door, circled wide to the other side of the street and walked along in a lane of shadow provided by a row of poplars. He let himself be seen, but furtively, and when he stationed himself at the far end of the wall, near the bird-house, he was visible but you'd have sworn he meant to be otherwise.

Satisfied, I went quietly down the hall, out the cute little door under the sun-deck, and stationed *myself* on my stomach, near a stone bench close to the gate, where I couldn't be seen from the house or the road.

Then I waited.

It just might work, I hopefully told myself. Unless all my deductions were faulty, Miss Marvin had duped me with a set-up very similar to this, last night. That goofy letter in the bird-house had glued me to the window of my room, enabling her to slip out for a meeting with her boy-friend, here at the gate.

He had come once — he might come again.

He did.

I heard him before I saw him. That is, I heard the car. The air was so still, the night so quiet, that the sound of the motor was plainly audible. The car climbed the hill and stopped, before the glow of its headlights turned the corner.

That was a dead give-away. This was not the season for outdoor spooning, and any machine climbing the hill could have only one destination — the home of Edgar Standish. Sure enough, the fellow emerged from the shadows a few minutes later, on foot, and furtively approached the gate.

The little door under the sun-deck opened, and out came Grace Marvin in a hurry.

They met at the gate and began talking. It was a sin and a shame, the way I eavesdropped.

"It's no damn use," the fellow said.

"She won't come back. Says this town is too hot for her."

"She's got to come back! She's got to! I need those letters!"

"You know Josie," the fellow said, shrugging. "Nothing short of dynamite can change her mind, once she gets it made up. You'll get the letters, though. She —"

"I tell you I've *got* to have them! Some of them, anyway — to show him I'm not bluffing. He's no fool, Nick. He can't be bluffed forever. You don't seem to realize what I'm up against in this place."

"You'll get the letters," he said. "She's mailing them. I'll bring them out tomorrow. Is he seeing you tomorrow?"

"I don't know. He as much as told me he was through fooling around. I'm scared, Nick. Those damned letters!"

"Keep your chin up."

"You'll come again tomorrow, sure?"

"I'll be there."

She kissed him. It wasn't much of a kiss, just a quick, desperate peck, aimed haphazardly at his face. Then she turned and ran back to the house.

The fellow faded into the shadows.

The rest of it was easy. I knew just about where his car was parked, from listening to the sound of its approach. I cut around the house, over the stone wall, and got there before he did. When he opened the door I stepped up behind him from the rear of the car and nudged him with a gun.

He all but screamed.

"Get in, brother," I said, "and we'll go for a ride."

H E WAS A big fellow, with long, beefy legs to balance an oversized head. First impressions are generally worthless, but he looked like a college athlete with about three years of professional wrestling under his belt. Battle-scarred, I mean, but not old. Hardened but not hard.

I frisked him and acquired a .45 that looked as battle-scarred as he did. Also, and more important, I acuired a couple of letters.

"What's your name?" I asked him.

Not exactly frightened he glared at me and countered with: "What's yours?"

I had an idea he knew my name, and that it might be some time before I learned his. We were wasting time. "We'll stop at my apartment," I told him. "Try any tricks and you'll arrive there feet-first."

Nothing much else was said until we got there. He tried no tricks, and after pulling the car to the curb in front of my apartment, he got out without protest, preceded me up the stairs, and entered my humble suite of rooms, without balking.

I waved him to the divan, took a pair of handcuffs out of the table drawer and tossed them to him. "Put them on," I ordered.

"You can't get away with this," he said. "You're not a cop any longer."

I laughed and said: "Neither are you."

He snapped the cuffs over his wrists. I produced a second pair and linked him to a floor-lamp, which would give him a heap of trouble if any bright notions happened to occur to him. Then I read those letters.

The first was in a ten-cent-store envelope. It was addressed to Mr. J. C. Smith, 10 Flodin Street, and was merely a typewritten note:

> THANKS FOR THE TIP, PAL. I HAD NO INTENTION OF SHOWING UP IN THAT HORNET'S NEST AGAIN, NOT AFTER JOSIE'S BRAINSTORM. LUCK TO YOU. SEE YOU WHEN I SEE YOU.

It was unsigned and bore no return address. The postmark was Chicago, dated a week ago.

"Who," I said, "is J. C. Smith?"

"I wouldn't know. I got the letter by mistake."

"Do tell," I said. "Is your name Smith, too?"

He hesitated, shrugged his shoulders. "Yeah. They put that in my post office box, by mistake. It's Greek to me."

"You never lived at 10 Flodin Street?"

"No."

I looked at the other letter. This one had been mailed yesterday, from Boston, and was addressed in feminine handwriting to Mr. Richard Andrews, P. O. Box — but no number — White Street Station, our city:

NICK:

I CAN'T COME BACK THERE. THE TOWN IS TOO HOT. I'LL MAIL YOU THE LETTERS
AND BE DAMNED GLAD TO GET RID OF THEM. MAYBE I DID GO TOO FAR WITH THAT
PESKY DICK BUT YOU'RE NO ONE TO TALK, NOT AFTER THE MESS YOU AND MARGE
DOVE INTO. GOOD LUCK TO THE TWO OF YOU, BUT COUNT ME OUT OF THIS. WAY OUT.

REGARDS,

JOSIE.

I stared at this letter for some time. It was more than just a letter — it was a
voice out of my past.

Remember my telling you about sweet Mary Anderson, who accused me
of conduct unbecoming an officer? Remember that scarf in Miss Marvin's
room? Ha!

Scowling at Mr. Smith, I said pointedly: "You're in a hell of a mess, aren't
you?"

"Am I?" he growled.

"You and Josie," I said, "who called herself Mary Anderson the time she
went riding with me out to the Four Corners."

He must have known the letter would tell me that much. All he did was
shrug his shoulders.

"You know," I said conversationally, "this is beginning to take an interesting shape. I didn't know what to make of it when Josie pulled that gag.
I had a hunch, of course, she was part of the blackmail business that I was
investigating, but it was only a hunch. Now we're really getting somewhere."

"Are we?"

I nodded. "You're quite a guy," I said. He really was. While living on Flodin
Street he had called himself Smith. At the White Street Post Office he was
known as Richard Andrews. Josie and Miss Marvin, whose other name was
Marge, called him Nick. Quite a guy.

"Just what," I asked him, "are these letters Miss Marvin is so anxious to
acquire?"

"That's for you to find out."

"More blackmail?"

"Look," he said. "I'm deaf and dumb."

"Must I work on you?"

"Go right ahead."

"I lose my temper real easy," I said.

"Lose it," he said. "You're no sap, Cardin. The law took away your license
to get rough. Kick me around and you'll pay for it." He smiled at the ceiling.

"For all you know, I may have a bum heart. One little poke might kill me. Then where would you be?"

He was smarter than he looked.

I THOUGHT it over. Apparently this lad was Grace Marvin's boy-friend. For all I knew, he might be married to her. Josie, the charming young lady who had skipped town after blackening my reputation, was evidently a friend of theirs, as was the author of the note from Chicago.

Judging from the tone of those two letters, the four of them had worked together until Josie's joust with the law had made the town too hot for them. Josie had fled to Boston. The other lad had skipped to Chicago. But Nick and Miss Marvin were still here and up to their necks in trouble.

The trouble involved some letters. These Josie had taken with her, much to Miss Marvin's apparent perturbation, when she hit the highroad. The letters were being sent to Nick by mail.

"You know what?" I said.

"What?"

"You're going to spend the night with me."

"Suits me," he said. "I sleep good anywhere."

"And in the morning," I informed him, "we're going down to the White Street Post Office, just you and I — just a couple of chums — to pick up those letters."

He shrugged.

That was a long, weary night. Twice, for the sheer hell of it, I waked him and told him for Pete's sake to stop snoring. By nine A.M. I resented him intensely.

We went down to White Street. The post office there is not exactly gigantic, neither is it a mere niche in the wall. One entire side of it was pigeonholed with boxes.

I kept a hand in my pocket, but the threat I held over Smith's head was not a threat of gun-play, and he knew it. What held him in line was the knowledge that if he made a break I'd grab him, yell my head off, and turn him over to the police.

I steered him toward the boxes and said gently: "Open it up, chum."

He drew back, staring.

"None of that," I said, putting a hand on his arm.

He fooled me. He began to shake. A look of concern widened his eyes.

"We're too late," he muttered. "That fat guy — he's a dick. He's at my box!"

I bit. The stout gentleman had his back to us and was down in a crouch, fumbling with the combination of a box on the lowest tier. I took a step toward him, for which even now I offer no apologies, and Nick slammed into me. , What it looked like to the few other customers, I don't know. I lost my feet and ploughed into the fat fellow face first, arms and legs flying, and we wound up on the floor like a pair of drunks wallowing in someone's gutter.

I didn't see Nick dive for the exit but he was gone when I got to my feet again, and a demure little lady with an armful of bundles was doing her best to restrain a giggle.

I felt foolish. The fat boy shot up like an erupting volcano and began sputtering at me. I tried to get past him to the door, but he climbed all over me, calling me names, demanding an explanation. By that time, Nick was no doubt half way to Little America.

I said petulantly to Fatso: "Who are you, anyway?"

Prepare yourself for a chuckle. He had a name six syllables long and played the piccolo in a symphony orchestra!

I got rid of him and walked over to General Delivery. Nick may have slipped through my fingers, but the letters hadn't — not yet, anyway — and I was still determined to possess them.

"The lad who pushed me," I said to the clerk, "is a phoney named Richard Andrews. That's just one of his names. He has a box here. I don't know the number, but I want what's in it!"

He frowned, shaking his head. "I'm sorry," he said, "but —"

"I'm a detective."

"You'd have to see the postmaster."

"What's the number of Andrews' box?"

He looked it up. "One seventeen," he said.

I looked through the little glass door of one seventeen, and the box was empty. I walked back to the window again. "Before I see the postmaster," I said, "find out if there's any mail for Andrews, will you? There should be a package. If there isn't, I'm wasting my time here."

He was a good egg. He spent ten minutes prowling around, but was shaking his head when he came back. "Not a thing."

So she hadn't mailed the letters after all, and I had sat up all night, listening to Nick's snores, for nothing.

Sore as a bunion, I hiked across the street to Nick's car, which still stood where we had parked it. Half an hour later I was back in Green Hill, at the home of Edgar Standish.

Something had happened. Three cars were parked there in the road, and two of them were scout cars.

## CHAPTER FOUR
### Back on the Front Page

THE CENTER of interest was Miss Grace Marvin, whose other and perhaps more authentic name was Marge. She didn't know she was the object of all that attention. She lay on the divan in the living-room. No one had yet thought to cover her with a sheet.

The room was full of cops. Dr. Truett was talking to them, his face at least ten years older than when I had last seen it. Edgar Standish stood by the door and told me brokenly what had happened.

She had fallen, he said, over the edge of the cliff, out back of the house. No one had seen her fall, but Mrs. Meade, while cleaning one of the bedrooms, had looked out of the window and seen her standing there at the cliff's edge, just a short while ago.

"Doctor Truett arrived about twenty minutes ago," Standish said mechanically, "to see her. We couldn't find her. Mrs. Meade remembered having seen her outside, so I went out there to look around. I just happened to look down . . ." His voice trailed off, then came back again, tinged with bitterness. "I blame you for this, Cardin. You were hired to keep an eye on her! Why weren't you on the job?"

I blamed myself. I walked over to get a closer look at the girl, and one of the cops gave me a queer stare of recognition but made no comment.

She wasn't something you'd want to look at for too long. From the top of Green Hill cliff to the rocks at the bottom is a sizeable piece of distance, and the rocks are jagged Her sweater and slacks were soaked with sea-water and blood. One of her sneakers had lost a heel. I scowled at her and thought queerly: "You'll never again write meaningless letters and put them in the bird-houses to fool Jeff Cardin." Then I went outside. I thought it wouldn't do any harrn to have a look around.

A city dick named Grayson was out there, prowling along the edge of the cliff. He glared at me as I approached He was an apple-for-the-teacher lad, one of the commissioner's pets, and he said unpleasantly: "So you finally landed a job, did you?"

"I finally did," I said, looking for footprints.

"You'll answer for this, Cardin. Standish says he hired you to watch the girl."

I ignored him. The ground there at the brink of the bluff was soft, and Grayson, despite his ugly disposition, had been smart enough not to tramp on the girl's sneaker-prints. You could see where she had walked along the edge. You couldn't see where she had gone over, because the prints led to a cowlick of grass and ended there.

I turned to Grayson.

"How do you figure it?" I said. "She slipped on the grass?"

He gave me the broad of his back and walked away.

I toed closer to the edge and looked over, and got a nasty sensation in the region of my stomach. I backed up and examined the grass again. Then I measured the distance roughly. The stone wall was about ten feet away.

Bare ground separated that narrow peninsula of grass from the wall. From the wall to the road, which lay a hundred feet away, the lawn was thick. I studied that patch of bare ground.

Grayson had gone back into the house.

I hopped the wall, went out to the road, and walked along to where the cars were parked. It began to rain. I opened a car door and snooped around inside, opened the door of the glove-compartment and took out a pair of expensive suede gloves. They were smeared with dirt.

With the gloves tucked carefully into my pocket, I went back to the house.

Edgar Standish was sitting on the piano-bench, glumly staring at the carpet. Someone had mercifully covered the dead girl with a shawl. Truett, parked in a chair, was saying to the cops:

"... unable to get in touch with her folks in Europe, so Mr. Standish generously offered to take her in. The young lady was definitely improving, gentlemen. I don't for a moment believe this was done deliberately. It was a ghastly accident."

"Guess again," I said. "It was murder."

Doctors don't frighten easily. This one didn't, anyway. He turned his head toward me, thinned his eyes a bit while staring at me, and then said: "I beg your pardon?"

I moved over to a chair and sat down. Grayson glared at me. I said: "In the first place, her name isn't Grace Marvin. It's Marge Something-or-other, and you know it. Moreover, if she has folks in Europe, they're probably in the blackmail business, or in prison."

I remember reading somewhere or other that Lincoln's Gettysburg Address met with a dead silence. My little speech won the same.

"What did she have on you, Doctor?" I asked.

He reacted to that. His face paled, and a space widened between the chair and his shoulder-blades. Then he shrugged, spread his hands in a gesture of bewilderment and said to Grayson: "I'm afraid I don't understand this man's insinuations."

"If you've got anything to say, Cardin," Grayson snapped, "say it!"

"This girl and her boy-friend," I said, "had some letters of vital importance to Doctor Truett. It's a little involved. They began to put the pressure on Truett quite a while ago. He wasn't the only one. They were really in the business.

"You wouldn't remember it," I said, favoring Grayson with a belittling smile, "but I was working on this blackmail set-up just before my resignation. The gang evidently thought I was warmer than I actually was, because they went to a lot of trouble to put the skids under me. That is, Josie did. Then Josie skipped town, along with at least one other co-worker, leaving Miss Marvin and Nick with their hands full of the good doctor here."

Compared with the vacuum that met this statement, the previous silence had been an Independence Day celebration.

"The trouble was," I said, "Josie left in a hurry and took with her the letters. And the good doctor absolutely refused to play ball until the letters had been produced."

THE GOOD doctor's hands were wet with perspiration.

"Well," I said, "the letters arrived this morning. I'm turning them over to the commissioner."

That did it. For one long moment Truett looked like a man watching the removal of his own appendix. Then he shuddered, shut his eyes and put his hands up to his face. And I knew the doctor was finished.

"What's Miss Marvin's real name, Doctor?" I asked him. "Marge what?"

"Margery," he said. His voice belonged in one of those midnight radio dramas. "Margery Knott. She — used to be my nurse."

This *was* something.

"Is there a ghost of a chance, Doctor," I asked, hunching myself forward, "that the victims of this gang were all patients of yours?"

He nodded, refusing to look at me.

"Margery Knott had access to your files?"

He nodded again.

It's really wonderful, how simple these things are — after you've solved them. For weeks I had tried in vain to find something that would tie those blackmail victims together, but blackmail is the meanest racket in the world to uncover, because those who get snared by it are never eager to talk. They prefer to pay up and shut up.

"Well, Doctor?" I said.

He thought I knew. He said helplessly, with a shuddering glance at those around him: "I made the mistake years ago, and she found out about it while she was working for me. She found the letters. God knows I should have destroyed them, but I hadn't. She took them. Later on, I learned that she and her colleagues were blackmailing some of my patients. I tried to put a stop to it, but she had those letters to hold over my head. Then . . . ."

"Then?" Grayson said, taking over.

"I suddenly realized that I had a hold over her, too. About six months ago, before any of this happened, she brought her brother to me — her brother Nick. Her brother was in a bad way that night. He told me he had been mixed up in a drunken brawl. I removed a bullet from his leg. There was nothing in the newspapers the following day about a drunken brawl, but there was an account of the wounding of a policeman in a gunbattle. I — I suppose I should have reported Nick's wounds, but Miss Knott begged me not to, and I was quite fond of her at that time, and . . . ." He sobbed a little. "It hardly matters now, does it?"

This was beginning to have angles. There were a couple of questions I wanted, to ask, but Truett went on with his recital.

"I kept that bullet," he said. "Later, when she threatened me with the letters, I was able to fight back. I told her I would turn the bullet over to the police, with a statement concerning it, unless she handed over my letters. But she didn't have the letters."

"Josie had them," I said.

He nodded. "So I forced Miss Knott to come here to the Standishes until the letters could be turned over to me. It seemed the best way to keep an eye on her. I lied to the Standishes about her and brought her here, and told her that if she attempted to leave, I would go straight to the police. You see, we — we were playing a kind of game of blind man's buff," he explained eagerly.

Grayson said darkly through a scowl: "This is all very ducky, isn't it?" Glaring at me, he added: "Where do you fit?"

"Standish hired me," I said. "He thought the girl was really goofy and needed watching."

"Standish hired you. Now isn't that a coincidence, him hiring you of all people?"

"Think what you like," I said. As a matter of fact, it wasn't such an astounding coincidence, when you stopped to analyze it. Men like Edgar Standish are not usually chummy with a horde of private detectives. Needing one, they wouldn't know where to turn. My name had been smeared all over the front pages. If you wanted a private dick and the papers told you you could pick up an ex-cop cheap, what do you think you would do?

"Well," Grayson growled, still eyeing me, "you were yelling murder a while ago. What about it?

"Truett pushed her," I said.

The doctor began to cry. And I almost felt sorry for him.

"These gloves," I said, carefully removing them from my pocket, "came out of the compartment in his car. They're dirty because he used then to wipe up his footprints."

WE ALL looked at Truett. He came out of his trance, began shaking his head like a ventriloquist's dummy and said rapidly: "No. No, I didn't. She was standing there and I came up behind her and she was startled when I spoke to her. I didn't push her. I had no idea of pushing her. She was startled. She didn't know anyone was there and when I spoke, she was frightened. She slipped." He stood up. Every inch of the man's body was shaking. "Come here," he said. "I'll show you." With quick, mincing steps he went across the room to a window. We watched him. It was a French window and a big one. Truett opened it. "Come here," he said. "I'll show you. She was standing there at the edge and —"

Then he leaped.

It was a fool thing to do. Even if he had landed on his feet, in full flight, there'd have been a broad lawn in front of him, then the stone wall to hurdle, then nowhere to go except down the road. He didn't land on his feet, though. He stumbled, lost his balance, and went to his knees.

Someone began shooting.

The good doctor staggered to his feet and clutched at his chest. He screamed. His legs turned to rubber and he fell, but he was finished before he fell, and the last two bullets of the assassin were not needed. Truett collapsed, his toes tapping the turf, and I looked past him and saw his murderer.

The fellow was in full flight behind the stone wall, racing as fast as his legs would carry him, toward the road.

Grayson, though a heel, was a first-class shot. He fired twice, and the fleeing man folded.

We walked over. It was Nick. I dropped to one knee beside him, put my hands on his shoulders and was staring into his face when he opened his eyes. I said gently: "You're in for it now, chum."

He could take it, that boy. He'd been hit where there was no getting over it — the red stain spreading into view on his shirt was directly under his heart. But he made a fist of one hand and weakly aimed it at my face, and the blow actually hurt.

"I have a date with Josie," I said "and Boston is a pretty big town. You could save me some trouble by telling me where to find her."

"You go to hell," he snarled.

"This wouldn't have happened," I told him, "if Josie had been on the level with you."

"What?"

"She didn't send those letters, chum. No doubt she figured they were much too valuable to be wasted on you and your sister. Your little stunt in the post office was unnecessary. The box was empty."

His lips curled and he whispered an unprintable epithet.

"All for nothing," I said, "you killed Truett. You might as well tell me. Where do I find her, chum?"

"Peterboro Street," he snarled. "She has an apartment. Mildred Blainey is the name . . . the name she's using. Peterboro Street . . ." His lip formed the number.

He died while we were toting him to the house.

Grayson put his chin out at me. "I don't get this," he said darkly. "Why'd this guy kill the doctor?"

I said: "He thought I had those letters. He figured the game was up and Truett's next move would be to turn that bullet over to the police; in retaliation. "

"What do you mean, he *thought* you had the letters?"

"I haven't them."

"What?"

"It's a funny thing," I said, "but here we are, with most of this mess cleared up, and I still don't know what Truett did to make himself a candidate for blackmail." I gave him my best Sunday smirk. "Isn't that odd?" I said, in a puzzled tone of voice.

He turned away and began talking to himself.

THE END OF the trail was in sight when I stepped into that apartment house on Peterboro Street and found the name Mildred Blainey in the list of tenants, but when I held a thumb against the bell, no one answered.

I had to round up the janitor, tell him a tall story about my being the girl's uncle from Tuscaloosa. He finally decided to let me in.

The apartment was empty. The letters were in a suitcase, under a mess of soiled clothes. I read two or three of them and learned that the fatal mistake committed by Dr. Truett was an illegal operation.

For six hours I cooled my heels, awaiting Josie's return. But when a key finally turned in the lock and the door opened, I found myself face to face with an officer of the law. He was a big, good-looking Irishman.

I was surprised. So was he. We talked it over and he informed me that Josie was in the jug. "Picked up," he said, "for shoplifting, yesterday, and I'm just making a routine check. We found her address written out on a sales-slip in her purse."

Half an hour later I was talking to her. "It's all over," I told her. "Nick's dead, the doctor's dead, the whole business is about to be spread out for the airing it needs. All I want from you is a statement about our little buggy-ride, the night you wore Marge's scarf and very nearly wrecked my career and my reputation."

Staring at me, she wet her lips and said mechanically: "Nick's . . . dead?"

She couldn't seem to believe that.

I nodded.

She went to pieces and I had to call the matron. It was the matron who got from her the statement I had wanted to get for a long time.

You'll be reading that statement in the papers real soon, and unless the war takes some dazzling new turn, you'll be reading it on page one. And a nice little story it will make, too.

That doesn't mean, however, that Jefferson Cardin will go back to being a city detective. I sort of like this idea of being independent. And look at the publicity I'm getting.

So, if you want any murders unmuddled or a tail hung on your rich Uncle Abner, just look me up.

●　●　●　●　●

# STRANGER
# IN TOWN

PUBLISHED IN APRIL 1941. I'M NOT GOING TO COMMENT ON THIS STORY. TO DO SO
MIGHT GIVE IT AWAY, AND I THINK IT'S THE BEST STORY IN THIS COLLECTION. NEVER
MIND WHAT ELSE I WAS DOING FOR THE PULPS AT THIS TIME. I WAS A YEAR AWAY FROM
DOING MY FIRST NOVEL, *FISHERMEN FOUR*, PUBLISHED BY DODD, MEAD. AND A YEAR
AWAY FROM SELLING MY FIRST TWO *AMERICAN MAGAZINE* STORIES, ONE OF WHICH,
"TWO WERE LEFT," HAS BEEN REPRINTED MORE THAN 100 TIMES IN ANTHOLOGIES
AND SCHOOLBOOKS. AND IN JANUARY 1944 *THE SATURDAY EVENING POST* PUBLISHED
THE FIRST OF 43 STORIES OF MINE, AN EXCERPT FROM ONE OF FIVE BOOKS I WROTE AS A
CORRESPONDENT IN WORLD WAR II. BUT YOU KNOW SOMETHING? I WISH THE PAPER
SHORTAGE IN THAT SAME WAR AND THE ADVENT OF POCKET-BOOKS HADN'T KILLED OFF
THOSE GRAND OLD PULP MAGAZINES. THEY WERE GREAT FUN TO READ — AND TO
WRITE FOR.

HBC

*When a man knows there are killers after him that's bad enough — but to
be the unconscious clay-pigeon for a trio of sharpshooters — as Ed Corley was,
knowing nothing of the why's and wherefore's that made him a target, then
it's really time to muster a miracle or two and take a lesson from the
cat in adding extra lives to the ordinary span.*

LINK LATHAM was a big shot and looked it, wearing his two hundred
pounds of beef as easily as he wore his transparent suspenders, his
balloon-seated trousers, and the three-carat diamond on his left little
finger. He paid no attention to the runt sidling up behind him.

Latham's attention was centered in its entirety on the pool table against
which he leaned, on the array of colored balls and the difficulty of the shot
with which he was confronted. He considered himself good at this sort of
thing. Difficult shots intrigued him. He seldom missed.

"Corley's back," the runt whispered, standing close behind him.

Latham grunted, "Don't bother me!" and sighted across the cue ball, carefully, to the number twelve. The cue slid across his knuckles. The balls clicked. Number twelve lightly rubbed one of its neighbors, caromed off and plopped into the corner pocket. Not until then did the runt's words strike home. Link Latham stiffened as though some part of his spine were a spring suddenly drawn taut.

Turning, he said huskily: "What Corley?"

"Ed."

"You're crazy!"

"No, I ain't, Link. With my own eyes I seen him in Kepner's place drinkin' beer, less'n ten minutes ago."

Link Latham wet his lips with an unsteady tongue. He left his cue leaning against the table and started across the room, his round, lumpy face yellowing with each step. He walked slowly on stiff legs, like a man struggling to walk straight with too much liquor in him.

Three or four men in the pool parlor straightened to watch him, aware that something unusual was happening.

Latham stepped into the phone booth and mechanically pulled the door shut. His eyes held a hunted look as he unhooked the receiver and fumbled for a nickel. His fat finger trembled in the dial slots.

He got his number and sent a furtive glance through the door's glass panel. Then, though no one stood within ten feet of the booth, he put his mouth close to the instrument and spoke in a whisper.

"Tony," he said. "Get me Tony."

Beads of sweat formed on his lip while he waited.

"Tony? This is Link. Tony, listen to me. Ed Corley is back . . . *Ed Corley!* . . . What? — No, I ain't seen him yet. Palumbo just told me. Why is he back, Tony? What does he want? . . . Yeah. Yeah, that's what I think, too. And listen, Tony, I'm gonna need help. You understand? I'll be at my place in twenty minutes. You hustle over there. Bring some of the boys."

ALDERMAN Harlan Grossman, alone in a small private office on the seventh floor of the Grayley Building, turned the pages of his evening paper idly. The war news failed to interest him — he was not high enough in politics to turn the war into personal profit. He was weary this afternoon anyway. Sometimes the boys were stubborn. Sometimes it wore him out haggling with them. They were saps to haggle. They should know by now that Harlan Grossman always had his own way in the end.

An item in the paper stopped him and he scowled, pulling the page closer to his eyes. It was about the new high school under construction on Laydon

Street. The new Laydon Street High School, destined to be the city's pride and joy.

Something had happened. A night watchman named Moriarty, father of four kids, had been crushed to death last night under a falling ceiling. The contractor was on the carpet. There was to be an investigation.

Grossman turned quickly to the editorial page. His lip curled as he read a long article on city politics. Moisture formed in the palms of his hands as he read on.

FOR SOME TIME, THE THINKING PERSONS OF THIS CITY HAVE SUSPECTED SKULLDUGGERY AMONG THOSE WHO GOVERN THEM. THE STENCH HAS BEEN PARTICULARLY ODIOUS IN THE MATTER OF AWARDING CONTRACTS FOR PUBLIC BUILDINGS. NOW, IN A NEW BUILDING WHICH HAS BEEN CALLED THE CITY'S PRIDE, A CEILING COLLAPSES AND A HUMAN LIFE IS SNUFFED OUT. WE ASK WHY? WE DEMAND A THOROUGH INVESTIGATION, NOT ONLY OF THE ENTIRE CONSTRUCTION SET-UP BUT OF MATERIALS USED, AND THE SOURCE OF THOSE MATERIALS. IN SHORT, WE DEMAND, AND THE PUBLIC IS ENTITLED, TO KNOW WHERE LIES THE RESPONSIBILITY FOR WHAT HAS HAPPENED.

Harlan Grossman reached for his phone. "Get me Creeley," he muttered. While waiting, he ran a finger under his collar and squirmed uncomfortably in his chair.

"Creeley? Hank. About the school —"

The receiver chuckled against his ear and a voice said softly: "Forget it, Hank. No one knows a thing."

"You sure?"

"Positive. The investigation is just so much hooey."

Grossman put the phone down and exhaled noisily through his mouth, regaining his composure. The phone rang and he picked it up, his hand steady again. "A Mr. Heffler is calling, Mr. Grossman."

"Put him on."

The phone did not chuckle this time. The voice was so low that Grossman had to center all his attention on it. "Grossman, listen. I got scary news. Ed Corley is back."

Grossman wet his lips, stared at the phone and weakly, stupidly, said, "What?"

"Ed Corley. He's been seen around. He's staying at the Minmar."

"My God!" Grossman said, the words strangling him.

"I figured you ought to know, Hank."

Grossman hung up. When his secretary entered a few moments later with some letters, he was in the same position, his hand on the phone-cradle. She glanced at him wonderingly. Harlan Grossman was shaking. One thin hand was white and tight against the edge of the desk, and his bony body was queerly tense. Too tense. Sweat gleamed on his high white forehead.

"Is something wrong, Mr. Grossman?"

He stood up and reached clumsily for his hat, dropped it, bent his knees and picked it up again. "No, no. I'm all right. Look, Miss Allen, I'm going out. I may not be back this afternoon. Take care of things . . . ." The words tumbled over one another and were unintelligible as Grossman stumbled on the threshold.

He went home.

The telephone in the hall closet of Harlan Grossman's suburban house was not listed in the book. He preferred to have this number known only to himself and a few selected confidantes. He used the phone now — three times — and then went nervously into the living room, where he mixed a drink at the small mahogany bar and spilled most of it before getting it to his lips. He was alone in the house.

Between five and six o'clock he had three callers. Matt Downey was a police sergeant. Philip Patterson, peering near-sightedly through rimless spectacles, was a politician. Rigney, the third caller, was a wiry, white-haired little man who spoke scarcely a dozen words but listened attentively and did a lot of nodding.

At six, Grossman took a cab downtown. He emerged from the cab on Green Street and walked two blocks, furtively, to the step-down entrance of Club 13. The headwaiter called him by name and admitted him to the private sanctum of the club's proprietor, Nick Vierick.

He thought Vierick would be surprised to see him. He was mistaken.

A SLENDER, sleek-haired man of unguessable age, Vierick nodded without rising, without extending his hand. "I thought you'd be around," he said as Grossman shut the door. His voice was soft. Men who worked for Nick Vierick had to pay close attention to everything he said, so gentle was his voice, so swift and savage his anger if they asked him to repeat.

"Ed Corley — " Grossman began.

"I know. The boys keep me posted."

Grossman sat down, uneasy in Vierick's presence. He dabbed a handkerchief at his high white forehead and it came away damp. He wet his lips — they were thin and taut and trembling. "What am I going to do, Nick?"

Nick Vierick's smile was very slightly a sneer. "Aren't you getting the jitters a little early?"

"Early? My God!"

"How do you know he came back to look you up?"

"What — what else would bring him?" Grossman moaned.

Nick Vierick held a match to a cigar, blew the flame out and carefully shredded the match with his immaculate fingernails. He touched the tip of his tongue to the backs of his upper teeth and let smoke curl lazily from his mouth-corners. He appeared to be enjoying himself at Grossman's expense.

"A lot of others had a hand in what happened to Corley," he said.

"I know, but —"

"He could be here to see any of them. Why should *you* be jittery, Hank? You're supposed to me smart."

"For God's sake," Grossman said hoarsely, "talk sense, Nick. What am I going to do?"

"I wouldn't know."

"You won't — help me?"

"I help anyone," Vierick said soberly, "for a price. The price will be high, though. The night-club business is lousy lately."

"How much?"

"I'll send one of the boys up to see you," Vierick said, "after I give it some thought." A look of shrewdness entered his eyes. "There's one thing I don't quite get, Grossman. Link Latham used to do your dirty work. Why the sudden shift to me?"

"This is too big for Latham!"

"You think so?" Vierick smiled. "That's good, Grossman. That will jump the price at least five grand." He stood up, yawned, gently patted his mouth with a slender hand. Opening the door he said softly: "It's a shame, in a way. I always thought Corley was a pretty right guy, in spite of you. Still, business is business."

S HE HAD A spacious and expensive apartment, but the furnishings were just over the border-line of good taste. A shade too flashy. Impressive enough at first glance, perhaps, but too garnish, too dazzlingly brilliant. She herself was like that.

At first glance she took a man's breath away with the slender perfection of her body, the studied grace of her step, the easy sparkle of her smile and the provocative way she held her head. Men stared and wet their lips, and felt old. Or felt foolishly young and reckless.

But her smile was too easy, too mechanical. Behind it lay a hardness acquired through four years of show business. The subtle shadows in her voice could vanish instantly in crisp, metallic accents of anger. She was a lady, but she could be a tramp.

Shapely arms aloft, she wriggled into an eighty-dollar evening gown that hugged her hips, tautened and pointed her breasts. Then she sat before the full-length mirror of her dressing-table and carefully dressed her face. Getting old, she thought angrily. Twenty-nine next month, wasn't it? Or thirty. She had lied so much about her age, first to Ed Corley — the sap! — and then to Nick Vierick and others, that the truth was hard to remember. But anyhow, she wasn't getting any younger.

A key turned in the entrance door and for a moment she was motionless, her hands upraised, dark eyes impassively studying her reflection in the glass. She did not turn when Nick Vierick's voice called softly: "Where are you, kid?"

"In here," she said.

He walked up behind her and her eyes watched his image in the mirror. She lowered her arms and Nick's cool hands pressed her shoulders, pulling her against him. He stooped and kissed her. "Hot stuff, that dress," he said.

She smiled up at him. "It ought to be. Did you get the bill yet?"

"No. How much?"

"Eighty dollars, Nick."

"Stiff," he said, scowling.

"You want me to look nice, don't you?"

His scowl faded more slowly than it usually did. He looked her over, not amorously but critically, withdrew his hands from her shoulders and stepped back. "Hurry it up. I want to talk to you."

She put the very best of herself into the languid look she gave him then. The slow parting of her lips, the softly indrawn breath, the studied subtlety of her body-movements. She could do no better and knew it. Even her voice was just right when she murmured: "Can't we talk — here, Nick?"

Nick Vierick laughed shortly, mirthlessly, with his lips tight. "I never said a sensible thing in this room yet, kid. We'll talk over a drink, in decent light." He turned abruptly and walked into the living-room.

He had a cocktail mixed for her, on the bar, when she emerged. Handing it to her, he raised his own, stared at her for an instant without touching his lips to the glass. Then: "Ed's back," he said.

She didn't hear it. She was studying the amber liquid in the glass and wondering if she ought to get a little bit drunk tonight. Nick liked her to get drunk once in a while. He liked to think she was being herself, being "natural," when liquor loosened her tongue and melted the cloak of restraint which ordinarily kept him from getting too rough. Perhaps tonight, to thaw him a little . . . .

"Why the hell don't you listen to me once in a while?" Nick said with sudden anger.

She came out of her thoughts, stared at him in amazement. "Are you talking to *me* in that tone, Nick Vierick?"

"I'm telling you," he said darkly. "I'm telling you Ed's back."

She got it then. Under the eighty-dollar gown her body was suddenly taut and cold, her flesh was shrinking. There was a hand at her throat, squeezing her breath back. She could feel the bones of her face aching, and realized that her tongue was jammed against the back of her teeth.

"*No*, Nick!"

"You didn't know, eh?"

She knew what he meant. She sensed that he was stabbing at her, testing her, and realized numbly that she must meet the test — or else.

"I didn't know, Nick," she whispered, cringing. " My God, I never dreamed!"

Nick Vierick gripped her shoulders, held her at arm's length and stared at her. His face wore no expression that she could analyze. It was the face of a shrewd card player studying his hand.

"You haven't been hearing from him, by any chance?"

"No!"

"Women don't usually lie to me, kid."

"Nick, I'm not lying! I'm not!"

Nick Vierick held her for a moment, then gave her a light shove that sent her stumbling into one of the ultra-modern chrome-and-satin chairs.

"O. K., I believe you," he said softly. "But get this. You're staying here — right here — until Corley's taken care of. I wouldn't go out if I were you, sugar. When I give the boys an order, I never soften it with any 'ifs' or 'buts' — I just give the order. Understand?"

Her hands were wet and white on the gleaming arms of the chair, and she watched him as a terrified bird watches a snake.

"Understand, sugar?"

She nodded, her lips too dry to make words.

Nick Vierick put a hand on her head, roughed her hair and kissed her. He was smiling, but men who knew him feared that particular smile, knowing its implications. With a gentle, "So long, kid," Nick went out, closing the door behind him.

Mrs. Ed Corley sat where she was, motionless in her eighty-dollar evening gown.

E D CORLEY stepped from the doorway of the Minmar at nine o'clock that evening into a drizzle of rain. A tall, too-thin man, he wore a limp-brimmed felt hat, and a gray raincoat that hung shapelessly to a point about six inches above his knees. The brim of the hat half-covered his face. His hands were in his pockets. He limped.

Pausing for a moment on the sidewalk, he looked up and down the street, then lowered his head against the turned-up collar of his coat and began walking. He appeared to be in no hurry.

A year ago, Ed Corley had weighed fifty pounds more. A year ago he had worked for the mayor as special investigator, his job the smelling out of the crime and corruption that had made this city the joke of the nation.

The mayor was gone now. The job of special investigator no longer existed. And after six months in the hospital, six more months in a convalescent home out West, Ed Corley was a slow-moving, transparent ghost of his former self.

He walked slowly along Firth Avenue, through the drizzle.

Behind him a wiry, white-haired little man moved methodically from a drugstore doorway on the far side of the street, to tail him. In a parked sedan at the corner of Firth and Murray, two other men came to life and exchanged scraps of words. In the Minmar lobby, still-another man stepped into a telephone booth and gravely slotted a coin.

The wolves were watching. Waiting. This was at nine o'clock.

At ten, Harlan Grossman downed his fourth drink in half an hour, put a match to his eleventh cigarette and resumed his pacing of the living-room carpet in his expensive suburban home. Sweat glistened on Grossman's high white forehead. He dabbed at it with a handkerchief. His round, fleshy face was colorless.

Grossman could stand just so much of this, and no more. He lacked the stability for enduring suspense. The moments crawled by now and he cursed the phone for not ringing. Damn Rigney! Why didn't he report?

Grossman tried to comfort himself and soothe his nerves with a cool analysis of the situation. He had done all he could, hadn't he? His private troubleshooter, the white-haired little man, Abel Rigney, was on the job and could be trusted to end this suspense at the first opportunity. Nick Vierick's boys were on the job, too. It was just a matter of time.

But time was precious. If Ed Corley got a chance to open his mouth and talk for even ten minutes to the right people, the fate of Harlan Grossman was sealed.

Grossman stopped before a mirror and stared at his reflection. Talked to it, in a voice tense with fear. "I could pay him a visit myself," he whispered. "By God, that's it! I could talk to him, hand him a song-and-dance about a lot of innocent people who'd be blasted if he turned on the heat too soon. That would give the boys time —"

It seemed a good idea, perhaps because Grossman had drunk too much and was in a mood to snatch at straws. He went to a window and looked out, and heard a downtown clock strike eleven. "I'll wait ten minutes more."

He waited five, and the minutes were hours. Then the mutter of the rain against the windows got him. The silence of the house set up a reactionary shriek inside him. He snatched his coat and hat from the hall closet, stormed out to his car at the curb, and drove downtown.

He entered the Minmar at twenty past eleven and forced himself to walk slowly through the empty lobby, past the desk and the sleepy-eyed clerk, to the stairs. He knew the number of Ed Corley's room. Two-one-nine. Rigney had reported that much, damn him, earlier in the evening.

The second-floor corridor was as empty as the lobby. It should be, of course. The Minmar was a small hotel, far removed both in spirit and distance from the pretentious hostelries of the bright-light district.

Grossman nervously paused before the door of two-one-nine and raised his hand. He wet his lips, caught and held his breath. He knocked.

The unlocked door creaked open a couple of inches when his knuckles made contact. Grossman stepped back, startled. But the door stopped swinging, stopped creaking, and there was no further sound except the noise of his own harsh breathing. The room was dark.

Grossman furtively pushed the door wider and stepped over the threshold. "Is — is anyone home?" he asked. No answer. The hall's dim light filtered in to reveal a floor-lamp near the door. He switched it on.

**H**E CLOSED the door and advanced to the center of the room, stood there looking around. Until tonight, Harlan Grossman had prided himself on his lack of nerves. Now he was jittery. His hands shook and he was hypersensitive to every slightest sound — the whisper of the carpet under his feet, the muffled noise of a car moving along the street outside.

Mopping his forehead, Grossman sat down to wait. He sat facing the door, in the overstuffed chair under the lamp. His gaze roved the room again, stabbing at seedy hulks of furniture, at the stains on the wallpaper. It was an old-fashioned room, a small room. The walls were too close, too crowding. The window, to Grossman's right, was a grimy rectangle opening on an interior court.

"I'll tell him he's got to give me twenty-four hours," Grossman schemed. "I got to have that, I'll tell him, or else a bunch of innocent people will go down with me. If I lay it on thick I can convince him. Then Rigney — or Nick's boys — will have time enough."

He began to get over his jitters. "Why, hell, it will be easy! Ed Corley was always a sucker for a sob story. If I just shed a few phoney tears, it will be a cinch!"

A shadow moved at the window, but Grossman did not see it. He was mired in thoughts of what he would tell Ed Corley. Perched on the fire escape outside the grimy glass, the shadow slowly straightened and peered into the room.

It was the white-haired little man, Abel Rigney.

He saw the lamp burning yellowly beside the overstuffed chair. He saw Harlan Grossman's legs, and the back of Grossman's head. The chair hid the rest.

The white-haired little man slid a revolver from his pocket. Carefully he fitted a homemade silencer, shaped like a musical sweet potato, over the muzzle. A little while ago, things had looked pretty dark, he mused. Ed Corley had given him the slip down on Nixon Street somewhere. " But they always come home to roost, " the little man thought. "You just got to be patient."

He pressed the gun delicately against the glass and took aim at the back of Grossman's head. He squeezed the trigger — once, twice, thrice — with the cool deliberation of a man shooting tin ducks in a target range. Then, without undue haste, he noiselessly descended the fire-escape, dropped into the court and walked away.

A little while later he stepped into a cab and gave the driver Harlan Grossman's suburban address. Grossman would be relieved, he mused, to know that Ed Corley was dead.

E D CORLEY came out of the Elite Bar on Nixon Street at twenty past twelve. He was tired, and his limp was more pronounced. He looked both ways along the street, hunched his coat collar higher and turned south. It was still raining.

In a sedan parked at the opposite curb, some fifty yards distant, a sallow man nudged his dozing companion. "He's on the prowl again, Joe. Let's move."

The stocky, block-shouldered man at the wheel looked at his watch, cursed softly, and put the sedan in motion.

Ed Corley walked along Nixon Street, under neon signs and street lamps. This was a middle-class neighborhood of middle-class theaters, restaurants, dance-halls. The lumpy rhythm of a boogie-woogie piano seeped from a second-floor casino. Hot odors of deep-fried food emerged with a noisy foursome from the opening door of a restaurant. Traffic was thin but steady. A drunk weaved along, peering gravely in store windows.

Ed Corley turned left into Mabel Street and entered a small, brown-front eating place noted for its Armenian food. The sedan turned left into Mabel Street and slowly stopped with its tires hugging the curb.

"One damn joint after another," the sallow man muttered. "What the hell *is* he up to?"

"Plenty, most likely. Go phone in," Joe said.

The sallow man let himself out of the car and walked back to the corner, to a seedy drupstore. There he shut himself in a booth and spat disgustedly on the floor while dialing.

"Lester, chief. Drugstore corner of Nixon and Mabel. He's in that Armenian dump."

The answering voice of Link Latham was an angry snarl. "What's the matter with you two saps? Does it take all night to snag a man off the street?"

"Now listen, chief —"

"Listen yourself! I told you what to do and how to do it. Do I have to attend to every damned little detail personally?"

"We ain't had a decent chance at him yet," the sallow man snarled back with rising bitterness. "It's too early and he's been stickin' close to the bright lights."

"There are no bright lights on Mabel Street!"

"Well — maybe not. Maybe when he comes out of this Armenian dump we'll get him."

There was silence for an instant, then the voice of Link Latham came thoughtfully, with less venom. "Listen, Lester. Is he alone?"

"Yeah, chief. There ain't been a soul with him since he left the Mimnar."

"Good. Watch him, but don't make a move until I get there. I'll see this through myself — then there'll be no hitch."

Lester went back to the sedan. "The boss is comin' down himself," he announced.

Joe sluggishly turned his head, raised an eyebrow. "Yeah?"

"Mm."

"Well, well," Joe said. Without further comment he centered his attention on the door of the Armenian restaurant.

Ed Corley had not emerged when Latham arrived. Driven by a lantern-jawed chauffeur, Link Latham got out at the corner, walked up to the sedan. His own car purred away again.

"He still in there?"

"Still in there," Joe said.

"Take a look at me," Latham ordered softly. "Will he know me?"

The two hoods looked him over and were surprised. Link Latham hardly resembled a big shot racketeer in this garb. He wore a threadbare coat, a battered brown hat, scuffed shoes. The three-carat diamond was missing from its customary place on his left little finger. Link Latham was physically as huge as before, but less impressive. His eyes blinked behind ill-fitting glasses.

"What's the idea?" Joe said.

"We're going to play this smart. Me, I'm going inside that dump and size things up. Now look. When Corley comes out, I'll be on his heels, see? You move this car across the street and be ready. It's raining, see, and if we do this right, no one will smell any trouble. Corley comes out. I'm right behind him. I shove a gun into his ribs and walk him to the car and push him in. That's that."

The two hoods exchanged glances. Joe said: "You want to be careful, chief. There's a rod in Corley's coat pocket."

"Is there? What's the coat look like?"

"One of them wrap-around raincoats, silver-gray, sort of."

"I'll take care of the rod," Latham said. Turning, he walked across the street to the restaurant.

E D CORLEY was lighting a cigarette at a corner table when Latham entered. A waiter was clearing dishes from his table. The waiter poured a cup of strong, black, oily coffee, straightened without comment and went away. Ed Corley stared straight ahead into space.

There were a dozen persons in the place, and it had accommodations for only that many more. The light was bad. Cheap dark tapestries adorned the walls. The floor was concrete, painted black. Dim lights on each table provided illumination barely sufficient for eating.

Link Latham removed his seedy coat and hung it on a crowded coat-tree. He ordered coffee and a sandwich, his gaze furtively fixed on the man at the corner table. Something of the terror that had tagged him in the poolroom, when the news of Corley's return had first been whispered to him, began now to creep into him again. What caused it was the sight of Ed Corley so casually, confidently sitting there.

Latham moistened his lips with a nervous tongue, put his hands in his lap and gripped his napkin savagely to keep the hands from shaking. His coffee came and he downed half of it in one gulp, scalding his throat. Had Corley seen him?

Ed Corley indifferently lit another cigarette, sipped his coffee, found it too hot and pushed it aside to cool.

Latham looked for the wrap-around raincoat, "silver-gray sort of," and thought he saw it. It hung from one of the coat-trees scattered about the room, this one not far from the door. He could see no other like it, and further scrutiny showed him a suspicious-looking bulge in the right-side pocket.

He glanced fearfully at Ed Corley, but Ed's back was turned. With an attempt to be casual, Latham stood up.

No one would say anything, of course. Plenty of times, in a public eating place, you hung your coat up and then went to get something out of a pocket. A handkerchief, maybe, or a pack of cigarettes. The place hummed with low conversation and was sufficiently crowded for his actions to go unobserved.

He walked over to the coat-tree and pawed aside the other coats to get at that bulging pocket. Once the gun was in his possession, he could walk up behind Ed Corley without fear. But he was nervous. His hands shook. A couple of coats flopped to the floor.

A waiter appeared at his side, scowling.

"Sorry," Latham mumbled, the silver-gray raincoat now in his hands. "Looking for my cigarettes."

The waiter said ominously: "You hung your coat over there." He pointed. "I saw you." He spoke gutturally, with an accent, and Latham was acutely aware of the omission of the customary "sir."

"What?" Latham mumbled.

"You sure this is your coat?"

It was too much for Link Latham. First the nerve-wracking sight of Ed Corley so indifferently sipping coffee at the corner table, then his own frantic fumbling at the coat-tree — now this Armenian waiter guardedly accusing him. People were staring. A second waiter was closing in.

Latham sent a frantic glance at Ed Corley's table and saw with a rush of relief that Corley's attention had not been attracted by the incident. This gave Link Latham a measure of his old bravado. He shoved his thick arms into the coat sleeves, hauled a dollar bill from his pocket and flipped it to the floor.

"Listen, you," he snarled. "I didn't come into this cheap dump to be insulted. There's for the coffee and sandwich!"

Then, with little bravado left, he fled.

The silver-gray coat flapped about him like a flag as he reached the sidewalk. He was actually running, though he did not know it. Too soon he reached the curb and braked himself. The curb was slick with rain. Latham slipped, fell to one knee and lost his balance in the gutter.

He was on his knees again when he saw the blunt black nose of the sedan bearing down on him. He screamed. Had the car's headlights been turned on — which they weren't — Link Latham's face would have appeared as a chalky gargoyle in the glare of them. Terror stiffened him, and for three seconds he stared motionless into eternity.

The car was in second speed, roaring its challenge at the night, when it struck him. A deft twist of the wheel threw Latham against the curb and pinned him there while the forward surge of the machine dragged him along for twenty feet. Then the car veered to mid-street and roared away.

Link Latham was pulp in the rain-filled gutter.

Behind the car's wheel, the stocky, block-shouldered man named Joe sucked up a slow breath, exhaled heavily and said "Neat, if you ask me. That will save Link a heap of trouble."

He switched the headlights on.

His companion said matter-of-factly: "Make for the Gray Street Garage and we'll get this hack cleaned up before the cops snoop. Then we'll mosey over to Link's place. There'll be extra dough in this for us. Link always pays big for smart headwork."

He flipped open the glove compartment, took out a pint bottle and uncorked it. "Well — here's to what's left of Ed Corley."

CORLEY frowned at the Armenian waiter and the waiter said again to the cop with the notebook: "The coat he's wearing belongs to this gentleman here."

"To you?" The cop stared at Corley.

"Yes," Ed Corley said, "it's mine."

"What's your name, mister?"

"Philip Smith," Ed Corley said.

"He must've swiped your coat on purpose, hey?"

"I don't know."

"Well," the cop said, "it's a cinch he'll never tell us, one way or the other." He snapped the notebook shut and turned to shoulder the crowd back. "All right, now, all right, get back! Get back, I'm tellin' you! There's nothin' to gape at. The guy got run over, is all. Get *back!*"

The waiter said solicitously: "You'll need a coat of some sort, sir, to go far in this rain."

"I will," Ed Corley agreed.

"Well, sir — turn-about is fair play. Why not take *his* coat? I can point it out to you. Of course it's all very irregular, but you left a handsome gratuity, sir, and what the management doesn't know won't hurt." He smiled, and his smile was as smooth as his voice. No accent now. That, evidently, was merely a part of the Armenian atmosphere, to be discarded in more serious moments.

Link Latham's coat was a few sizes too huge for Ed Corley, and seedy in comparison with Corley's own. It offered protection, though, from the rain. Engulfed in it, Ed Corley walked leisurely down Mabel Street to Fourth. A corner clock read two A.M.

He kept on walking.

It was on Seventh Street, twenty-five minutes later, that the black and yellow cab fell in behind him. The driver, his cap pulled low, had two passengers. When he spotted Ed Corley he slowed to a crawl, slid the glass partition behind him and said: "Is that him?"

The two passengers peered through the wet window. One was a slim, jet-haired youth with sultry eyes. The other was not much older but had a slack, wet mouth and was slower of motion, less crisp of speech. Nick Vierick picked his men carefully, though, and Wet Mouth was more dangerous than he looked.

"That's him, ain't it, Al?" Wet Mouth said.

"Yeah. " And to the driver: "Get ahead of him, Andy."

The black and yellow machine passed Ed Corley at normal speed, then slowed. Al, the slim sultry-eyed youth, got out. The cab moved on again and turned a corner. Al sent a swift, stabbing glance at his approaching victim and stepped into a tenement doorway.

It looked perfectly natural. It looked as though Al lived in that tenement and had just arrived home by cab.

Ed Corley walked past.

Al's feet were noiseless as the pads of a cat when he stepped from the tenement doorway and closed the gap. The automatic in his pocket nudged Ed Corley's hip. "Keep right on goin'," he said.

Ed Corley glanced at him and frowned. He missed a step. The gun's pressure increased and the sultry-eyed youth said with sudden venom: "I ain't afraid of you, Corley! Get that out of your head! You try any stunts and I'll blast you!"

Ed Corley's mouth thinned, but he did not again look at the man beside him. At the corner, the pressure of the automatic steered him in the direction Al wished him to go. The black and yellow cab was waiting.

Wet Mouth had a gun in his hand and the cab door open when Ed Corley came abreast of the machine. "Nice going, Al," was all he said. His free hand slid over Corley's clothing and he seemed surprised to find no weapon. He moved back on the seat and Al crowded Corley against him.

Al got in and closed the door. "Stop at Carey's place, " he told the driver. "I'll phone Nick."

His gaze slanted to Ed Corley's face. "You surprise me," he added with a trace of a sneer. "I had you figured for a tough guy."

Ed Corley stared straight ahead of him and was silent.

They rode across town. Grey's place, a bar-room, was on lower Eustace Street, and Al was inside but a moment.

"Nick says bring him to Flo's apartment."

"O.K.," the driver said.

"Nick says don't rush it. He wants to get there first."

"O.K."

NICK VIERICK stepped briskly out of a cream-colored coupe, a very swank job, in front of the apartment house toward whose upkeep he so generously contributed. The rain had stopped. A stoop-shouldered man lounging near the entrance lit a cigarette, holding the match overlong to his face, and nodded. Nick favored him with a short syllable in passing.

It hadn't been so tough, Nick thought. You learn early in the day that your deadliest enemy is in town gunning for you, and before the night is out, you have the situation under control. Neat. Organization was the answer. "Give me the right boys, smart enough to think for themselves in a squeeze, but level-headed enough to take orders," Vierick mused, "and I could run the country."

He was in good spirits. He hummed softly on his way up the stairs. For a moment he listened outside the door of Mrs. Ed Corley's apartment, then thrust a key into the lock, opened the door and stepped inside.

"Where are you, kid?"

"Right — here, Nick."

He walked into the living-room and stared at her, and for an uncomfortable moment wondered what he had ever seen in her. She looked worn. The eighty-dollar evening gown had been swapped for an old black satin housecoat, her hair was in her eyes and her face was bird-tracked with fatigue lines.

"Why aren't you in bed?" Nick demanded.

She gazed at him out of bloodshot eyes, holding her head up with an effort. "I did go to bed, Nick. I — I couldn't sleep." Her voice dropped to a whisper, rough at the edges. "Nick . . . . Why did he have to come back? What does he want?"

Smiling a tight little smile that looked skimpy on his lean face, Nick Vierick sank into a chair and lit a cigarette. She would know what Ed Corley wanted, he thought, a lot quicker than she expected. He relaxed, and Flo watched him, afraid of him. Nick was on his third cigarette when footfalls in the hall caught his attention.

He looked at the door, and someone knocked. He got out of his chair and said tautly: "Who is it?"

A voice replied: "Us, chief."

Nick opened the door.

The girl's eyes widened when she saw Ed Corley. She sucked a breath and put a hand to her throat, stared at Ed as though she were seeing a ghost. Nick stared at him, too, but if Nick expected a display of emotion on Ed Corley's part he was disappointed. Ed glanced at the girl, veered his gaze around to Nick, then showed no further interest in either of them and stared, instead, at his feet.

Vierick's two hoods shoved him deeper into the living-room, one on each side of him. "What now, chief?" Al asked.

"Tie him up. Tape his mouth."

"We go ridin' before daylight?"

"There's a big burlap sack in the trunk of my car, out front. You, Pete"— to Wet Mouth — "go get it." He tossed Pete a key. "Al, you go down and tell Andy to move the other car around back, to the alley."

"It's there already. We come in the back way."

"Go down and sit with him, then. After you tie this mug up."

Al was efficient with a roll of adhesive tape. Down on one knee, he slapped Ed Corley's feet together and deftly secured them. A nurse with a roll-bandage could have done no neater job. Rising, he pulled Ed Corley's arms back, but found the ill-fitting coat too cumbersome, and paused to yank it off. He tossed the coat onto a chair and finished his taping.

A neat thrust of his foot spilled Corley to the floor, and Al sat on him, taped his mouth. Ed had nothing whatever to say before his lips were sealed, and after that could utter no sound loud enough to travel ten inches.

Al and Pete went out. Nick Vierick took a step forward, looked down at Ed Corley and said with a slow, curling smile: "You know, Corley, I've been wondering just how much you're really wise to what happened to you. This business of coming back — it was a noble gesture, sure — tough Ed Corley, fresh out of a rest home and determined to get even with the boys who put him there. But it had a lot of angles, guy.

"First place, I didn't have a thing to do with snatching you that time. Grossman ordered it, but I wasn't doing Grossman's dirty work then — Link Latham was. Link's boys grabbed you, Corley — not mine. And they never figured you'd live through the workout they gave you. When they dumped you on Toole Street that night they thought you were finished. You surprised them, hey?

"But if you think I had a hand in that little bit of business, guy, you're wrong. I'm no angel, understand. Oh, no. Fact, I was having ideas about doing away with you myself. But my motives were a mite different from Grossman's. I had an eye on the little lady here. Husbands are a nuisance."

Ed Corley lay on his back with his taped wrists under him, his knees drawn up. His eyes were open, returning Vierick's gaze. The eyes closed and Nick Vierick shrugged, moved away.

Corley's coat — Link Latham's coat — lay there on the chair, and Vierick picked it up. He picked it up to move it, so he could sit down. Something clinked in one of the pockets, and curiosity led Vierick to investigate. He pulled out a cigarette lighter.

IT WAS worth something, that lighter. Small, exquisitely made of yellow gold with a deep red stone, not of the semi-precious variety, winking above the engraved name *Flo*, it weighed but an ounce or two in Vierick's palm — yet he almost dropped it.

His eyes thinned to slits and ominously darkened. His mouth thinned with them, spreading in a tight white line across his face. He put the coat back on the chair, walked to a table and placed the lighter on the table and backed up, staring at it.

The door opened and Pete came in. "Here's the sack, chief."

"Leave it and get out," Nick Vierick said, his voice strangely metallic. "Come back with Al in ten minutes."

Pete gave him an odd stare. The door closed. Nick Vierick looked at the lighter again. "I paid a lot of money for that, kid," he said, without turning his head toward the girl.

Flo looked at the lighter, too. Puzzled at first, her gaze flicked from the lighter to Ed Corley and back again, like a humming-bird. Then she was too scared to be puzzled. Every last touch of color ebbed from her face, and her hands tightened jerkily on the gleaming arms of her chair. She knew she had to say something. She knew that every passing second was of enormous importance, that if she were not quick with an explanation she would not be believed.

But her mind was trapped. Nick Vierick had given her the lighter months ago. Last week, last Monday, she and Link Latham had been fooling with it, looking it over, wondering how much Nick had been stuck for it. Last Monday night, late — Nick safely out of town. Only when Nick was out of town did Link and some of the others drop in for their surreptitious visits.

Link must have walked off with the thing, by mistake. Now it was in Ed's pocket. How in God's name —

She looked up, white as wax, and Nick Vierick was standing over her. His hands were reaching for her. Cruel as trap-jaws, they closed on her shoulders and yanked her out of the chair.

"You dirty, two-timing little tramp! You knew Ed was back! You had him up here!"

She tried to say no, but his right hand shifted lightning-like to her throat and burned the denial before it was born. And she knew then that she was through. This was the end. Nick Vierick's anger was not this time the kind that could be softened with a melting glance, a few whispered words of endearment.

He had caught her in the one crime which in his code of ethics was inexcusable. Two-timing.

She found her voice, finally. "Nick, it — it isn't what you think!" But it was a waste of breath and she knew it. Nick Vierick flung her back into the chair.

"Say your prayers."

"No, Nick! Oh my God!"

He put a hand in his pocket. The automatic he kept there was a tiny thing, a special job weighing but fourteen ounces. She had seen it, she knew what it looked like. She knew that he carried it always but used it only for those rare tasks too intimate or too personal to be entrusted to the hired help. And now suddenly Flo was out of her chair, fear-crazed, clawing at him with a savagery that surprised even herself.

Vierick stumbled, fell over Ed Corley and went down. And Flo was on him, tearing at his face with her crimson nails, biting, kicking, clawing.

She heard the gun go off and felt the burn of the bullet under her shoulder, felt a sudden sickening rush of pain to her stomach. But she had both hands on his gun-wrist now and his upturned face was a ghastly shade of gray. One of her sharp knees had struck something sensitive and inflicted agony.

The gun went off again. But this time she was writhing over it. Both her hands were clawing at it. When it exploded, Nick Vierick's agonized eyes were looking into the muzzle of it, and the bullet ploughed his face like a torpedo churning through sea-water.

HE STIFFENED convulsively and the girl lost her balance, fell away from him. She rolled into the legs of a table, lay there and listened to Vierick's horrible groans of torment, saw him twisting and curling like a snake under a heavy stone. It lasted but a moment, then he thrust his legs straight out and was still, but his groans continued.

She staggered erect, the pain in her own body forgotten in her desperation. She knew all at once, with crystal clarity, that she had only a few minutes in which to do what had to be done. Al and Pete would be coming. "Hurry, hurry, hurry!" she whispered. But Nick Vierick wouldn't stop groaning and the blood in his gaping mouth bubbled like a fountain with every outpouring of sound.

She tore a coil of adhesive tape from Ed Corley's ankles and slapped it over Vierick's lips. It wasn't enough. Blood and groans seeped from under it. She ripped tape from Ed Corley's wrists and used that, too. Scrabbling about on hands and knees, she snatched up the burlap sack and knelt between Vierick's legs and tugged the sack over his head, down over his shoulders, his hips.

The sound of her own breathing frightened her. The redness of Vierick's spilled blood, smeared on her hands and wrists, churned up a sickness inside her that vied with a physical pain steadily growing more acute. She jammed Vierick's legs into the sack and pulled tight the rope that closed the sack's mouth. Frantically, she tied knot after knot until the rope was hopelessly snarled. Then she fled into the bathroom.

A towel cleaned up most of the blood. The puddle on the carpet, where Vierick's face had been, she covered with a scatter-rug. Then she seized Ed Corley by his shoulders and dragged him into the bedroom, pushed and kicked him into a closet and slammed the door shut.

When Al and Pete came in a moment later, she was finished. She sat in her favorite chair, languidly smoking a cigarette. The burlap sack lay against the legs of the living-room table.

There were spots of blood on her housecoat, but her arms were draped to cover them, and over the greater blotch of blood beneath her shoulder she had drawn a red satin jacket for which the man in the sack had paid thirty-five dollars only two weeks ago.

The shoulder throbbed like an impacted tooth. Pain poured through her, so that it was torture even to lift the cigarette to her lips. But she said in a casual voice: "Nick's gone out front to his car. He'll meet you in the alley."

"We got time for a drink, you suppose?" Al said hopefully.

"No. Get that damned thing out of here. It gives me the creeps."

Al gave her a look, grinned. "I wouldn't be surprised," he said. Matter-of-factly, he and Pete lifted the sack from the floor and went out with it.

Flo was on her feet almost before the door closed. Ghastly pale, she clung to the arm of her chair to steady herself. "Got to — hurry," she whispered, the words brittle against her teeth.

She stumbled into the bedroom. The pain was growing worse, but in spite of it she propped herself against the end of the bed and removed her housecoat. You couldn't wear a bloody housecoat on the street and hope to get anywhere without being picked up.

She wanted to look at herself in a mirror then. To look at the hole in her body made by the bullet. But she had strength left for only one thing more — a dress — something heavy, through which the blood would not soak too soon.

Somehow she got the thing over her head, down over her heaving breast. Then she was out of the bedroom, weaving drunkenly through the livingroom to the door.

She got as far as the stairs and looked down them. They seemed steep as the drop of a Coney Island roller-coaster, and up from the depths in a gray, swirling cloud, shot through and through with streaks of lightning, came agony.

She swayed there, took a step forward. Scream after scream ripped from her lips as she fell. Like an uprooted tree on a mountainside she crashed downward, and was still tumbling, still reddening the walls with her blood, long after her screams had stopped and the pain inside her had gone away — forever.

POLICE SIRENS wailed as Ed Corley emerged from his wife's apartment. He stood in the hall, listening, his swollen lips hooked in a scowl. He went to a window down the hall and looked out.

A police car-stopped at the curb and uniformed men piled out of it. Another squealed to a halt behind it. There was a rush of uniformed shapes.

Ed Corley backed away from the window, muttered something under his breath, and hurried to the rear of the hall, to the rear stairway. He walked stiffly, because the adhesive tape had numbed his legs. His wrists were numb, too, and sticky. His lips were torn.

He descended the rear stairs slowly, hearing echoes of the pandemonium that dinned in another part of the house. He opened a door and it led to an alley. He went through the alley — which was empty — and kept on walking.

He supposed he had done enough walking for tonight, even though the doctors had told him to walk as much as possible if ever his legs were to be strong again. By rights he should return to his hotel now and go to bed, but the thought left him cold and scowling.

This was a strange, unfriendly city where strange things happened. He had liked it a while ago. Certain things about it had seemed familiar. But now he hated it, and wanted to be out of it.

The frightening thought occurred to him that maybe, after all, he had made a mistake in running away from the sanatorium. Maybe the doctors had been right in telling him that a man without a memory, a man with no recollections of his past, would be no good in the world.

He had wandered for weeks now in search of that past. Cities, open roads, odd jobs here and there, handouts . . . . He had been away for ages and was mentally no better for it, physically so weary that he longed to lie down somewhere, anywhere, and sleep for days on end.

"Maybe — maybe I ought to go back there and take things easy, like they told me to. Maybe if I do that, the old brain will get right again — in a while."

A policeman turned the corner ahead of him. Ed Corley hesitated, then made up his mind. Quickening his step, he closed the gap.

"Officer, listen. I used to be a cop, too, they tell me, and I got to have help. Look, officer . . . I want to go home."

● ● ● ● ●

# A Checklist of the Books and the Detective and Mystery short stories of Hugh B. Cave

- ## Books

*Fishermen Four*. Dodd Mead, 1942.

*Long Were the Nights: The Saga of PT Squadron X in the Solomons*. Dodd Mead, 1943; reprinted 1981 by Zenger.

*The Fightin'est Ship: The Story of the Cruiser Helena*. Dodd Mead, 1944; reprinted 1981 by Zenger.

*We Build We Fight: The Story of the Seabees*. Harper, 1944.

*Wings Across the World: The Story of the Air Transport Command*. Dodd Mead, 1945.

*I Took the Sky Road* (with Comdr. Norman Mickey Miller). Dodd Mead, 1945; reprinted 1981 by Zenger.

*Haiti: Highroad to Adventure*. Henry Holt, 1952.

*Drums of Revolt*. England: Robert Hale, 1957.

*The Cross on the Drum*. Doubleday, 1959; reprinted by Dollar Book Club; Literary Guild bonus book; paperback by Ace Books; British edition by Werner Laurie; Dutch edition by Fontein-Boekerij.

*Black Sun*. Doubleday, 1960; British edition by Alvin Redman.

*The Mission*. Doubleday, 1960; reprinted by Best-in-Books Club.

*Four Paths to Paradise: A Book About Jamaica*. Doubleday, 1961; British edition by Alvin Redman.

*The Witching Lands*. Doubleday, 1962; reprinted by Best-in-Books Club; British edition by Alvin Redman.

*Run Shadow Run*. England: Robert Hale, 1968

*Larks Will Sing*. England: Robert Hale, 1969.

*Murgunstrumm and Others*. Carcosa, 1977; selected stories published in German and French editions. A collection of Hugh B. Cave's shudder-pulp stories, assembled by Karl Edward Wagner. Winner of the World Fantasy Award, and one of the entries in *Horror: 100 Best Books*, by Stephen Jones & Kim Newman.

*Legion of the Dead*. Avon (paperback original), 1979.

*The Nebulon Horror*. Dell (paperback original), 1980.

*A Summer Romance & Other Stories*. England: Longman, 1980, published in their "Simplified English Series" and by Eichosha-Longman (Japan), where it is used for teaching English in schools and is in its 12th printing. A collection of Hugh B. Cave's *Good Housekeeping Magazine* stories.

*The Evil*. Ace-Charter (paperback original), 1981.

*Shades of Evil*. Ace-Charter (paperback original), 1982.

*Spicy Detective Encores . . . No. 2, Three Stories of "The Eel," by Justin Case*. Winds of the World Press, 1987. Three pulp stories by Hugh B. Cave originally published in *Spicy Detective Stories* under the pseudonym "Justin Case."

*The Voyage*. Macmillan young adult novel, 1988; British edition by Collins.

*Disciples of Dread*. Tor Books (hardcover), 1988; reprinted 1989 as a Tor paperback.

*Hugh Cave's The Corpse Maker*. Starmont House, 1988. Published both in hardcover and paperback. A collection of Hugh B. Cave's pulp shudder stories assembled by Sheldon Jaffery.

*Conquering Kilmarnie*. Macmillan young adult novel, 1989; British edition by Collins.

*The Lower Deep*. Tor Books (paperback original), 1990.

*Lucifer's Eye*. Tor Books (paperback original), 1991.

*Magazines I Remember: Some Pulps, Their Editors, and What it Was like to Write for Them*. Tattered Pages Press, 1994. Reminiscences based on Hugh B. Cave's correspondence with fellow writer Carl Jacobi.

*Death Stalks the Night*. Fedogan & Bremer, 1995. A collection of Hugh B. Cave's shudder-pulp stories, assembled by Karl Edward Wagner. Nominated for World Fantasy Award.

*Bitter/Sweet*. Necronomicon Press, 1996. A booklet of 2 new short stories.

*The Dagger of Tsiang*. Tattered Pages Press, 1997. A collection of Hugh B. Cave's "Tsiang House" Borneo adventure stories from the pulps.

*Escapades of The Eel*. Tattered Pages Press, 1997. A collection of Hugh B. Cave's "Eel" stories originally published in the *Spicy* line of pulps under the pseudonym "Justin Case."

*The Door Below*. Fedogan & Bremer, 1997. A selection of Hugh B. Cave's mystery, horror and detective stories, from the 1930s through the 1990s.

*The Death-Head's March and Others, The Geoffrey Vace Collection, Four Far East Detective Tales*. Black Dog Books, 1998. Stories of India from the pulps by Hugh B. Cave and his brother Geoffrey Cave, compiled by Tom Roberts.

*White Star of Egypt*. Black Dog Books, 1999. Two stories originally published in *Spicy-Adventure Stories* under the pseudonym "Justin Case."

*The Desert Host*. Black Dog Books, 1999. Long novelette originally published in *Magic Carpet Magazine*.

*Isle of the Whisperers*. England: Pumpkin Books, 1999.

*Dark Doors Of Doom*. Black Dog Books, 2000. Three stories originally published in the *Spicy* Pulps under the pseudonym "Justin Case."

*The Dawning*. Leisure Books (paperback original), 2000.

*Officer Coffey Stories*. Subterranean Press, 2000. A two story collection of Hugh B. Cave's Officer Coffey stories originally published in *Dime Detective*, with a foreword by Richard Chizmar.

*Bottled in Blonde*. Fedogan & Bremer, 2000. A nine story collection of Hugh B. Cave's Peter Kane stories originally published in *Dime Detective Magazine*.

*The Lady Wore Black and Other Cat Tails*. Ash-Tree Press, 2000. A collection of fantasy stories.

*Long Live the Dead: Tales from Black Mask*. Crippen & Landru, 2000. A ten story collection originally published in *Black Mask* with an introduction by Keith Alan Deutsch; prefaces to each story by Hugh B. Cave.

*Dig the Grave Deeper*. Black Dog Books, forthcoming. A seven story collection of Hugh B. Cave's Shane Kelley stories originally published in *The Feds, Federal Agents,* and *Public Enemy*.

*The Evil Returns: Mindstealer*. Leisure Books (paperback original), forthcoming.

*Satan's Red Mist*. Black Dog Books, forthcoming. A two story collection originally published in *Strange Detective Mysteries*.

• MYSTERY STORIES APPEARING IN PULP AND DIGEST MAGAZINES

---

Hugh B. Cave has written nearly 1200 short stories, and a complete check-list would almost fill an entire book. The following is a list of all of his known stories in the mystery, crime, and detective genre.

*Ace G-Man Stories*: "Federal Trails to Glory," November-December 1938

*Ace Mystery Magazine*: "The Horde of Silent Men," May 1936.

*Alfred Hitchcock's Mystery Magazine*: "The Catbird Nest," August, 1965; "The Isle of Truth," October 1983; "The Lady Wore Black," March 1984 (reprinted in *Mystery Cats*, Signet-Penguin, 1991; collected in *The Lady Wore Black*, 2000); "Appointment with Yesterday," June 1984 (reprinted in *Tales from Alfred Hitchcock's Mystery Magazine*, Morrow, 1988; reprinted [as by Geoffrey Vace] in *100 Crooked Little Crime Stories*, Barnes & Noble, 1994; collected in *The Lady Wore Black*, 2000); "Mistress of Shadows," February 1985 (reprinted in *Murder Most Cozy*, Published Signet-Penguin, 1993); "The Hard Luck Kid," November 1992 (reprinted [as by Geoffrey Vace] in *100 Crooked Little Crime Stories*, Barnes & Noble, 1994); "The Caller," November 1993 (reprinted in *Mystery Cats 3*, Signet-Penguin, 1995; collected in *The Lady Wore Black*, 2000).

*All Detective Magazine*: "The Black Brotherhood," November 1932; "Hands Down," February 1934; "Sign of the Serpent," 1935.

*All Fiction Detective Anthology*: "Monkey See Murder," 1948 (reprinted from *Street & Smith's Detective Story Magazine*, March 1943).

*Amazing Detective Stories*: "Four Minutes after Midnight," August 1931 (as by Maxwell Smith; actually written by Cave's brother Geoffrey, although Hugh Cave used the pseudonym Maxwell Smith on a later story).

*Black Book Detective*: "The Prophecy," October 1934; "Maxon's Mistress," February 1935; "The Grisly Death," August 1934 (all three stories collected in *Murgunstrumm and Others*, 1977).

*Black Mask*: "Too Many Women," May, 1934; "Dead Dog," March 1937; "Shadow," April 1937; "Curtain Call," November 1938; "Smoke in Your Eyes," December 1938; "Long Live the Dead" (as by Allen Beck), December 1938; "Lost — and Found," April 19 40; "The Missing Mr. Lee," November 1940; "Front Page Frame-Up," February 1941; "Stranger in Town," April 1941 (all ten stories collected in *Long Live the Dead: Tales from Black Mask*).

*Candid Detective*: "Something for Nothing," January 1939.

*Clues Detective Stories*: "Seven to Be Slain," October 1936; "Dance Macabre," April 1937; "The Dead Speak Softly," November 1936.

*Complete Detective*: "The Devil Has Flaming Eyes," August 1938.

*Detective Fiction Weekly*: "The Infernal Web," March 21, 36; "No Way Out," May 9, 1936 (reprinted in *100 Sneaky Little Sleuth Stories*, Barnes & Noble, 1997); "You Just Can't Lose," June 13, 1936; "Nuts about Mutts," October 17, 1936; "Trail of the Torch," December 19, 1936; Queer Street," April 10, 1937; "The Smoke of Vengeance," May 22, 1937; "Deadline," November 13, 1937; "You Could Be Next," January 15, 1938; "Match Ya for It," April 9, 1938; "Murder Makes a Frame," April 30, 1938; "Joker in the Deck," June 18, 1938; "Desperate Character." July 9, 1938; "Scandal Sheet," September 17, 1938; "Murder at Hand," October 1, 1938; "No Trial by Jury," November 19, 1938; "I Am the Law," November 16, 1938; "Death Writes a Policy" (4-part serial), December 10, 17, 24, 31, 1938 "Cops Are Not Heroes," January 7, 1939; "The Pushover," January 14, 1939; "John Bum's Body," March 4, 1939; "Red for Rebellion," April 1, 1939; "According to Hoyle," April 8, 1939; "Death Comes for a Diva," April 15, 1939; "The Mystery of the Maudlin Mermaid," April 22, 1939; "The Head of J. James," April 29, 1939; "Hideout," May 6, 1939; "Seven Dirty Dollars," May 13, 1939; "Wit's End," May 27, 1939; "Time for Murder," June 17, 1939; "And Sudden Death," July 1, 1939; "Footprint," July 8, 1939; "Treadmill," July 22, 1939; "Mr. Petrie Ties a Fly," July 29, 1939; Beards Grow Slowly," August 5,1939; "But the Kill Was Gold," August 12, 1939; "Symphony in Shrouds," August 26, 1939; "A Den for Daniel," September 2,1939; "Seven into Murder," September 9, 1939; "Come into My Parlor," September 16, 1939; "But Few Are Chosen," October 21, 1939; "My Old Man," November 11, 1939; "So Long, Slicker," November 25, 1939; "Laugh, Clown," December 9, 1939; "The Barricade," December 23, 1939 (collected in Hugh Cave's *The Corpse Maker*, 1988); "The Signature of Murder," January 13, 1940; "Phantom Trap," February 3, 1940; "Big City Blackout," February 10, 1940; "Certainly, Sister," April 20, 1940; "Killer's Exit," June 8, 1940; "Weak Sister Act," June 29, 1940; "Coffin Cargo," July 20, 1940; "A Picture of Guilt," August 3, 1940;

*(Detective Fiction Weekly con't.)*
1940; "Prowl by Night," September 14, 1940; "Easy to Kill," October 18, 1940; "Murder off Key," November 2, 1940; "Terror's Twin," March 1, 1941; "Appointment with Yesterday," May 24. 1941; "Shadow Man" (5-part serial) May 31, June 7, 14, 21, 28, 1941; "Two Kinds of Snake," July 5, 1941; "Photo Finish," September 17, 1941; "Homicide Highway," November 19, 1941; "Faith for Rent," December 27, 1941

*Detective Short Stories*: "Black Fury," August 1937; "Madmen Laugh by Moonlight," February 1938; "The Gentleman Is Dead," April 1938; "Masters of Midnight," October 1938; "The Careless Cadaver," January 1939; "Death's Door," November 1940 (collected in *Death Stalks the Night*, Fedogan & Bremer, 1999).

*Detective Story Annual*: "Seven to Be Slain," 1943 (reprinted from *Clues Detective Stories*, October 1936); "As Does a Spider," 1946 (reprinted from *Street & Smith's Detective Story Magazine*; February 1943).

*Detective Tales*: "Murder — the Matchmaker," August 1937; "Odds to Die for," February 1938; "Neither Gold Nor Glory," June 1939; "A Gun for Galahad," March 1940; "The Cat and the Killer," June 1941; "The Richest Cat in Town," February 1951; "Seven Dirty Dollars," April 1951(reprinted from *Detective Fiction Weekly*, May13, 1939).

*Detective Yarns*: "Satan Wears a Mask," December 1938.

*Dime Detective Magazine*: "The Late Mr. Smythe," August 1, 1934 (collected in *Bottled in Blonde*, 2000); "Hell on Hume Street," November 1, 1934 (collected in *Bottled in Blonde*, 2000); "Bottled in Blonde," January 1, 1935 (collected in *Bottled in Blonde*, 2000); "The Man Who Looked Sick," April 1, 1935 (collected in *Bottled in Blonde*, 2000); "The Screaming Phantom," May 1, 1935 (collected in *Bottled in Blonde*, 2000); "The Brand of Kane," June 15, 1935 (reprinted in *Tough Guys and Dangerous Dames*, Barnes & Noble, 1993; collected in *Bottled in Blonde*, 2000); "The House of Sudden Sleep," December 1935; "The Lady Who Left Her Coffin," June 1936; "Footsteps to a Finish," August 1937; "Twenty after Murder," November 1937; "Farewell with Trumpets," January 1940 (collected in *Officer Coffey Stories*, 2000); "Deal from the Bottom," August 1939; Loose Loot," April 1940; "He Didn't Know Nothin'," July 1940 (collected in *Officer Coffey Stories*, 2000); "Ding Dong Belle," August 1941 (reprinted in *Hard-Boiled Detectives*, Gramercy, 1992; collected in *Bottled in Blonde*, 2000); "The Dead Don't Swim," November 1941 (collected in *Bottled in Blonde*, 2000); "No Place to Hide," February 1942 (collected in *Bottled in Blonde*, 2000); "The Fugitive Face," September 1942; "This Is the Way We Bake Our Dead," June 1943.

*Double Action Detective*: "Ticket to Trouble," October 1938.

*Double Detective*: "Crazy Guy," January 1938; "There's Always a Way Back," April 1938; "Worth Fighting for," May 1938; "In this Corner — Death," June 1938; "Rifles at Dawn," July 1938; "The Forgotten Man-Killer," August 1938; "The Education of a Killer," September 1938 (reprinted 1996 in German Anthology, *Back in the Ring*);"Three Rats, One Hole," October 1938; "Counsel for the Damned," December 1938; "Special Delivery," January 1939; "Time Out," February 1939; "Payroll Heist," September 1939; "The Melancholy Mask of M. Montreau," October 1939;

*(Double Detective: con't.)*
   "No Errors," February 1940; "Murder Me Him," May 1940; "Not Dead but Sleeping," September 1940; "The Guardian Angel," October 1941.

*Ellery Queen's Mystery Magazine*: "Alike under the Skin," April 1955; "Naked in Darkness," August 1965 (reprinted in *100 Dastardly Little Detective Stories*, Barnes & Noble, 1993); "The Course of Justice," October 1965 (reprinted in *100 Dastardly Little Detective Stories*); "Many Happy Returns" April 1966 (collected in *Murgunstrumm & Others*, 1977; reprinted [as by "Justin Case"] in *100 Crooked Little Crime Stories*, Barnes & Noble, 1994).

*Exciting Detective*: "The Silken Snakes," Summer 1941.

*Federal Agent*: "Killer's Exit," March 1937; "Wings of Death," May 1937; "Holiday in Hell," July 1937; "The Dead Talk Back," September 1937 (all four stories collected in *Dig the Grave Deeper*, 2000).

*The Feds*: "Death Hogs the Highways," February 1937 (reprinted in *Dig the Grave Deeper*, 2000); "Blood in His Eye," October 1937.

*15-Story Detective*: "Guilt Frame," February 1951.

*Flynn's Detective Fiction*: "Blackguard's Book," December 1942.

*G-Men Detective*: "Death on the Program," January 1941.

*Green Ghost Detective*: "An Eye for the Future," Spring 1941.

*Mike Shayne Mystery Magazine*: "The Woman at the Pond," February 1965; "Run for Your Life," October, 1984

*New Detective Magazine*: "Passport to Hell," March 1943.

*Pocket Detective Magazine*: "Sense of Humor," December 1936; "The Hidden Eye," February 1937; "The Dead Samaritan," July 1937.

*Popular Detective*: "Marked for Murder," July 1935; "The Silent Men," March 1936; "Greetings to You," January 1937.

*Private Detective Stories*: "Sleep Baby Sleep" (as by "Justin Case"), September 1937; "Dizzy Dame," October 1937; "Design for Death" (as by "Justin Case"), January 1938; "She Slept Too Long" (as by "Justin Case"), June 1938; "Bad Water" (as by "Justin Case"), November 1943 "Hangman's Chain," December 1943; "P. D. File 213 (as by "Justin Case"), March 1944 (*Note:* although credited on the title page to Hugh B. Cave's pseudonym, Cave did not write this story).

*Public Enemy*: "Dig the Grave Deeper!," February 1936; "The Red Butcher," March 1936 (both stories collected in *Dig the Grave Deeper*, 2000).

*Red Star Detective*: "Copper's Exit," August 1940.

*Romantic Detective*: "The Gorilla Will Get You" (as by "Justin Case"), December 1938.

*Secret Agent X Detective Magazine*: "Killer's Test," June 1935.

*The Skipper*: "Doll of Death," April 1937.

*Spicy Detective Stories* (all by "Justin Case"): "I See by the Papers," May 1936 (reprinted as "Headline Bait" in *Private Detective*, March 1938, under house name J.C. Cole); "Women Are Damned Fools," September 1936; "Death to Cops," January 1937; "Eel Poison," August 1937 (collected in *Spicy Detective Encores* . . . #2, *Three Stories of "The Eel,"* 1987 and in *Escapades of the Eel*, 1997); "Death Wears No Robe," October 1937 (collected in *Spicy Detective Encores* . . #2, *Three Stories of "The Eel,"* 1987 and in *Escapades of the Eel*, 1997); "The Eel Slips Through," December 1937 (collected in *Escapades of the Eel*, 1997); "Prison Pay-off," August 1938; "Eel's Errand," August 1940; "The Widow Wears Scarlet," October 1940 (collected in *Escapades of the Eel*, 1997); "The Last Laugh," December 1940; "Annie Any More," March 1941 (collected in *Spicy Detective Encores* . . . #2 , *Three Stories of "The Eel,"* 1987 and in *Escapades of the Eel*, 1997); "On Ice," April 1941; "Death Has Green Eyes," June 1941; "The Second Slug," July 1941 (collected in *Escapades of the Eel*, 1997); "Krock's Wife," October 1941; "A Pile of Publicity," January 1942 (collected in *Escapades of the Eel*, 1997); "Eel's Eve," April 1942 (collected in *Escapades of the Eel*, 1997).

*Star Detective Magazine*: "Death Stalks the Night," August 1935 (reprinted in *Death Stalks the Night*, 1995).

*Strange Detective Mysteries*: "The Crystal Doll Killings," May-June 1939 (collected in *Satan's Red Mist*, 2000); "Satan's Red Mist," May 1941 (collected in *Satan's Red Mist*, 2000); "The Guardian Angel," November 1943.

*Strange Detective Stories*: "Half Way to Hell," December 1933 (reprinted in *Pulp Review* July 1994).

*Street & Smith's Detective Story Magazine*: "You Forgot Something," February 25, 1934; "Tiger Face," February 1938; "Necktie Party," July 1939; "Two Can Fight," August 1939; "The Albino Butterbugs," November 1941; "Too Tight the Grave," July 1942; "As Does a Spider," February 1943; "Monkey See Murder," March 1943; "Steve Takes a Hand," January 1944 (reprinted in *Second Mystery Companion*, Gold Label Books, 1944, and as "Gramp Takes a Hand" in *100 Little Spy Stories*, Barnes & Noble, 1996); "Southbound Special," March 1944.

*Super Detective Stories*: "Terror Island," June 1934 (collected in *Death Stalks the Night*, 1995); "The Corpse Crypt," September 1934 (collected in *Death Stalks the Night*, 1995); "Vale of Inferno," December 1934; "Fall Guy" (as by "Justin Case"), February 1944.

*Suspense* (British): "Lonely Journey," February 1959; "High Man on the Mountain," August 1960.

*Ten Detective Aces*: "Sinister Street," July 1937.

*Ten Story Gang*: "Stand in for Death," November 1938.

*Thrilling Detective*: "Rendezvous," December 1934; "Murder Backfire," November 1936; "One Way — Dangerous," February 1938.

*Top Notch Detective*: "By the Neck Until Dead," March 1939.

*True Gangster Stories*: "Headstone for a Heel," February 1942; "This Way to Death," June 1942.

LONG LIVE THE DEAD

*Long Live the Dead: Tales from Black Mask* by Hugh B. Cave is printed on 60-pound Turin Book Natural (a chlorine-free and acid-free stock) from 10-point Palantino over 12 for the Text and Poppl-Pontifex for the titles. The introduction is by Keith Alan Deutsch and the prefaces to each story are by the author. The cover painting and book design are by Tom Roberts. The first printing comprises two hundred copies sewn in cloth, signed and numbered by the author, and approximately eight hundred copies bound in softcover. Each of the clothbound copies included a separate pamphlet, *Danse Macabre* by Hugh B. Cave. The book was printed and bound by Thompson-Shore, Inc., Dexter, Michigan, and published in October 2000 by Crippen & Landru Publishers, Norfolk, Virginia.